THE LAST DUSK

Tempest Rising Book 2

Elliott VanDruff

Belle Rose Press

Edited: Cayce Berryman at Kingsman Editing
Cover Design: Elliott VanDruff
Cover Background: Purchased from IStock.com
Artist: a_Taiga
Sword Image: Pixabay: jerycho1960
Dragon Image: Purchased from IStock.com
Artist: ChrisGorgio
All Rights Reserved
ISBN-13: 978-1-7344783-3-4

Dedication

This book is dedicated to my father, Joe, and mother, Rachel, who cultivated my love of stories.

Map of Lyrica

Chapter 1

"THERE ARE BUT TWO THINGS in life, Rowyn, duty and choice. Always know where your duty lies, and it will lead you to the right choice. Always." Mother's voice was so faint, I struggled to hear the words. Tears coursed down my cheeks as the fever and boils ravished her body until nothing remained but a ghost of who she once was. I didn't have the heart to tell her Grandmother had died the night before. Could she see the empty pallet beside hers? The knowledge that Mother wouldn't be alone in the afterlife offered little comfort.

My heart wavered when I thought of my mother's last words, her voice so faint that I struggled to hear. It wasn't until I considered leaving my home of Espiria that I knew what she meant.

It seemed like forever since I'd ventured beyond the shroud and found my way to Solridge, though it was merely a year ago. I didn't regret it, either. I'd made friends and earned an odd sort of acceptance since I'd proven myself. But then, the Spring Equinox festival happened a few weeks ago, and it felt as though everything had changed since then. Elias Lyon, the son of the most powerful man in the Western Empire, had finally gone too far in tormenting me. His death and the banishment of his brother, Seith, from Solridge would undoubtedly haunt me.

My memory of the fight with the golgeman was filled with fog and uncertainty. I had no memory of why I'd left. Was the fear of Lyon retribution enough to cause me to turn tail and run?

"Are you trying to remember again?" a voice asked as the stable door creaked shut.

I nodded to my closest friend at Solridge, Fin, and turned my gaze back to the empty stall. No tack hung on the wall. No Espirian saddle blanket folded on the shelf. No Ally, stamping his foot in greeting. He was my only friend from home, and he was gone.

"I just wish I remembered," I said for the hundredth time. "I wish I remembered why I tried to leave. Why I risked so much."

Fin patted her horse, Breeze, who snorted into her hair. Blonde strands the color of straw billowed out. "Later," Fin whispered, addressing Breeze's question.

It was always a marvel to watch Fin hold entire conversations with a flock of blackbirds or exchange pleasantries with a tiny frog on a branch. I would have thought those abilities and Fin's sweet temperament would make her welcome in any home in the empire. But Fin was born of a tryst between a nobleman and a commoner. Given the circumstances of Fin's birth, none of the other nobles bothered to befriend her.

I knew what it was like to be an outsider. I was born of a rebel clan who didn't hold sway with the empire. I knew that the others whispered "traitor" behind my back.

"Galena said that your memory loss was to be expected. You were traumatized, Rowyn. You nearly died," Fin said.

I rose from the stool. "I know. I'll try to be better. I just . . ." I wiped away a tear. "I don't want to think I lost him for nothing."

Fin came and hugged me. "I know you loved him."

I leaned into her shoulder. If anyone knew how I felt, it would be Fin, whose bond with animals meant she built deep relationships with them. The fact that they tended to have shorter life spans was a sorrow she often spoke of.

"I just wish I could remember why I was in such a hurry. I suppose I could've been afraid of Duke Lyon, but why that night? Why would I risk leaving by myself and not tell anyone my fears? Why try to take the golgeman on when I knew I couldn't handle it?"

Fin broke away and studied me. "I've no idea. I just remember that you were scared. People do crazy things out of fear. Maybe it's something that can't be explained."

I nodded. "You're probably right." Perhaps there was some truth to her words.

"Master Gillius is looking for you," Fin said after a moment. "The council needs to see you."

I took one last look at the empty stall and left, letting the stable door slam shut behind me. Though the sky was cloudy, it was a warm spring day. The smell of sweetgrass and laughter drifted through the air as I made my way through the garden.

Master Gillius smiled at me from the steps of the school, but a wariness in his eyes made me distinctly uncomfortable.

"There you are," Gillius said, reaching out.

Though I couldn't explain it, I shrank from his touch. I should've been grateful for everything he'd done for me. If it weren't for Gillius, I would have lost my life in the fight with the golgeman. But whenever I found his eyes on me, I felt a low thrum in my bones as if I were afraid of him. I'd never been fearful of him before. What was I missing?

Gillius let his hand fall to his side. "We've been looking everywhere for you."

"I'm sorry," I said, smoothing my skirt. "If I'd known we were to meet today, I'd have made myself ready."

Gillius nodded as he led me into the school. "It's all right. I know it's been hard since the incident. But you need to focus on the trials ahead, rather than dwell on struggles of the past."

"I suppose," I sighed.

Gillius stopped at the council doors. This time, he put his hands on my shoulders and leaned in, his green eyes watching mine. "We care about you here, you know that, don't you? The other sorcerers and myself, we want you to be safe. We want you to see growth and make a name for yourself out in the world."

"Thank you," I said, a false smile stretched over my face. "I know you all care about me, and I'm sorry I've been in such a mood."

Gillius nodded and thrust open the council doors. It didn't escape my notice that he said nothing about the sorcerers wanting to see me *happy*. I supposed it was a small thing, but it was cause to wonder, nonetheless.

The council of sorcerers sat in their usual circle. I was shocked at seeing Lord Alexander in their midst. The last time I'd seen him, he'd been heading to Seaport to escort the body of Elias Lyon to Ayastaren. I wondered how his audience with Duke Roland went. Was he able to smooth over the incident? I doubted it. Now, I supposed, I would hear the verdict. Perhaps I would be sent to the Ayastaren prison for what happened to Elias. Though I knew I wasn't to blame, I was sure the duke would feel differently. I would not escape that incident unscathed; Duke Roland

Lyon would make sure of that.

"Rowyn," Lord Alexander's deep voice grumbled. "I trust you've healed properly since your ordeal. How are you feeling?"

"Well enough," I said, dropping my eyes to the floor. "How is Seith?"

Lord Alexander grunted. "As well as can be expected. Duke Roland grieved at the news of his son's death. He didn't accept my account of the situation, and it's been getting . . . complicated."

I glanced over at Gillius, who had taken his seat next to Master Haris. He was watching me, a crease between his brows.

"What is to be my sentence?" I asked, standing straight and tall. I was weary with fear and ready to face something head-on. Even if it meant Ayastaren.

Gillius glanced at Lady Vianne. Her purple gem was hidden behind the dark hair that she swept over her fore-head.

"Stop being so dramatic," Vianne ordered. "The duke has no claim to you, and we won't be sending you to Ayastaren, so you can forget those thoughts right now." She turned to the other sorcerers who shifted uncomfort-ably in their seats. "We don't need to worry Rowyn over the political implications of an event she had little control over."

"Will he come for me?" I asked, voicing the fear that kept me awake at night. Given the past events at Ayasta-ren, I knew the duke would have some sort of punishment in mind. The question was whether the council would let the duke act on his anger.

Lady Vianne's eyes narrowed. "Rowyn, we didn't bring you here to discuss bureaucracy, although I appreci-ate you taking your studies more seriously."

"To be sure," Lady Madeline agreed with a wizened smile. "There's no need to frighten the poor girl."

"We brought you here," Master Haris said, "to admin-ister the Trial by Stone."

I raised my brows. "So soon? I was given to under-stand that most students studied at least two years before their trial."

Lord Alexander and Gillius exchanged glances before Gillius spoke. "There's no specific length of time for an initiate to study before their trial. It's up to the council to deem whether or not they're ready, and we've deemed you as such."

"For some, it may take two or three years of study," Lady Madeline added. "Given that you've been struggling with control, we've decided to quicken your retrieval of the gem to give you more time to practice using it. Does that make sense?"

My mind raced as I nodded. I remembered Master

Gillius mentioning the possibility of the Trial by Stone. Still, I hadn't realized it would be so soon.

"Well then, let's get on with it!" Lord Obi snapped. His dark skin had grown in wrinkles since I'd come to Solridge, along with his irritability. "I don't recall the requirement that we must ask students their feelings about the matter, or explain ourselves to them. By all the gods, you all tiptoeing around this girl's emotions is enough to make one queasy!" Lord Obi turned to me and leaned in. "You don't have a choice, no matter what these dandies will tell you."

I smiled. At least Lord Obi was honest about it.

Master Haris rose and cleared his throat when no one else spoke. "So, we will begin then." Haris walked over to the table and lifted a tray that held a cup and a small clear stone. He brought them before me. "The Trial by Stone is a step that all sorcerers must take on their path to mastery. You will be called on a quest for a stone that beckons you, and only you—"

"And so on and so forth," Lord Obi grumbled before turning back to Lord Alexander. "May I be dismissed to my studies now?"

"No, you may not, and if you continue to behave in such an untoward manner, we'll take away your books as well." Lady Madeline's voice was soft but tinged with anger.

"By the gods, woman, if you so much as touch my books, I'll—"

"Enough!" snapped Vianne.

She waited a moment for Lord Obi to respond, but he only glared at everyone, mumbling curses under his breath.

Lord Alexander rubbed his temples. "Master Haris, if you would be so kind as to continue."

Haris turned back to me. "A sorcerer wields his power from a gem. It allows us not only to store our magic but also to concentrate and control it better. Certain gems call to us because they are the best conduit to our powers. Before your training can truly begin, you must mine your own gem. After this test today, you must use all available free time to prepare for your quest."

I took a deep, shuddering breath. "I'm ready. What must I do?"

Haris smiled. "It's pretty simple, really. You drink this potion, then hold the stone in your hands. The stone will show what gem you seek, and your mind will show you where to find it."

My heart drummed rapidly in my chest as I lifted the cup from the tray. Holding the stone carefully, I put the cup to my lips. The bitter scent of herbs filled my nose, and I wavered.

"Drink up," Gillius said simply.

Tipping my head back, I downed the whole mess in one gulp.

The sorcerers leaned in, watching me closely.

"By all the gods," I breathed. "That tasted awful."

"Don't speak," Vianne said sharply. "Close your eyes and look within. Where does your mind take you?"

I closed my eyes, my stomach churning as the potion wrapped me in its grip. A tingling sensation started at my throat, then raced through my body until I was bursting with magic. My head grew fuzzy, and suddenly, it was as though I were floating above my own body, looking down.

The cup had fallen next to me, and I sat with the clear stone cradled in both hands. The sorcerers leaned toward me, watching with wide eyes. Haris's balding head stood out stark against the others.

I giggled.

"You need to focus," Lady Vianne said, her voice breaking through the fog. "Let the magic carry you."

Suddenly, there was a pull, and my dream-self soared through the air. Clouds rose around me as I moved farther and farther away from school.

"I think I'm going north," I said as the air around me grew chillier. "It's getting darker."

I glanced below and saw a spattering of mountains and a port city. There was a river, and then more mountains, as the sun faded away entirely behind me. It was dark, with only the moon to guide the path. I flew farther until, suddenly, I froze above a plain bordered by dark mountains.

There was a gasp, and my eyes flew open as a jolt of energy ran through me. The vision vanished, leaving me in the council chambers. The translucent stone in my hands had been transformed. It was deep black, with veins of blue, red, and green creeping across it.

I looked up and saw a range of expressions on the sorcerers' faces. Vianne cradled her head in her hands while Lord Alexander's mouth was slightly agape. Lord Obi stamped out of the room after shooting me a look that, on anyone else, would've been one of sympathy. Lady Madeline and Master Haris were horrified.

Gillius looked merely resigned. He rose and stepped toward me. "We should've known," he murmured, taking the stone from my hand to study it. The colors faded almost immediately. Gillius met my eyes. "Black opal. You're to go to the Nightlands."

My face paled. "The Nightlands?" I croaked, my throat plummeting into my stomach. My body rebelled against whatever poison they'd given me. I couldn't shake the face of Imor from my vision. He looked as though he was leering at me, daring me to enter his domain.

I leaned over and retched.

Chapter 2

THE NIGHTLANDS WERE the lands beyond the mountains north of Morgania. I'd heard stories about the beasts that dwelled there, monsters that could consume you whole. Even if you survived the predators, eventually, everyone went mad and perished from lack of sun.

"How am I to endure it?" I asked. "I'm from the north, and even *I've* never heard of anyone foolish enough to venture there. This is impossible!"

"Actually, you're better equipped to survive than most," Gillius said. "Morgania already receives less sunlight than the south, so your body could withstand long periods of nightfall, which will be an asset to you. Make it easier to bear."

Master Haris was nodding. "You will need to prepare yourself by studying everything you can about the place. The library will be your best ally. I don't know much other than the darkness causes some animals to lack color. You'll need to seek out more information on where the gems are hidden as well."

"You must work fast," Lady Madeline added. "You'll have to journey there this summer since it gets far too cold during the winter. You could wait another year before you leave, but I'd advise against it. You're running out of time, Rowyn."

"There is no choice," Lord Alexander said, his eyes narrowed at me. "You will leave in six weeks."

Gillius rose and motioned me to the door while Vianne and Alexander whispered to each other. I obeyed and tried to process what had been said.

"Master Gillius, why did you say you should have known? About the opal?" I hated how trembly my voice was.

Gillius glanced behind him then dropped his voice low. "There have been many weather sages over the centuries, but the last wielder of an opal was Morius the Black. Though your powers are very similar to his, I'd no idea you would be just as powerful. It was still . . . surprising."

"All I've heard are the legends about him, but they scarcely seem real."

"Seek out any papers and writings on him and his time. It may give you some guidance."

"Isn't there someone who will accompany me? Will you go too?"

Gillius cleared his throat. "We'll confer on who your companion will be. The council has to send communications to those whose talents would be an asset to your quest. We'll meet with you soon to decide."

Master Gillius went back into the council room to join the others. As the door shut, I heard an excited murmur. I went to the door, put my ear to the keyhole, and tried to catch what they were saying.

Lord Alexander grunted something, then Master Gillius said, "No, not yet, he was firm about that."

"Do you think that wise, Master Gillius?" Lady Vianne asked. "If you continue to toy with her, she'll rebel again."

Master Gillius said something else that I didn't catch before the sounds changed. Footsteps. I bolted down the hall, turning the corner just as the door opened and Master Gillius stepped out. He strode down the corridor toward his chambers, followed by Lady Madeline.

My head pounded from the after-effects of whatever was in that cup as I leaned against the wall, trying to keep my knees from collapsing. I couldn't help but think I'd been set up for failure. The Nightlands? What folly! How was I to survive such a journey?

I walked somberly out to the garden. Fin and the other sorcerers were waiting for me by the herb patch, joined by Araceli and Pedr. All of them seemed to be holding their breath as I approached.

"Well?" Fin asked, her eyes wide with excitement. "It was the Trial by Stone, wasn't it? Which gem is it? The men have all taken bets."

I faced their stares. Even Idris and Marc, two nobles

who usually showed little interest in me, were waiting with bated breath. Lord Destrian of Helena, who I hadn't spoken to since I'd woken from my ordeal with the golgeman, glowered behind them.

"Black opal," I said. "I'm to go to the Nightlands."

Whatever the others were expecting, it certainly wasn't that. My pronouncement was met with stunned silence.

"The Nightlands?" Marc repeated. "I heard that's where the dragons retreated to."

Idris nodded. "My nurse used to tell me stories of vermin as big as a grown man that would prowl the mountains, picking off wayward children who wandered off."

I raised my brows at him.

"She was from up north," Idris added then ducked his head when Fin glared at him.

"Rowyn can hold her own in a fight. Let's not forget that," Araceli assured us, but her face betrayed doubt.

"But that was a one-on-one fight," Pedr said. "To battle the forces of the Nightlands, the harshest terrain in the world, is another matter entirely." He flushed when Araceli glared at him, then added, "But Rowyn will be fine. If there is anyone who could survive the Nightlands, it would be her."

For the first time in weeks, Destrian addressed me. I tried not to look away. "Where in the Nightlands are the opals to be found?"

I thought back to my mental journey in the council chamber. "Quite far, I think. I passed two mountain ranges before I stopped at the plain."

Destrian nodded as if that meant something. Fin, her voice becoming quite shrill, asked, "How far is that?"

Destrian cleared his throat. "The first range is The Bitters, the second, The Dires."

Fin glared at him. "How far?"

"From the maps I've seen, it will be at least a month's journey, more likely two, if all goes well."

A hush fell over the group. I was sure they were each contemplating the numerous ways I could die. I'd avoided doing that myself.

"When do you leave?" Araceli asked. There was no mistaking the tremor in her voice.

"Spring's end."

"The council must be mad. So soon?" Fin shrieked, looking to the other sorcerers for support.

"You must be mistaken," Pedr said, his hand on Fin's shoulder. "Fin's been studying a whole year for her quest to Horan this summer."

Destrian met my eyes with a frown before looking away.

"I'm not."

Fin gasped, and Araceli, wide-eyed, seemed to be looking for an explanation from the others. Neither seemed to want to believe me, as if the men around us would have something better to say that would prove me ill-informed.

Marc crossed his arms. "I heard the meeting with Duke Roland didn't go well. I imagine they're trying to get Rowyn out of Solridge so they can figure out this mess with Ayastaren. If she's off questing in the Nightlands, the duke can't enact vengeance, can he?"

"Was it so bad?" Pedr asked.

"Yes," Idris said. "Marc and I were working in the practice field last night when Lord Alexander got back. I've never seen him so worried."

My brows wrinkled. "What could the duke do to me?"

"He's the most powerful noble this side of the Ballerian," Idris said, his eyes grim. "What couldn't he do?"

"She falls under the Articles of Clemency," Pedr said. "Even the Duke of Ayastaren has to honor that."

Araceli smiled. "You're quite right, Pedr. See, Rowyn, you have nothing to worry about. The law is on your side."

"Nothing to worry about?" Fin exclaimed, nearing hysterics. "She has to quest into the Nightlands! Who could survive such a journey!"

Galena's blue-tinged hands signed urgently to Fin, who continued to shake her head in disbelief. I caught a couple of words. Something about plants and sun, but I'd not learned enough of her signs to follow how fast she was moving.

"What does Galena say, Fin?" Pedr asked.

"She says we have some plants and herbs that will help her not go crazy from the darkness."

Galena nodded, patted me on the shoulder, and shouldered her basket before making her way out of the garden on a delivery.

Fin and Pedr stayed with me as the others drifted away, lost in their thoughts. Destrian watched me for a moment before retreating into the forge, and I felt a pang of anger. It was he who shot me in the gut, nearly killing me. I didn't care if it was an accident or not. He had no right to act so wounded.

No matter. He'd be rid of me in six weeks.

As Ena brushed my hair out that evening, I noted that the crescents tattooed outside of my eyes were fading. I turned my head and inspected the rose vine blessing curled over my shoulder blade and around my neck. It was fading a bit too. I would stop home before venturing to the Nightlands. I could visit my clan and ask Conal to touch up my blessings before I left. I didn't think the council would mind. It seemed appropriate that I say farewell to what was left of my family and clan before I ventured to certain death.

"I've gone to the market and commissioned some warmer tunics and breeches for you," Ena said as she plaited my hair.

"That's a good idea," I agreed, studying the star blessing on my chest. It still looked fresh, being the newest one. "They can warm my corpse when I inevitably meet my end."

Ena chuckled, though I wasn't joking.

"I knew a boy who had gone to the Nightlands," she said, placing my brush gently on my dressing table.

I stopped fidgeting and looked up. "Really? My clan has always been close to the border, but we never have reason to go that far north."

"Yes," Ena said, releasing me from my looking glass. I lay on the bed. Ena bent down and began gathering the clothes I'd worn that day. "It's a common dare in the villages near the river. They say you aren't really a man unless you summit the peak of the first mountain and look the Lands of Death in the eye."

"Did they all return?"

Ena nodded. "Most did. Granted, they weren't traveling as far in as you must go, but still, it's not as impossible as you may think. Especially for a girl of your talents."

"Hmph," I grunted, checking to make sure my weapons still hung in their places on the wall. Even though the golgeman was gone, I still grew nervous at night. "I wonder who they'll send with me."

"I'm sure they'll choose someone experienced to ensure your success."

I turned over in bed and leaned on my hand. "I'd thought to visit Espiria on the way there—see home and all. You're welcome to travel with me to visit your family. There's no sense in you being here if I'm at the edge of the world."

Ena beamed. "I would like that. I've so much to tell Father and the girls. Are you sure you won't need me?"

"I've not had a handmaid for most of my life," I said with a shake of my head. "I'll get along well enough."

Ena smiled then ducked out of the room as Fin entered. I didn't bother to move but felt some comfort when her weight sank part of my bed. "I've spoken to the others," Fin said, throwing her leather riding gloves on the table and pulling off her boots. "Most are betting you'll survive, though some think you'll lose your mind."

I raised my brows. "I bet that was Marc. He always had a morbid mind."

Fin laughed. When she doused the light, I remembered Marc's words and her talk of bets were forgotten. What had the duke said to Lord Alexander that would cause them to send me on my quest so soon?

Chapter 3

FOR THE FIRST TIME SINCE I'd been at Solridge, Lord Alexander seemed to take an actual interest in my training.

"Harder, Rowyn. You must master this if you wish to survive the wilderness," Lord Alexander urged. The weight of his blows increased. My sword arm trembled, but I strained and attempted to beat his sword back. Sweat streamed down my face and back, making my hands slip on my practice sword.

"Move your feet," he bellowed. "Move!"

I darted, feeling as though I were at home on a raid. Swinging my sword as fast as I could, I regained the upper hand.

"Come on!" Lord Alexander yelled.

It felt as though I were fighting for my life. I swept my sword into his with a crack. Whipping the blade to the other side, I smashed into his chest.

"By the gods!" I gasped, dropping my weapon. "Lord Alexander, I'm so sorry." Though it was a practice blade, that didn't mean it couldn't do some damage.

Lord Alexander was bent over, clutching his side. Sweat rolled off his nose and onto the grass. "No, it's all right. It's just a bruise." He took a deep breath. "I want you down in the practice field in your spare time. You must build endurance for battle. You've gone soft over the past year."

I narrowed my eyes at him, but Lord Alexander held up a hand. "I know it's my fault," he said, "but how could I have known the dangerous journey you now have to take."

"All right, I'll practice more," I agreed, wiping the sweat from my forehead and accepting Fin's waterskin. "Though it would help if I had someone to practice with. I know you can't spend every morning with just me. Fin and Araceli don't do sword work, and the boys refuse to practice with me."

Lord Alexander spit into the grass and nodded. "We'll figure something out."

To the side, I noticed several boys who worked in the stables and kitchens using horses to drag rocks to the hillside.

"Excellent," Lord Alexander said, turning and addressing the youths. At the movement, he bent sharply and sucked in his breath. I hoped I hadn't broken a rib. Then again, Master Gillius could set him to rights quickly enough. Lord Alexander went on, though his usual bellow was pained. "Make sure to build them up a bit. We want it to be mountainous."

"What are they doing?" I asked.

"Building you a mountain. Since your foes are likely to be familiar with fighting among the rocks and boulders, so should you be if you're to survive."

"I suppose that makes sense," I said, hoping we wouldn't start that very day.

Lord Alexander saw the look on my face and laughed. "You can finish out the morning by helping the lads arrange these stones. Tomorrow we'll start the real work."

I rolled up my sleeves and let out a breath of relief.

"Lord Alexander," a reedy voice called out. We turned to find Master Haris standing awkwardly at the side of the training field. "I was hoping to borrow Rowyn for the rest of your session. I have some books and scrolls I wanted to discuss with her for her upcoming trip."

Lord Alexander's mouth twitched. "She also needs to practice for the battles she's sure to face."

Master Haris paled, but he went on. "Be that as it may, Rowyn is already well-versed in battle, but when it comes to the route through the Nightlands or the animals she may face . . ."

"Fine," Lord Alexander grunted. "You may have her this morning, but next time pull her from writing."

Master Haris nodded quickly. "Quite right, Lord Alexander. Next time I'll remember that. Come along, Rowyn. I've much to show you."

Master Haris led me to the library. He motioned me to sit at a study table littered with papers, books, and scrolls. The bright morning light fell over the clutter in rays, giving the library a more cheerful appearance than I was used to, having gone only in the evenings.

"Now, Rowyn, we have much to cover in the short time we're here before I leave with Fin for Horan. You don't mind, do you?" Master Haris was bouncing his foot so quickly that it jostled the table. Even his hands were shaking. By all the gods, did I make him nervous?

I nodded, pulling the papers toward me. "I would appreciate any help you can offer, Master Haris."

Though I'd spent time with the other sorcerers who made up the council at Solridge, Master Haris and I hadn't crossed paths in any meaningful way. The ring of brown hair around his head looked even odder up close since he wasn't very old, and he had an ugly scar on the back of his hand. His mysteriousness only increased my interest.

"What is your power, Master Haris?" I asked. "The others don't speak of it."

The table shook harder. "Memory."

I blinked. "Memory? What does that mean?"

Master Haris laughed nervously. "I have a perfect memory. I can recite every page from half the library here. This is why I write with Fin and anyone else who could add to the world's store of knowledge."

"Do you remember when you were a baby?"

Master Haris nodded. "I remember the day I was born."

My eyes widened. "How does your gem help you?"

Master Haris stopped shaking the table and ran his hand over his bald spot. "I can store memories there that I don't want to be so . . . present."

"Bad memories?" I murmured.

Master Haris nodded. "I'm told that most memories fade until they are fuzzy, like shadows. Even when others do remember more clearly, they only focus on certain aspects of memory—the smell, the sight, or the emotion. For me, I remember everything to the last detail. It's mentally taxing, so I mostly use my gem to store memories."

I nodded. I didn't think I'd like that skill at all. To remember every bad thing that ever happened to me in perfect detail? No, thank you. That being said, Master Haris probably had his share of bad memories he'd like to forget. And I had something I wanted to remember.

"As you know, the Nightlands are huge, covering a large swath of land running far to the east, west, and north. Horses won't venture into the darkness, so you'll have to travel on foot. Due to the cold, the animals tend to be large and dangerous, covered with thick fur and layers of fat. Some of the smaller animals are translucent, using their glow to find their way through the darkness."

"Why are animals so much bigger?" I asked.

Master Haris blinked and held up a finger. "Very good. I'm glad you asked. Many times, when it's colder, animals adapt by growing larger. This could be due to the need to travel long distances to find food. Either way, the Nightlands is inhabited by a mix of animals ranging from very large to incredibly tiny. According to that map," he said, pointing to the one in my hand, "there are vents that pump steam into the sky. Some smaller creatures can be found there, living off the heat. Legends say the dragons didn't die out but retreated to the dark mountains. The gods only know if that's true, but you'd be wise to prepare yourself for anything."

I pulled an old journal from the stack and leafed through the pages.

"Ah, you found Batice's notes. Very good."

"Gillius said I should seek out information on those who survived the journey."

"Oh, Batice didn't survive," Master Haris said, running his hand over his bald patch. "They found his pack on a mountain path when a few boys crossed the river to gather Nightweed." Master Haris noticed the look on my face and hurriedly added, "But that won't happen to you. You'll be fine."

He cleared his throat and moved on. "Within the mountains are caves. You live in a cave system in Espiria, do you not?"

I nodded.

Master Haris went on. "Then you know that it's easy to get lost in them. Take the utmost care that you don't try to use the systems for passage. They might do well enough as a shelter to rest, but don't go adventuring within. You're sure to get lost."

"I know," I said, walking my fingers on the map over the distance from Espiria to where my opals would, hopefully, be found. "Do you know what a black opal is good for?" I asked.

Master Haris thought for a bit. "Power. It can gather and use enormous quantities of power. You'll require quite a bit of control to wield all of it."

"What happens if I fail?" I asked honestly. "What if I can't control it?"

Master Haris rubbed his hands on his knees and looked away. "You either succeed or die trying."

My eyes widened. "Really?" Every sorcerer either succeeded or perished on the journey? That couldn't be right. I began to reassess the whole reason I was at Solridge. Dying was not one of them. "And if I succeed, what then?"

Master Haris started bouncing his leg again. "You will always have a place with us, Rowyn. Why would you think otherwise?"

I shrugged. "I don't know." I didn't dare tell him about

the nagging feeling that kept me wary. Like a well-kept secret, every face I saw seemed to know something I didn't, but instead it was I who held the secret. So well, in fact, that I still couldn't remember it, and it burned me to think I never would.

"You know," Master Haris said, "many sorcerers have to make their own way, as all abilities are rarities in their own right. It just depends on the gem. I know you may feel like this is an impossible task, but with enough study and training, you're sure to succeed." His bouncing leg stilled, and he smiled.

"Thank you, Master Haris, your words are a comfort to me," I said then bent over the parchments as he continued his explanation.

"Most cross the river at the Last Dusk. There is a seer there, Arda, who you may be asked to visit before you leave."

My stomach somersaulted. "I don't want to see a seer," I stammered. The creature that stalked me for a year was sent by Chassandre, the seer to the Eastern Empire. I was loath to revisit any of those memories. Would Arda try to hurt me to appease her counterpart?

Master Haris raised his brows. "Arda is daughter to Imor. Though you may have had bad experiences with seers in the past, she is unlikely to hurt you. Her life's work has been to aid the Morganites."

I groaned inwardly. I already had a host of misgivings over my journey to the Nightlands, but now I had to visit a seer too? Dread filled every fiber of my being, and I found it difficult to concentrate on Master Haris's lectures.

I left the library a bit later. Destrian passed by in the hall, glanced in my direction for a moment, then ignored me. My mind was so filled with Master Haris's information that I barely even noticed and chose not to care.

The others seemed to look to me with new respect, something I'd once hoped to earn.

But if I was so all-powerful, as Master Haris claimed, then why was I so frightened? What was this feeling of dread?

Chapter 4

"ROWYN, THE COUNCIL needs to speak with you about your quest," Master Gillius said, pulling me aside as I ventured toward my writing class. I'd been doggedly training for a week. My muscles were overworked, my brain was mush, and my temper short.

I followed him to the council chamber and seated myself in the center chair as before, noting how much more familiar I felt with the sorcerers looking back at me.

"I'm pleased to report the progress in your studies," Lord Alexander said. "The quest for a gem is an important step in the life of a sorcerer."

Lady Madeline was nodding. "I don't think we need to explain the dangers and tests of resolve to come."

"It's never easy, Rowyn, not for any of us," Gillius added. "You'll need to plan your journey with care."

I nodded. Already I'd seen how seriously the council was taking my trip. In addition to the instruction I was getting from both Master Haris and Lord Alexander, I could feel the north calling me, beckoning me into the darkness. I was growing excited about the journey and how it could change the course of my life.

"You're allowed one companion to help you on your

quest, another sorcerer."

Finally, the council was getting to the purpose of my summoning. With such a short time to prepare, I felt like I had one hand tied behind my back, not knowing who would accompany me.

Then fear struck me, and I felt uneasy. What if it were one of the sorcerers who hated me? What if it were Marc?

"Will it be you, Gillius?" I asked. Gillius's healing powers would be quite useful, given the amount of peril that awaited me in the north.

But Gillius shook his head. "I would be honored to go with you, but I wouldn't be enough help in the Nightlands. You need someone with great strength, someone who can survive the environment. I'm no fighter."

I looked at the others expectantly.

Lord Alexander spoke first. "We sent missives to the palace, but we don't think we'll get a response in time."

I wiped my sweaty hands on the folds of my gown. Who would want to join me on a seemingly suicidal quest?

Lady Vianne's black eyes studied me as she spoke. "We have discussed it at length. You need someone with skills in the fighting arts and survival. Their magical abilities must be an asset to you in surviving the Nightlands. They must be available to train with you and leave on the short notice required. It left only one choice."

I raised my brows. "Lord Alexander?"

Lord Alexander shook his head. "Though I'm skilled in the fighting arts, I would not be an asset to you. You already have powers in controlling the weather. There is nothing my ability over water would do to help your journey in the Nightlands. You must be accompanied by someone who has powers over something you will need, but lack."

Vianne was staring at me awfully hard, her amethyst glowing. She was reading my mind. The hackles on the back of my neck rose, and I shrank away from the purple glow.

Gillius met my eyes. "Lord Destrian should go."

I tore my attention away from Vianne as Lord Alexander and Master Haris nodded. A sick feeling pulsed through me.

"No, absolutely not! How can you ask this of me?" I tried to keep my voice steady, but I was wound to my last nerve.

Lord Alexander turned his level gaze to me. "If any sorcerer here could help you, it would be Destrian. You could use his fire for warmth and light. He would be the difference between life and death in the brutal cold. Destrian is also an experienced fighter, which will be a necessity for the path into the mountains. I've heard there are terrors there you can't even imagine."

"He's also from the north, like you," Master Haris

added, "and already used to longer periods of darkness. It may be too much to bear for the rest of us."

I tried a different angle. "Destrian hasn't achieved mastery yet. I thought only sorcerers who've completed all their tests could be companions."

"Not always," Lady Madeline said. "It only depends on the skills needed for the quest. This is no exception."

I was in utter disbelief. "You mean it would be just Destrian and me, nobody else, for a month *or more*?" My gaping mouth betrayed the horror inside.

Lord Alexander's eyes flashed annoyance. "He's experienced, Rowyn. Don't discount his abilities. You're incapable of completing this quest on your own, and Destrian is the key to your success."

"What of my honor?" I asked, throwing them my last reserves. "What will people say if I go gallivanting into the wilderness with only a young man for company? What will I tell my family?"

Master Gillius almost laughed.

I glared at him, gritting my teeth.

"Rowyn, I don't want to get into personal matters with you," Master Gillius said, "but I know you've heard what's already been said about you on the road."

Lady Vianne tried to hide her smile. "Gillius is right. Nobody has faith in your virtues. Nobody of rank anyway. What does it matter what they'll say as long as you get your gem?"

A deep flush rose to my cheeks. "I can't believe this is your decision. We aren't even friends anymore!"

Lady Madeline swept her hand around the table. "Look at us. Who among your peers and instructors could better help you in this task?"

I tried to find another tactic to persuade them, but despite my inhibitions, I knew what they were saying was true. Still . . . *Destrian*?

"Have you spoken to him yet?" I asked, proud that my voice had calmed.

They shook their heads.

"We thought he'd appreciate hearing the request from you," Vianne said.

"Fine," I grumbled, resolved to my fate. "I don't agree . . . but I will ask." Curtsying, I left the room and walked blindly outside, letting the sun warm my face.

Unwilling to go to writing, I looked toward the road behind me. The council would assume I'd go back to class. It might be a while before anyone came looking for me.

I ran to the beach. Discarding my boots, I walked to the surf, watching the waves while my mind wandered. The journey to the Nightlands was approaching fast, and I didn't feel like I was prepared for it. In truth, I didn't think I would ever be ready.

I replayed the meeting with the sorcerers in my head.

I still couldn't believe they expected Destrian to go with me. What would my family say? What of his father? In the end, Destrian might not even agree. That thought shifted my thinking as I let the waves lap lazily around my ankles. *If not Destrian, then who?*

I wouldn't deny that the lord of Helena had grown on me over the past year. I even counted him as a friend for a time. I thought back to our dance in the marketplace at the Spring Equinox festival. He seemed on the verge of revealing something, but the moment had passed. Then again, I couldn't think of that dance and not remember Fin's face as she watched us. The memory tore a wound in my heart at the possibility of hurting my dearest friend.

Then Destrian had nearly killed me. It seemed impossible to move on from such a terrible experience. His face only reminded me of the fear and pain of that moment. The moment when all seemed lost, though I still couldn't remember what I was running from. Why I'd been so scared.

I sat on the smooth rocks that made up the coastline and stretched out. I loathed thinking of the terrors that awaited me in the Nightlands. Instead, I thought of home. I was sure my family would try to talk me out of it. But I didn't have a choice. I had to go.

The sun dipped low in the sky. I'd been gone for most of the afternoon, and it was sure to be noticed now. As if to prove me correct, I looked over my shoulder and saw someone riding a horse down the switchbacks. The red hair was unmistakable in the bright afternoon sun—Destrian.

I turned back to the sea as he dismounted and sat a distance away from me. He pulled off his boots and tossed them over his shoulder before plunging his bare feet into the cool water.

"Greetings, my lord," I murmured, watching the waves roll over each other. I wondered again why fate continued to throw the consul's son in my way. Something tied us together, and try as I might to break it, it just wouldn't split.

Destrian leaned back on his hands, eyes to the sea. "They sent me to find you."

"I'm surprised you came, considering," I said, unwilling to meet his eye.

"They wouldn't let me refuse," was his simple answer.

We sat quietly for a moment. I knew Destrian waited for me to explain why only he was sent to fetch me rather than Pedr or Fin. Still, I hadn't yet convinced myself that the council was right in their assertion that it should be Destrian.

Destrian broke the silence. "Why did you come here?"

"I had to collect myself. Gillius has made me feel as if I've been imprisoned."

"They treat all ladies this way. No one takes the liberties you do," Destrian muttered darkly.

"I'm unused to a cage," I said, "no matter how gilded. I'm used to coming and going as I please. Now that Chassandre's creature is gone, I see no need to be cooped up behind the gates."

Destrian shook his head. Looking out to the ocean, he grew quiet again, his mind elsewhere as we watched the waves. It took me a moment to realize I hadn't been alone with him for weeks. Not since the day of the festival had we really had a chance to talk.

Destrian seemed to read my mind. "Have you forgiven me yet?" His dark eyes met mine, but I looked away.

"I don't know." I scooped sand into my hand and let it spill back to earth, watching the little granules fall. "You did nearly kill me."

Destrian ran his hand through his red hair, making it stand on end. "I was trying to save you. In that effort, it feels like I lost everything." He sighed before looking at me, eyebrows raised. "Gillius mentioned you needed to talk?"

I cleared my throat while trying to think of the best way to go about it. "What can you do? Specifically, what are your strengths?" I prodded.

Destrian's jewel flashed, and an orange ball of flame, as large as a small boulder, appeared above us and rose over the water. I felt the warmth radiating from the fire as it burned from within, a bright smokeless blaze. The light burst, exploding into a million tiny cinders that sizzled as soon as they hit the seawater.

"Is there anything else you do?"

Destrian snorted. "Subtle. You don't listen at all to Lady Vianne's lessons, do you? I know you need something from me for the Nightlands. So, you might as well spill. What do you want? Safe passage through Helena? An unending burning lantern? A fiery sword?" Destrian picked up a stone from the beach and hurled it angrily into the water. "Just tell me what you wish of me, and I will give it."

"I wouldn't be so quick to hold yourself to that," I muttered. "That's quite a promise."

"Anything to get you away from here. I want to feel like myself again."

That startled me. "What do you mean?" I heard a pang of resentment in his words. Had I done something to him that I couldn't remember? Had I wronged him in some way? For the past two weeks, Destrian seemed to look at me as though he were waiting for something. For the life of me, I had no idea what it was. The uncertainty of it only fueled my irritation . . . and fear.

Destrian threw another rock. "Get to the point. What do you want?"

I really wished the sorcerers had spoken to him first. I didn't know half of what Destrian was speaking of, and it was clear that he would refuse to go with me anyway. Was there even a reason to ask? *By all the gods, get it together, Rowyn!*

Hating myself, I turned and faced Destrian, my eyes meeting his. "I need you to be my companion."

Destrian's face froze. "You're joking."

I shook my head.

"Did you choose me?"

"The council wants you to go."

Destrian scoffed. "What are *your* thoughts, Rowyn?"

"Truthfully?"

Destrian nodded, his dark eyes staring into mine.

"I think you have the skills for it. I agree that, out of anyone here, you would be best suited for the quest," I said before adding, "I just wonder if we might kill each other first."

Destrian was silent for a long time, shaking his head and staring out to sea. "Sometimes, I feel as though Sol is toying with me."

He didn't add further insight into his thoughts. I wondered what was going through his mind. He was probably cursing my name or something.

We sat silent again. Gulls dove into the sea, plucking fish from the water and soaring away. Imor had risen as if to watch and judge, which made me wonder what my mother and father thought of my path. Father would've been excited about the Nightlands. He'd almost ventured there, but an attack from a sable panther had sent him back to the shroud.

"How will we trust each other?" Destrian asked suddenly. "You've already shown that you don't trust me."

I thought for a moment. "That's not necessarily true. You've never been truly unkind to me. I could never trust your father, though." I waited for him to say something, but he didn't. "How will you trust *me*?" I finally asked.

"I don't know," Destrian murmured. "You would be a powerful ally and an unholy enemy. I *do* know that I don't want to be your enemy."

An unholy enemy? What did that mean?

"So, you want me to go?" Destrian asked as if he'd not said anything out of place, watching me out of the corner of his eye.

I let out a gusty sigh. "Yes, I want you to go."

Destrian frowned. "That sounded like it was pretty hard to say."

I glowered. "You just said you wanted me to be away from here, away from you. So let's not pretend you'll actually agree."

Destrian sighed. "That's not what I meant. Can't you understand my perspective? I poured my wounded heart out, and you threw it back in my face."

Was he talking about the festival? The dancing? Had he tried to tell me then, and I rebuffed him?

"Listen, about that—"

"I don't want to talk about it," Destrian said. "Let's have one hard conversation at a time, please."

I sighed. "Fine, so will you do it? Will you be my companion?" I held my breath, waiting for his answer.

Destrian looked me straight in the eye before speaking. "Yes, I will." An odd mix of relief and uneasiness washed over me. "I was jealous when I heard." His dark eyes sparkled as he looked back over the sea. "The Nightlands, into a great unknown. The adventure of a lifetime."

"Really? I think it's suicidal myself."

Destrian stared at the horizon. "Do you believe in fate?"

"Fate?" I asked, wrinkling my brow. "No, I've always hated portents and fortune-telling. Fate is nothing more than an excuse we give ourselves to make us feel better about our choices."

Destrian shook his head. "The gods have their reasons for everything, Rowyn. It's fated that you're here, fated that we go into the Nightlands together. We would be fools to turn away from such obvious signs." Destrian's voice was heavy with the weight of his words.

It was as though he was trying to tell me something,

urging me with his words, but I knew not what it was. Not for the first time, I wished I had Vianne's power of reading minds.

"The gods have never been kind to me, so if they want something, they damn well better just come out and say it. I'm tired of reading the signs."

Destrian frowned. "Don't speak ill of the gods, Rowyn. They have a way of punishing blasphemy."

I thought to shoot back a hateful retort but reconsidered. Destrian agreed to go on the quest. A quest that could kill either one or both of us quite easily. I'd expected more of a fight despite disliking this as much as he did, but he'd not said no at all.

I rose, dusting the sand off my skirt, and held my hand out to help him up. "Thank you," I whispered when he rose. "You will be risking your life for me."

Destrian's face was close to mine. Our eyes met, and he nodded. "An eye for an eye."

Chapter 5

FIN WAS SITTING at the study table when I arrived in our room that evening, a robin perched on her shoulder. She was strangely quiet. For a moment, I thought to leave my news for another time, then reconsidered. Fin wouldn't appreciate hearing from another student, and it would encourage the thought that I had something to hide.

Better to just be out with it, I told myself, clearing my throat to speak.

"They want Destrian to go with you, don't they?" Fin murmured, continuing to write on the parchment.

My stomach plummeted to my knees. Fin's nose was red as if she'd been crying, and there was a tremor to her voice.

I let my breath out in a gust and nodded. Fin was smart. She was always better about reading signs than I was. I should've known she'd figure it out already. "Fin, I don't know what to say," I admitted. I didn't want to have the conversation, but we couldn't leave each other with anything left unsaid. I had too much experience knowing life could change in a moment. "You care for him, don't you?"

Fin whispered something to the robin who flew out the window. Fin set her quill down and turned to me. "Yes, I do care for him. But I also know we could never be."

I sat on my bed. "Why is that? Why do you not tell Destrian how you feel?" Fin was not a coward. Since that moment in the marketplace, I often wondered if Fin had spoken to Destrian about how she felt. I'd also wondered why she never had.

Fin studied her hands, her fingers brushing over an ink stain. "He doesn't feel that way about me, Rowyn. He never has." A tear leaked out of her eye and flowed down her cheek. "I see the way he looks at you. He's never even looked at Ingrid that way. I don't want to be a fool."

I was at a loss. What else was there to say? "How long have you cared for him?"

Fin sniffed. "I don't want to talk about it. It's just wishful thinking."

"I had someone like that," I said, then hesitated. I'd never told Fin about Luc before and wondered why that was. "At home, there was a boy I grew up with, a childhood love. We were engaged to be married if you can believe it."

Fin's eyes went wide, and she wiped away her tears. "*You* were engaged to be married?"

I nodded. "We were best friends growing up, our

fathers being close and all. I have very few childhood memories without him. When I found out he felt the same way, it seemed like it was meant to be—like fate."

"What happened?"

"He was conscripted when he went to the city. The doghunters came to the inn, drugged the ale, bought rounds for all the young men, then took them late in the night when they were all asleep."

Fin nodded. "They would do that at Lark Harbor, too, in the slums along the dock where I lived. One of our neighbors was taken one night. Have you heard from him since?"

"No, Imor only knows what happened to him, and those from Morgania never make it back."

Fin rested a cheek on her hand. "Do you think you will ever see him again?"

"I hope I do," I said, relieved I could unshoulder the burden of wilted hopes. At home, I could have shared my worries with Pria, had she been speaking with me. But to share with Fin, it felt like I'd released myself from the last bad memories from home. "I hope I get to see him again, but at the same time, he could already be dead from the war. I don't know whether to grieve or try to find him. Even then . . ."

Fin waited expectantly while I drummed up the courage to say what I feared most. If anybody could understand without judgment, it would be Fin.

I took a deep breath and went on. "Even if Luc is alive, which is very unlikely given the number of deaths in the war, I would have to find him. They take the conscripted men to the Fields of Forgotten Men or the fighting pits. Even if I manage to free him from there, will he still want me?"

"Of course he would want you. Why ever would you think that?" Fin asked, sitting straighter.

"Because, Fin, feelings change. People change. I've been away from home for a year and can't deny the changes I've gone through. We were so young when we were engaged. We only knew of life behind the shroud. Neither of us will be the same person now that we've left."

"What of him?" Fin asked. "Would you still want him?"

I sighed. "My heart wants to say yes, but my mind—I don't know. I suppose it depends on how much Luc's changed."

Fin sat next to me on the bed. "So, this is why you won't let yourself close to Destrian?"

I nodded. "It's the biggest reason. My family and clan would still want nothing to do with him, nor is it easy to forget what his father and family have done to us. Luc was in Helena when he was taken. Did the consul know about it? Did he authorize the doghunters to come? They seemed to be targeting Morganites in their raids. If it was the consul, did Destrian know?"

"I don't envy you," Fin said. "You must quest to the Nightlands with Destrian, with all of this going on in your mind."

I nodded. "Who told you Destrian was chosen?"

"It was the likely choice. I first thought Destrian would be most advantageous to you. You would need heat and light in the Nightlands, and there are only a few fire sorcerers scattered across the empire, and many are getting on in years."

"Are you upset?"

Fin met my eye and shook her head. "I don't have a right to be."

"Still, how you—"

"Stop." Fin held up her hand. "Yes, I care for him. Since the moment I arrived here, I've had feelings for him. Sometimes that would lead to daydreams, wild thoughts, and fantasies, but I also care about you. Ever since you've found out, you've withdrawn yourself and tiptoe around my feelings. I want us to go back to the way things were. Your friendship means more to me than my feelings for Destrian."

A tear escaped from the corner of my eye. "I don't want to lose my friendship with you, either" I said, wiping the tear away.

Fin didn't speak for a moment. She stared at the floor then, as if she'd determined something, and nodded. "I'm going on my quest this summer too. Master Haris told me this morning that we would be leaving at the same time. I want to go with a clear head, focusing on my journey, rather than fretting about where our friendship stands."

"I would choose you over Destrian, over anybody. I would choose our friendship first."

Fin smiled. "But what I'm saying is you don't have to. A friend wouldn't make you choose. Not if it's meant to be. You have enough to worry about with everything coming up and all that you've told me. Please don't worry about me too. I'll be here for you, regardless of what happens, or which path you take."

I let out a breath that I didn't realize I'd held and hugged her.

"Thank you," I whispered. "Not many have been as forgiving with me as you've been."

Fin hugged me back. "Now, let's speak of other things. What do you plan to take on your journey? Master Haris said there won't be any inns or anything in Horan, so we'll be carrying everything with us to camp. Can you look over my list and recommend anything?"

I smiled and nodded, glad that our friendship was finally back on the right foot and that, if I could leave here with one surety, it was that I would always have a friend in Fin.

"DESTRIAN?" ARACELI ASKED, looking to the men's practice yard at weapons work the next morning. "Does Ingrid know?"

"I've no idea." I shrugged. "I don't hold the Caldeaon sisters in confidence."

Araceli narrowed her eyes. "I wouldn't make light of the anger you're sure to be subjected to by the Byrnes. Though you may think Ingrid and Lisbet are silly, as a friend, I would warn you against openly attracting their anger."

"What does Rowyn have to fear from Caldeaon?" Fin scoffed.

"I've never been to The Fens," I added, "nor am I nobility to worry about arousing their anger. None of their family are sorcerers, either."

Araceli raised a single eyebrow and pursed her lips. "Caldeaon is the most popular court in the Western Empire. It's a hub of art and music, begun by the first Byrnes to rule Caldeaon. Unlike the other consuls, the Byrnes are original Adarites and remember when they were kings in the area. They have quite a following with the people, and they get along well with the emperor. Tread carefully is all I'm saying. There's been many a reputation ruined at their expense. That family knows well the games and intrigues to be had at court. I should know, my mother is a Byrne."

"You are cousins with Ingrid and Lisbet?" I asked, dumbfounded I didn't realize it sooner.

Araceli nodded. "I take more after my father, but yes, we are cousins. That's why I came to Solridge instead of going to the capital, though Calla is in the Eastern Empire. Mother wanted me to spend more time with her side of the family."

"Oh, I suppose I hadn't put that together," I said.

"Just be careful of them," Araceli urged. "They can be ruthless in their own way."

"I'll remember that," I muttered, stepping out into the sun where Lord Alexander was waiting for me.

MY MUSCLES SCREAMED as I collapsed in the library seat across from Pedr that evening.

"If I ever complained that Lord Alexander didn't pay attention to me in weapons work before, I take it back."

Pedr chuckled as he set up our chess game. "You did well fighting downhill."

Lord Alexander had me run through drills on the large stones he'd placed at the bottom of the hill, going uphill and maneuvering to get the upper hand. Of course, that meant my muscles felt like butter the rest of the day.

"How do you feel about the journey? It's all the others are talking about."

I shrugged. "Well enough, I suppose. Some days, I think I will most likely perish. Other days I'm more hopeful."

"Is it really so perilous?" Pedr wrinkled his brows as he studied the chessboard. "One would think the Nightlands would be void of much life. Granted, I've not heard much about it, other than no one should go there, the stuff of nightmares, and the lot." He smiled as he moved one of his pieces. Looking over the board, I couldn't tell if it was a strategic position or not.

"The Morganians have lots of stories about the Nightlands," I said. "My grandmother used to swear that's where the fairies went when man spread west. The Woltari called it the Land of Terror, for even they refused to cross the river unless they were searching for a vision."

"I pulled what I thought would help you," Pedr explained, motioning to a stack of books next to him. A couple had to do with exotic plants and animals of the north. I thanked him.

Lord Obi rose from his desk by the library door and

wagged his finger at me. "Just don't smudge the letters, and *don't* you *dare* eat while you read, or I'll have your neck!" Satisfied with his scolding, Lord Obi sat and took a shaky sip of ale.

Pedr took my knight with his bishop. "So you and Destrian are to go to the Nightlands together."

I bemoaned my poor chess skills as I tried to rally what few pawns I had left. "Yes, it will be quite the adventure, to be sure."

The door to the library screeched open, and familiar voices came in. Pedr and I were tucked away in our corner, screened from the rest of the room. Although Lord Obi always knew when we were in there, he mostly chose to ignore us.

It was clear that Ingrid and Lisbet were having a heated discussion as they walked, looking for a tome on remedies for blood sickness.

"Aren't you worried, though?" Lisbet asked softly.

"No, why should I be? Noblemen of all stations bed gutter wenches, but they never marry them," Ingrid said, her voice dripping with disdain. "So what if they have a tryst in the mountains. When he returns, things will go back exactly to as they were. Honestly, I'd much rather he get it out of his system now before we wed."

Pedr glanced at me with wide eyes, and we both shrank into our seats, hoping to the gods that we wouldn't be seen. Thankfully they found the book they were looking for and headed back toward the door.

"But he hasn't officially asked you. Surely you must realize that it may not be a sure thing."

"How dare you say such a thing," Ingrid hissed. "You're just jealous of the attention he's paid to me all these years. Father plans on another union between our families. The wealth of Morgania forever intertwined with the nobility of Caldeaon. Destrian and I are both devoted to the idea."

"He did seem devoted . . . in the past. But you're kidding yourself if you haven't noticed that his devotion has fallen away since her arrival," Lisbet remarked.

The door slammed shut behind them, and I smiled. I hadn't known Lisbet to have such a backbone on her. Her sister had always seemed the bold one, but Lisbet was rising in my esteem.

Pedr looked astonished. "How can you smile after the insult Ingrid just paid you?"

I waved my hand away. "Oh, bother Ingrid. I've never cared for her good opinion, and she would never bestow it. What's the point of getting upset about it?"

"You don't care about the rumors that are spreading?"

"Oh, please, the Lyons have called me far worse than gutter wench."

"But you . . . and Destrian."

"What of it? I'm not remotely interested in him as a . . . you know." I paused. "As someone to even think about. My mind is on other things, Pedr, and we'll be traveling for months in one of the most dangerous places in the world."

Pedr shrugged. "If you say so. You know, he's really not a bad guy. Nobody should be judged by the sins of their parents."

"I know he's nice. Nobody will let me forget it."

FIN WASN'T IN THE ROOM when I returned that evening, presumably still out riding with Breeze. But Ena was waiting to help me ready for bed, her mouth drawn into a tight line.

I waited patiently as she helped me undress, knowing that Ena liked to ponder her words before she spoke.

"Your mother . . ." She paused then shifted awkwardly. "Before she died, did she talk to you? About men?"

My brows furrowed. "What about men?"

Ena seemed at a loss for another moment. "Well, about what it means—how it works when you are alone with a man."

My eyes grew wide. "Ena!"

Ena's hands flew to her cheeks. "I just want you to be prepared. You're going off to the wilderness, and Imor only knows what will happen. This is most unusual! All the servants are talking about it, which means all the lords and ladies are speaking of it."

I rubbed my temples with my fingers and chuckled. "Romance will be the very last thing on my mind."

At that, Ena swiped my shoulder. "Maybe, but is it the last thing on his?"

"Well," I sputtered, "that is so obviously not the point. Nothing will happen, and that's the end of it. I don't know what everyone is making such a racket about!" I threw off my gown and jumped into bed. "We are not having this conversation."

"No, wait!" Ena said, her hands flying up. "It will make me feel better. Just tell me your mother spoke to you."

I paused, poised to blow out the candle. "Yes," I said. "Mother spoke to me at length! With elaborate description! There, do you feel better now?"

"Yes," Ena said, going to the door with a relieved sigh. "All right, we won't speak of it again."

"Good!" I snapped, then blew the flame out as she left.

By all the gods, was everyone in an uproar. I had

known they would be, but still it stole my patience. It certainly wasn't a proper arrangement. Now it felt as though the entire Western Empire were watching us and gossiping. I didn't like that thought. Not in the least.

Chapter 6

THE NEXT MORNING, Lord Alexander beckoned me to the makeshift mountain. Destrian, Marc, and Idris were waiting at the base, and all seemed to be avoiding my eye. The air was fraught with tension, so I stood away from them, awkwardly silent until Lord Alexander finished giving directions to the other young men and joined us.

"Now that Lord Destrian has agreed to go," Lord Alexander said, "I want you to practice fighting over the stony terrain. We will work a bit on these stones and, in a week or two, move down to the beach. I also want us to spend some time practicing after dark. You must get used to this type of fighting if you're to succeed in the Nightlands. Marc and Idris have graciously offered to help."

Marc and Idris glared at me so hard I was taken aback. What had I done to them?

"Come, Rowyn, hop up on that stone there and practice fighting with weight in your favor. Marc can help you. Destrian, I want you to practice with weight in your opponent's favor. See if you can maneuver to a better position."

Lord Alexander called for us to start. I bore down on

Marc, my practice sword whipping about speedily until he stumbled back, duly disarmed.

Marc picked himself off the ground and shot me a look so filled with contempt that I almost loathed him for it in return.

"Excellent, Rowyn," Lord Alexander said as he returned from the practice field. "Now, Marc, it's your turn. Let's see if Rowyn can get the upper hand."

I moved to the lower position, while Marc towered above me. He seemed to dance over the stones and rocks, whipping his blade about as I struggled to withstand the blows made all the more forceful with his weight behind them. Marc's mouth was drawn into a hard line, his eyes searching for an opening.

One blow knocked the sword out of my hand, and another threw me to the ground. Looking up, Marc stood above me, his sword pointed at my throat.

"Try again," Lord Alexander said from behind me. I groaned as I got to my feet and wiped the sweat from my brow. "This time, pay close attention to the rocks. Close the distance between you so he can't sweep down so hard. Move over the rocks so you are constantly changing placement and elevation."

I nodded, holding my sword up. Marc swept about just as quickly as before, the corners of his mouth drawing up into a sneer. Within minutes I was sprawled on the ground, my shoulder bruised from hitting a rock on the way down.

"Again," Lord Alexander demanded.

An hour later, with weapons work finally ended, I limped back toward the school. I hadn't been able to maneuver to a better position to best Marc, who was merciless with his technique. I was so absorbed with my misery that I hadn't paid any attention to Idris and Destrian's matches.

"Rowyn, can I speak with you a moment?" Marc asked from behind me. The others had gone on, and we were alone.

Curious, I stopped and gave Marc my full attention.

"Listen, I know you asked Destrian to accompany you to the Nightlands, but have you really thought of the danger you are placing him in?"

I was taken aback. I'd no idea Marc felt so strongly about his friend, nor did I realize his anger toward me might be for his concern. I could respect as much. "Destrian is aware of the dangers."

Marc shook his head. "That's not the danger I'm talking about. Things are already bad between Ayastaren and Solridge from Elias's death. You will foment anger with them at Destrian and Morgania if he goes with you. They will see it as him aligning himself with you over them. There will be unrest."

"Why . . ." I stopped, my heart skipping a beat. I hadn't considered what Marc was saying, so focused was I on the journey to come. Was it true? Would it be detrimental to Destrian's standings with the other nobility if he came with me?

"Have you mentioned this to him?" I asked. "I don't feel as though it's my decision, but his."

Marc's eyes narrowed. "I did." He stopped for a moment as if to choose his words carefully. "The other nobles don't want to choose an alliance between Helena and Ayastaren. Though Ayastaren holds the highest seat and is the emperor's chosen warden of the Western Empire, Helena is the wealthiest. It could get rough diplomatically if we are forced to choose."

"But you would choose Destrian, surely. He's your friend!" I stammered, wondering how Destrian had responded to him.

Marc shook his head. "Did you not hear what I just said? Ayastaren was placed by the emperor as the ruling seat, and we don't want to make that choice."

"Would you wish me to talk to him? I make no promises. He's his own person, after all."

Marc shook his head, clearly disappointed with me. "If you cared about him at all, you wouldn't let him go. He would do the same for you in a heartbeat if it were the other way around." Then Marc stormed into the building, leaving me to wonder what in the gods just happened.

Was Marc correct in his assessment? Given everything that I'd heard, I was beginning to have severe misgivings about Destrian being my companion. I wasn't entirely enthusiastic about the idea in the first place. Now that it endangered Destrian's standing with the other nobles, I began to doubt the council's wisdom in their choice.

There was something else Marc had said. *He would do the same for you.* How could I ask Destrian to give up everything, just for my gem? He was risking his political standing, his friends, his very life for me. Could I ask him to take such a risk?

DESTRIAN'S WORK SHED was smoking away as I approached it. I ducked inside, trying not to inhale the fumes, and looked around. I'd rarely entered before, not ever having a purpose to. The fire burned at the center of the stone shed. Destrian stood at its side, a leather apron wrapped around him as he pounded away with a hammer. He was covered in black soot, while droplets of sweat streaked his face, making it look like he'd been painted.

Destrian seemed utterly different, so . . . messy. In a way, he reminded me of home.

I had to shout to get Destrian's attention. He set the hammer down and used his arm to wipe his brow, which only served to blacken it further. "What is it?"

"Marc spoke with me this morning," I began, the flames of the fire retreating into the pit. "He brought up some issues I hadn't considered. I'm wondering if you should go."

Destrian frowned. "What did he tell you?"

"That Ayastaren could turn their backs on you. That the other nobles would have to choose," I said, eyes on the floor.

Destrian shook his head. "Well, he shouldn't concern himself with my business."

I waited for Destrian to go on, but he didn't. He only waited, eyes on me.

"Do you not care at all for the consequences that Marc spoke of? What *would* happen if the other nobles had to choose?"

Destrian shrugged. "I suppose I'd find out who my true friends are, wouldn't I?"

"What will your father say?"

Destrian scuffed his foot in the dirt. "We shall see. I wrote to him yesterday. I suppose we'll find out when we reach Helena."

"I've changed my mind. I don't think you should go," I said, trying to put weight behind my words. "I didn't consider the position it would put you in, and I'm sorry for that, but given everything I know now, I can't let you take the risk." Destrian was shaking his head, but I took a deep breath and continued. "You have a duty as heir to remain in diplomatic standing with the other consuls and rulers of the west, not to mention the danger to your life, which is no small thing. I'm resolved. I can't let you go."

"Have you spoken to the council yet?" Destrian asked, moving abruptly around the firepit. "You didn't say anything to them, have you?"

I shook my head, realizing that was precisely what I should have done if I wanted my little speech to work. Destrian looked relieved.

"Good, I'm going with you."

"No!" I said, stamping my foot. "I can take someone else, someone nonmagical, like my cousin Ferris. I'm sure he would go with me if I asked." If my uncle let him.

Destrian crossed his arms. "No, your companion will be me. It is decided."

I let out a gust of frustration. "Why are you so insistent on this, with everything you may have to sacrifice?"

Destrian stepped forward again, looking down on me from his great height. "You once called me a coward. Now, when I actually have a chance to prove my worth, you ask, no, demand this of me? I'm not fooled, Rowyn. This is a test, and I *will* pass."

My eyes widened at my own words being thrown back in my face. I didn't think Destrian was a coward anymore. In fact, I thought he was one of the bravest nobles at Solridge. "Don't listen to me!" I exclaimed. "This isn't about that! This is entirely different."

Destrian shook his head. "No, it's not. Besides, I've already spoken to the council. Being your companion is my final test to mastery. If we make it back with your gem, I will have finished my Trial by Self."

Destrian's announcement threw me off guard. To know he'd benefit made the situation easier on my mind, but at the same time, the risks were the same. "Oh," I said finally. "I hadn't realized you would have a stake in this journey."

Destrian sighed. "I suggest we move on from this. I've made my choice, and I will face the consequences of my actions. You don't have anything to do with it, and I refuse to let you feel guilty about it. It's my choice. Let me *choose*."

"But, Marc . . ." I started then didn't know how to finish.

"Go on, what about Marc?" Destrian growled.

I took a deep breath but was unable to look him in the eye. "He said you would do the same for me."

I heard but didn't see him sigh. Destrian tilted my chin up, so my eyes were on his. "I would," he answered simply, "but you would have responded no differently."

He was right. How often had I shown that I cared nothing for the consequences of my actions and simply hurtled forward with whatever I deemed was right at the moment.

It seemed that Lord Destrian knew me better than I knew myself, which wasn't a welcome thought. In fact, with all that had been said of late, it was downright disturbing.

Chapter 7

"I WISH WE WERE GOING TOGETHER," I said to Fin as she gathered her bags. I was sprawled out on the bed, my single pack already propped in the corner, carefully arranged. We were to leave early the next morning and were enjoying a much-needed day off.

"Me too," Fin said. "Master Haris is not what I would call welcome company. He'll be more interested in studying the Woltari for his next book than helping find my gem." Fin tossed down a heavy pack. "Have you gotten any of your gifts yet?"

"Gifts?" I asked, sitting up in bed. "What are you talking about?"

Fin raised an eyebrow. "They didn't tell you? Whenever a sorcerer leaves on a quest, they are given gifts to help on their journey. It's meant to be a show of support."

"Oh," I said, crestfallen, "maybe they weren't planning on it since we're leaving on such short notice."

Fin smiled. "No, they will have something for you. But you must wait till tomorrow morning for mine."

"You don't have to give me anything," I said, holding up my hands. "I don't—"

"I won't take no for an answer."

Well, at least that gave me a day to figure out her present now that I knew the custom.

Gillius was waiting at the dining hall door when Fin and I went down for breakfast. "The council would like to see each of you when you are finished." He reached out as if to pat my shoulder but seemed to think better of it and turned and walked away.

We entered the dining hall, where the other students glanced at us before returning to their whispered conversations. Araceli smiled when we took our seats at the ladies' table.

"Are you two ready? There is a big journey ahead for each of you."

"As ready as I'll ever be," Fin muttered before taking a bite of her sweet roll.

I nodded. "I feel as prepared as I would be if I knew a year ago, and I don't have to dwell and fret on it for very long. So, I think I'm lucky that things happened quickly."

Araceli nodded. "Well, I know I speak for the rest of the ladies when I say, I hope you find your gems and that your journeys are safe from peril."

"Thank you, Araceli," I said, reaching my hand out to her. "I've always valued your friendship."

"Yes, Araceli," Fin added, "you're a young woman of true merit."

Araceli blushed then held out both hands, one fist to

Fin, and one to me. "I know the sorcerers give each other tokens before their trip, so I would like to give you these."

Fin and I held out our hands, and she dropped a small key onto each of our palms. It was iron, with ridges in the shape of sun rays. The head had a sunburst carved in the center.

"It's beautiful," I said, turning to smile at her.

Fin nodded. "A stall sold these in Lark Harbor."

Araceli's ears turned pink. "It's a good luck token from Calla. Our sigil is a key, so we use keys as gifts and charms. They can mean all sorts of different things. This one is for Sol to watch your journey, and it's supposed to ward off malevolent spirits."

"What a marvelous gift. I shall treasure it," I said, clasping her hand and beaming.

Fin agreed then rose. "I'm going to join the council now. Wish me luck!"

"Good luck to you," I said to her retreating back.

"I didn't know if you'd like it," Araceli whispered. "I know Morganites follow Imor, but . . ."

"No," I said, shaking my head. "It's lovely and thoughtful. Do they normally wear it around the neck?"

Araceli nodded and grinned before turning back to her breakfast and the other ladies. I took another bite of my roll, unable to stop the joy spreading through me.

After a while, I rose and went to the council chambers.

Fin was nowhere to be found, but the sorcerers were inside, waiting.

"Ah, Rowyn, there you are," Gillius said, standing and beckoning me in. "It is customary for the council to bestow gifts to help you on your journey. We trust all of your preparations are in order?"

I nodded, glancing at the others as I walked inside the chamber. "Lord Alexander and Master Haris were kind enough to go through my list. I also have several weapons I am borrowing from the armory."

Lord Alexander nodded but didn't smile. I'd slaved away the past several weeks during weapons work. Though my muscles ached after every practice, he always seemed to think it was never enough. I wondered if he thought I'd ever be prepared.

Lord Alexander rose. "I am gifting you this waterskin. It will hold double the amount that you think, and weigh half the amount that you see."

It was an excellent gift given the nature of my journey. Weight was always a problem when traveling long distances on foot, and water was essential. "Thank you, Lord Alexander," I said, my cheeks warm.

He stepped back so that Lord Obi and Master Haris could step forward. Lord Obi held up a scroll while Master Haris gripped his robes with trembling hands. I couldn't imagine him trekking the Canyonlands of Horan and meeting with the fierce Woltari.

"This is a map," Lord Obi said. I waited for him to continue, but he didn't.

Master Haris glanced at Lord Obi and cleared his throat. "Yes, this is a map of the Nightlands. It won't tear or stain and, if lost, will find you again in a moment."

My eyes widened. "It's sure to be essential to our success," I said, curtsying. Lord Obi nodded shakily, while Master Haris stepped back to allow Lady Madeline and Gillius to step forward.

"From us, you have a variety of medicines," Lady Madeline said, sweeping her hand to a few velvet bags. "The sachets won't spill. The directions and use for each are on this list."

I nodded and scanned down the parchment. "So, the arnica is for bruises?"

Lady Madeline nodded. "For these to work, you must pinch a bit of the herb into a boiling pot, let it cool, then rub onto the affected area."

"What will help with the lack of sun?" I asked, scanning the little bags.

Lady Madeline lifted a small cloth sack and opened it up. Pulling out a mushroom, she said, "Put one of these in your waterskin each time you refill. There are more than enough for both you and Destrian."

I nodded. Seemed simple enough.

"I've included my own magic to them," Master Gillius added. "Not only are the herbs more potent"—he nodded to Lady Madeline—"they contain a magical dose that will help you heal. They will last a year if you're careful."

"That's so wonderful," I said with feeling. The medicine would probably be the difference between life or death in the wilderness.

Lady Madeline smiled and went back to her seat at the council table.

Lady Vianne stood. "I would like to give my gift in private."

The other sorcerers nodded, letting Vianne lead me to the room where she held her classes. As soon as I entered, I felt the hair on my arms rising. Vianne's presence always set my nerves on edge. I didn't think I'd ever get used to someone sifting through my thoughts at their will.

Vianne motioned me to the couch and filled two goblets with wine before sitting beside me and offering one. I took a sip as she did.

Leaning back against a cushion, Vianne regarded me for a moment. "You shouldn't take your brooding to the Nightlands. I know the past several weeks have been difficult, but you will need your mind completely devoted to your task to succeed."

I raised my brows. The lost memories *had* been haunting me the past week, but Vianne's words gave me a sudden idea. I sat up, clutching the goblet in my hands. I didn't know why I didn't think of it before. Surely Vianne would be able to find the answers I sought.

"Are you able to recover memories lost to trauma? Can you tell me why I left that night?"

Lady Vianne took another sip of wine. Her gem glowed, and I could tell she was poring over my thoughts, something I usually detested. Then again, she would know that.

After a moment, Vianne turned her gaze to the window, refusing to meet my eye. "When a memory disappears due to trauma, it's to protect the bearer. This is why Master Haris is so anxious all the time. He doesn't possess the skill to forget, though I know he wishes he did." Vianne's eyes darted to mine, then looked away. "I would not restore your memory to you, even if I could."

The swell of excitement deflated, and I ran my fingers over the lip of the goblet. I'd gotten myself worked up for nothing. I should've known it wouldn't be so easy. I'm sure my disappointment showed, but Lady Vianne cleared her throat. It occurred to me that she'd brought me to her room for another reason.

"Tell me, what was Lord Destrian's reaction when you asked him to go?"

"Oh, I don't know," I said slowly, unwilling to look up. "Destrian was . . . excited, I suppose. He said he wanted to come."

"Aye, do you know why?"

"Well, for the adventure," I said, nervously taking another sip.

Vianne shook her head. "No, you and I both know that is a lie."

"Then why did he agree to go?"

"Do you really want to know?" Vianne asked, taking another sip and regarding me thoughtfully.

"No, actually, I don't."

Vianne laughed. "Very well, I won't give you an answer you already know, even if you won't tell me. I see you're planning on returning home before heading to Helena. I hope you won't dally long, for summer in the Nightlands is short."

"I won't," I said. "I just want to see how everyone is doing. I haven't been able to send letters or anything, so I want them to know I'm all right."

Vianne nodded again, but her eyes narrowed. "What will your clan say when they find out who will accompany you on your quest? Destrian's family is their great enemy, no?"

Vianne *would* choose that wound to salt. "I don't know. Nothing good. I almost thought to skip Espiria before I left, but . . ." I shrugged. "I want to have said goodbye, in case anything happens to me. They'd never forgive me if I didn't say goodbye."

Vianne nodded then cleared her throat. "I can't give you my gift now. Not yet, anyway."

"Oh?" I asked, then rallied. "That's all right. I didn't expect any gifts at all until Fin mentioned something this morning."

Vianne tilted her head. "You have a sweet side, don't you."

I didn't know what to say to that, so I said nothing.

Vianne went on. "I have a gift, but it must wait until you return. Though there is someone else who wanted to give you something."

Rising, she opened the door to Galena, who clutched a small, wrapped parcel in her blue hands. She held out the package to me.

I glanced at the note on top. "Silphium for courses," I read, my brows knitting together. Where had I heard that name before?

Galena nodded then signed very slowly.

"What do you mean, Destrian and I?"

Vianne cleared her throat. "Whenever you refill your waterskin, put a pinch of this inside. It will make sure you keep your courses."

"I still don't . . ." I said, then remembered Ena's words, and it dawned on me. "No! Nothing is going to happen. Has everyone gone mad?"

Galena signed something else, and a deep flush rose to my cheeks. She couldn't be serious.

"Galena ... I ... Please, even the thought is improper."

But Vianne was insistent. "Rowyn, Galena came to me for help because she values you as a friend. You may not intend for anything to happen on this journey, and you may well be right, but just in case, please make sure to use this."

"So ... this will keep me from being with child?" I asked slowly.

Galena nodded, then signed again, "Just in case."

I thought to make a scene of it, but Galena was trying to help. It would be rude to repay her assistance with pitching a fit. "Fine," I relented, "I will include it—just in case. But know that there isn't a need for it."

Just in case, indeed.

Of course, no sooner had I left Vianne's room, I ran straight into Destrian himself.

"I was looking for you," he said as I hastily shoved the silphium into a pocket of my gown.

"Yes, did you want to finalize our packs?" I asked, trying to sound distant and formal.

Destrian shot me an odd look and shook his head. "No, I have a present for you as well. It's customary for the companion to gift something of great importance to their pilgrim."

Now, this was getting out of hand. I'd never received so many gifts in my life. Some exceedingly useful, and some . . . not so much.

"You really don't have to," I mumbled.

Destrian rolled his eyes and headed down the corridor. When I didn't follow, he turned. "Well, are you coming?"

I sighed but followed him out to the grounds. Galena's and Vianne's words still ran through my mind. Even Ena seemed to expect something of the time between the Destrian and me. In fact, the whole of Solridge did. Just the thought made me profoundly uncomfortable.

I followed Destrian to the forge. The place seemed oddly silent with the fire out. I stood inside the doorway and waited patiently as he pulled down a sword from the wall, still encased in a black scabbard.

"Here," he said, offering the weapon to me. "I know you gave up your sword in Ayastaren. I didn't think it would be right for you just to grab any old sword from stores. It seems only fitting that you should have your own."

I was stunned. "Did you make this?" I whispered, inspecting the black leather scabbard. The hilt was simple and smooth, but within the pommel was carved a ten-point star with a sideways crescent in the middle. It was the same design tattooed on my chest. Heat flooded my cheeks.

Destrian shifted his feet, his eyes watching my face. "Yes, and I hope you like it. I made one for myself, too. I wanted to make sure the swords wouldn't crack in the cold, so I found some old concoctions in the library from a blacksmith up north who came up with a metal called bitter steel. I experimented with it a bit and am quite happy with the result. Pull it out—take a look."

Nervously, I slid the sword from the sheath and held it up to the light. The blade was bright silver and the perfect weight. I tested the balance and found it perfect as well. There was an etching at the top of the blade. I looked closer and saw a shadow falcon in flight, emblazoned above Morganian rose blossoms. I was flabbergasted at how much thought he'd put into the design. We'd barely spoken since he'd become my companion. To think he'd been in his forge, slaving away for me, was utterly unexpected. A tear coursed down my cheek.

"You like it?" Destrian asked, taking a step toward me.

"It's the most beautiful thing," I said, wiping the tear away.

"I'm sorry, you said you had a marking of a shadow falcon on your back, and that it was your favorite, so I did my best to . . ."

"Destrian, I have no words."

Suddenly, Destrian smiled. It had been months since

I'd seen him look genuinely happy. I was startled out of my tears and found myself smiling back at him.

"I'm glad you like it," he murmured.

"I love it," I said with feeling, testing the blade on my finger. It sliced clean, and blood welled up from my thumb.

Destrian handed me a handkerchief and leaned against the forge. "You've drawn first blood. What will you name her?"

"Name her?" I asked, dabbing my thumb with the bit of cloth. "I suppose I don't know."

Destrian lifted a large sword that was leaning against the forge and held it out to me. Within its pommel was carved a star whose points looked to be flames from a fire. His blade was bigger and heavier, with a pale gold sheen. "Every good sword must have a name. I've decided to call this one Phyranox. It's Old Mortongue for the flame in the night."

"That's fitting," I said, running my hand down the cool blade of my sword. "Did you find one that would work for mine?"

Destrian shrugged, but his lips curled up at the corners.

"What is it?" I asked, still grinning at him. "I'm not creative in the least."

Destrian bowed his head with a chuckle. "All right. I

may have put one together that might do in a pinch."

"Out with it," I said when he paused.

"Iranoct. It means night rain."

"Iranoct," I repeated, holding the blade up. I nodded. "Iranoct it is."

Destrian fiddled with the hilt of Phyranox for a moment then leaned it back against the forge. "Marc gave me your gift."

"Oh?" I asked, still admiring the designs on the blade. "Why could Marc not give it himself?" He was probably still angry I wasn't able to talk Destrian out of coming with me.

Destrian tilted his head to the side. "He helped me make the swords and added his essence to them." Destrian fiddled with his hilt again, refusing to meet my eyes. "I hope you don't mind—it seemed dead useful at the time, though I second-guessed myself when it was too late."

I frowned. "What did you do?"

"Since Marc is a tracker, his essence linked the swords. One can lead the bearer to the other." Seeing the look on my face, Destrian hesitated. "It was in case we get separated, so we'll have a way to find each other again."

"Hmm," I said, taking a practice swing. "I suppose that would be useful. How does it work?"

"He said to hold the sword up and concentrate your entire mind on the other blade." Destrian's smile returned.

"Here, try it with Iranoct." Destrian took his sword and left, shutting the door of the forge behind him. I waited a moment before holding Iranoct's blade up and closing my eyes. In my mind, I could see Phyranox, its golden sheen, the pommel with the flaming star.

My sword gave a gentle tug. I let the hilt lead my hands down, and it pulled me to the door. I left, following the pull of the blade until I reached the stable door. Opening it, I found Destrian inside. Phyranox rested on his shoulder as he leaned against his horse's stall, absentmindedly patting Valor.

"It works!" I said excitedly. "Did you feel anything?"

Destrian shook his head. "No, we decided against the other sword responding, just in case it was stolen. We didn't want to let the bearer know they were being tracked."

"Good thinking," I said in agreement. "I will be sure to thank Marc before we leave."

Destrian crossed his arms and regarded me somberly. "Are you ready?"

"As ready as I'll ever be. It feels like the stone is beckoning me."

Destrian nodded. "Yes, once you go through the Trial by Stone, it will torment you until you've accomplished the task."

I glanced back to the empty stall that once held Ally.

Destrian followed my gaze.

"I'll leave you to the rest of your day," he said shortly. Then he strode out of the stable. As he passed, I grabbed his hand.

"Thank you," I said. "Thank you for everything. I don't know how I could ever repay you."

Destrian met my eyes then pulled his hand from my grasp. "Pedr's looking for you. Best to say your goodbyes today."

Chapter 8

"**D**O YOU LIKE IT?" Pedr asked, his eyes bright. I smiled, running my fingers over the smooth dark wood of a chess piece in the shape of the queen, strung on a simple silver chain. "It's wonderful, but the queen might be a little ambitious, given my chess ability. A pawn might be closer to my skill set."

"I didn't make it myself," Pedr went on. "I had it commissioned a few weeks ago, but I thought it would suit you as a reminder."

"It's perfect," I said with a smile, pulling the chain over my head, "and will remind me of the wonderful memories where you bested me at the game."

Pedr laughed as we continued walking along the road outside of Solridge. I readjusted my pack, groaning under the weight. For the past couple of weeks, I opted to practice carrying my backpack instead of going to the library. Pedr joined me most nights to chat about our classes, the other students, or our homes.

Destrian had been practicing with his pack too. I'd seen him carrying it to the beach, accompanied by either Idris or Marc. Once or twice, Ingrid went with them.

"When do you leave?" I asked Pedr. His lover, Will,

had been writing to Pedr daily in anticipation of his return.

"At the end of the week," Pedr replied.

I nodded and took a deep breath, relishing the scent of sweetgrass and wildflowers that grew over the moors, mixed with the brininess of the sea. "You will come back at the end of your visit, won't you?"

Pedr nodded and smiled. "I'll actually look forward to it this year. I never have in the past, but now that things are different, I've begun to feel quite at home."

"Do you think the issue with the Lyons is over?" I asked, trying to sound hopeful. "Marc doesn't seem to think so, but I wonder . . ."

Pedr's face darkened. "One can only hope, but I don't think it will be that easy."

"Maybe it would be best if I didn't return. I wouldn't want to put the council and other students at Solridge in a bad position with Ayastaren."

Pedr stopped and turned to me. "Don't say that. You're the reason I'm excited to come back. We would miss you, Fin and I. Destrian would, too, if he was returning."

My stomach twisted into an unexpected knot. "What do you mean? Why wouldn't he come back?"

Pedr frowned. "Your quest is his test for mastery. Once the sorcerers gain mastery, they don't need to continue their studies. Some stay, like Galena and Master

Haris, to work at the school, but Destrian is an heir. He has to be at home to help rule Helena."

"I didn't realize that," I said slowly.

"Yes, Destrian's farewells tomorrow will be his last. Everyone will miss him."

We fell silent, admiring the sunset over the meadow. The sky was washed with pink and orange while the indigo of night peeked over the ocean.

"Can you imagine not seeing another sunset for more than a month?" Pedr asked. "I can't."

I breathed deeply, trying to imbue the images of Solridge in my mind. It seemed impossible to believe that merely a year ago, I'd left Morgania for the first time. Solridge was so different from home. I'd traded views of giant morwood pines and mountains for meadows, bogs, and a sea view.

"I'll miss this, but it's mostly dark in Morgania. The council was right about that, at least."

Pedr turned, his gray eyes somber. "Why do I feel like this may be the last time I see you for a long time?"

"I know," I murmured, reaching out and grabbing his hand. "I feel it too."

"Be careful," he said. "Be careful, and know that I love you and am rooting for you to succeed."

I threw my arms around him. "I love you too. Send Will my love as well. I can't wait to meet him."

Pedr nodded. "We should head back. You have quite a journey ahead of you, friend. You'll need your rest."

I smiled. Together we made our way back to Solridge as the sun disappeared from the sky, and the sound of waves splashing against the beach filled our ears.

WAKING IN A COLD SWEAT, I looked to the sky outside the window. Dawn was coming.

Fin sat up. "Today's the day," she said, wrapping her arms around her knees. "How do you feel?"

I smiled and rolled out of bed, letting the bad dream disappear into the sun's rays. "Nervous," I said honestly. "You?"

Fin took a deep breath. "Nervous," she agreed with a smile, "but excited."

I drew a tunic over my head then pulled on my breeches, dressing in what I would typically wear at home in Espiria. I strapped Iranoct to my waist then hid my other weapons until it was just my bow and quiver left, which I slung over my shoulder.

"Come, I have your present," Fin said, pulling out a trinket with a metal face bearing symbols that turned. On the side was a knob.

"I know you were worried about keeping track of your time in the Nightlands," Fin said, "so I found this for you. It will measure the days. There's a tracker that you can re-start here, and you just have to make sure to wind it before you go to sleep. Here are the directions the merchant gave me. I figured you could tinker with it on the ship to Dark-port to figure it out."

I smiled. "Fin, you're a godsend." I retrieved Pedr's necklace with the chess queen and strung Araceli's key and the timepiece on it as well.

"I've got your present too," I said, reaching into the table beside my bed and grabbing my best dagger. It was a little thing of beauty, and Fin had spent quite a bit of time admiring it over the past year. The handle was rose-wood, and the sharp blade cut clean. "I know it's not much," I said, holding the handle to her, "but I want you to have this."

Fin gasped, her eyes round. "Rowyn!" She flipped the blade, caught it by the hilt, and took a few practice swipes. I hoped it made up for the fact that I didn't know about the gift-giving custom and was going with what I had.

"I would bid to write, but chances are it would be worthless," I said, giving her what I hoped was a brave smile.

Fin hugged me. "I'll see you when you get back."

"I'll miss you," I whispered into her blonde locks as I

returned the hug with a squeeze.

"I'll miss you too. Next time I see you, you'll be this famous person. Too grand to mess with the likes of me," Fin insisted, pulling away.

"Never," I assured her. "That will never happen."

Ena knocked on the door and came in, handing each of us a roll to take with us. "Are you ladies ready? They're expecting you outside."

Fin nodded, and we made our way down the stairs where the council waited for us.

Destrian was standing awkwardly next to a weeping Ingrid. Marc and Idris were with them, speaking under their breaths.

The council had lined up beside the stairs, so Fin and I stopped by them first.

Lord Alexander raised his hands and placed them on Fin and my forehead. I took Fin's hand in mine and squeezed it. "May Sol shine his light on both your journeys as you embark on this pilgrimage."

Lord Alexander moved to the side, and Vianne took his place. Her hands were soft and smelled of jasmine. "May those whom you encounter aid you on your path."

"May your power within shield you from harm," Lady Madeline said.

Lord Obi delivered his blessing with a scowl. "May the earth make your feet swift to quicken your journey."

"Whatever the path, may you embrace the sage you've become," Master Gillius finished.

Fin went to say goodbye to the other students. I lingered next to Gillius, wishing I knew why he'd been so distant after all the time we'd spent together.

"Thank you for showing me that I can control this," I said, meeting his eyes.

Gillius frowned. He opened his mouth to say something then seemed to think better of it. Finally, he shook his head. "I just want you to know, I wish there had been another way." He put a hand on my shoulder. Was he speaking of my quest to the Nightlands? He seemed to be mourning my death already. Perhaps he didn't believe I would be successful.

No, I refused to believe that Gillius didn't believe in me. He probably just didn't relish sending a student on such a dangerous mission. "If I don't see you again, thank you for all you've done for me," I whispered.

Gillius nodded then stepped away so I could say farewell to the others.

"Thank you for the gift," I said to Marc.

"I didn't do it for you." Marc glowered, his eyes darting to Destrian. "Guard him for us."

I nodded. "I will, my lord."

Pedr came and hugged me. "Don't do anything rash," he said into my ear. "I'm still counting on you to visit me in Livian sometime. So you can meet everyone."

Fin gave me a final hug as well. "You'll be fine," she assured me, but it felt as though she was trying to convince herself more than me. "We'll see each other again soon."

I nodded then brushed the tear out of my eye. "Don't let the Woltari keep you once they find out what a marvelous person you are."

Fin laughed. "I won't. Master Haris says they don't like outsiders, so I'm sure they'll be ready for me to leave."

I squeezed her one last time before I leaped onto a borrowed horse and nudged it next to Destrian's. Ena was mounted as well since she'd be journeying with us back to Morgania.

We rode out of the gate together. At the fork, Fin and Master Haris rode west, while Destrian, Ena, and I turned north toward where the ship was waiting for us.

I'D NEVER SAILED ON A SHIP BEFORE. I meandered over the deck and let the wind whip my black hair behind me. Ena was chatting with one of the young sailors adjusting the rigging. Her sweet laughter filled the air, and I smiled before turning my attention to the figure leaning against the prow.

Destrian was studying something in his hands as I cautiously approached. Seeing me, he folded up a slip of paper and slid it into a pocket in his breeches. I recognized Ingrid's elegant penmanship.

"So, the journey begins," Destrian said, watching the waves crash against the hull.

I ran my hand over the smooth, lacquered wood. "So, it does. I hope your farewells went well."

Destrian glanced down at me. "All my friends are acting like I'm dead already. It'll be nice just to escape the dramatics."

"They care about you, that's all."

Destrian sighed, his eyes on the sea. "Did you receive some useful gifts?"

I was immediately reminded of Lady Vianne and Galena thrusting the silphium on me. "I did, but none so useful as this sword." I patted Iranoct's hilt at my waist.

Destrian laughed. "I'm pleased you like it. I just ask that you don't use it on me." Destrian looked down and noticed the necklace I clutched. "I see Araceli gave you a key as well."

"I'm hoping it brings the good luck she promised. I'll need it." Destrian's eyes strayed to Fin's timepiece, so I explained its use. When I was finished, he lifted the small chess piece in his hand.

"This must be from Pedr," he muttered, glancing up

at me. "A queen . . ." He trailed off, rubbing the ebony wood with his fingers before letting the piece fall back to my chest. "It's fitting."

"I couldn't disagree more," I said, scratching my nose. "I'm queen of nothing and terrible at chess."

Destrian snorted then fell silent. Ena laughed again. She was taken with the sailor, and I wondered if she'd even leave the ship with us when we docked. I'd be happy for her, though I'd feel sorry for myself.

"What if you were?" Destrian asked suddenly, interrupting my thoughts.

"What if I were what?"

"What if you were queen? What's the first thing you would do?"

"Well . . ." I said, trying to stall while I thought. "If I were queen, and therefore could have whatever I want, because both of us know that every whim of a queen is honored."

Destrian grinned. "Of course."

"Then, I would destroy the Fields of Forgotten Men and send them back to their homelands. I would end conscription too." I'd always detested the empire's laws that allowed them to steal men away from their homelands and force them to fight in unnecessary wars.

Destrian's red eyebrows shot up. "That wasn't the answer I expected."

THE LAST DUSK

"What did you expect?" I asked, leaning against the railing next to him.

Destrian flushed. "I thought you'd say something about kicking all the Lyricans out of Morgania."

I shook my head. "No, I don't think I would want to do that. That's what my family would want, and I agree things need to change, but I wouldn't want all of the Lyricans gone." I turned to him and smiled. "What about you? If you were king, and your every whim were to be honored, what would you do first?"

Destrian looked back over the ocean, his smile gone. "I'd stop the endless wars."

His answer wasn't what I expected either. "Why?" I asked.

"I had to go to Yliria to get my gem." Destrian studied his hands. "I still have nightmares about it. We fought them over nothing more than the emperor wanting more land to control because of some sick devotion to his father's memory. It was senseless. The Ylirians are good people. They didn't deserve the bloodshed that we brought to them."

I hadn't realized Destrian harbored such terrible memories from his time in Yliria. I'd heard stories of the disastrous war we'd fought in the Desertlands, but I'd never seen it.

I laid my hand on his arm. "You will be a good consul

someday."

Destrian looked down at my hand then met my eyes. "You would make a good queen."

ENA'S FAREWELL TO HER SAILOR was not without tears when we drew anchor in Darkport several days later. The sweet scent of morwood pines filled my nose. Shadow falcons swooped overhead as though they heralded my return. It wasn't long before we reached the Espirian pass.

"Remember, don't dally long. We want to be in the Nightlands as soon as summer begins," Destrian said. "I'll check the library for anything that may be helpful."

I nodded. "Thank you, my lord. It will just be a couple of days to visit and say goodbye."

Destrian glanced at the guards and dropped his voice low. "We can wait for you on the road. I don't like the idea of you traveling back alone."

I shook my head. "The only thieves in Morgania are us. I'll be fine, my lord. Don't worry."

"If you're sure," Destrian mumbled, but he didn't look entirely convinced.

I turned to Ena. "Tell your family I send my love." I pulled out a purse filled with coins I'd saved up from a small allowance Gillius had given me. Unused to having money to spend, I didn't use hardly any of it. I counted out plenty of coins for Destrian and my journey so I wouldn't be beholden to the heir of Helena, but there was still quite a bit leftover. Ena was the best use I could make of it. "Take this," I said, handing her the purse. "Get the girls some ribbons in the market, and get little Vic some sweets."

"No, my lady," Ena said, pushing the purse back to me. "I can't accept it. Gillius's wages are more than enough."

I tossed the purse to Destrian. "Make sure she takes this," I ordered.

Ena sighed then hugged me. "Thank you," she whispered. "I won't see you in Helena, but be safe on your journey. When I hear of your return, I'll come to Helena right away."

I nodded and waved as I turned toward the forest. "Blessings on your visits. I'll see you in a couple of days."

I watched the small band continue down the road then turned and regarded the trees. "You might as well come out," I shouted. "I know you're there."

Ferris stepped from the trees. His black hair glistened in the sunlight, and a broad smile stretched across his face. "Welcome home, Rowyn."

Chapter 9

"HOW ARE YOU TO SURVIVE in the cold?" Ferris asked as we walked through the forest toward the shroud. I led my horse by its reins, finding myself in no hurry to face the stares and whispers of my clan.

"I'll have Lord Destrian with me. He can control fire, so I'll be able to stay warm," I said, watching Ferris out of the corner of my eye. I hadn't forgotten the spectacle Ferris made in the market on the Spring Equinox. Given Ferris's expression, he hadn't either.

"By all the gods, Lord Destrian?" Conflict flitted across his face, first anger, then resentment, and finally, relief. "Fire magic. That may well save your skin in the Nightlands, I'll warrant you that. But of all the people to go with you, Lord Destrian would be my last choice, simply out of principle."

I shrugged. "He wasn't my first choice."

Ferris glanced at me out of the corner of his eye. "I'm afraid my mouth got the better of me when I returned. I might've said that you and Lord Destrian were on friendly terms."

"Why would you do such a thing!" I moaned.

Ferris hung his head. "I know, I'm sorry. I should've let you deliver the news yourself. I was still angry."

"So, what am I to expect with my return? Does everyone hate me?"

"Some do," Ferris replied, "but many will be happy to see you."

We'd reached the shroud. Ferris barreled in with no hesitation, but I hesitated at the border. A tendril of mist brushed my fingertip as it welcomed me back.

I plunged through, making my way through the familiar path, though I was blind to it. The scent of the shroud dredged up memories of long ago that overtook my senses.

I PULLED ON THE BLUE DRESS then smoothed it down as Mother draped my hair over one shoulder and began lacing the black cords crisscrossed over the back of the gown's bodice. "That looks lovely, my dear." Orange rays shone through the open window, illuminating my family quarters with the color of the sunset.

Looking in the mirror, I admired the embroidery. Amid the dusky blue fabric was black stitching of animals and flora from our homeland. My fingertips traced the outline of a shadow falcon. Farther down, a sable panther prowled near my feet, winding through the lines of thorny vines covered in Morganian rose blossoms. Grandmother and Mother had done the embroidery together as they did most things for as long as I could remember.

Grandmother perched on her chair by the fire and dabbed her eyes. "You look so beautiful, my dear."

I smiled in the mirror. Mother turned me to her and pinched my cheeks. "For color," she said as she always did when I had to be presented to the clan.

There was a knock on the door. Mother opened it to Father, who strode into the room, took one look at me, and shook his head. "That does it. He doesn't deserve you."

He always ruined that statement with a smile.

"Are you ready, sweet?" he asked, his blue eyes sparkling down on me. Mother's arm wrapped around Grandmother's waist, helping her stand. They followed Father and me as we left for the great hall.

The stamping of feet and clapping of hands reverberated against the walls of the long corridor.

The clan cheered at our family's entrance. Large men clapped Father on his back while the women pulled my mother and grandmother to them to gossip. I stood, holding my breath, and stared at Luc.

His dark hair was bound away from his face. Like all

Morganite men, he had a beard, though his was trimmed shorter than most. Hazel eyes shone with admiration as they darted over me.

I stepped toward him as Father called the clan to order.

"I thought you'd come to your senses and reject me," Luc whispered, his eyes on the crowd. "It's not too late for you to run."

I lightly punched his arm.

"You should be so lucky, Luc," Ferris grumbled next to me. "How can you marry someone who routinely bests you with the sword?"

Luc raised an eyebrow. "Easily. Who else would you want to watch your back?"

"Family, friends, a happy day to you all!" Father said, his voice bouncing off the stone walls. "Today, we celebrate my daughter's nameday." The clan clapped as I went to stand beside Father. I smiled, though I was sure I looked as stiff and awkward as I felt. Father held up his hand. "But, we also have another announcement we are delighted to share. Rowyn has promised herself to Luc Butler. They will be married at midsummer!"

A cheer rose from the crowd, though everyone had expected the announcement.

Conal, Luc's father, held up his hands to quiet the crowd. He'd worn his best robes, midnight black with silver embroidery of Imor stitched down the chest. "As many of you know, it has been a great wish of our families to unite as one."

Conal looked over to Father. I was close enough to see the sparkle of a tear at the corner of his eye. "I've always been grateful to count Chief Weldon as my dearest friend. But now Imor has blessed me twice over, for I will gain a fearless daughter!" Conal held his hand out to me. There was applause, though it wasn't as joyous as before. The clan never knew what to think of me, given my curse. Conal put his hands on my shoulders and kissed both of my cheeks.

"I can't tell you how proud I am to count you as family," Conal said.

Luc's large hand found mine and squeezed it. We faced the clan, our arms raised, and they began to hoot and holler, pounding their mugs on the tables and cheering.

Nothing could dampen my joy. Mother smiled from her seat next to my father. Grandmother winked cheekily before clapping her hands with exuberance when Luc bent me back and kissed me, his beard tickling my chin.

We walked through the crowd as clan members offered their congratulations. I tried to focus on their words, but my eyes kept drifting up to Luc's face. I'd always admired how his infectious laughter filled the room. Out of all the clan members, Luc was the best-loved. Perhaps the clan would be more relaxed in my company, knowing that Luc held me in such high favor. I hoped it would end their stares, and they'd finally accept me as one of their own, instead of the changeling that I was rumored to be.

The crowd drank and ate as noise filled the hall. My eyes found Pria seated next to Mother, her eyes watching Luc and me with longing.

"Come with me," Luc whispered, tugging me away. I took one last look at Pria and ran after him, down the stairs, and into the bright moonlight outside of our mountain home.

"They'll wonder where we've gone," I whispered, my eyes on the gate.

"Let them wonder." Luc took my hand and led me to the path that overlooked the shroud and forest beyond. He stood behind me and wrapped his arms around my waist. Resting his cheek against mine, he stared into the lands of our fathers. "Your father said he'll announce me as successor on our wedding day."

I smiled up at him. "You know this was his and Conal's plan from the start." Though I was Father's only child, the clan always whispered behind my back about my curse. It would fragment the clan if Father named me his successor. Luc had always been the natural leader. He was who people brought their troubles to in times of need. Luc was who led the raids against the Lyricans on the road. What did it matter, anyway, if I was by his side regardless?

Luc shook his head. "Baylin wasn't happy to hear about it, but the man shrinks at the sight of blood. He's not fit to lead the Morganites to greatness."

I frowned as I often did when I thought of my uncle. "He thinks I should be sent away."

I felt Luc's chest bounce as he chuckled behind me. "You know I would never let that happen. This will be ours to rule. Father says we will bring about the rise of the Morganites. Fate is calling us to our destiny."

He spun me around and lifted me in his arms. "You look best in moonlight," he whispered. He leaned down and kissed me softly. I couldn't help the trill of excitement that coursed through my bones each time his lips met mine. I wove my fingers into his hair and pulled him to me, relishing the scent of morwood and leather that always seemed to emanate from him.

Luc broke the kiss and ran his fingers over my cheeks. It was as though all my dreams had come true.

I EMERGED FROM THE MIST, wiping a tear from my eye. How perfect my life had seemed then. How swiftly my feelings of joy turned into those of sorrow. I'd lost everything that year. After that, my clan's feelings of distrust only festered like a sore that refused to heal. I'd give anything to go back to that moment. I wished I'd known then what I knew now. I would have treasured it as the precious gift it was. I would have told my family that I loved them, one last time.

Chapter 10

I HEADED TO THE STABLE with my horse trailing behind me. Inside, a giggle and a deep voice murmured something.

"Hello?" I asked, looking around the stalls.

A giant stepped from the shadows, followed by the hostler's daughter. I recognized Haplin, the Morganite warrior from a different tribe I'd encountered on the road the year before. I'd met with his chief, Urdua, and sent the clan to Espiria so they could live in safety.

Haplin's eyes grew wide as the girl shot me a wary look and snuck out. "How are your travels?" he grumbled. "We hadn't heard of your return."

"Well enough, Haplin," I said, shaking my head at him. I grabbed the pack from my horse while Haplin took its reins. "How has it been here in Espiria? Was it everything your clan was hoping it would be?"

Haplin dropped his voice low. "It's been even better. It's a credit to your family."

"I'm glad to hear it," I said with sincerity. "How is Urdua? Has she made a bid for chief behind Baylin's back?"

Haplin laughed nervously. "You seem to know her well despite your short acquaintance, but no, she took another path. I'll let her speak to you herself. She'll be happy to see you."

Haplin led my horse away and glanced over his shoulder at me as I left. I wondered about his odd behavior but dismissed it as I made my way through the granite arch and up the stairs, into the fortress dug into the side of the mountain. The scent of roasted goat wafting down the corridor whispered of suppertime. The halls were already dark, with torches lighting the way. I followed a natural cavern that lay on the outside of the mountain and into the great hall.

Dinner was chaotic compared to Solridge. Men and women had scattered around the hall, setting about platters and bowls of wildberry tarts, roasted goat, and wild carrots and garlic in a goat milk sauce. Dogs barked and whimpered in the corners, their eager tongues lolling. They surveyed the scene with mounting excitement, quick to grab any scrap that happened to find its way to the floor.

Pandemonium broke loose when one of the young boys crashed into a woman holding a platter of stuffed pigeon. Dogs leaped upon the morsels, tripping the boy even more, and he fell to the ground, covered in a yipping mass of fur and flesh. His father strode over and hauled him to his feet. After a sharp slap to the face, he sent the boy to the table.

To the right lay a series of arched windows that looked to the east, with shutters embedded in their frames that could be closed on stormy nights. Stone hearths stood at either end of the hall, draped in black flags with silver crescents. They were lit with roaring fires, for though the evening was warm, the nights still carried a chill in the northern spring. Pria occupied Grandma's chair by the hearth, busily spinning at her wheel. I took in the familiar sight, letting the feeling of home wash over me.

My father used to sit in the ox-hide chair at the head of the table, his long hair and beard blending into the sable panther fur he wore around his shoulders.

Uncle Baylin sat in that seat now. He and Father had always looked alike. The same black hair, pale skin, and blue eyes of the Blythe family. Traits that I had inherited. Father used to have a hint of mischief in his eyes and seemed always on the verge of laughter, whereas Uncle Baylin was cold and humorless.

Sitting to his right was Urdua, the female chief I'd met on the road to Solridge a year ago. On Baylin's left was Conal, our Imorati, or priest.

Everyone looked exactly as they had before I'd left, though gray now tinged Conal's dark hair and beard. Ferris leaned over them, murmuring in his father's ear. A hush fell over the dining hall as the Espirians registered my presence. Pria rose from her spinning wheel, and Conal leaped to his feet, while Uncle Baylin slowly lowered his goblet.

"It's true," Conal said. "You've returned."

I took a deep breath. "Only for a visit. I'm questing for a gem and came to say farewell."

Conal strode from the table and embraced me. "Welcome home," he whispered, squeezing me tightly. I returned the hug, for Conal was as close to a father as my own. He would've been my father had things turned out the way they were supposed to.

Uncle Baylin seemed to breathe a sigh of relief. "Ferris, bring her a chair and plate," he said, tipping his goblet in my direction.

Conal led me to a seat across from Uncle before retaking his own. Talk gradually filled the hall as the denizens of Espiria went back to their evening meal. Several clansmen seemed apprehensive, but some raised their mugs to me when they caught my eye.

Ferris carried over a goblet and plate of food then sat next to me. I looked over to the hearth, hoping for Pria to join us, but her seat was empty. Ferris saw the direction of my gaze and shook his head. "Maybe later," he said shortly before falling on his meal.

"So, you leave without a word, but to Ferris and Pria, and now the great hero has returned," Uncle Baylin said, his voice dripping with disdain.

"This is her home. This is where she belongs," Conal growled. "She's always welcome to return to her people."

Urdua rolled her eyes and smiled at me. "Great hero indeed. We heard that one of the seven sons of Ayastaren met his end because of you—is that true?"

I nodded, casting a sidelong glance at Ferris, who was there that day in the market. "It wasn't me who killed him, but the crowd. They didn't appreciate him attacking a girl." The villagers had felt beholden to me in some way because I'd made their harvests fruitful. However, I didn't want to spread that news around for fear of what others would say.

"I warned her about traveling to Ayastaren," Urdua was saying to Conal and Uncle. "It seems I should have saved my breath."

"Rowyn is a match for the Lyons any day," Ferris said. "I doubt any of them will try to best her again."

"Pawl seemed nice enough," I admitted, "but the others are terrible. I would be happy never to see another Lyon in my life." My mind flitted back to Marc's warning. Duke Roland was angry and wouldn't take his son's death lightly. His fury was enough to worry Lord Alexander to send me on my quest prematurely, possibly saving me from the consequences of my involvement. But what awaited me when I returned to Solridge? I pushed those thoughts aside. I could worry about that when I returned.

"How goes your training, Rowyn?" Urdua asked, pulling me from my thoughts. "Do you feel you get the help you require at the school?"

I nodded. "I get along well enough. I've made friends and most times feel quite happy there." I didn't add that my closest friends were Lyrican, though I was sure Conal and the others would figure that.

"Your quest, dear girl. Tell us about it," Urdua urged, reaching her hand out to mine. "I've heard so much about you since arriving here, and you've been on all of our minds."

I took a deep breath, trying to quell the butterflies in my stomach. "A sorcerer must go on a quest to retrieve their gem. I underwent my Trial by Stone and found that I must venture for an opal, the same as Morius the Black."

Despite himself, Uncle's eyebrows shot up with interest. "Where does one go for black opals? I know it's in the legend, but I can't remember."

"The Nightlands," I said quietly, staring at the table. Nobody said anything, so I glanced up, only to find Urdua looking upon me with respect, Baylin with disbelief, and Conal with horror.

"People don't venture into the Nightlands to retrieve anything," Baylin said. "How will you accomplish such a task? Do you go with a group? Are there other sorcerers attending you? What of the beasts that lurk beyond the mountains?"

"I'm allowed only one other companion," I said then stopped. Seeing Conal's expression, I didn't think I could go on.

"Well?" Urdua's brows had shot up. "Who is it?"

Ferris patted my shoulder, knowing that the worst was yet to come.

I decided to be out with it. Raising my head, and looking Uncle Baylin straight in the eye, I said, "Lord Destrian Everett of Helena."

There was no mistaking it; all three adults looked at me with utter horror and revulsion.

"By all the gods," Urdua whispered under her breath.

"Who decided this?" Baylin asked calmly, though his raised eyebrows suggested another internal conflict.

"The council at Solridge," I said, then hurriedly added, "and it makes sense given the circumstances. Since he has fire magic, we can use it as light to see, and keep warm . . ."

Uncle's eyebrows crawled even farther into his hairline. "So, you agreed to this?"

"I always told you she was a sorcerer," Conal interrupted, anger creeping into his voice. "Weldon dismissed my concerns that she should be trained somewhere, but here we are. The first Morganite sorcerer in a hundred years, and she's now beholden to Lyrica for her training. What would Chief Weldon say, one of our greatest enemies accompanying our most favored daughter into the wilderness? What if he means to kill her? She is a threat to his reign!"

I was shaking my head. "Destrian would never—"

"Chief Weldon is gone," Uncle Baylin interrupted, glaring at Conal. "You know we must do what's best for the clan, even if it leads opposite to what's best for family. We have to put our people first. Let's count ourselves lucky that she's found the help she needed."

Conal scoffed. "I didn't realize you were such an expert on sorcery, Chief, that you feel confident in the matter! Do you not remember the conversation we had two seasons ago? I warned you and Weldon of this, and you didn't heed it. Shea Innes and Yliria both have academies suited to their needs. As it stands, we have little *choice* but to send Rowyn back to the Lyricans, who are turning her into no better than a Lyrican whore!"

My cheeks flamed red as those around us eavesdropped on our conversation. Urdua grabbed my hand and held it, though her eyes betrayed her own misgivings. Ferris only stared at his plate.

"Can we not make other arrangements for her now? Is it truly too late?" Baylin asked.

Conal snorted in frustration. "If we don't tread carefully, we could have the Butcher of Bruin at our doorstep! This is all due to your careless disregard for Imor's word!"

I'd never seen Conal so angry in my life. Only he would be able to speak to Baylin that way and live to tell the tale. But instead of being awed at his boldness, I was fearful of his words.

Conal went on, slamming his fist onto the table. "They will never let Rowyn go after realizing she has powers rivaling those of Morius the Black!"

"Your regard for old legends aside, she's already well on her way in her studies. This business with the lord of Helena may well get her the gem she needs. I don't claim to be an expert in sorcery, and neither should you. If they feel it's best, and if Rowyn trusts their judgment, then so be it. It's done."

"They took my son," Conal said, his eyes on Baylin. "Now you freely give them your brother's daughter? Your own niece? How much more will we give before we have nothing left?"

"We have a whole clan to care for! Other children who depend on us!" Uncle's eyes gleamed.

"Imor has decreed that all children stolen from us will be returned," Conal said, rising from his seat. "When they do, they will seek vengeance on those who forsake them."

Baylin turned to Conal, his eyes narrowed. "Leave," he hissed. "I've put up with your disrespect for a year, but you are out of line. You may return when you've calmed yourself."

It looked as though Conal wanted to hit Uncle, but instead, with a nod to me, he turned and strode from the hall, his black robes billowing behind him.

Uncle glared at me. "Luc is never coming back, Rowyn. As much as you and Conal may hold out hope, the truth is there for all to see."

Urdua cleared her throat, but Uncle was watching the door that Conal had left through.

"Come," Urdua said, rising from her seat and reaching her hand out to me. "Let us walk together. There is much I'd like to hear of your travels."

I took her hand, thankful for the excuse to leave.

Urdua pulled me to the maze of corridors that made up the family units. Luckily, most clansmen were still at dinner, so the halls were empty.

"There now, that's better," Urdua said, turning to me with a smile. "Now, tell me about your studies. Are you doing well at Solridge?"

"They are well enough," I said, kicking a pebble along the corridor.

"What path will you take on your journey?"

"Well, first we must go to the Last Dusk. From there, we will take the Pass of Shadows over The Bitters, then through the plains toward The Dires. Over that range is the Land of Iriset, where the opals lie," I finished.

Urdua's jaw clenched. Of course, it seemed like an

endless journey. It may well be one.

"Do you not have control now?" Urdua asked as she continued to walk.

"Some. I can call rains and snow, but I don't have enough control over where it falls. Some say Morius the Black could channel lightning when he chose. I can't do anything like that now, but I may with my gem."

Urdua's eyes widened as I spoke. She shook her head, turning away from me. "That is fearsome to be sure, but we'll pray for you, as we always have."

"Thank you for your prayers," I said, touched at her concern. "How has your clan been acclimating? It must be quite a change from the traveling they're used to."

"It's so much better. We were tired, ready for a rest, and your uncle and his people have been most welcoming."

"Aren't you still chief in their eyes?" I figured it would be hard to follow someone else's leadership, especially if they didn't know the person.

Urdua cleared her throat. "Your uncle and I married over midwinter."

"Why?" I asked then felt immediately ashamed. I couldn't imagine my uncle—who at best was described as grumpy, and at worst, was downright hateful—as a husband. I'd never remembered his wife, who died while giving birth to my cousin Pria. I'd heard from Conal that

Baylin had simply never recovered from it.

"I wanted my clan to fully integrate here in Espiria," Urdua said, taking a drink from her goblet. "But my people's loyalty wouldn't be divided. So, there was nothing to do but marry. Nothing binds like a blood tie."

"But, he's so ill-tempered."

Urdua studied me. "When you're a leader, your clan must come first. My people follow me. They trust me always to do what's best for them. I must ensure they fully integrate here in Espiria. Traditionally, uniting two bands under one banner has been done through marriage."

I was reminded of words my father always repeated. In our world, the clan came first. Before family, before dreams, before life itself.

"My father had expected me to help lead Espiria when he was gone," I said then hated how accusing it sounded. I wasn't bitter that my life wasn't turning out how I thought it would. Well, not overly bitter.

Urdua took my hand in hers. "So I've heard, but I wouldn't despair of not achieving that dream yet. You have greatness in you that others will want to follow. I think we'll make a leader of you yet."

Chapter 11

THE NEXT MORNING I awoke in a cold sweat. Looking around the room, I realized I was home, and it was dawn. I decided it was as good a time as any to get up, so I dressed in the gown my mother had carefully stitched for my nameday.

I left my room and aimlessly walked through the halls. A woman I recognized was walking down the hall with her young daughter. The mother bowed her head low as she approached and pulled the little girl close to her side. I smiled, but she didn't seem to notice.

Farther on I passed two other women. They watched me from the corners of their eyes, and as soon as we passed each other, I heard the hiss of whispers. It was just as it was before I left.

The marked looks.

The fear.

I found myself at the temple. When I peeked inside and found it empty, I stepped in and kneeled in front of the statues of Queen Helen and King Philemon.

"Am I doing the right thing?" I whispered after a moment. My mind was in a tumult, and I began to second-guess my quest. Was Conal right? Should I try to attend a school of sorcery elsewhere so I wouldn't be beholden to the Lyricans? Even if I did, would the results be the same? I'd still have to go to the Nightlands. I still needed to journey for my gem. More than anything, I craved control of my power. I didn't want to have to be afraid of another Lyon again, or the empire, or anyone. I wanted to be respected.

I wished the statue could answer me, but her stone gaze only studied the chamber within. I waited for a moment longer then sighed and rose.

"Rowyn, there you are," Conal said, stepping into the temple and shutting the door behind him. The gentle clink of the lock startled me. I couldn't remember a time when the temple doors had been sealed. "You mentioned you wanted me to retrace your markings."

I nodded but glanced back at the locked door before taking my seat at the blessing alter. Conal opened his cabinet and placed a pot of ink, a needle, and a small wooden hammer on the table in front of him.

"She was a great lady, you know," Conal said, nodding to the statue as he dipped the needle into the morwood berry ink. "Not just because she was the first queen, but because she always took Imor's word as sacred. It's what led to the rise of the Morganites and the building of our great cities."

I held still as Conal dipped the needle in ink and

scratched along the border of my imorets. "Whenever I thought of Queen Helen, I always envisioned Mother."

Conal nodded. "A fair comparison. Your mother had many of the attributes that were celebrated in the first queen. Beauty, judiciousness, wisdom beyond her years, and a responsibility for those whose needs were greatest."

"I always wished I were more like her," I said. I'd always felt a sense of emptiness that I would never grow into the woman my mother was.

Conal moved to trace the other side. "You take more after your father, it's true, but I see Hania in you. She would be proud of you if she were still here."

Conal worked silently, scratching at my skin to retrace the outlines of the numerous tattoos that decorated my body and told my story. The rose vine on my neck symbolized my mother's family. The band on my upper arm showed that my father was a Blythe, a chief, and that I was his oldest child. The shadow falcon on my back celebrated a feat of courage I received in a skirmish against Lyrican guards. Finally, the ten-point star on my chest, with the sideways crescent within, announced that I was blessed by Imor.

"You know, ever since you were young, I always thought of you as a daughter," Conal said as he finished. "When you and Luc were promised to each other, it seemed like our families' greatest wish was coming true."

I grabbed Conal's hand and squeezed it. "You've always stood up for me against the whispers of the others. We will always be family."

Conal nodded and dropped his voice low. "May we speak together in confidence, then, as family?"

"Of course," I murmured.

Conal breathed deep, relaxing back into his chair with a look of triumph. "Imor sent me a dream last night. A vision of how you could be of use to the cause."

"I'm learning to bring rain. I plan to return and ensure Morgania is as fruitful as ever," I said, suspicious of his smile. "Surely, this will please Imor."

"That's all well and good, no doubt. But there's something more you can do. Something that could catapult us into achieving an independent Morgania, one free of the yoke of Lyrica. It's what the Morganites have dreamed of since The Fall."

"What must I do?" I asked, wondering at his sudden meaning.

"Lord Destrian—if he doesn't come back from the Nightlands, Consul Colman won't have an heir. We could revolt and take charge of Helena upon his death."

"You want me to kill him?" I gasped. "I can't, Conal. How can you ask such a thing of me?"

"It's not I who ask, Rowyn, it's the people. This is our chance to reclaim the throne. For too long, we've felt the chains of the capital at our throats. We must be free of them. Your people need this, Rowyn."

I shook my head. "I can't, Conal. I have to trust him. He has to trust me, or we'll never make it out alive."

Conal leaned toward me. "He could fall from a precipice or get attacked by an animal. Who knows what terrible fates will befall him there? You may not even have to do anything; your conscience could remain clear. Just make sure he doesn't return."

I shook my head in disbelief that Conal would ask such a terrible thing of me. Such a wretched betrayal was not within my nature. "He's not a bad person," I said, choosing my words carefully. "He's shown me respect at Solridge, and now is risking his life just by going on this journey. I can't repay that kindness with deceit. I refuse to believe that Imor would ask such a terrible thing of me."

Conal leaned forward. "What have they done to you, Rowyn? Can you not see how they deceive you?" The expression on his face was so fierce, so full of rage and passion, that I shrank away from him.

I tried to make my voice calm, fearing him as I spoke. "I'm sorry, no."

Conal sighed. "I never thought you would abandon us."

"I would never abandon Espiria," I whispered, torn by his words.

"Show us then. Show us that you aren't abandoning us all," Conal murmured, unfolding himself from the seat and walking to the door. "The heir's death could bring our people new life. You must decide where your loyalties lie."

When Conal left, I was still shaking my head in disbelief that he would ask me to do such a terrible deed. I was almost frightened at the prospect. But he said that Imor wished it of me. Was that true? Or was it merely his interpretation of a dream?

I left the temple and walked the halls but couldn't ease my anxiety over the encounter. I was so focused inward that I almost passed Pria without noticing. She certainly was trying to avoid me, given the way she stepped to the far side of the corridor. But I refused to let her slip by.

"Pria, how goes it?" I asked, my smile overly bright. I didn't want to return to our past conversations. I wanted to start over and be a family once more. "How is it with the other clansmen?"

Pria stopped, which was more than I had hoped. She leaned awkwardly against the wall, her gnarled foot resting on her toes. "Well enough. They're hard workers at least, which helps given the number of mouths we have to feed."

I fiddled with an embroidered rose that decorated my gown. "How do you get along with Urdua as a stepmother?"

Pria shrugged. "Well enough. She's different from your mother, active with the guard and patrols."

I nodded but didn't know what to say next. I wanted to ask if she'd forgiven me yet. If she was willing to put our past behind us.

"I'm to be married at midsummer," Pria said suddenly.

My brows shot up and I smiled. "Really? To whom?"

"Haplin."

"What?" I hesitated, my mind returning to the day before—Haplin in the stable, dandling the hostler's daughter. I'd laughed about it then, but now I felt an overwhelming sense of dread.

Of course, Pria noticed my apprehension. "You know, I've always craved a simple life."

"It's not that, Pria," I said, unsure of what to say next. Was I to tell her that her betrothed wasn't as attached to her affections as she? "I know he was Urdua's right hand," I said, unable to think of anything else. I knew Pria well, and she would be angrier with me for being the one to break the news than she would be at Haplin. "He's just so much older."

But Pria could read my misgivings. She scowled. "He is a nice man, and he *likes* me."

"Pria, I didn't mean . . ." I said, worried that I offended her. Why couldn't I've just kept my mouth shut? "It's a great match, and you will be the lady of the fortress, especially if Urdua is working with the warriors. It's perfect."

"I never wished to be destined for greater things, like you," Pria said, holding her head high. "I know my place in the clan. Haplin thinks it's an honor that I've accepted, and he will treat me well enough. It also brings our clan closer as one. First Father and Urdua, now Haplin and I, bound by blood."

"What about Ferris?" I asked. "Does Uncle seek to make a match for him as well?" Would he seek the same for me? Though I'd left Espiria to train, I still planned on returning. What would Uncle do with me? Would I be expected to marry one of the strangers from Urdua's clan to tighten the blood bonds?

"Well, I must attend to the laundry," Pria muttered. "I'm glad you found the help you need. Make sure you're careful in the Nightlands."

"Thank you," I said. "I look forward to talking more when I return." Pria nodded then limped down the hall, holding the wall for support.

I glanced outside the window and saw the warriors down by the horses' paddocks. A large man barked orders from the side, his long beard roped into his belt. I made sure my sword was secured to my waist before making my way down the never-ending staircase.

Maybe I didn't dare to say anything to Pria, but I had

plenty of courage to deal with Haplin myself.

Chapter 12

"UP-SWING, DOWN-SWING," Haplin's voice roared to the men and women practicing with large staffs. I stood at Haplin's side, watching the training and waiting for an opportune moment to speak with him.

We never really used staffs to fight in Espiria. Apparently, Haplin's presence was changing that. Looking over the group of warriors in the practice yard, I spied Urdua in the corner, whipping her staff about in practiced measure. Ferris practiced next to a young woman I didn't recognize.

"All right, find your partners, and go through the drills we practiced yesterday!" Haplin bellowed before turning to me with a frown. "Did you need something?"

"Yes," I said, holding my head high and meeting his eyes. "I wish to have a word."

"Can it wait? I've got to get this lot ready for raiding season."

"No." I shook my head. "It won't take long."

I led Haplin to the stable. "I'm given to understand that you and Pria are betrothed," I said with the air of authority I always used when Father sent me to address the clansmen. It felt different speaking in such a way now, but I knew none would question it. "I appreciate that it will bring the clan closer as one. However, I'm going to be clear to you that I have doubts about the match."

Haplin scratched the back of his neck, his eyes uncertain. "Yes, Chief Urdua encouraged Baylin to set that up. She's a sweet girl. I think we could get along well."

I raised a brow. "Baylin is your chief and should be addressed as such."

"Yes, of course," Haplin said quickly. "Don't be angry with me. It's just, habits die hard."

Given Haplin's fearful look, it seemed word of my powers had gotten around to the new clan members. Good, his fear meant I would be taken seriously.

I narrowed my eyes. "I know some other clans have had allowances in terms of marriage and duty. However, here in Espiria, when you enter into a marriage contract, it is with the expectation that you will be faithful."

Haplin's cheeks blossomed to a dark scarlet. It was an interesting sight, seeing such a formidable man so wholly uncomfortable. "Of course, I will fulfill my duty. I don't want you to worry over her on my account."

"Just so we're clear," I continued, "Pria is of great importance to the clan. She's been lady of the fortress since my mother died. She will probably continue that role given Urdua's interests in fighting and patrols. Pria demands a certain level of respect from the clansmen and women who live here, and I will personally ensure that she's treated with the respect she deserves."

"N-n-now, just listen for a moment," Haplin said. "I'd never hurt the girl, I promise."

"No, you will make certain you do not," I agreed. "I'm sure you've heard all about me from the rest of the clan. Most, if not all of it, is probably true. So know this, if I hear of you behaving inappropriately outside of your marriage vows, you will find your fear of me quite warranted."

"Yes, your ladyship." Haplin's eyes were bugged out of his head, and his hands were shaking.

"I look forward to hearing of your wedding when I return from my quest," I said, breaking into a smile. "You may return to the training yard."

"Y-y-yes, your ladyship," Haplin stuttered again then strode from the stable as fast as his legs could carry him.

"What was that about?" a voice asked from outside. Ferris peeked into the stable. "I was wondering if you wanted to go on a ride in the forest. I have to check in with the patrols."

A ride sounded perfect. Within no time, Ferris and I were mounted and riding through the mist to the forest beyond. Birds called out to one another through branches still light with spring's leaves. We nodded and waved as we rode past another clansman who was returning to the mist from his morning post. The clansman smiled cheerfully to Ferris, but when he saw me, his expression fell away. The man ducked his head and continued on. I bristled as he hurried past. Ferris whistled an off-key tune, unwitting to the man's rude departure.

"What were you talking with Haplin about?" Ferris asked.

"Nothing," I said, trying to sound innocent.

Ferris wasn't fooled. "I already told him that if anything happened to Pria, my father and I would have his head." He laughed.

I shrugged. "The point just needed to be reiterated. It seems Haplin is afraid of magic."

"The clan had a bad brush a few years back with another sorcerer," Ferris explained. "They were all a bit skittish when we spoke of you."

"When I have my gem, I'll be able to control my power."

Ferris understood how much I'd longed to have a choice in my affliction. He'd put up with my complaints about it for years. "So, your school is sending you to the Nightlands. Couldn't they view your power as a liability? Did you ever consider that they may be trying to get you killed?"

Did Ferris know what Conal had asked of me? Was only one of us supposed to return from the Nightlands?

No, it didn't have to be that way. Destrian would have no reason to hurt me. He'd done nothing but try to help me since I'd met him. But could I hurt him? Was it really what Imor wanted me to do?

"I have to go to the Nightlands," I said finally. "I know in my heart I'm nothing without my gem."

"You'd be something to us. We'd accept you, gem or no." Ferris tried to smile, but I saw the lines of worry between his eyes.

It gave me the courage to share what I was really feeling. "Sometimes, I worry that I could never live up to everyone's expectations. That my failure to do so will be my ruin," I said softly.

"I guess we all have to live to someone's expectations," Ferris agreed. "I suppose there is no escape for anyone."

"I just feel like this journey, with Destrian—I have this feeling of foreboding."

Ferris didn't appear to be listening to my words. He was watching my eyes. "You look different," he said. "Something is different with your eyes."

I glared at him. "What are you talking about? There is nothing wrong with me. I look the same as ever."

Ferris would not be put off. "What have you been doing lately?" His blue eyes flicked across my features as he studied them.

"I'm getting ready for my trials," I said, completely thrown off guard by his behavior. "What's wrong with you?"

"What sort of trials?" he persisted, not dropping his gaze in the slightest.

"Well, I have to get my gem. Then, I need to practice, learn control, and study what I can do. We get very focused in the years after we retrieve our gem, so I guess I will probably be working a lot with the weather and being wet and cold most of the time. I don't know. They don't talk to me much about the future," I grumbled bitterly.

I cast my eyes down from his, completely unnerved while he continued to scrutinize me. When he spoke, it was slow and soft. "I have given it some thought, and I wonder, could you conceivably end the drought?"

"I don't really know . . . Maybe . . . Possibly," I admitted. My mind raced through different scenarios. "I've been wondering if that's what they expect."

"I thought of it, so you know it has to have at least crossed their minds. Aren't you doing this kind of hurriedly?"

"Yes," I said, "but the other issue is that Duke Roland of Ayastaren is very unhappy with me. I've heard from multiple students that the council is sending me away so he won't retaliate against the school."

Ferris's brows shot up. "Can he do that?"

"I don't know." I shrugged. "But I am glad to be away from the duke for now. Perhaps, when he has had some time to think, he'll see that it wasn't my fault." I was proud of myself for being so optimistic in front of Ferris, but I wasn't stupid. Duke Roland seeing reason was as unlikely as Sol rising at night.

"We've missed you," Ferris commented, startling me out of my reverie. "Nothing suspicious has happened . . . has it? I can't help but feel there is something wrong with you. Something you're not telling me."

I sighed. "Ferris, I'm serious when I say that I have no idea what you are talking about."

"Please, just let me look." Ferris held my arm tightly and we stopped our mounts. With his other hand, Ferris grasped my face and turned it toward him, his eyes searching mine.

I laughed nervously, a chill shooting through my spine. "What is it?"

Ferris shook his head and dropped his arms. "I don't know. I can't explain it. There's just something off about you." My mind went searching for a memory, anything that would give me a clue. I found none and looked back at Ferris and shook my head.

"Nothing comes to mind," I said to his frown, but even he could see that I wasn't sincere. Could Ferris's worry have anything to do with my lost memories?

Was there truly something wrong with me?

I WALKED AROUND my old family quarters, drinking in the memories of my childhood. Uncle Baylin dwelled there now. It hadn't changed much. The bearskin still lay on the floor, mouth open in a growl. The Blythe tapestry still hung on the wall next to the fireplace that featured stitchings from five generations of mothers. I wondered if Urdua had added embroidery yet to commemorate her addition to the family. I looked closely over the scene but found nothing added.

The only item that marked the room as different was a table underneath the window littered with papers. I walked over to it, curious, and found a map of Morgania. On the map were two black rocks painted with silver crescents. One sat at a fertile valley near Darkport. The other sat at a tower called Caymir's Rook, south of the mountains. I reached out to touch one of the stones.

"What are you doing?"

I jumped, jostling the table and sending the rocks to the floor. I hurriedly picked them up and put them back in their spots before facing Uncle Baylin. "I was just looking around."

Baylin frowned, shutting the door behind him. "You shouldn't be in here. These aren't your family's quarters anymore."

"You're still my family," I said.

Uncle fiddled with the rocks on the map. "I suppose, but you should wait to be invited instead of just barging in."

"What is that?" I asked, suspicious. "Are you mounting an attack?"

Uncle Baylin scoffed. "Of course not. Only your father would've risked men's lives so needlessly."

"What do the rocks signify?" I asked, wondering at the secrecy and choosing to ignore his jabs. Was he afraid I would say something to Destrian? Did he think I was getting too close to the consulship?

"Times have changed," Uncle Baylin said. "The people are tired of fighting. We crave peace."

"We've tried peace before," I said, leaning against the wall with my arms crossed. "It only ended in bloodshed. What makes this time different?"

Uncle shook his head and watched me. "This past autumn, the empire sent a messenger. They are willing to talk, grant us farmland and the tower, so we can finally have peace and go back to our ways. We never enjoyed fighting, you know. We were farmers, taking more pride in tending our land than bearing a sword."

I laughed. "What makes you think the Lyricans will fulfill this promise? We've been fighting them for years. Now, all of a sudden, they want to give us the most fertile valley in the region and a tower? You're a fool if you think they'll give that up for nothing."

Uncle Baylin looked outside the window. "You weren't there when the consul called the chiefs together for a truce. Your father wouldn't hear of us relenting our attacks for some Lyrican lord, no matter how the clan would suffer."

"They would've gone back on their promises," I said. "We've never been able to trust them. Father knew that."

Uncle shook his head. "That time it was different, but your father would not be swayed. He'd always been pig-headed. Even your mother couldn't sway him."

Uncle had always said rude things about Father, who was decisive and brave—everything Uncle wasn't. "So now you seek to make a deal with the consul?"

"No, not the consul, the empire," Uncle said, his eyes back on me.

"Consul Colman would never agree to give away land for a mere promise to stop raiding." I couldn't help the disbelief that eked into my voice.

"Even the consul has to bow to the empire, and I didn't say it was for a promise." Uncle refused to meet my eye. "They've asked for something in return, and I fully intend on giving it for the good of the clan." Pulling a scroll from his pocket, he tossed it to me.

I caught the parchment, unfurled it, and read.

As blood guardian of Rowyn of Espiria, commonly known as Rowyn the Morganite, I hereby relinquish all guardianship and claim to her person and place her care to the Empire of Lyrica. I understand that as a ward of the empire, her guardianship will be at the discretion of Emperor Arthello II, including all rights of person and fortune.

Blood drained from my face, and the parchment fluttered to the floor. "Uncle, what have you done?"

"I've not signed it yet," Uncle said, his eyes on me once more. "But, I intend to."

My hands shook as an icy chill crept down my spine. "The empire doesn't allow women to claim their own person when they reach majority. Conal was right. You would sell your own family to the empire. You would sell me into *slavery!*"

Uncle's eyes narrowed. "I would do anything for our clan. Can you really claim the same?"

"How dare you!" I shouted. "Everything I've done since I've left, I have done for us, for my people!"

Uncle shook his head. "You've done nothing but bring us lower. At least in this, you can be of some use.

I'm sorry it has to be this way, but if you truly cared about the clan, the sacrifice would be easy to make."

"Conal will never stand for this, and neither will the rest of the clan."

Uncle balled his fists. "Conal may come around when he sees that it brings us closer to being our own people once more." Uncle strode over to the map and slammed his hand down. "This is our ancestral valley, and this tower is a strategic point, which we'll be able to man without firing a single arrow, or spilling a drop of blood."

"What about my blood?" I demanded. "My father would've never stooped so low as to sell a clansman to the empire."

"Weldon cost the clan countless lives over his years of raids, and for what? What did we gain other than a reputation for being robbers and thieves?"

Heat raged through me. "No wonder the clan chose Father over you," I hissed. "Even Grandfather backed his younger son because he knew you wouldn't have the stomach to lead. He could see how weak and unprincipled you were. If only they could see the monster you've become!"

Uncle slapped me across the face. Without a word, he strode from the room. The sound echoed in the air as I raised a hand to my burning cheek, trying to regain my breath. I let it take control as I walked to the temple balcony that jutted from the mountainside. I threw my feelings to the heavens, a frigid wind sweeping through the once warm valley. I sent all of the anger, frustration, and pain spilling out of me to the clouds blanketing the sky.

I held out my hand, and a snowflake landed softly on my finger. Heavy snow began drifting to earth, giving the valley a sense of peaceful stillness I'd always loved. The men and women below stared at the sky, whispering and pointing.

Snow collected on the ground and melted on my palm. The coming night held a mournful glow that crept through my bones and sent gooseflesh over my arms. I shivered but was unwilling to leave for fear of meeting someone in the halls. Wrapping my arms around myself, I found the thin dress provided little comfort from the temperature.

Uncle couldn't go through with it. I knew he'd never liked me, but I never imagined he would betray me so utterly. Conal would fight for me, and he would win. Especially if I returned from the Nightlands with my gem. Given the other sorcerers' comments, if I returned from the Nightlands with a black opal, I would be one of the most powerful sorcerers in the empire. My clan would not allow Uncle Baylin to sign over my rights after that. I could be an asset to them. I just had to show them I could do it. I had to prove loyalty and win over their hearts once more. I felt the gems pulling me north more forcefully than ever.

There was no time to lose. My life, my very freedom, depended on it.

I lost track of how much time passed when I heard footsteps behind me. Turning, I found Ferris draping his cloak over my shoulders.

"I leave for Helena tomorrow morning," I said.

"Please, Rowyn, stay for one more day," Ferris said, his hands clenched into fists.

"Ferris, I can't," I said. "I must journey in haste."

I thought to tell him of his father's deception, but I couldn't do it. What if Baylin was able to convince Ferris it was the right move? What if Ferris abandoned me too? No. I had to prove to them that I was worth keeping. That I was worth my salt as a Morganite.

Chapter 13

THOUGH I ENJOYED THE QUIET solace on the road, relief flooded through me when I finally reached Helena and made my way through the city. Children darted in front of my horse, begging for coins. I pulled one from my purse and tossed it to a little girl, who bit it before running down the street toward the market. I watched her for a moment before turning to the towers of the citadel, bracing myself for the next trial to come.

"You there!" someone shouted behind me. I turned, only to meet a hand that shoved me out of the saddle.

I leaped to my feet and drew my sword as mounted soldiers surrounded me. Their deep blue tunics bore the Everett sigil, a gold star with flaming points. The same design on Destrian's sword.

"How dare you!" I seethed, brandishing Iranoct. "I demand safe passage to the castle. I'm expected there."

"Likely story," sneered one of the guards. "She's a thief! The baker said he was robbed this morning, claimed it was Morganite scum."

Something slammed into the back of my head, pain searing through my vision as I pitched forward, dropping Iranoct. One of the soldiers put his metal-tipped boot back into his stirrup as I lifted my head.

Blood dripped sluggishly down my neck. The men dismounted, one unfurling a length of rope. It was too bad the marketplace was filled with people or I would have happily unleashed my anger. As it was, there were too many innocents around.

"They are expecting me!" I shouted when the soldiers grabbed me. I kicked as hard as I could while the four guards hauled me to my feet, pulled my hands behind my back, and tied the rope tightly.

They patted me down, pulling the knives from my sleeves and the dagger at my waist. My bow and arrows were slung on one guard's saddle, while another man unbelted Iranoct from my hip.

"Make sure you get them all," the lead guard ordered.

Lightning struck a roof, followed by thunder that shook buildings around us. But the guards were not deterred. They strung a rope around my waist and mounted, pulling me through the market behind them.

"You will pay for this!" I continued shouting. "I know the heir of Helena, and he will not stand for this!"

The guard riding in front laughed. "Oh? I know the heir of Helena, too, and Lord Destrian will be happy to find we're cleaning the streets of vermin."

The other guards laughed as rain fell from the sky in thick sheets.

The guard holding my rope gave it a cruel tug. "We'll see how you feel after a night in the Helenian dungeon. Then, we'll find what happened to the baker's purse."

The people in the market openly stared as I was pulled through the streets, covered in blood and muck. The little girl I'd tossed a coin to was hidden in the shadows of an alleyway, her eyes wide in fear.

I slipped on a loose stone, wet with rain, and fell to my knees with a cry of pain. The guard holding the rope didn't stop. He kept riding, dragging me on the ground behind him.

"Wait!" I pleaded, trying to keep my face out of the mud as it piled up in front of my dragging body. My cheek smashed into a stone that jutted out from the road, and despite myself, tears snuck out from the corners of my eyes. Thanks to the rain, it was impossible to tell.

The guards stopped for a moment to let me stand before pulling me along once more. Judging by their crude language, it seemed the jailer took liberties with female prisoners. My heart dropped to the pit of my stomach, and I frantically pulled at my fetters.

"Oy! Check out the beauty of this sword!" one of the guards said, holding up the blade that Destrian had gifted to me.

"I've heard the Morganites are swift as deer," another said, glancing back at me.

"That's easy enough to test," the guard holding my rope said, kicking his horse forward. I tried running to keep up, but the speed of the beast pulled me down, and I landed on my shoulder. The guard dragged me several feet before he slowed again. Peals of laughter rang through the air, followed by another flash of lightning and a thunderclap.

I stumbled to my feet again and staggered toward the castle. Rain still beat down, darkening the sky and making the going hard to see. Thankfully, most of the city people were driven inside their dwellings, so fewer would witness my misery.

We reached the ward and were met with pandemonium. Destrian was mounted, shouting to a host of castle guards through the rain as they scrambled for their horses. I recognized Bernard, the kind old soldier who'd accompanied me to Helena with Gillius a year ago. He turned when my captors pulled me through the gate. Bernard's hand went to his sword when he saw me, his eyes wide. The castle guards froze, their eyes going from the city guards to Lord Destrian, whose eyes had filled with what I assumed was either disbelief or uncertainty.

I glared around defiantly, still tugging at the fetters tied painfully around my wrists. I was sure I looked a sight, rain-drenched and caked with mud.

I met Destrian's eyes as we approached. His face

darkened, and he urged his horse toward us. I didn't envy his position. The city guards were known to harass and arrest unsuspecting Morganites, but Destrian had always claimed ignorance to that fact.

He wasn't ignorant anymore.

"Untie her, Karl," he said slowly, his voice trembling. Judging by the steam rising from his hair, Destrian was livid. Well, I tried to warn them.

The guard holding the rope didn't move. Instead, he glanced back at the others and laughed nervously. "Lord Destrian, the baker said that someone lifted his purse from behind his stall. He thought he saw a Morganite girl nearby, so we picked her up."

Destrian's hair was definitely smoking. He nudged his horse, Valor, closer. "Release her!"

Given that Destrian knew the guard's name, it appeared that they did know each other. Karl jumped down from his saddle, drew a dagger, and cut my bonds. I rubbed my wrists, trying to get some feeling back. It didn't seem I'd drawn Destrian's questions at all, but with Karl's words and my position, it did sound as if I were rightly accused. At least, in the eyes of an ignorant Lyrican brood.

"Bernard," Destrian said before I could speak, his eyes not leaving Karl's, "see to her."

The old soldier stepped toward me and leaned in to inspect my face. "So, we meet again, lass," he muttered.

The last time I'd seen Bernard, he bore the sigil of Rudin, a small village with a tower on the southwestern border of Morgania. Now he wore the garb of Helena. "By all the gods, they've roughed ye up something fierce." Bernard dabbed at the blood on my face with a dirty handkerchief he pulled from his pocket, but I shoved his hands away and glared at the guards.

"I did nothing wrong," I said forcefully. "I was simply riding to the citadel." I turned to Destrian. "I told them I was your guest, but they ignored me." I thought to disregard that last part—they'd done their job, after all—but then I remembered their treatment of me, and a part of me enjoyed the look Destrian gave his own people as my anger flourished. There, if he'd not seen before, now he understood the discrimination of my people.

Destrian glared at each of the guards, finally ending once more on Karl. "Why did you not come to check with me? It would've been easy enough to do."

Karl glowered. "Why would a Morganite have business at the citadel? The merchants complain of them constantly, and your father asked us to take them in hand."

Destrian drew his sword. "Guards!" he shouted behind him. The castle guards stood at attention. The leader stepped forward.

"Dru, arrest these four. I'll deal with them later."

"But, my lord!" Karl cried, stepping toward Destrian.

The castle guards glanced at the heir of Helena with uncertainty.

"Do it!" Destrian yelled. The castle guards jumped
then swarmed the four, dragging them off of their horses
and hauling them into the citadel.

"Rowyn," Destrian said, coming to my side. "I don't
know what to say, except that I'm sorry." Taking my chin
in his hand, he turned my face to what meager sunlight
broke through the clouds that remained.

At least it had stopped raining, though not to quell my
anger, which hadn't ebbed with Destrian's actions. On the
contrary, I felt justified in my previous accusations, my
fury anew with an almost boiling feeling that reminded me
how much I used to hate all Lyricans.

Bernard patted Destrian on the shoulder. "How could
ye have known, lad? It's not yer fault."

I scowled, turning my face so his hand fell away. "You
didn't believe me when I spoke of it before. Now, do you
see? They called me Morganite scum!"

Bernard shifted uncomfortably, but Destrian had the
grace to meet my eyes, though his gaze was one of despair.

"They tied me up and dragged me through the market!" I shouted. Here I was, about to start my quest, and
now I was bruised and wounded because some city guards
felt like brutalizing someone that day. Of course, given my
luck, it just happened to be me passing by. Thank you,

Imor, and fate, and whatever other machinations controlled my life.

"This is your city," I said finally, trying to calm myself. "This is your city, so lead it. If there is injustice here, it falls on you to correct it. You may have jailed the guards who attacked me, but what happens to the Morganites of the city once we've left for the Nightlands? Disciplining one injustice doesn't mean the problems are solved. Your guards spoke of such loathing, such contempt for me and the other Morganites. Tossing them in jail will do nothing to prevent future mistreatment."

I turned to Bernard. "Show me to my room, please. I would like to make myself more presentable."

"Yes, yer ladyship," Bernard said when Destrian nodded. "The window's fixed in the room ye were in before. Will that do?"

"That will be fine," I said, then angrily collected my weapons that had been strewn across the ward when the guards were arrested. Destrian pulled the pack off my horse and handed it to Bernard, who walked to the steps of the citadel.

I was about to follow when Destrian grabbed my arm. "I promise no more harm will befall you in my city."

His eyes seemed to be pleading with me, but I couldn't hold back my emotions. Sharp pain pierced through my conscience, making it difficult to think or feel anything other than contempt for everyone around me. I scoffed. "Don't make promises you can't keep, my lord."

Destrian lowered his gaze as I turned and walked away.

Chapter 14

I'D LAIN MYSELF OUT ON THE BED to rest in pain and peace. I resolved to avoid marketplaces in the future, considering I'd been attacked twice in them. My mind wandered back to the incident with the Lyons several months before. How the people had reacted when they found me being brutalized. Of course, the people of Helena would be used to seeing a Morganite harassed by the guards.

I thought my harsh words to Destrian were completely warranted, though I knew it pained him to hear them. He had the power to do something. He could be a force for good if he chose.

After a while, it became clear that I hurt too much to move, but the silence only served to send my mind wandering back to Conal's words in Espiria. Could it be that simple? A choice between Destrian's death and loyalty to my clan in Espiria. Was that what Imor wanted from me? My mother's words swam to my ears. "There are but two things in life, Rowyn, duty and choice."

Growing up, Father had echoed her sentiments almost daily. "The clan must come first." But Destrian?

There had to be another way.

I couldn't stand thinking anymore. So I closed my eyes, letting blessed sleep overtake me.

A BOY PLAYED IN THE DIRT, little wisps of wind swirling around him as he laughed. His hair was jet-black, and he had imorets tattooed around his eyes. The wisps of wind grew larger, swirling cyclones of air and dirt that danced over the earth. I realized I was watching him through the eyes of another when he looked up and grinned.

"Come see," he said, reaching out to me. A hand appeared in my vision, my hand, and I kneeled next to him on knees that weren't my own. I was a little girl in ornate robes that clashed with the boy's simple dress.

"Will they hurt?" my dream-self asked, watching the cyclones as they shrank.

The boy shook his head.

I touched one. The cyclone jumped onto my hand and darted about, tickling my skin. I giggled.

We played in the dirt, tossing sticks and leaves into the tunnels of wind until an older boy joined us. He wore robes embroidered with the Morganite sigil, and he regarded the boy with distaste.

"They sent me to get you," the boy told me.

I took his outstretched hand and stood.

The swirling air disappeared. A cloud of leaves and dirt drifted to the ground as the boy I was playing with angrily watched us walk away.

"You spend too much time with him," the regal boy told me as I looked over my shoulder. "Not only is he below your station, but he's odd. Even his mother admits it."

"He's my friend," I insisted.

"I'll speak to your father. He'll put a stop to it."

Fear swelled in my gut as I looked up at the older boy. "Promise you won't tell him, Mony. He'll be so angry."

"Promise me you won't play with him anymore," the boy said, turning to me with a frown.

"I promise," I sighed in my small voice. But I could tell it was a lie.

I AWOKE TO A KNOCK at the door. By all the gods, what an odd dream. I'd never dreamed of myself as someone else before. The clothes the children wore were from olden times. Why had my mind led me to those children?

After another knock I let in Daisy, a maid I'd known from my previous visit. She took one look at me and hissed through her teeth.

"You poor thing," she said, her voice dripping with honey. "You poor, poor thing. We should take you to see a sage."

I shook my head. "I'd rather not go to all that trouble." Really, I didn't think I could make it down the stairs to the sage's dwelling, wherever that was. Then, I had an idea. "Bring me my pack, please," I said. "Then, if you would be so kind, draw me a hot bath."

"Of course, my lady," Daisy said, bringing over my pack before pumping water into the bathing basin. I sat on the bed to rifle through the contents. Pulling out my herbs and medicines, I checked over my list and grabbed two bags. Rising slowly, I staggered to the tub.

I pinched some of the herbs into the bathwater then tossed the bags back on the bed.

Daisy helped me step into the tub and I sank into the water, feeling the magic from the herbs swim over my wounds.

"His lordship asked to receive you in the great hall for the midday meal whenever you're ready," Daisy said, soaping my back and hair. "He would like to properly introduce you."

"Will the consul be there?" I asked. "I'm going to guess that his feelings toward me haven't improved."

Daisy sighed. "When his lordship came home from

schooling, there was a bitter row. My lord consul was most upset upon hearing the news of your travels. I would watch your back here, my lady. There are many hoping for you to fail."

"They may well get their wish too," I grumbled, sinking below the water to rinse. At least the bath was reviving my spirits and leaving my bruises a bit paler.

Daisy helped me pull a fresh white tunic over my head and held my boots while I slid into a pair of dark breeches. I belted the sword Destrian made for me around my waist. After a quick check in the mirror, I asked Daisy to plait my hair into a simple braid. Finally, I left for the great hall.

I heard a heated discussion as I reached the corner of the hallway. Recognizing Destrian's and Bernard's voices, I slowed and eavesdropped.

"I have to do something. She has no faith in me to make this right."

"They are yer men, my lord," Bernard grumbled. "Acting on yer father's orders. How can ye punish them for that?"

"Did you see what they did to her?" Destrian hissed. "I can't believe Karl would do such a thing!"

"I know, I know," Bernard said. "Just keep them out of her sight while she's here, then release them when ye leave. That's not too hard, is it?"

"They wouldn't have learned anything!" Destrian

huffed.

I rounded the corner. Bernard motioned to Destrian, who turned and greeted me with a frown.

"I was told you wanted to introduce me in the hall," I said, eyes on both men.

"Go, I'll speak to you later," Destrian said to Bernard.

"My lady," Bernard mumbled, dipping his head.

"Am I?" I asked with a raised brow. When Bernard looked confused, I approached. "Am I a lady? Do all guards at Helena treat the *ladies* here in such a way? Those behaviors are common enough for the great men of Ayastaren, but I was given to understand that Helena was different."

"I'm sorry," Bernard grunted. "I'm going in." He strode away with surprising speed for a man his age.

Destrian reached out to touch my swollen cheek.

I stepped back. "It hurts, my lord."

"What would you have me do?" Destrian asked, dropping his hand. "I know this harsh treatment is what you've spoken of time and again. But now that I've seen it, I'm at a loss."

The first response that came to my mind was to flog them before the others to teach them a lesson. I opened my mouth to say as much but then reconsidered. Destrian was a ruler, and Lord Alexander had told us that being a leader meant striking a balance between what you want to do and what others want you to do. Was I angry at those men for beating the living tar out of me and dragging me through the street? Indeed. But I didn't want to fall into the trap of reacting how everyone expected me to. Then, I had an idea.

"Release them," I said.

Destrian's mouth fell open. "I don't believe you mean that."

"I do mean it," I insisted. "With the demand that the guards sit by me at dinner this evening."

Destrian frowned. "What will that do?"

"Maybe nothing, maybe something," I said. "Maybe the solution isn't to punish them but to allow them to see that I'm also a human being. I hated all Lyricans until I got to know you better. Now, I only hate some of you."

Destrian stepped closer. "What if I don't want to let them off so easy? What if I think they should be punished?"

"Well"—I held up my hands—"then so be it. But I won't ask you to treat them as they have treated me. I won't give the Lyricans here the pleasure of believing their fears are warranted."

"You surprise me," Destrian said, but it didn't sound like it was a good thing. "I thought you'd be out for blood."

I turned and started for the door. "If the guards

disrespect me at dinner, I'll duel them. Does that make you feel better?"

Destrian grabbed the door and opened it for me. "If they disrespect you at dinner, I'll defend your honor."

I rolled my eyes. Defend my honor, indeed.

Consul Colman sat at the head of the table picking at his food. His navy overcoat boasted several dark stains, and his red hair had gone even whiter since I'd seen him over a year ago. He took enormous swigs from his goblet while listening to the talk with a frown.

"I'm not optimistic," Destrian muttered under his breath, "but let's see how it goes."

Seated at the table were a handful of knights and soldiers. They laughed and told bawdy jokes to each other while drinking their ale and wine. When Destrian strode through the door, many of the men raised their glasses to him but froze when they noticed me.

The consul looked me up and down and shook his balding head. "So, here she is," Consul Colman growled. A sinister smile crawled over his features. "I see the boys have given you a warm Helena welcome."

Destrian opened his mouth to speak, but I cut him off. "Indeed, Lyrican nobility seems to relish the art of beating women in the street. No wonder the people love you so much."

The consul scowled. "Destrian told me about the

Lyon boys. If I had any respect for you, I would tell you to beware the duke. He's one of the most slippery fellows I've ever met, and he takes all discourtesy to heart."

"And if I had any respect for you," I said with a brittle smile, "I would warn you that if another one of your guards comes near me again, they should be prepared to breathe their last."

The consul leaned back and studied me. "I thought school would've softened you into a lady like my daughters. I see I was wrong." The consul shook his head. "You look like the same wild girl who entered my hall last summer. It makes me wonder if I'll be getting what I paid for when Destrian is finished."

"Father, cease this talk at once," Destrian said. "Rowyn is becoming a well-known Morganian. We should be proud to host her."

I was amazed at how even his voice sounded.

The consul glared at his son. "Is it not bad enough that you insist upon parading this creature through my halls, but now you ask me to be proud she's here? She should grace my castle in chains, not honors as you so claim!"

I cleared my throat. "If it pleases my lord, I can stay elsewhere in the city. I need not burden you with my company."

"No, Father!" Destrian exclaimed. "We spoke of this. She must be able to stay safely in our halls."

The consul rose and gestured to Destrian with his goblet, spilling wine all over the table. "It troubles me that you would risk your life on some traitor's errand! I've sent a complaint to the Council of Five at Somme, and I've already given word to those southern sorcerers that I'll be sending no more gifts to that damned school. Had I known they would allow such vermin into that place and put your life in needless danger, I would've paid the extra expense to send you to the capital!" The consul flung his goblet into the fire and collapsed into his seat. "Go, take your meal in your rooms. Don't disgrace me with your burdensome company."

In the consul's pitiful display, I saw a genuine fear for Destrian.

Destrian turned and strode swiftly from the great hall. I followed him down the corridor, nearly running to keep up. We passed by the door to my room but Destrian didn't stop. Instead, he continued until we reached the library.

"Wait," I said, grabbing his arm outside the doors. "Are you all right?"

"I'm sorry," Destrian said, his voice husky. "Coming here has been a disaster. I don't know what I was thinking."

I couldn't even muster a comforting smile. "We should've expected it. Gillius isn't here to protect me this time."

Destrian scowled and looked away. "But I thought I could."

I pulled Destrian's arm around so he would face me. "I didn't realize this would put you in a bad position with your father." Though I had wondered if it would and hoped for the best. I couldn't even count the number of times I tried to explain to Destrian that our families' contempt for each other was an obstacle to our friendship. But Destrian always seemed to dismiss it. Still, knowing I was right in my worries didn't make me feel like gloating. Not when he already looked so defeated.

Destrian sighed. "I'm sorry, this just isn't going how I'd planned."

"If it makes you feel any better, my visit home wasn't much better."

Destrian's eyebrows rose as he pushed open the library doors to let us in. "Did something happen? Is everything all right?"

"Yes and no," I said, "but it's complicated. We don't have to talk about families anymore if you'd like. I've certainly had my fill of them. Venturing into the Nightlands now feels like a welcome task in comparison."

Destrian shook his head as he pulled back the curtains to let in more light.

Looking around the library, I noticed it had been cleaned thoroughly since my last visit. There were no more cobwebs in the corners or dust blanketing the hundreds of leather-bound volumes lining the shelves. Destrian had said before that none of the maids or servants cleaned the library, and I wondered at the change.

"I've gone through the titles and found one or two books we might want to read over," Destrian said, waving me to a table in the corner of the room that held a pitcher of water and a stack of books. "I found one in particular I thought would interest you." Picking up a small book from the table, Destrian handed it to me.

I pulled out a chair and sat, taking the small book Destrian offered. The cover was leather, stamped in gold lettering that read, *Morius*. "My lord," I said, running my fingers over the cover. "Thank you."

Destrian smiled as he took a seat beside me. "I found this the first day I arrived home. I thought it might help."

Opening to the first page, I read. The court healer, Orzo, who served under Philemon and Helen, had written the book after Morius's violent death. I remembered reading Orzo's account of Philemon and Helen's reign with my grandmother. It was one of the few books we had at home.

The book described Morius as having black opal gems on the back of each palm, where he called the rains to nourish the lands. He would travel Morgania, blessing the mountains and valleys. The area flourished, with villages and hamlets popping up in the valleys to the south, allowing Philemon and Helen to expand.

I stopped when I realized Destrian had gone, and set the book carefully on the table, wondering when he would return. Deciding it was as good a chance as any, I rose to inspect the shelves nearest the door.

When I had been to Helena the year before, a book had fallen from the shelf. When Destrian and I investigated, we found no one in the library but us. Destrian had refused to show me what book it was, and I wondered at its significance. Walking over to where I remembered the book falling, I looked up, studying the titles on the topmost shelf. I could barely read them from where I stood, but one was the history of Philemon and Helen's reign, the first king and queen of Morgania by Orzo. Next to it was the reign of Philemon II. It continued, and I read the names of each successor until I came to an empty space. The last book was missing. The history of the final successor of Philemon and Helen, Theramon the Conquered—whose family didn't survive the invasion—was nowhere to be found. Had Destrian taken it? Did he know I would come to these shelves to try to find it?

"*Lost.*"

I jumped at the whispered word in my ear. Looking wildly around, I saw no one.

"Hello?" I asked warily, walking to the end of the

bookcase and looking over the empty library. I saw a flash from the corner of my eye and turned, still finding no one.

I walked up and down the rows of books, looking for the hidden specter, but it was nowhere to be found. I remembered the voice from my dreams the year before. Bernard had told me a woman haunted the library. It must've been her.

But why was she speaking to me?

After a half hour of fervent searching, I returned to my table of books disgruntled. Destrian had lit the candles before he left as the day was proving to be dark and cloudy. The wax had melted onto the table and crept toward the books. I moved the stack away and went to clean up the mess.

Letters had formed in the candle wax. I bent closer to get a better look.

Lost.

Gooseflesh prickled over my arms as I tried to listen for my unknown companion.

I wasn't able to concentrate after that. My ears were searching for the faintest noise until I stood with the book, *Morius*, and doused the candles. Shutting the doors to the empty room, I went back to my chamber and read for the rest of the day, my mind going between my book and the figure that haunted Helena.

Chapter 15

"THERE YOU ARE, MY LADY," Daisy said, stepping back.

I grinned at the girl in the mirror. I'd asked Daisy to make me look like a "lady," and she had delivered. My hair was piled on top of my head in curls fashioned from a pair of round irons that she heated over the fire. The bruise on my cheek was still ugly, but I could do nothing about it.

Standing, I smoothed the skirt to my nameday dress and grinned. Though the dress wasn't anything fine, it would have to do. Daisy let Destrian in and left with a few new coins jingling in her purse.

"What do you think?" I asked absentmindedly as I patted and smoothed my hair in the mirror. The rose vine tattoo on my neck was highly visible with my hair piled up, but I liked its appearance.

Destrian leaned against the wall, his arms crossed. "You look very nice, though it's missing a proper dress."

I tilted my head to the side, making sure the hair wouldn't fall. "I know, but this was all I brought since I didn't think I would need anything fancy on the road."

"If you had mentioned it, I could have sent one to you.

My sisters keep a couple of gowns here for visits. You and Onora are of similar size."

"It's all right," I said, straightening and joining Destrian by the door. "Is your father going to remove us from dinner, or are we free to dine?"

Destrian offered his arm to me. "I spoke with him, and he knows to leave you alone. Karl and the other city guards are waiting at the table for you as well."

The consul didn't even bat an eye when I entered. The only empty seat available to me was next to Bernard, which lifted my spirits somewhat. He rose and pulled my chair out for me with a smile.

On my other side was Karl, and across the table were the three other guards who attacked me in the market. They glared at me over their plates, but I thought back to Vianne. *There is always power in grace, if one simply knows how to wield it.* I smiled, lifting the pitcher of wine to pour myself a large glass, then stopped myself. *A lady never overdrinks.* I poured myself a little glass instead.

"Good evening, sirs. I didn't catch all of your names," I said by way of conversation.

"What do our names have to do with anything?" Karl grunted, taking a swig of his ale.

"Watch it," Bernard growled next to me, his eyes on the others. It seemed Destrian had assigned the old soldier as my social guard.

"If we are to be dinner companions for this evening, then I must at least know your names. Potatoes?" I offered the youngest one a tureen. His ears stuck out from his dark hair, reminding me of Pedr. The young man glanced at the head of the table where Destrian glared at him.

"The name's Dell," the young man said, spooning the potatoes onto his plate with a shaky hand.

I flashed back to the morning, being dragged through the street, my face smashing into loose paving stones. *A lady doesn't vary speech whether she's talking to a maid or to the emperor. Always be polite.* I supposed that meant young guards who assaulted you as well.

"It's a pleasure to meet you, Dell. It's a pity we weren't properly introduced on the road, but my name is Rowyn Blythe."

Dell nodded and ducked his head down to eat.

I looked at my plate and was about to lift a large piece of potato to my mouth, then I paused. *Always eat your food in tiny bites, like a bird.* I never thought I'd thank Solridge for lessons in decorum. I'd made a conscious effort thus far to show my worth in their language, so I drew a knife from my sleeve and delicately cut my meat with it. Dell watched the blade with wide eyes.

"I was able to retrieve my knives from the ward," I explained. "I appreciate you holding on to them for me so they wouldn't be lost."

Bernard choked on a bit of food. I patted him gingerly on the back. He'd not understand my choice of actions and surely not my words, though compared to my first experience in this hall, I surprised myself with how much more easily a forced resolve came. "So, are you from Helena?" I asked, trying to draw them into the conversation.

"I'm from Dimtown," Dell muttered, pushing food about on his plate.

"Where is Dimtown?"

The guard next to Dell spoke up. "It's the poor district in Helena." He met my eyes. "I'm from there too."

I smiled. "And what is your name, sir?"

"Asher," he muttered.

"So, Asher, do you have a mother in Dimtown? A sister or wife, perhaps?"

"What's it to you?" Karl snapped, then he hissed and dropped his fork. Tears eked from his eyes as he waved his hand about. I glanced at his plate where the fork blazed red. We all looked at Destrian. His face was clouded with fury as the glow on his gem dulled.

I would be a fool if I told myself I didn't enjoy that just a little.

"I just wondered how the women in your family would feel knowing you took pleasure in the violence displayed today," I said, taking another bite.

Asher glared at me. "My mother's dead."

"Oh," I said, my voice dropping, "I'm sorry to hear that." I didn't know what else to say. I took a sip from my goblet and fiddled with my knife. "My mother perished from the plague," I murmured.

"Plague took my sister," said the last guard, "and my brother was lost in the war." When I looked at him, he added, "The name's Guy."

Bernard slapped his hand on my shoulder and shook me a bit. I was glad the goblet was out of my hands, at least. "Rowyn here is headed to the Nightlands with his lordship."

The guards gaped at me.

"To be sure?" Dell asked. "Aren't you frightened?"

"Of course," I said, glaring at Bernard while taking the teeniest sip from my goblet. "But, I am on a quest for a gem, so I must go."

"Like Lord Destrian?"

I nodded. "I'm a sorcerer as well."

The guards looked at each other out of the corner of their eyes. I was surprised they didn't already know that but admonished myself for such a conceited thought. Most people wouldn't have heard of me.

"So you have a great journey ahead of you. Do you feel prepared?" Bernard asked.

"Is anyone ever prepared for a journey such as this?" I asked, taking a tiny bite.

"That's where my gran says the dead go to have relief," Guy whispered.

I frowned. "I'd not heard that one. She thinks there are ghosts there?"

Guy looked down at his plate. "That's what she says, but I've never left Helena."

"I'd never left Espiria before last summer," I said with a smile. "I'd not even been to Darkport, even though it's so close."

"What is Seaport like?" asked Asher.

After that, dinner could've even been called pleasant. None of the guards had left the city of Helena, so I described the lands around Solridge and Seaport as well as the citadel of Ayastaren. Although the guards didn't say very much, they weren't outright rude to me anymore, either. I was sure Vianne would have been proud of my display. My mother would've been too.

My eyes flicked back to the consul, who was drinking too much. My feelings of hatred were diminishing to those of pity as he slunk further in his seat, his eyes on the table.

The dining hall gradually emptied when the consul left for the night. Bernard and I chatted for a bit longer before I rose to grab one more book from the library before bed.

Torchlight flickered in the empty halls. Shadows seemed to dance over the walls and crevices while the arched windows looked out to the starry sky. A fresh breeze wafted in, carrying with it the scent of spring. On my way back from the library, I took a wrong turn and hit the end of a corridor. Frustrated, I turned to go back when I was met by the consul.

Despite my hackles rising in warning, I curtsied. "My lord," I said, taking a step back. I glanced around the corridor as my heart raced. There was no one in the hall but the consul and me. Dread coiled in the pit of my stomach when I realized there was no escape. Consul Colman's eyes glittered with malice, and his mottled face turned a deep scarlet.

"Don't 'my lord' me," Consul Colman snarled as he staggered toward me. "My son might be blind to what a minx you are, but I'm not. You'll be the death of him. I'm sure of it."

I stopped breathing. The hatred behind his gaze froze me to the spot, and I was wracked with indecision. I couldn't move past him. I couldn't go back.

The consul grabbed my hair and yanked me toward him.

I shoved his chest, trying to break away. Did I dare draw a weapon? I might as well sign my death warrant if I did. He'd be well within his right to execute me if I injured him, even if it was in self-defense. By all the gods, the consul had truly trapped me.

"Stop," I cried, trying to pull his grip loose. "What

would Destrian say if he saw you like this?"

The consul slammed me against the wall. His hands gripped my throat and he squeezed.

"Please, my lord," I rasped, clutching his hands and attempting to loosen his grip. Tears sprang to my eyes as I tried to peel his fingers off. A streak of lightning lit the dark corridor, and thunder grumbled against the stone walls.

The consul's eyes were glassy, filled with anger and resentment, and above all, fear. It was as though he knew what Conal had asked of me and was going to prevent it by any means necessary.

"Please," I mouthed again as I tugged and pulled at his arms. The consul only grew more determined. He pushed me toward a window, the sill rising just below my waist. Consul Colman leaned against me, pushing my upper half into the night air. A strong wind picked up my curls and flung them behind me.

Never in my life had I predicted I would be in a position to end Consul Colman's life, nor in one where I'd stay my hand. But there I was, and unbelievably, I didn't want to hurt Destrian's father.

I glanced down at the sickening drop and panicked. Stars glimmered over my eyes as lightning struck the roof of a nearby tower. It was too late to defend myself now, I realized, darkness closing from the outside of my vision. I didn't have the strength to reach into my sleeve to grab my knife, let alone use it. Consul Colman would get his way after all. In a way, it seemed almost fitting. Almost fair. For if this were not my fate, I was but a gift to the empire.

"What is this madness!" someone shouted. An arm reached around Consul Colman's neck and dragged him back. His hands released me, and I crumpled to the ground below the window, coughing and gasping for breath.

Lightning crackled outside as the pitter-patter of rain fell over the sills of the open windows. The corridor brightened, and I saw Destrian standing with his back to me, facing his father.

"You're drunk," Destrian snapped, sparks alighting from his fingertips. "How could you stoop so low?"

"She's bewitched you," the consul sputtered as several guards stamped down the hall. "Why can't you see her for what she truly is?"

Destrian turned to the guards. "My father is unwell. Escort him to his room." His eyes brooked no argument.

The guards glanced uneasily at Consul Colman who shrank into himself. "Son, please, don't leave."

Destrian shook his head. "You're better than this. Go to bed. I'll see you in the morning."

Consul Colman opened his mouth to say something

else, looked at the guards, then nodded. He trudged down the hall, flanked by the castle guardsmen, leaving Destrian and me alone.

I couldn't move from my place on the floor. Every step I'd taken since leaving Solridge had been met with bad omens. First, Conal's demand that I do the unthinkable, then my uncle Baylin threatening to sell me away to the empire for a parcel of land, the guards' terrible treatment in the marketplace, and now the consul's attack. By all the gods, we hadn't even entered the Nightlands yet. My life was an ever-increasing series of torments.

I drew my knees to my chest, unable to stop the tears streaming down my cheeks. Embarrassed, I buried my face in my arms as exhaustion and misery took hold of me. I couldn't help but hate my life.

"Rowyn," Destrian murmured, kneeling next to me. "Rowyn, please don't . . ."

I could only shake my head. I wished he would leave me alone and let me cry in blessed peace.

But Destrian didn't leave. He sat next to me and wrapped his arm over my shoulders, drawing me into his warmth. "I've utterly failed you," Destrian said, his voice hard. "I've failed you in every way imaginable."

I sniffed, raising my head and wiping my cheeks with my sleeve. "It's not your fault," I said, trying to calm my trembling voice.

Destrian shook his head. "No, it *is* my fault. Just like everyone else, I accepted the way things were here. I can't tell you how many times I've seen Morganites dragged to the citadel in the name of justice. I told myself they must've done something wrong. They deserved it. I didn't ever think to question my father's methods until I met you."

I shuddered as the storm outside quieted to a light rain. I'd used my magic twice in one day. No wonder I felt so weary. "It was lucky you happened upon us so quickly," I muttered, my eyes on the floor. By all the gods, a minute more, and I would've been dead. I was sure of it.

Destrian furrowed his brows. "I was coming for you."

I finally met his eyes. "You were?"

"Of course," Destrian said as though it were something I should've already known. "The weather always reveals your feelings. I was getting ready to look for you earlier when the guards showed up at the castle. I knew you were scared."

"Oh," was all I could think to say.

Destrian leaned his head against the stone wall, watching the flickering flame of a torch mounted across from us. "I noticed it on the trip to Solridge. By all the gods, it was cloudy and depressing the whole way there." Destrian shook his head at the memory. Then, he smiled. "But, on the second day back, I noticed the sun shining through my window. The sky was clear without a cloud in sight. When I went down to breakfast, I saw you laughing with Fin. I figured you must've been happy."

My tears disappeared at his words. I couldn't believe he'd noticed those details. I also couldn't believe how comforted I felt with his arm around me.

Destrian was watching me, as though willing me to acknowledge his thoughts. But I couldn't read them. I didn't know what he wanted me to say.

"I'm tired," I muttered finally.

Destrian sighed. "It's been a long day. Let's get you back to your room." He rose then held his hand out and pulled me up.

Destrian and I walked slowly through the halls. I rubbed the bruises on my neck, my pity for the consul fading.

"When we come back from the Nightlands, it'll be different. It has to be," Destrian said, watching me out of the corner of his eye.

I thought back to home. "You can't force it." At least Destrian hadn't been with me in Espiria. I was sure the visit would've gone much worse if he'd been. I didn't want to think about what Conal would've said.

"Did you read enough in the library? Would you be ready to leave tomorrow morning if I cut our stay short?" Destrian asked.

Thinking back to the library, I remembered the specter and missing book from the long line of Morganite rulers. "There was one book I'd wanted to see that wasn't in the library. Perhaps you may know where it lies," I said, studying Destrian's reaction.

Destrian crossed his arms and leaned against my door. "Which one?"

"The history of Theramon the Conquered. I wanted to read about the Lyrican invasion."

A dark look crossed Destrian's countenance. "What does that have to do with our quest to the Nightlands?" he asked huffily. "You're not focused as you should be, Rowyn."

"I can't seem to shake it from my mind. I've even had dreams about it. Why do you keep it from me?" Annoyance rose within as he glowered.

"You need to be focused on our trials to come, not some history that happened long ago."

"What are you hiding?"

"I'll meet you here at first light," Destrian said, opening my door. "Try to get some sleep."

"Fine," I muttered, walking through the door.

"I'm warding your door tonight. Don't open it until Daisy comes in the morning, or else it will go away."

I nodded then shut the door and bolted it. Stepping back, I watched the door glow red.

Chapter 16

"YOU WILL WAIT FOR ME, won't you?"

I recognized the boy from my dream, but he was older. His black hair was longer and knotted at the back of his head. Dark eyes looked into mine. On his shoulder was a marking of the moon enshrouded in a cloud. I recognized the band below it. It was nearly identical to the band I had on my arm. The symbol of the Blythe family.

Behind the man stood a crowd of people carrying packs and holding walking sticks. Many were kissing loved ones farewell. It felt like a funeral procession, though I couldn't see any dead. A woman next to me had tears in her eyes as she traced the imorets on a young man's face in blessing.

"If we don't return, take them across," someone whispered to me from behind.

An elder, with a crown on his head and robes the color of midnight, patted a young man's arm. I recognized the regal boy from before. The elder grabbed Mony by the shoulders and embraced him. "I love you, son. Take care of the others while we're gone, and if anything happens . . ."

My dream-self was crying. "Please stay," I whispered.

"You don't have to do this. You have nothing to prove to them."

But the man in front of me shook his head. "Imor is calling me. They need my help."

"Please," I begged, holding fast to his tunic. He released my hands and stepped away. The procession of people moved north in single file. The dark-haired man swung a pack over his shoulder and joined the end of the line. He looked back once and waved, his eyes filled with fear and sorrow.

"We can only pray for their safety," a voice said in my ear. I turned to find Mony standing next to me, his eyes watching me closely. "Imor will show them the way. We must have faith."

I shook my head. "Imor has deserted us."

I AWOKE AN HOUR BEFORE DAWN. Groaning, I sat up in bed, rubbing my neck. The bruises were worse than the night before, but I refused to put a healing salve on them. I wanted others to see the price I paid for being in Helena, though I knew it would hurt Destrian to think of it.

I wondered about the dream. Who was the man and woman parted by some great journey? The sights and sounds seemed so real. It didn't feel like a dream at all. It felt like a memory of long ago.

I dismissed that foolish thought. How could I have a memory of something I never experienced before?

I readied for the day. After pulling on my tunic and breeches, I belted Iranoct to my side. Fin's timekeeping device, Araceli's charm, and Pedr's chess piece dangled from my neck. The map was tucked into one of my pockets, the waterskin draped over one shoulder.

I'd decided to use my cape from home rather than the new one Gillius had purchased for me. There was something special about wearing the black fabric embroidered with the silver crescent and stars of my clan. I was traveling as a Morganite, not some Lyrican sorcerer.

Destrian came in armed to the teeth. Phyranox was at his side, and a dagger was tucked into his belt next to a small ax. His scarlet cape peeked beneath the pack slung over his shoulder.

I followed Destrian down the stairs and out into the ward. The guards were there to see us off, though Destrian's father was noticeably absent. Bernard held the reins of my borrowed horse and smiled at my approach.

"So, the great journey begins. Are ye ready?" he asked, taking my pack from Daisy and tossing it onto the horse's back.

"As ready as I'll ever be," I said with a smile. I patted

the old soldier's arm. "Take care of yourself. I wish you and your family well."

"Aye, they'll be coming to join me soon enough. I'm posted at Helena for good, it seems."

I tilted my head to the side. "What brought about that change?"

Bernard glanced over his shoulder and dropped his voice low. "Your Lord Destrian requested it in the letter to his father about his visit. The consul called me up straightaway."

"Hmm," I said, musing aloud. "I wonder why Destrian did that. Do you mind it?"

Bernard shook his head. "Nay, I don't mind it. Helena's a more interesting place to be anyhow. Besides, there's nothing that says I can't visit the folk of Rudin if I get to missing them."

"Are you ready?" Destrian asked over his shoulder.

I nodded. "If you're finished with your farewells, then yes."

Destrian put his hands at my waist, but I stepped back. "I can—"

"Mount yourself, I know," Destrian muttered, pulling me toward him again. "I wish to show you honor," he whispered, nodding to the guards in the ward. "So there is no doubt. If I honor you, so must they."

I hadn't thought of that. Destrian lifted me gently into

the saddle. His hands lingered for a moment, brushing down my leg as he met my eyes. I looked away, the tips of my ears growing hot. He stepped away quickly and mounted his own borrowed horse.

"May the gods bless you, my lord," someone shouted. The men all joined in cheering blessings while Destrian waved.

We rode silently through the city. The busy roads and market were a welcome distraction, but after riding through Helena's northern gates, an awkward silence stretched between us. I felt Destrian studying me, but I watched the stony path instead.

"Do you want to talk about what happened?" he asked after a while.

"Not really," I said, studying a granite outcropping for no reason other than to avoid looking at him.

"I've spoken to Father."

I raised my brows. "What did he say?"

"Rowyn, you have to understand—"

"No, *you* have to understand. I told you how your father and his soldiers treated Morganites, and you didn't believe me. You called me a liar."

I'd lain in bed the night before, fuming about my visit to Helena. It was Destrian's city, and all I'd found there was the same cruelty exhibited by the Lyons. Not to mention he insisted on keeping that damned book from me.

"That's not fair," Destrian retorted. "Can't you see I'm trying to make it right?"

"You think that defending my honor will suddenly make it right?" I scoffed. Dread filled my thoughts. I knew my resentment of Destrian was unwarranted. I knew I wasn't being fair. But now that the Nightlands were looming ever closer, I couldn't help but feel that the journey would end in tragedy. The trip had barely begun, and I could already count it as disastrous. What dangers awaited me behind the mountains where even the eye of Sol feared to go?

Even if I did survive, what was the point? My uncle would sell me away for peace and a parcel of land. My life might as well be forfeit. I found myself wishing, for the first time, that Destrian could read my thoughts.

Finally, I sighed. "You didn't bat an eye to the other Morganites in the city. How many of my kin rot in your prisons as we speak?"

"I . . . that's completely beside the point," Destrian exclaimed.

I shook my head. "That's precisely the point. These are your people, too, you know. How can you show me honor, yet let your family and laws degrade my kin? That makes absolutely no sense."

Destrian's hair began smoking at the ends. "What would you have me do?"

I threw up my hands. "Anything, Destrian! I would have you do anything to make the plight of my clan better. Who is in a better position to make a difference than *you*? You'll be consul one day. Can't you see the divisions between the clans and Lyricans weaken Morgania?"

"I know!" Destrian growled, then fell silent. He gritted his teeth, staring at the horizon as though it held the answers he sought.

I concentrated on the road. We rode silently for the rest of the day, passing merchants and farmers, as well as a band of Helenian guards who eyeballed me as they headed south. Destrian had pulled the hood of his cloak up to hide his face and gem, so nobody gave him a second glance.

Gradually, my anger seeped away. I'd said my piece. It was up to Destrian to correct it, and he knew that. I didn't envy his position. How did you go about amending centuries of persecution? At least he voiced a willingness for change. I couldn't expect our world to become equitable overnight just because Destrian saw reason. I supposed I should celebrate those small victories.

"Bernard mentioned you wrote asking him to be stationed at Helena," I said, trying to relieve the tension.

Destrian nodded. "I thought you would appreciate a friendly face. You like him, and I wanted you to feel comfortable. Much good it did you."

"Thank you for that kindness," I muttered. I couldn't help but feel conflicted. I could see the steps Destrian had made to make me at ease in Helena. He'd sent me Daisy who was sweet. He'd picked through the library so I would have all the books I needed ready. By all the gods, he'd even had the library cleaned so we could study in comfort and peace. Was it his fault it wasn't enough? Not entirely, but he had to know that surface gestures weren't going to bring peace to his lands. If he wanted my respect, he had to bring about true change, not just favors because it suited him.

"Do you see it?" Destrian asked suddenly, pointing to the sky.

I shielded my eyes and looked up. A shadow falcon was gliding through the air, its gray feathers camouflaged with the coming dusk.

"You have a good eye, my lord," I said, smiling up at him.

Destrian looked unsure, but after a moment, he returned the smile. "Let's stay at an inn for the night. We'll only be able to camp when we cross the river, and I like a soft bed."

Destrian and I stopped at a small village that boasted an inn and not much else. We dismounted and led our horses to the door, the promise of a warm meal wafting in the night air. Destrian pulled his hood down to hide his gem and nodded to me. After a quick knock, the innkeeper opened the door, glanced out, and shook his head.

"We don't serve Morganites. Best be on your way."

My stomach flipped. Destrian's eyes darkened, and I could tell he was about to lose his temper. "By all the gods," Destrian exclaimed. "You dare turn us away?"

The innkeeper nodded. "I wouldn't have no more customers if I served a Morganite. The people around here don't hold with their kind."

On first thought, I wanted to shove the door open and fight past the innkeeper to be served. I'd been looking forward to a hot meal and a mug of ale. But, it would only give credence to his feelings about Morganites. My conversation and dinner with the guards were a far more pleasant outcome than seeing them whipped in the ward.

I placed my hand on Destrian's arm and gave a slight shake of my head. "You must have something," I whispered to the innkeeper.

The innkeeper sighed, glanced over his shoulder, then stepped outside and shut the door. "You all can sleep in the stable if you'd like. Just make sure none o' the others see and be gone before light." He walked to a large outbuilding farther down the road, opened the door, and ushered us in.

One stall held a mule that was chewing away at his oats. The other three stalls were empty. The straw looked clean enough, and there was plenty of it, so Destrian would get his soft bed after all.

As the innkeeper passed, I grabbed his arm. "Thank you," I said. "We appreciate your kindness."

The innkeeper looked surprised. "You're welcome, lass," he said, brushing my fingers away from his sleeve. He turned to Destrian. "Remember, be gone before light." Then the innkeeper was gone.

Destrian and I stood awkwardly for a moment, looking around.

"Well," I said finally, "I suppose we can make a little soup from the dried food I packed."

Destrian sighed and began taking the saddle and packs off our horses. He seemed at the end of his patience by the way he gritted his teeth.

"Where is your ruby from? How did you get it?" I asked in an attempt to distract him.

"The Desertlands. I had to ride a camel most of the way," Destrian answered, frowning at the memory. "Horses are much easier to deal with—not as stubborn. Also, camels spit."

I laughed. "I've never seen a camel. I read about them in books but have never seen one."

"Don't worry, you aren't missing out on anything. It was sweltering too. I had to wear special clothing to protect me from the sun. It was more dangerous to go without a shirt on than it was to be covered."

"Who was your companion?"

Destrian sat across from me, leaning against the empty stall. "Lord Alexander. We met up with a tribe who'd fled the invasion from Lyrica. They weren't very friendly, but Lord Alexander drew water from the ground and created an oasis in exchange for guided passage. They were the ones who led us to the dried-up river valley where the rubies were."

I nodded, worrying again about finding my opal. "Fin mentioned that the Woltari were supposed to guide her."

"Normally, that's what happens. There was a sorcerer at the capital who had to get his gem underwater. He said a clan of sirens ended up taking him there."

A gem underwater? How on earth did that work? Then, I had another thought. "How did you know which ruby to take?"

"The rubies had been mined for generations, so I had to dig pretty deep. But, as I dug, I saw a glint in the earth. When I picked it up, I knew instantly when it shone."

Would mine shine too? I still felt the pull; was that my gem speaking to me? Or was it me searching it out? "What's the ceremony like? Embedding it into your head and everything—does it hurt?"

"Not really. Stings some. The ceremony isn't very long. Gillius pulled me aside before we left and gave me the specifics. You'll be fine."

I nodded grimly. Destrian noticed.

"The first sorcerer in centuries with the ability to wield a black opal, and you're afraid of it stinging." Destrian chuckled.

I stuck my tongue out at him. "Does it feel the same now as it did before your quest? Preparing and being so nervous?"

Destrian plucked a bit of straw from his tunic and tossed it to the side. "Actually, I'm anticipating it more than my own quest."

"You know, there's a reason people don't just waltz into the Nightlands," I said, hoping my tone wasn't too dismal. "Most of them don't come back."

"I think we'll be fine, Rowyn. Something about this trip—my decision to go—just feels right." Destrian leaned toward me, resting his arms on his knees. "You know what I mean? Like we were meant to do this."

I nodded, though his answer wasn't at all what I expected. "I suppose that's how I feel too. But, I feel like if we *do* succeed, it will change everything." I chastised myself. I shouldn't be revealing those thoughts to Destrian of all people. But still, if we were to gain each other's trust, I should at least be honest about my feelings. "People will expect me to end the drought."

Destrian's mouth twitched. "Would helping people be

such a bad thing? Why does it matter if they are Lyrican? It can't be mere coincidence that the first weather worker in centuries appears in the middle of a drought that has impacted the entire empire. I'd argue that fate put you here."

"I suppose it shouldn't." I sighed. "I just wish I had a choice in the matter. But that's not the only thing. What if . . . What if I can't? I suppose if I believed in fate, I wouldn't worry about that. But I don't, so I do worry. People seem to want so many things from me. How can I possibly please everyone?"

The crease between Destrian's brow grew. "Within fate, there is still a choice. Don't think that you have no control over your own path." He was so matter-of-fact, as though he really believed it.

I smiled. "Thank you. That makes me feel a little better, actually."

"You know, we all get nervous right before we leave. Just keep your head up."

Chapter 17

THE SUN SET EARLIER and earlier each day. The Last Dusk only received two hours of sunlight, nightfall coming around early afternoon.

It was a depressing place, with only meager gray light illuminating the huts, revealing what few denizens resided there. A house served as the inn, and we were the only guests. It was a dingy place where we could relish our last moments of comfort before we crossed the river to the land of night on the other side.

Several people had congregated at the inn's tavern, curious about the wealthy visitors who arrived just before nightfall. Destrian enjoyed speaking to them, telling the villagers of our intent to venture into the Nightlands, though leaving out the gems. I heard a whispered frenzy around the tavern when Destrian mentioned our journey. I caught the name Arda several times and looked around in curiosity.

"Arda, the seer?" I asked a group of men clustered around us as we ate.

The man standing next to Destrian spoke up. "Arda insists on telling the fortunes of everyone who crosses the river."

"How much?" Destrian asked, intrigued.

"Two silvers a person. I can show you the way to her hut," the man offered.

Destrian nodded and stood. "Are you coming too?" he asked while I scraped the last of the stew from my bowl.

I sighed. Even though Master Haris said I had nothing to fear from Arda, I still didn't like the idea of visiting a seer. Especially considering one tried their hardest to murder me for a year. "I suppose I will."

This sent the villagers whispering anew, more excited than ever as Destrian and I followed the man from the inn into the night. He took us down the road to a small hut near the river. Knocking on the door, he ducked in and spoke to someone inside.

The door opened again, and the man came back out, looking at Destrian and me in turn. "Which of you first?" he asked, setting his hands on his hips. "She only sees people one at a time."

My eyes went to Destrian's.

"I'll go," he said.

The man waved his hand to the entrance and stood on the outside, eying me. "Why do you and your companion seek to cross the river?" he asked, probably to buy time as we waited.

"I'm to go on a quest. I must find something in the Nightlands and bring it back," I said, again wary of giving away the true nature of my venture.

He frowned at me. "*Hmph*, very few go over the river and even fewer return. You should ask yourself if it's really worth it."

"I'm afraid I must make the journey. I don't have a choice," I said with finality.

His eyebrows shot up. "You don't have a choice? Everyone who crosses the bridge has a choice, whether they want to see it or not. Many a great warrior have lost their lives on this foolish Nightlands business." The man was getting on my nerves. I wished Destrian would hurry up and finish so I could be rid of this man.

Soon enough, Destrian opened the door and stepped back into the night air, breathing deeply as he held the door open for me to enter. I ducked inside and approached the small fire at the center of the hut. Sitting behind it was a woman so old and frail, it looked as if a brisk wind could carry her away altogether.

"Sit." Her voice was gruff and no-nonsense, like a fed-up grandmother. I kneeled on the other side of the fire, peering at the old woman's face in the flickering light. My heart skipped a beat when I realized what I was seeing. She had two blue irises in each eye, which meant four irises were gazing back. No, that wasn't right. One of her eyes was clouded, blinding her. But the pupils were still there. The sight of two such different eyes made me catch my breath as the elderly seer peered at me curiously over the flames.

"We don't get very many visitors this far north. You're bound for the land of night?" she asked, her eyes narrowed to slits.

"Yes," I said as I studied her in return. She wore rags, her white hair knotted and hanging in disarray over her head. It made her look quite wild.

"I see you're an exceptional woman, just as he viewed you. What would you like to know?"

My heart caught. Was she talking about Destrian?

Arda sneered knowingly at me, but I drew myself back up. "You're a seer of Imor," I said, recalling my research of the golgeman. "You're one of his daughters."

Arda nodded. "I heard that you dealt with my cousin's servant. I told her it wouldn't work. Prophecies can't be dismissed so easily."

My head perked up. "What prophecy?"

Arda's voice became low and distant, as though another spoke through her.

"The daughter of an ancient queen,
aided by Imor,
protected by Sol,
whose fire will rage through broken cities,
whose rain will quench parched earth,
whose coming will unite children of the empire,

she will rise."

"Who does the prophecy speak of?" I asked.

Arda coughed, a great hacking sound that filled the hut. I stood and went to the corner where a stone water basin sat. Stooping down, I ladled water into a cup and brought it to her, offering it as I would to a shrine. Arda smiled gratefully and took a sip of the water. She was missing some crucial teeth.

"You don't know her yet, but you will come to find her in time."

A rising woman. Rain quenching the parched earth. That had to be me. The fire could be Destrian, of course, though Fin had said there were other fire sorcerers across the empire. So much was running through my mind that I resolved to think about it later. I still had questions I needed answered.

"Conal, our Imorati at home, said that Imor spoke to him."

"Yes, he did, didn't he," Arda wheezed. "Are you troubled by the task you've been assigned?"

"Well ... yes!" I dropped my voice to a whisper. "How can I kill Destrian? How can that be right?"

Arda shrugged. "Imor commands no one. He merely suggests. You can choose for yourself what you would like to do."

I tried a different tactic. "Uncle is going to sign me

away to Lyrica. Will that work? Will I find myself at the capital?"

Arda blinked. "If your red lord doesn't return, maybe not." Arda blinked again and leaned over the fire, studying me. "There's magic in your mind. It's an impenetrable cloud that I can't break through. So I can't see your path clearly."

"There is magic blocking you from my mind? It could be mine, couldn't it? The instructors at school say I'm near bursting with magic."

"No, it's not you. I see your power now, spilling out of you and all over my floor. That's what this eye is for." Arda pointed to her good eye before lifting her finger and placing it below her blind one. "This eye sees the future, your past, things I can't see in front of me. And this eye sees almost nothing right now. It's as if I'm blind."

I'm sure I looked confused because, really, she was blind.

"Do you know who it was? Who magicked me? Is there nothing you can read?" I was pleading with her now, unwilling to leave her hut until she gave me some actual answers.

Arda hesitated then waved her hand, beckoning me to her. I approached, kneeling next to a pile of white bones picked clean and discarded in the corner. Arda grasped my hands in her cool, wrinkled ones. She leaned closely to stare into my eyes while smacking her lips. Her breath blew into my face repeatedly; it stunk, the musky smell of age and decay. I did my best not to wrinkle my nose and return her stares.

When Arda spoke, flecks of spit landed on my cheeks. "*Hmph*. I see fear, great fear, probably for the Nightlands, to be sure. But there is something else . . ." Arda continued staring. "Ah, there it is." Letting go of my hands, she turned away, satisfied.

I was bursting with anticipation. "What is it?" I asked, trying to stop myself from shaking her frail shoulders. She would surely break under my hands.

"Two silvers!" Arda said, smacking her lips in satisfaction. I produced the silvers from my purse and thrust them into her hands.

"Well?"

Arda grinned at me, her eyes sparkling in mirth. "Coveting. That is what I found when I looked into your eyes. There is great coveting in your life."

That wasn't what I expected. "What do you mean, coveting? I want what I can't have?"

Arda laughed. "Yes and no. You covet what others have, being able to choose their lives without the peskiness of fate. You covet a life where you don't have power. You covet those who live without fear. But those are all normal covets, things everybody wishes for. You have something unique in your coveting."

"So, what's unique about wanting what everyone else wants?" I was growing more confused by the minute.

"I just said it wasn't unique. You need to listen. It's not what *you* covet, it's the number of people who covet *you*." Arda smiled at me.

"People covet me?"

"Yes, people covet you: your power, your beauty, your skills. You draw them in like flies to honey. Much like you naturally draw your magic to you, people are attracted as well. The magic flows around them and toward you, leading them right along with it." Arda's eyes flicked back to the fire. "I've heard your name uttered before, Rowyn the Morganite. You can be sure it's whispered in the halls of the Golden Palace this very day."

"What do they want of me?"

"Many things. Too many to tell. I got more from Lord Destrian than I did from you," Arda whispered, glancing at the entrance of the hut. "He knows things about you. Things even you don't know."

"Tell me!" I hissed, but she only shook her head while her hand flapped toward the door in my dismissal. I stood, angry at what Arda had confirmed.

"Farewell, and remember, the red one is a lover I would be wary of," Arda said as I looked down at her. Nodding, I walked swiftly to the entrance and pulled back the door, stepping out into the cool breeze. The air was much colder away from the fire, and I clutched my cloak to myself as I found Destrian and the man waiting for me at the bank of the river.

"How was it?" Destrian asked, eying the look on my face. I was sure I was glaring at him.

"It was fine," I replied, though my voice was pitched too high.

That night I lay in bed, contemplating Arda's words. The prophecy spoke to the future of the empire rather than my personal path. But what did it mean?

More importantly, at least for the time being, Destrian was keeping something from me. He knew something and he'd purposely not told me. Arda made it seem as if it was more than one thing. I thought back to the library. The hidden specter trying to communicate with me. The book Destrian had hidden time and again. There was something in the book he didn't want me to see, and now more than ever, I wondered what it was.

Chapter 18

I HAD NIGHTMARES of unseen creatures scratching and clawing me while I twisted, trying to get free. Awaking in a sweat, I found dawn peeking through the window. The last sunrise I would see until I got back.

My hands shook as I got ready, making sure my gifts, weapons, and tools were tucked in their spots. The pack, coupled with my furs, was bulky in the narrow indoor space. Going down the stairs was hazardous. I slipped on the last two steps and slid to the bottom on my rear with a clang from the pot dangling at my side. Destrian laughed as he helped me up, looking like a hulking giant to my fat partridge.

The people in the small town, mainly miners, were used to adventurers crossing the banks and never returning. Their eyes twinkled under their dirty faces, watching as we asked the innkeeper if there was a crossing nearby. A young boy came to lead us to a bridge on the edge of the town.

The "bridge" was a series of ropes and planks running from each bank. It didn't look like it would hold a lizard, let alone the weight of two carrying heavy packs. Shadows seemed to stretch toward me, beckoning me to the

Nightlands, but I couldn't take the first step. Seeing that, Destrian stepped forward.

"I can go first if you like. If it holds my weight, then you should be fine."

I hated the flood of relief that filled me at his words, but I nodded all the same.

Destrian stepped forward. I grabbed his hand. "Be careful," I said.

Destrian looked over his shoulder and smiled nervously. "Of course," he said, then turned to concentrate on the bridge.

I clutched Araceli's key charm hanging around my neck and began to sweat as Destrian took the first step. The bridge bowed under his weight, touching his boots lightly to the water.

Holding my breath, I sent silent prayers to Imor. But, were my prayers for naught? What if Conal was right? What if Imor demanded Destrian's blood? The wind picked up, and the bridge swayed to the side. Destrian gripped the rope handholds with white knuckles. His boots were nearly enveloped in the rushing river below, but the bridge held. Finally, he stepped onto the outer bank. Turning to me, he reached out his hand.

"Come on! It wasn't so bad," he shouted.

But I couldn't do it.

Looking over my shoulder, I wondered where I could

go, what I could do if I chose not to take the quest.

"I can come back if you're scared," Destrian yelled.

Seeing the look on Destrian's face—wonderment, excitement, and yearning—I decided my fate and took that first step.

The bridge swayed so I grabbed the rope handrails. Taking a deep breath, I took another step, then another.

"That's it," Destrian shouted from the other side.

The rushing river pounded in my ears, but I refused to tear my eyes away from Destrian. I knew if I looked down, I'd freeze up.

My foot slipped. I went down on my knee, my heart flying to my throat and thrumming in my ears.

"Rowyn!" Destrian shouted, stepping onto the bridge.

"No, wait!" I yelled back, my hand raised to stop him. I was probably right in thinking the bridge could only hold one of us.

Destrian nodded and backed off, letting me rise, shakily, to my feet and continue onward. Before I knew it, my feet hit solid ground, and I could breathe a sigh of relief.

"Well, we managed the first test," Destrian said, smiling down on me. "How do you feel?"

"Nervous," I answered, rubbing my sweaty palms on my furs.

Destrian nodded to the rocky mountain path before us. "The going only gets harder from here."

We didn't speak, only climbed, and we watched our surroundings warily. The faint call of insects gradually faded as we scaled the first mountain.

After hiking for hours, we finally reached the first peak. The innkeeper had packed a nice lunch, so we sat and ate, looking toward the pitch beyond.

"There's no going back now," Destrian said beside me. A vast expanse of stars blanketed the sky, the only light in the land of darkness.

"Do you think we'll make it out alive?" I asked, turning to him.

"I don't know," Destrian admitted. "I asked as much to Arda, but her answer wasn't reassuring."

I raised my brows. "What did she say?"

Destrian leaned against his pack, studying the flickering stars in the sky. "She made it seem like it was up to you, or something."

My breath caught in my throat. Arda knew about Conal's request, and yet she didn't tell Destrian.

"Anyways, it didn't go how I expected," Destrian finished. "Her answers weren't exactly clear."

"What did you ask?" I probed, unable to help myself.

Destrian was silent. At first, I thought he didn't hear my question.

"I don't really want to talk about it. I didn't understand half of it," Destrian said finally.

I wondered what was going through Destrian's mind, but he provided no clues. He brushed the crumbs from his fingers and stood. "Come, we gain nothing in dallying."

I nodded and rose, heaving my pack to my shoulders.

Checking my map in the moonlight, I led the way through the mountain pass. Enormous boulders and rocky outcroppings shadowed the ground, making it difficult to see. I watched for errant pebbles and cracks that would turn an ankle when given a chance.

"Rowyn," Destrian said behind me. "Come, look at this." He was crouched several yards back, studying something lying off the path. A red orb hovered next to him, dimly lighting whatever had caught his attention.

I turned. Something weighty dropped onto me from above, and a terrifying snarl ripped through the air. I choked back a scream as I fought to stay upright. Claws tried ripping through my leathers, but the animal had landed on my pack, otherwise my back would've been slashed to ribbons. Jaws clamped onto my braids, and the beast yanked its head from side to side, nearly scalping me.

I unsheathed Iranoct, my heart pounding, and slammed backward into an enormous boulder. The animal yowled and fell before launching itself at me, catapulting me to the ground. Teeth flashed inches from my face as the roar turned into a yelp. The enormous cat had speared itself on Iranoct's blade. Rolling away, I rose quickly and stabbed the animal again, but it was already dead.

"By all the gods," Destrian said next to me, white knuckles clutching Phyranox as he stared at the body. "It's lucky you're fast."

I kneeled and wiped my sword on the animal's black fur. "It's a sable panther," I said, sheathing Iranoct.

Destrian whistled. "We had a guard killed by one a few years back. Took him right off the road."

I eyed the rocks around us. "Let's get out of here. Sable panthers live in mating pairs during the warm months. This one's female may be close."

Destrian looked over his shoulder and nodded. We continued hiking, warily studying the shadows around us. It was quite a while before either of us felt comfortable enough to camp. Destrian found an entrance to a small cave that widened dramatically farther in. Without wood nearby, he made a fire sustained by his magic.

While the soup bubbled away, I made sure to wind the time tracker hanging next to Araceli's charm and Pedr's chess piece. We'd been gone a day. One down, more than a month to go. Finishing that task, I began mending my tunic, which had ripped in the sable panther's attack.

Destrian noticed what I was doing, dug through his pack, and tossed me a pair of breeches. "Can you fix these also? I meant to get it done in Helena but forgot."

I glared at him, indignation bubbling to the surface. "You're not doing anything. Mend it yourself."

"I don't know how to sew," Destrian admitted, although I heard a hint of laughter in his voice. "It's not like it's required learning for men of my rank."

"You act like it would be silly for you to learn," I accused with a scowl.

Destrian threw up his hands. "Well, it *is* silly. When would such a skill prove useful? There's always someone around to do the mending."

"It's probably about as useful as weapons work has been for me," I said, throwing his breeches back to him. "I'm not your maid. If you want your things mended, I'll happily teach you, but I refuse to do it for you."

Destrian sighed. "I don't have a needle or thread."

I shot him a saccharine smile. "Lucky for you, I have extras of both. Come here, and I'll show you how it's done."

Destrian scooted next to me. I handed him my extra supplies and demonstrated how to thread the needle. Destrian attempted it, but the thread frayed at the end. I licked the end of the thread and took his large hand in mine.

Suddenly, I was entirely too conscious of his touch. My skin tingled, and heat rose to my cheeks. Instead of watching what I was doing, Destrian's eyes were on my face, darting over the features. Nervously, I guided his big hands to thread the needle and tie off the ends.

"There," I whispered, handing the needle to him with a tentative smile. I then showed him how to make even stitches. Destrian bit his lip while he concentrated on his work, his brows furrowed. Despite his protests, he was giving it an honest effort. Though Destrian's stitches were entirely too large, I figured he would learn in time.

"There, don't you feel better now that you did it yourself?" I asked.

"I suppose," Destrian mumbled. "I still don't see where this will be useful to me outside of here."

I leaned forward and ladled half the soup into my mug. "My father used to say your greatest resource will always be yourself. You give others power if you rely on them too much."

Destrian blew on his portion of the steaming meal. "I don't believe for one minute that your giant of a father sewed."

"He didn't embroider, but he could fix a ripped seam," I assured him. "If you hopped off your high horse and actually gave it any thought, you'd see how useful knowing 'women's work' is. It's not like your friends are here to judge."

Destrian grumbled to himself, probably admitting I was right.

Chapter 19

I T WAS ODD WAKING UP to darkness. I tried to rub the sleep from my bleary eyes and noticed Destrian was already up, pouring water into the pot and setting it over the fire. I yawned widely, stretching my arms and discarding the furs I used to make a nest for myself.

"Care for a game of dice?" Destrian asked. Reaching into a pouch hanging from his neck, he produced two dice carved from bone.

I blinked. "By all the gods, where did you learn to roll dice?" We played dice at home. It was a peasant game, but my clan and I were hardly nobility. Destrian, however, didn't seem the type to have learned, seeing as he thought not to sew.

Destrian grinned. "My grandfather taught me. We would play with the guards after dinner." Destrian handed me one of the dice.

"Wasn't your grandfather a fire sorcerer?" I asked, folding my legs beneath me. I rolled my die against Destrian, winning the higher number.

He nodded. "My grandfather, my great-grandfather, and great-great-grandfather all had the skill."

"It passed to every generation except your father?"

How could the skill, once so predictable, suddenly pass over Consul Colman entirely?

Destrian cleared his throat. "Yes, and it has always bothered him."

I rolled the die and grinned at the outcome. "Do you know why it skipped him?"

"No, though Father suspects it's because Grandfather was unfaithful to his wife."

I raised my brows. That's what happened to Fin. Her father, a general in the Lyrican army, had a dalliance with Fin's mother as he passed through Lark Harbor. His wife wasn't happy when she found out such an important trait was passed to someone outside the family.

"Do you believe that?" I asked, curious how Destrian would've gotten the skill if it passed outside of his grandmother.

Destrian shook his head. "There were no other fire sorcerers in Morgania or Lyrica around Father's age. But, I could see why he would think that. In many ways, my grandfather was not a nice man. He bullied Father when he realized he didn't have the trait, he was cruel to my grandmother, and he didn't pay any mind to my aunt nor sisters. The only one he cared about was me."

"It must've been hard for your father, growing up in your grandfather's shadow," I admitted, handing Destrian the die. Conleth Everett was a legend. The man had been a favorite of the old emperor, even fashioning the decorative sword the emperor used to knight those loyal to the realm. He was also a known womanizer. I'd never considered how that would affect his family.

"I envisioned being just like him someday," Destrian said. "It wasn't until I was older that I realized how Grandfather's behavior was so negative to everyone around him. I asked my father about it before I left for Solridge. He told me he'd vowed at an early age to become a different sort of man. Father didn't want to dismiss his daughters' affections, nor send his wife crying to her room every night."

I began to feel a begrudging respect for Consul Colman. I couldn't imagine growing up with a distant father. Deciding to make your own path took courage. Also, I had to admit he raised a good son.

We were silent for a while, each of us rolling our turn until the soup boiled. I pulled the pot from the fire and ladled half into my cup.

"Pedr said you aren't coming back to Solridge," I said, blowing the steam away. My voice trembled, and I couldn't look him in the eye. Would I ever see him again after the Nightlands?

"No, after mastery, I'm free to go my own way," Destrian said, his eyes on my face.

I wondered what he was thinking. Probably that he

was glad to be free of the place and finally return home. I knew Destrian missed Morgania in his absence, though he had plenty of friends to distract him. But my heart skipped a beat at the thought of him not being there anymore. For whatever reason, I never considered Solridge without Destrian. I hated the thought of it.

"What do you plan on doing with your time if you don't have school?" I asked, picking at a loose thread on my breeches.

"I've quite a bit of catching up to do when it comes to running Helena," Destrian replied. He watched me far too closely. "Father was going to show me some things before he left to visit my sisters."

I'd rarely heard Destrian speak of his siblings. "Where will he go?"

"Onora lives in Eslin. It's an easy distance, so he'll stay there for a bit before sailing to Caldeaon to visit Ilisa."

"Do they have children?"

Destrian nodded. "Onora has a little boy named Galvin, but Ilisa hasn't been blessed with children yet."

"Were you very close to them growing up?"

"Why all the questions?"

I shrugged. "I just wondered what it would be like to have siblings. I have a hard time imagining you as the baby brother to two girls."

"Well, they were terrors," Destrian said, chuckling at

the memory. "Sometimes they would dress me up in their frocks and have me take tea with them. Father put a stop to that the minute he found out, though."

"What of your mother?"

Destrian didn't speak for a moment. "My mother and twin died the day I was born," he said. "Ilisa is the only one who actually has memories of her."

"I'm sorry to hear that," I mumbled. Though my parents were gone, at least I had memories of love growing up. I couldn't imagine what Destrian felt. My heart tugged at the thought of him denied a mother's love.

"My sisters and I came to terms with it, though Father still struggles. Even after all these years."

By all the gods, I hated feeling sorry for the consul. "Why didn't he ever remarry? Second marriages seem common enough, especially among the nobility."

Destrian took a sip of soup and shook his head. "Father wasn't interested in traveling around and trying to court someone. So, my aunt Maureen helped raise us. She's at Eslin now helping Onora. Auntie always loved being around children. She's much happier there than she would've been at Helena now that we're all grown up."

"Your aunt sounds like a lovely woman," I said.

Destrian smiled. "Maybe you will meet her someday and find out for yourself." There was so much warmth behind his dark eyes. My heart raced, and I looked back down at my soup. I recognized what the fluttering in my stomach meant. The irresistible draw of his eyes to mine. It was starting to feel as though, with each passing word, Destrian was tempting me to love him.

But I couldn't let myself be tempted. I knew what it felt like to fall in love, but I also knew how it felt when it was ripped away. I didn't want to go through that heartbreak again, and heartbreak it was sure to be, given that he was a Lyrican.

We finished eating and began walking again. Gradually, the path narrowed to a ridge. The ledge was a mere four feet wide before dropping off. I knew what happened to foolhardy travelers who didn't take the dangers of mountain heights seriously. The entrance to Espiria was bordered by its steep drop-offs, with plenty of bodies littering the bottom.

"Should we turn back?" I asked, peering up the darkened path.

Destrian shook his head. "Let's keep going. Who knows how long it will take us to find an easier path?"

I swallowed the lump in my throat and relented. Destrian took it upon himself to go first, carefully picking his way over the path. I hugged the mountain as close as I was able, stepping over loose stones and cracks in the cliff. Destrian was getting farther ahead, looking back from time to time to make sure I was still behind him.

It was at one of those times the path started crumbling beneath his feet. I had a brief glimpse of his stricken face before he fell over the edge.

The world stopped in its tracks. Blood drained from my face and a high ringing filled my ears.

"Destrian!" I shouted, running to where he'd fallen. He clutched the edge of the ridge, his knuckles and face white as he strained to hold on.

I dropped to my knees and grabbed his pack, trying to heave him back onto the path. I wasn't strong enough. Even as I clung to him, one hand slipped, and Destrian fell an inch.

I threw myself onto my stomach and grabbed for Destrian's hand. Straining, Destrian pulled himself up the cliffside. I gripped his fingers so hard, they were sure to be crushed, but Destrian only grunted with the effort to pull himself onto the path. I helped as best I could, but Destrian, clever boy that he was, decided to use my pack to help him clamber up the ledge. I prayed my weight would leverage me enough not to go careening over the side while he dragged himself over. Finally, Destrian made it, and we scooted as far away from the edge as we were able.

I clutched Araceli's key, trying to calm my racing heart. Tears of relief sprang to my eyes, but I pushed them back. "By all the gods, be careful! You can't take the path for granted."

"I-I'm sorry," Destrian stuttered, trying to catch his breath. "I didn't realize it was so unstable until it was too late."

"You can't be so careless," I scolded, elbowing him in the ribs. "Stay closer next time. We shouldn't wander apart from each other here." I pushed my feet to rise, but Destrian held me back.

"I'm sorry," he said, putting his arm around my shoulder. "I didn't mean to scare you."

I tried to stop my hands from trembling. "I didn't mean to lose my temper, I just . . ." I took a deep breath. I didn't know how to go on, but Destrian was watching me intently, waiting. "I don't want anything to happen to you."

"Would you have missed me?" Destrian asked. Although I couldn't see his face well in the dim light, I heard the smile in his voice.

"What's this silly talk? If it's a jest, I don't find humor in it," I said, dismissing his lilting tone. Our journey was life or death. It wasn't the time nor place to be flirting with Destrian. Although Lady Vianne would have disagreed. My mother would've as well, come to think of it.

"Well," Destrian said, rising and holding his hand out to me. "I promise to be more careful, for your sake."

"That's all I ask," I snapped.

We hiked for several hours before finally stopping to

rest at the peak of a mountain. My fingers were near frozen with the cold, and our breath hung in the air. Though the soup was hot, it didn't keep me warm for long, and no matter how many skins I piled onto myself, I couldn't get warm. I didn't dare ask Destrian to make the fire bigger. We had to conserve magical energy in the same way we conserved everything else, so I cupped my fingers around my mouth and huffed. Rubbing my hands together, I prayed I would leave the Nightlands with all of my appendages.

"Are you cold?" Destrian asked from across his small fire.

"A little."

"Come here," Destrian said, waving me toward him.

I crawled over to where he sat. "What?" I whispered.

"Sit here, next to me. We can use each other's body heat."

"No!" I exclaimed, my cheeks growing hot despite the frigid air.

"Seriously, Rowyn, I read this in a book. To conserve energy and stay warm, we must utilize each other's body heat."

I paused, weighing my options. On the one hand, it made perfect sense. During the harsh winters at home, we would huddle together in the hall. On the other hand, I wasn't sure I wanted to be cuddled up with Destrian. What would the others say? What would Destrian think?

But the nagging voice of reason entered my mind. There was no one else present, so what did it matter? The bottom line was that I was freezing, and if I wanted to be able to sleep, I had to get warm. That thought decided me.

"Fine," I said, scooting closer.

Destrian raised his arm and I curled up beside him, resting my head on his chest. Destrian covered me with my pile of furs and draped his arm around me. He was surprisingly warm, warmer than he should have been. I wondered if he'd magicked himself to give off more heat. The scent from his sweat-soaked skins filled my nose while Destrian watched the night, listening.

"Are you awake?" Destrian whispered into my hair after a while.

"Mm-hm," I mumbled, returning to consciousness.

He shifted his arm. "Look."

I opened my eyes. A great swath of green light filled the sky. Thinner streaks of pink and purple hung like clouds, turning the canvas of stars into the most beautiful painting I'd ever seen.

"What is it?" I breathed.

"I've no idea," Destrian said. "Can you believe we're the only ones alive today who have seen this?"

It was as though the sky were dancing. Warmth poured through my veins as Destrian cradled me in his arms, resting his head on mine.

The light swam across the sky until it melted away as suddenly as it had come.

I was left with the feeling that I would cherish that moment for the rest of my life. Not because I'd glimpsed a sight that no other living soul had experienced. I would cherish it because, at that moment, I had someone to share that beauty with.

Chapter 20

FINALLY, WE STEPPED OFF the last mountain, and the Plains of Moranoct swelled before us. As we walked, we kicked up swirls of dust that choked and stung the eyes, making the trek almost unbearable. Thirst squeezed my throat, and my mouth felt like a muddy pit. We had lucked out finding some small water sources in the mountain range, but our supply was quickly dwindling.

Destrian tore off bits of one of his tunics during a rest break and tied it around his mouth. He did the same for me, and after gargling water, I found it helped some.

We walked for hours. I tried to distract myself by listening for creatures. I needn't have bothered. The cold and lack of resources made the plain uninhabitable. Though, on our third day on the plain, a faint rumbling noise grew behind us, something akin to hoofbeats.

"Do you hear that?" I asked. The stars were out in force, but the land was so dark that I couldn't distinguish anything on the horizon.

Destrian nodded, his eyes narrow as he looked over his shoulder.

The wind picked up, blowing dust around us, making

visibility even more limited.

"Over there," Destrian said into my ear, pointing west. "Do you see?"

I looked but saw nothing: no stars, no moon, nothing but an inky blackness.

"What is it?" I asked as the rumbling grew louder. Then I realized the blackness was streaming toward us. A burst of lightning tore through the wall, giving us a glimpse of raging clouds of . . . something.

"Run!" Destrian shouted, but I was already two steps ahead of him.

We were enveloped by a great cloud. The winds roared and swirled dust and debris into my eyes and ears. Thankfully, we had our rags in place, but I couldn't see where I was going. The map slipped from my hand. I tried to catch it, but the wind carried it away into the storm.

Dirt and grime flew into my mouth. I fell to my knees. Each ragged breath seemed to fill me with dust, smothering me. I'd lost Destrian in the cloud, so I stayed put, trying to cover my face from the gale and harsh sand.

A great weight crushed me. Gasping, I turned and felt Destrian over me, trying to cover me from the worst of the cloud. I clenched my eyes shut and breathed shallowly.

After what seemed like forever, the noise finally died down.

Ripping the rag from my mouth, I spat and coughed

up mud and dirt, gulping air desperately.

"Destrian?" I gasped. His weight was crushing me. I rolled him off. "Destrian," I repeated, shaking his shoulder.

Destrian wasn't moving. I wiped the dirt from my eyes and leaned over him. "Destrian!" I shouted, slapping him lightly on the cheek.

He still did not move. I began to shake as I desperately beat his chest. Conal's words flashed through my mind.

"Just make sure he doesn't return."

No, I couldn't consider abandoning him so early in the quest. We hadn't even reached the second mountain range yet. I hated myself for even thinking of it.

Destrian's rag had fallen loose and lay limp on the side of his face. A ring of dirt circled his mouth, making his face look even darker than it already was.

"Destrian!" I shouted again, turning him onto his stomach and beating him on the back, but my energy was failing.

He coughed, and my body flooded with the chilling relief. I let out a sigh as Destrian's eyes opened. I rolled him to his side so he could breathe easier. Uncorking my canteen, I gave him the last gulp of water. Destrian took it gratefully, swishing the mud out of his mouth before taking another drink.

I kneeled back, exhausted, but thankful Destrian was

alive.

"Thank you," he gasped, trying to see me through his dirt-crusted eyes. I ran my hand through his hair, shaking out debris as a cloud of dust fell.

"How are you feeling?"

"My breathing is troubled," Destrian wheezed.

I nodded, but nothing in the empty canteen could ease his aching throat. "We can't go farther without water," I said, already feeling the defeat set in. "I could make it rain."

"No, this whole place would be mud and ice if you made it rain," Destrian said huskily.

"What about snow? It would help with the dust and water, at least."

Destrian sat up, trying to brush off the dirt as he thought. "As long as you ensure it won't be too much, it might help."

"I can cut it off," I said with more confidence than I felt. It was possible that I was too tired, but I'd grow even weaker if I didn't have water.

Looking at the stars, I raised my hands. The night air was oddly still, given the loud storm from before. Finding the well of my power, it rushed through me and into the sky, clouds appearing out of nowhere to block the light from the stars.

A bolt of lightning shot to the ground leagues away,

and thunder grumbled over the plains. Thick, fat flakes of snow fell, dusting the barren landscape.

I let it go on for a bit, then attempted to cut it off.

It didn't work.

My eyes flew open. Desperately, I tried to stop the flow of magic, but if anything, it sped up. I fell to my knees. Ice sped through me and I began to fade.

"Rowyn," Destrian said, crawling over and grabbing my shoulder. "Rowyn, cut it off."

"I'm trying," I said. Something trickled down my lip. I brushed it with my fingers and looked at my hand. My nose was bleeding.

Destrian shook me. "Rowyn, it's too much. Cut it off!"

I concentrated on the magic billowing out of me. It wasn't like at Solridge or even home. It was like my power was being pulled from me. Snow piled up. The wind sent drifts of the white flakes over the plains in a glistening swirl.

I couldn't breathe. My stomach clenched, and sleepiness dragged at my eyelids. I'd never known such exhaustion. I fell. Destrian pulled the gloves from my hands and thrust my fingers into the fresh, white powder. The frigid ground shocked my senses and the power cut off.

It stopped snowing.

"It's over. I'm all right," I said, though I didn't move from my spot.

Destrian rolled onto his back, exhausted. "By all the gods, don't do that again. If you're too weak, it will pull from your life force."

"I know," I said, dredging up the last bit of energy I had to sit up. We propped ourselves against Destrian's pack, sitting side by side in the middle of nowhere.

"We're a miserable pair, aren't we," Destrian said, his eyes on the sky. "If something comes to finish me off, I'm of a mind to let it."

"I'm not much use, either," I said, gathering snow in my hands and washing my face. The frigid water strengthened me, and I shoveled more into my mouth.

"The map is back," Destrian said, pointing to my side. I looked down and, sure enough, the map was tucked into the pocket of my cloak.

"That's useful," I mumbled. I pulled the parchment out, studied it for a moment, then stuffed it right back where I found it.

The moon crested over the horizon. I pushed Conal's words to the back of my mind. I didn't think Imor would want me to traverse the Nightlands alone. But if I didn't want anything to happen to Destrian, why did I still consider Conal's demand?

Because Destrian was keeping something from me. Despite his kindness, despite the growing comfort I felt in his presence, the knowledge that he wasn't being entirely honest still nagged at me. I liked Destrian. I liked the person he was and the man he wanted to be. But I didn't trust him.

Destrian looked down on me. "What are you thinking of?"

"The book in the library," I admitted.

Destrian sighed. "Can't you just let it be?"

"No. I want to know what it said and why you insist on hiding it from me."

"Can you not trust me in this?"

"How can I ever trust you if you keep things from me?"

Destrian threw his hands in the air. "Stop it this instant. I don't want to hear any more about that damned book."

"Why won't you tell me?"

"Because it could get you killed," Destrian said, his cheeks reddening.

"How could knowing something get me killed?" I scoffed.

"You could easily die for something you know in Somme."

"I don't intend ever to visit the capital," I replied snarkily. Though, I did find his words worrisome. After all, the capital was exactly where I was headed if my uncle had his way.

"You may never intend to visit the capital, but you will find yourself there one way or another. I intend to tell you what I know in time, when it won't be a danger for you."

"I hate you," I said, staring at the face of Imor.

"No, you don't. You love my chivalrous company and winning personality." I could hear the smile in his voice. "You will never hate me."

I shook my head. "If you told me a year ago that I would be joking with Lord Destrian of Helena, I wouldn't have believed it. I couldn't stand you."

"The feeling was mutual. When I first met you, I despised you," Destrian admitted.

"It makes sense your father would've passed on his prejudice."

Destrian sighed. "I'd always heard Morganite women were free with their charms, and I thought you were flirting with Bernard."

"What?" I gasped, leaning forward to look him in the face. By all the gods, he was serious! "He's old enough to be my father, and I don't flirt!"

"I know," Destrian said, running his hand through his hair. A cloud of dirt fell, landing on the white snow below us. "But I've seen noble girls flirt with wealthy men three times their age. I honestly didn't know what to make of you. It took me off guard when you spoke so openly."

I waved my hand away to show how little I cared for

the intricacies of societal customs, which set Destrian to laughing anew.

"What am I saying? Rowyn of Espiria will act any way she damn well pleases."

I smiled. "You'd best remember it."

Destrian's fingers brushed mine. "Your hands are ice-cold," he said. Taking my palm in his, he rubbed it. "Here," he murmured, interlacing our fingers. I thought to pull away, but I was comforted by the heat. There was nothing wrong with holding hands, after all. It didn't have to mean anything.

"Ayastaren," Destrian said suddenly.

"What?"

"That's when my feelings for you changed. It was in Ayastaren."

"Why Ayastaren? What happened there was horrible." My stomach sank as I thought of the woman's fated family, killed to teach me a lesson. I didn't think I'd ever forget such a tragic mistake.

"Aye, it was terrible, but I admired how hard you tried to do some good, no matter how harshly it backfired," Destrian said.

I shook my head. I didn't want to think of Ayastaren. Every bad thing that happened to me since leaving home was connected in some way to Ayastaren. I could only hope that, upon my return, I would be powerful enough to avoid Duke Roland's retaliation. "Let's get some rest and not speak of it anymore."

Destrian lifted his arm and draped it over my shoulder, drawing me in. We covered ourselves in a pile of furs, and before long, I could hear the deep, even breathing that meant Destrian had fallen asleep, his head propped on top of mine.

I kept watch over the dark horizon thinking of Arda's speech and Conal's demand. Could I let Destrian perish in the Nightlands? I hoped to the gods I wouldn't have a choice in the matter. Knowing the gods, they wouldn't make it easy for me. Better to take things day by day than to dwell on what might be, or could've been, had I chosen differently.

Chapter 21

"YOU NEVER TOLD ME about your visit to Espiria," Destrian said, wading through slush. It had been two weeks since we'd crossed the bridge, according to Fin's timepiece. Puddles riddled our path as the snow melted around us. An acrid smell permeated the air, and I was again thankful for the masks Destrian had fashioned. According to the map, we were approaching vents that rose from the ground and belched out hot air.

"It was all right," I replied, hoping he would drop it.

"What happened?"

"Nothing, it just wasn't the homecoming I'd hoped for." From Conal's demand to Baylin's betrayal, I was beginning to regret the visit altogether. All hope lay in the quest for my gem. Baylin wouldn't dare sell me once he saw how strong I could be. I just had to show I was an asset to the clan. If I achieved control, they were sure to welcome me back. Or at least, that's what I hoped.

"Was your cousin there?" Destrian asked. In a visit to Seaport months before, Ferris attacked Destrian in a misguided attempt at protecting my honor. I wished he'd known to stay away, rather than call attention to himself.

I nodded. "He's doing well. How was your visit?"

"I made sure Bernard got Ena home safely, then Father and I went hunting. Several of my friends in the guard went with us," Destrian said, yanking his foot from the mud.

I didn't know what to say next. We both knew how the visit ended.

"I'm sorry for Father," Destrian added, meeting my eyes.

I shrugged. "It's not your fault."

Destrian hesitated. "When my mother and brother died, Father was away, dealing with a Morganite uprising."

I stopped and stared. "That's why he hates Morganites so much."

"He didn't even get to say goodbye. Aunt Maureen said that Mother was fine when Father left, but all of a sudden, we decided to come early." Destrian shifted, his eyes on his feet. "They died right after I was born."

I watched Destrian grapple with his story. In truth, I wasn't sure how it made me feel. "I'm sorry," I said, knowing those weren't the right words.

Destrian met my eyes. "I'm not telling you this to excuse his behavior. I just want you to understand him better. Sure, Morgania is the richest land in the empire. We're blessed as a noble family, but that doesn't mean Father's life has been easy, nor particularly happy. His melancholy has gotten even worse since my sisters and I left home. He never used to drink that much when we were growing up."

"I had no idea," I murmured. I couldn't help but feel conflicted. At least with the family I'd lost, I'd gotten to say goodbye. Did that excuse the consul's actions when it came to throwing bodies of plague victims in the river? No, of course not. Was he still the reason most of my own family was dead? Yes, he absolutely was. But Destrian was right. I was understanding the consul better.

A blink of light to my right caught my attention. Up ahead were hundreds of tiny flashes floating through the air.

Destrian squinted to get a better look. "Insects," he said after a moment.

He was right. Large rock towers loomed in the distance, emitting steam into the cold night air. Long tendrils of light spiraled down from the top and sprawled on the ground around them.

Destrian strode forward. I grabbed his hand and shook my head. "Who knows what could be hiding near there? Let's watch first."

Destrian nodded. I let go of his hand, but he wrapped his fingers around mine and we stepped forward together. Though I sensed movement from the glowing tendrils, everything was still and quiet.

"It's probably nothing," Destrian said. "Although the

light may be useful to help us see."

"During the summer, we struggled with flies in the family quarters. The little boys made a game of lighting candles on the sills to lure them out."

"You think the lights are alive?" Destrian asked.

I pulled my hand from his and dropped my pack to the ground. "Master Haris said that some of the animals glow."

Destrian shook his head but relented to making camp.

In short order, we had our pot of water bubbling away over a small fire. I peeled off my boots and examined my feet. Large blisters had formed on the back of my heels and toes. Lightly pressing my finger into one, I hissed from the sharp burst of pain.

"I have a few too," Destrian said, eying what I was doing. "If you want to watch the vents for a bit, we should probably treat our feet."

I studied the rock towers while Destrian worked, my eyes glued to the glowing tendrils. Out of the corner of my eye, something moved off in the distance. It was low to the ground and slithered like a snake would. Long feelers protruded from its head, probing the ground as it passed. The animal skirted around puddles, opting instead for the higher ground until it reached the rock tower closest to us.

"Destrian," I whispered, pointing to the vent. As the creature crept nearer, the tendril seemed to glow brighter, a vivid, luminous light that captivated the animal. It slith-ered closer and closer until it was directly next to the vine. One feeler tentatively reached out to inspect the glow and I held my breath.

As soon as the feeler touched the glowing vine, the tendril whipped up and curled around the creature. Hun-dreds of the animal's tiny legs flailed as it was towed to the base of the tower where the glow seemed to be concen-trated.

I glanced sideways at Destrian who was staring, wide-eyed, as a dark yawning mouth appeared. The creature still struggled wildly, but there was no going back. The tendril forced the creature into the mouth, which ate the animal painstakingly slow. It seemed to struggle forever, until fi-nally, it ceased, hanging limply from the gaping mouth.

I turned away, not feeling quite so hungry anymore. "I don't know what I should fear more, the tendrils at the vents or whatever that creature was that just got eaten."

Destrian's face had drained of color, or what I could see of it in our firelight. "Well, let's hope we can avoid them if we stay away from the vents." He handed me a mug of soup. "Let me see your foot."

I stretched my leg out, and Destrian guided my foot into his lap. Looking over the sores, he dipped his fingers into the mug filled with herbs and gently dabbed the paste onto my sores. "Hopefully this speeds the healing," he said. His fingers rubbed along the arch of my foot, kneading the muscle. It tickled, and I had to stifle a nervous giggle. Destrian looked up and met my eyes, a mischievous smile on his face.

"Don't you dare," I ordered, pulling my foot from his grip.

"I promise I won't do anything," Destrian said with a long-suffering sigh. He pulled a tunic from his pack, drew a dagger, and sliced a piece of linen off. I put my foot back in his lap and he tied the linen into place.

I held out my opposite foot and blew on the soup, my eyes back on the rock towers. The lighted bugs continued to flicker off and on, making the place seem fairy tale-like. Still, danger undoubtedly lurked around the corner, waiting for us.

After our respite, we continued, giving the rock towers a wide berth.

"Rowyn, stop," Destrian said, not long after we started walking again. "Listen." He eyed the hazy darkness around us.

I froze and tuned my ears to the breeze. The wind whistled as it passed between two rock towers that stood close together. A faint skittering to my right turned out to be a large bug that disappeared into a crevice in one of the towers.

Finally, I heard what caught his attention. A faint

chittering sound broke through the air before fading into the distance. I squinted, studying the landscape, but found nothing out of the ordinary. We heard it again. It was distant, but there. I grabbed my bow and nocked an arrow, just in case.

After hearing the chittering again, I had the sense to look up. A huge black silhouette was hurtling toward us. I shoved Destrian to the ground and felt the breeze from the creature as it swooped.

"Look to the sky!" I cried, scrambling to my feet as the great silhouette circled overhead. The hair on the back of my neck stood straight, and my pounding heart wanted to burst from my chest. Praying for courage, I lifted my bow and aimed, loosing a shot.

"It's out of range!" Destrian yelled as the arrow fell uselessly to the ground. "Find cover!"

The flying creature was getting ready to swoop again. Destrian and I bolted, my pack bumping behind me as I dodged rocks and boulders. The silhouette appeared again, right in front of us. I loosed another arrow. The beast shrieked as the arrow tore through a wing. The animal flailed for a moment before colliding with the ground several paces away.

Destrian and I glanced at each other before taking a step closer. The animal chittered angrily while it flapped and struggled. Destrian unsheathed his sword and walked cautiously toward the creature while I flanked him, my bow at the ready.

The creature's face was wrinkled and ugly. It had large, onyx eyes that glared at us over bared, dagger-like teeth. Perched atop the head were gigantic ears that turned in all directions. Out of all the creatures I'd studied from Master Haris's books, I feared these the most.

"It's a bat," Destrian said, stepping closer. His sword gleamed as it sliced down, beheading the monster. The bat twitched for a moment before the wings stilled and stiffened. Destrian kicked the head and sent it rolling away.

"Don't do that," I scolded.

My ears rang again.

"Rowyn, your bow," Destrian murmured as his eyes fixed on a blot fluttering through the sky. I rose and aimed. Destrian shouldered his pack and stood next to me, his sword at the ready in case I missed.

The bat dove. I held my breath and shot, missing the bat by a hair. I tried a second shot, and a third, but the bat dodged each one.

"Duck!" Destrian yelled. I threw myself to the ground as a mass of leathery wings flapped over me.

"Rowyn!" Destrian shouted. "Rowyn, get back!"

I rolled away then rose to my feet, unsheathing my sword as I went. Destrian and the bat were being dragged across the dirt, borne by a glowing tendril. We hadn't even noticed we were by a vent.

Another vine wrapped around Destrian's foot as he kicked and flailed. With my sword in hand, I darted over and severed the vine in two. A vile goo coated my sword arm and Destrian's leg as he attempted to kick himself free.

I tried to raise my arm, but the liquid from the vine was the stickiest substance I'd ever encountered. My hand was glued to my side. I frantically pulled, but it was no use. I was stuck.

"Destrian!" I shouted as another tendril wrapped around my middle.

An explosion, followed by a blast of hot air, sent me careening into the mud. Realizing the vine had let me go, I scrambled to my feet and ran away from the vent. Turning, I found Destrian untangling himself from the smoking carcasses of the bat and vine.

Snow fell heavily. When the soft, white flakes reached the rock towers, they turned into drops of rain. The water cut through the goo's stickiness, and I was able to wrest my arm free.

"Look," Destrian said, pointing to another vent. The tendrils' glow seemed to have dulled, and they looked to be curling back toward the opening of the rock tower. "They must not like the snow."

I studied the rock tower. "The vents give off heat. I

bet it's the cold they don't like."

"I wonder where these roost," Destrian said, poking the bat with his sword. Its crumpled body was the size of Destrian and me combined, not to mention its wings. "They have to live in caves nearby. The Dires are probably closer than we thought."

"By all the gods!" I said, sheathing my sword. "How are we to climb with those monsters after us?"

"Honestly, they may not be much trouble in the mountains. It would be difficult to grab us on uneven terrain. Their wings are so big that they'll need open space to hunt. That's probably why they're out on the plains instead."

"I suppose that makes sense," I admitted, eying the dead bat. I couldn't believe what I was about to say. There's nothing like an adventure in the wilderness to make one desperate. "Should we *eat* it?"

"The choices seem to be pretty slim," Destrian said, though he didn't seem enthusiastic about the idea either.

I walked toward the creature and pulled out my dagger. Kneeling, I cut away pieces of thin, stringy muscle while Destrian created his fire. It wasn't enjoyable, but it would have to do.

Chapter 22

FTER FOUR DAYS OF WALKING, we finally made it to the base of The Dires. The warmth of the vents was long gone, replaced by a bitter wind and freezing temperatures that made breathing difficult. The only way we survived the cold was by constantly moving and sharing each other's warmth during rest breaks.

As we approached the bottom of the first mountain, we came across what had once been a river valley with odd, ghostly shapes jutting up from the ground. At first, I figured it was a herd of animals but disregarded that thought when none of them moved. As we drew closer, the spikes took on more familiar outlines.

"Skeletons," Destrian said, his red orb glowing brighter as he stepped into the rib cage of an impossibly large animal. The skull had giant horns, bigger than Destrian or me, protruding from it.

I kneeled and studied the bones scattered over the dry riverbed. "They don't seem to be the same animal," I said, studying a skeleton that looked eerily human. "What do you make of it?"

Destrian came up next to me. "Maybe they died from thirst."

I clutched the good luck key and shook my head, glad that Fin wasn't in the Nightlands with me. The sight of so much death would have pained her.

"What do you—"

"Shh," Destrian whispered suddenly, his body still. He'd grabbed his dagger and held it out, facing the darkness. I pulled my bow from my shoulder and nocked an arrow. Rising from the skeleton, I aimed at the shadows but only saw ghostly white bones. The hair on the back of my arms and neck rose, and my eyes strained to see.

Still as statues, we watched and waited for what seemed like an eternity. But whatever it was refused to show its face.

Finally, I turned to Destrian. "What did you hear?"

"A whisper," Destrian said, his brows knitted together.

"Could it be the wind?"

"Do you feel any wind?" Destrian asked levelly.

I didn't, but what else could it have been?

"Let's keep moving," I whispered. Whatever it was would reveal itself when it was ready, probably while we were sleeping. But as we walked, I kept having a nagging feeling in the back of my mind. The sense that we were being watched.

Destrian and I found a large ledge to camp under, but I couldn't shake the sense of foreboding that seemed to lurk in the shadows. We stayed awake for a long while, just watching the darkness without speaking. Finally, I fell asleep, my head nestled into the familiar warmth and smell of Destrian's chest.

A gentle nudge from Destrian woke me up.

"Ready for your turn?" I asked groggily, sitting up.

"No, I'm ready to get out of here. I keep getting these chills up my back," Destrian whispered.

"All right, let me just get my things," I said, crouching underneath the stone roof. Destrian had the fire so low that I couldn't see even a foot in front of my face. I hit my head on the rock overhang and fell back into the dirt as pain seared over my eyes. Cursing, I felt a cut on my forehead. It was bleeding.

"Are you all right?" Destrian asked. He held my chin in his fingers and tipped my head down so he could see the wound.

"Some light would be nice," I snapped grumpily.

Destrian wasted no time in building up the fireball. I checked my hand, and surely, it was blood. I reached down to my tunic and ripped a strip from the bottom to cover my wound.

"Rowyn."

I was in a bad mood, and Destrian was getting on my nerves. I chose to ignore him.

"*Rowyn*," Destrian hissed again.

"What?" I said, maybe a little too loudly.

Destrian pointed to the ground. "Look."

The fireball grew brighter, and I leaned closer. In the dry dirt, all around us, as far as I could see, were hundreds of footprints. Destrian's face was ashen. It looked as though, whatever it was, had crouched over us while I'd slept.

I burst into tears. "Please, Destrian, tell me the truth," I choked out between sobs. "Did you fall asleep?"

Destrian took a second to answer, but when he looked at me, the pain in his expression was sincere. "Not a moment, Rowyn. They got this close to us, with me awake."

More crying from my end. I'd officially lost it. It didn't help that blood was dripping down my face, and a vicious pain throbbed from my head.

"Can you tell what it is?" I asked as Destrian crouched to study the prints.

My heart plummeted from my chest to somewhere in my gut when Destrian met my eyes. "They look human, Rowyn."

I nodded and sniffed back the remaining few tears.

"Maybe they could've been there already," I said, my hands trembling uncontrollably as I shoved my pack to our camp entrance. "Before we got here."

Destrian shook his head. "I've been looking for our prints but they aren't here. They must have gotten covered up by whatever . . . whoever *it* was."

Destrian led the way from below the ledge and back onto the mountain path. I checked that my weapons were within arm's reach before I shouldered my pack.

Destrian and I didn't speak. Instead, we watched our surroundings, listening for noise. As we walked, I kept thinking I saw flashes of movement out of the corner of my eyes. When I turned my head to find what it was, there was nothing there.

That went on for leagues as we trudged up the mountains, through the unending darkness. Destrian stooped and eyed the ground every hour or so to mark the footprints that seemed to follow us on our journey. Whatever it was seemed content to stay in the shadows and simply watch.

"What do you think they want?" I whispered when we took a break. The ever-present footprints were scattered around us as we warmed ourselves from the ball of fire Destrian had called.

Destrian shrugged. "Let's ask them." Raising his voice, he shouted, "What do you want?"

We held our breath as the stillness of the night filled the air.

Bodiless whispers rose around us. *"The daughter of Morius."*

Destrian and I looked at each other with wide eyes. It

was impossible to know what was going through Destrian's head, but it was obvious he was just as fearful as I was.

"Who are you?" I asked.

A long silence followed. A cold sweat broke out over my back and arms. Destrian glanced at me, grabbed my hand, and held it tightly.

The shadow of a figure stepped into the firelight.

"Destrian!" I gasped with shrillness, pointing my finger toward whatever creature it was. It melted back into the darkness. I saw no being, nothing to put my hand out and touch, only the shadow it cast on the ground. "Did you see it?"

Destrian nodded slowly, his eyes going back to the darkness looming around us. His grip on my hand tightened.

Another shadow stepped into the light, and another, and another, all of them leaving footprints in their wake. Tears sprang to my eyes as the shadows danced around the fire. The dark hands crept over the ground to where we sat. Disembodied laughter was carried by the breeze. They were toying with us.

Destrian's mouth was drawn into a tense line. Our shallow breaths formed curls of mist in front of us. Through one of the clouds, a face appeared, leaning toward us with a smile.

Destrian grabbed me, pinning me underneath him as a blast of fire exploded around us. The heat singed my leathers, but the blaze wasn't long enough for our things to catch. After a moment, Destrian lifted his head and looked into the darkness. The laughter had gone.

"Sorry, I just wanted them to stop," Destrian said, looking down on me. "Are you all right?"

"Yes, I think so. I'd be much better if you'd get off me, though," I grunted.

Destrian rolled off and sat up again. Another ball of fire had replaced the one he had blasted, though it was much dimmer than before.

"How do you still have hair?" I asked, furiously patting my own to make sure it wasn't singed. If I had one vanity, it was my hair.

"I don't burn, not with my fire. It's handy at times."

I studied the darkness but saw nothing. "Do you think they've gone?"

"For now. I don't think the blast hurt them. It might have scared them off, but I don't think they can be hurt. At least not in the same ways we can."

"Do you think they'll be back?"

"I don't know. I hope not," Destrian said, rising off the ground and holding out his hand to me. "Come, the sooner we get your gem, the sooner we can get out of this cursed place."

Destrian and I traveled for hours and hours trying to listen for any hint of our silent stalkers, but they continued to elude us. When we were near exhaustion, we made camp in a cave that fed deep into the mountain. We set up on a ledge that overlooked an enormous cavern. Towers of stone rose from the ground, while sharp rock formations hung from the ceiling, giving the cavern an eerie look. It was pitch dark except for the small orb Destrian had conjured to light our way. But it was warm, which I was thankful for. At least I could take a break from some of my furs.

"What do you think?" Destrian asked, turning to me.

"It's fine," I said as I pulled off my pack and tossed it down on the ledge. Destrian discarded his bag as well. I pulled out our foodstuffs. The last of the bat meat was wrapped with the soup mix, so I heated them in our pot over the fire Destrian had burning.

Destrian explored the cavern with the hope there might be water. I followed him, using the sound of loose stones crunching and rolling while he stepped throughout the cave. Finally, he returned and plopped down next to me.

I passed him his bowl of food. Destrian took one bite then wrinkled his face in distaste. "For all your gifts, Rowyn, cooking is not one of them."

I stuck my tongue out at him. "What would you know?

It might be the rotten bat meat."

"No," Destrian said with his mischievous smile. "Every time you cook, it tastes awful. I don't know how you do it. It takes some effort to be that bad."

"Fine, you can cook from now on," I muttered sullenly, crossing my arms and watching the fire. Destrian was right; I was a horrible cook. I hadn't even eaten my fair share of the soup because I could barely choke it down.

When Destrian was finished, he rinsed out the bowl then settled back onto his pack. "Hand me your whetstone. I want to make sure our blades are sharp."

Destrian refilled the pot with a bit of water while I dug out my stone and tossed it to him.

He pulled out Phyranox and inspected it in the dim light. I leaned against my pack, watching quietly as he worked. Destrian drew his blade back and forth over the stone, testing the sharpness as he labored, drawn into his task.

"Destrian?" I asked after a moment. "How could I be a daughter of Morius?"

Destrian glanced at me before he spoke. "Morius was killed in Adair, but his children and wife escaped. It would make sense if they took refuge in Espiria. Even in the olden times, it was used for sanctuary."

I continued to ponder. It most likely fell on my father's

side. His family lived in Espiria for hundreds of years. That meant I'd gotten my powers out of sheer luck. Morius's abilities could've just as easily gone to Pria or Ferris. Even Baylin could've been cursed with the gift. Perhaps when I returned home, I would tell him that. Maybe then he wouldn't be so quick to sell me to the empire.

Then I remembered. The dream I had in Helena. The boy playing with the wind. The man bearing the same armband that I had. His dark eyes swam into my vision as if he looked into my soul. Was that Morius? Where was he going when he left the poor girl? Where did that dream come from?

"I've been thinking," Destrian said, pausing his sharpening. "About my father, and the guards at Helena, and . . . well . . . everything." Destrian met my eyes.

I folded my hands in my lap, waiting for him to go on. A range of emotions passed over his face, first embarrassment, then excitement, then, oddest of all, longing.

"You told me before how Morganites viewed Helena, and I didn't believe you. But I believe you now, and I don't want to rule Helena like my father has. I want a Morgania that has a place for everyone. I just don't know how to end the bloodshed. How can our people find peace together?"

I narrowed my eyes. "You could give us back our land and return to the eastern shore where you belong," I said in a mocking tone.

But Destrian didn't find humor in it. "Forget it," he said, going back to his sharpening.

"No, wait," I murmured, ashamed I'd been so hurtful. Destrian was genuinely asking for my help. It didn't bode well that my first reaction was to mock him.

"We're still part of the empire, you know," Destrian said. "It's not within my power to do that, and honestly, if it were, I don't think I would. Idris was right, not everything that comes from the empire is bad."

"I'm sorry, I didn't mean that," I said. We'd been fighting for so long to regain our land that I never considered an alternate possibility. Could we unite as one? "Listen, I don't know off the top of my head, but I'll think about it. There has to be a way for most of us Morganites to live under your banner and still feel free like everyone else."

Destrian nodded and set his blade aside. "Our travels have opened my eyes. You're right. There are problems with how Morganites are treated, but I don't know how to fix it."

I nodded. "Like I said, let me think on it."

"I can do your weapons while you rest," Destrian said with a smile. I pulled the blades from my belt and handed them to him, hilt first.

It was easy to find rest with such a rhythmic sound

echoing from the cavern walls. The steady scrape lulled me
to sleep. My mind drifted away, imagining the possibilities
of a Morgania built for all.

Chapter 23

"*HE'S AWAKE*," a voice whispered.

I sat up. "Did you say something?"

Destrian stopped sharpening. "No," he said, his eyes searching for shadows.

"*He smells you*," the voice hissed. I turned sharply as a shadow melted into the darkness behind a nearby stalagmite.

"Did you hear that?" I asked Destrian.

"No, what do you hear?"

"The shadows are back. They're whispering to me."

The shadow peeked from behind the stalagmite. The dark figure crept over the cavern wall and reached toward me.

"Rowyn," Destrian cautioned, the color draining from his face. I held up my hand and listened, straining my ears as the shadow whispered once more.

"What does it say?" Destrian asked softly, his eyes wide.

"It says he comes."

"Who? Who is coming?"

"I don't know," I said, standing swiftly and gathering my pack while Destrian did the same, calling up the light to drift between us. I grabbed my weapons and thrust them into my belt before drawing the bow. The shadow was back, hissing so loudly even Destrian could hear.

"*Run!*"

"Go!" Destrian said, shoving me ahead of him. We bolted as fast as we could toward the entrance of the cavern. The hovering ball of fire grew brighter and glinted off something hanging above the cavern entrance.

"Wait!" I screamed. Grabbing Destrian's pack, I wrenched him back as a colossal head slammed into the spot where he'd stood only a moment before.

My eyes traveled with the diamond-shaped head as it rose back up. The long body was wrapped around an enormous stalactite. The beast flicked a forked tongue into the air and hissed, baring fangs the size of a grown man, dripping amber drops of venom.

"It's a snake!" I yelled, loosing an arrow that soared wide from my shaky hands. My heart pounded in my ears as the sheer size of the creature overwhelmed me. I'd never seen an animal that big in my life. I'd wondered if the bats were the masters in the Nightlands, but it seemed I was wrong. The snake could've eaten twelve bats with Destrian and me for breakfast.

"By all the gods," Destrian gasped. He made a throwing motion, and the fireball that lit our way went crashing into the snake's nose in a shower of sparks.

The snake recoiled with a hiss but wasn't dazed for

long. Its muscles coiled, and its eyes followed us as we retreated to the ledge. There was no way we'd be able to make it to the tunnel.

I loosed another arrow that glanced off the snake's scales. The third one bounced away as well. Then, the snake struck with lightning speed.

I stumbled, not sure whether I should jump off the ledge or move back.

Destrian hurled another fireball. The blast blinded the snake, and it crashed headlong into the cavern wall. The floor shook with the impact, and my trembling legs struggled to keep me upright. I staggered forward, trying to get out of reach of the snake's fangs.

"Rowyn, go! Run!" Destrian cried.

I glared at him. "I'm not leaving you!" I shouted back, drawing Iranoct.

The snake uncoiled itself from the stalactite and began slithering down the cavern wall toward Destrian. I stood near the entrance and had to resist the urge to dart through the tunnel to safety, even though that was exactly what Destrian had told me to do.

Destrian was backed against the wall, his sword raised. The snake's head swayed from side to side as it eyed him. A hiss and flick of the tongue were met with bitter steel as Destrian severed the forked appendage. Blood sprayed over Destrian, and the snake's writhing knocked me off my feet. The tongue fell with a sickening flop before it wriggled off the ledge and out of view.

The snake was infuriated. Instead of fleeing, it snapped at Destrian with renewed vigor. I rose and charged the beast with a yell, slashing at its scales with Iranoct.

The ledge trembled and shook. My sword slid under a scale and pierced the snake's flesh. As I drew my weapon out and darted backward, the colossal snake slid off the ledge and down to the cavern floor.

"Let's get out of here!" Destrian shouted, bolting toward me.

Breathing thanks to Imor, I grabbed my pack, and I ran as fast as my legs would carry me to the entrance. The stone floor rattled and quaked as we drew closer to our escape tunnel. The rumble grew deafening and the ground shook violently, but we were nearly there. I'd just lifted my foot to the entrance when the ledge crumbled. I screamed as the floor fell away. Down I went with the rocks, tumbling to the cavern below.

Thankfully, I landed on something soft. I lay there for a moment, checking my faculties and trying to catch my breath. Was I bleeding? No. Did I have my sword? Yes. Thankfully, I'd clutched it during the fall. But, where was Destrian? The cavern was pitch black, which meant he was either unconscious or dead.

I sat up, and the ground began to bend and slide

underneath me. I'd landed on the damn snake.

I scrambled to my knees and relentlessly stabbed below me with Iranoct.

The snake turned sharply, and I was flung off. I hit a wall and landed with a crunch. Dazed, I scrabbled back. In my flight, I'd lost my grip on my sword. I tore off my pack and blindly patted the ground with one hand while grasping the dagger at my waist with the other.

Suddenly, light blazed throughout the cavern. "Rowyn!" Destrian shouted, seemingly from far away. "Rowyn, where are you?"

The snake was snapping at Destrian, coming within inches of his head as Destrian darted from side to side, swinging his sword to hold the snake back.

Destrian gathered a weak fireball and sent it soaring through the air to erupt on the snake's eye.

"I'm here!" I shouted back, finding Iranoct in the light. Grabbing the hilt, I sprinted along the side of the beast. Seeing the creature on the cavern floor made me appreciate exactly how big it really was. The snake's body filled the space, its girth the size of a large cow.

The snake reared up, and I slid toward its underbelly. Hoping to Imor it would prove softer than the scales on top, I drove my blade into the snake's flesh. The creature hissed and writhed, knocking me back, but still showed no sign of slowing.

Destrian let loose another fireball, but it puttered out in the air, not even making contact with the snake before it burst into sparks. He was depleted but for a dim light that lit the cavern. If Destrian's light failed, it would all be over.

"Use your powers!" Destrian shouted as he was backed into a corner.

"I don't think they'll work here!" I shouted back, but it was becoming clear that it was my only option.

The creature's muscles coiled as it readied for a strike. Destrian held Phyranox up, his eyes on the snake. "Do it!"

Without another thought, I threw my power above. A bolt of lightning struck the interior of the cavern and seemed to bounce over the stalactites above. A blast of thunder echoed over the walls and the entire cavern shook.

I leaped onto the snake's back, screaming my frustration as another bolt of lightning blasted through the chamber. A stalactite fell beside me, its sharp point shattering as it hit the floor.

The snake's back was covered with broken scales exposing the weaker flesh underneath. The snake turned its attention to me and flicked what was left of its ruined tongue. The head rose, ready to strike.

A flood of energy streamed through Iranoct, gluing my hands to the hilt, and shooting out the tip of the sword in arcs of light. My hair rose, the ends sparking and crackling with the flood of energy. I slammed Iranoct's blade deep into the snake's belly. The power surged through my sword and into the snake itself. Its body convulsed, the tail shooting straight and rigid, while the arcing light danced over the snake's scales till it reached the head, flashing glimpses of the skeleton within.

Stalactites rained down onto the chamber floor, toppling all around me. I pulled Iranoct out of the snake. The cavern was collapsing.

Chapter 24

I WALKED IN A MEADOW. I recognized the man from my dream in Helena, but he was much older. My eyes caught a dark glimmer on the back of his hands as he stood, his arms outstretched. The sky darkened, and rain poured from the heavens, drenching the man as he bowed his head.

A rider approached in the distance. His face was set in grim lines, and he drew his sword. I shouted a warning, but the man didn't hear. The rider was coming closer, the sound of hoofbeats filling the air as I screamed for the man's attention. He didn't turn. He didn't speak. Not even when the rider cut him down.

The man fell, his robes darkening with blood. He breathed his last as the rain petered off.

AM I DEAD? I THOUGHT AS I was thrust back into consciousness. Pain made itself known throughout my body. *No, death wouldn't hurt this much,* I thought as I whimpered. It felt like fire coursing through me, and I wished for death with every fiber of my being, making me cry out in agony.

Opening my eyes, I saw nothing but darkness. My arm was the source of the fire. I felt my sleeve. It was wet with something, presumably blood. But I had one saving grace. Iranoct was still firmly clutched in my hand.

Destrian. I had to find Destrian. I sat up, but pain shot through me, and I cried out anew. I transferred Iranoct to my good hand and tried to rise to my feet. My fingers brushed against rock and scales. I froze, refusing to breathe, wondering if the snake was still alive. After a moment, when all was still, I let out the breath and relaxed. At least the snake was dead.

"Destrian?" I whispered to the darkness. "Destrian? Are you there?"

Nothing. Nothing but an abyss of silence.

I staggered to my feet. How was I going to find Destrian in a blackened tomb?

Then I remembered.

Iranoct.

I held my blade up and thought of Phyranox. I remembered its golden sheen and the flaming star on its pommel. Iranoct turned down sharply and pulled me forward. I stumbled into something, probably a large rock. I climbed over it shakily and continued, skirting around rocks and tripping over debris from the cave-in. Iranoct still pulled me along until I tripped over something soft.

"Destrian?" I hissed, patting the ground around me until I felt it once more. It was only one of our packs. I fumbled with the straps and pulled the bag over my shoulders.

I concentrated on Iranoct once more, and it pulled me forward. The trek felt perilous. I prayed there wasn't a drop-off every time I slid over a large stone. My pack was a hindrance, but I persevered until I hit a rock wall.

"Destrian?" I asked the darkness. But I received no answer. I concentrated on Iranoct again. It directed me straight into the rock wall, which meant only one thing. Destrian was on the other side.

I unshouldered the pack and put it to the side. I sheathed Iranoct, took a deep breath, then felt around with my hands and found a grip. Straining through the pain in my bad arm, I began to climb. I checked each foothold thoroughly before transferring my weight. I'd climbed for a good ten minutes when the rocks beneath me shifted and I tumbled back down with a host of stones and dust.

I sat at the bottom of the wall, coughing and spitting out dirt. Feeling around again, I found the pack and sat with my back to it, tears coursing down my cheeks.

Had fate intervened? Was Destrian lost, just as Conal had wanted? No, it couldn't be. I couldn't go on without Destrian. I didn't care anymore that he kept something from me. I didn't care that Arda cautioned me to beware. Destrian didn't deserve to die.

"*He lives*," a voice whispered into my ear.

I jumped, my hand shooting to my hilt. Then, I remembered. The shadows had warned us.

"Are you sure?" I asked, rising.

"*Trapped*," the voice said.

That was all the encouragement I needed. I attacked the wall, climbing in a fury. The stones shifted more than once, but I flattened myself against the rise and was able to keep going. My injured arm trembled with each movement, but I cried and endured the pain until I reached the top of the wall.

I sat for a moment, trying to catch my breath. Unsheathing Iranoct, I concentrated. The sword pulled me down, directly underneath me.

Descending the wall was uncomplicated. The second I stepped down, the rocks slid out from underneath me and sent me to the bottom in short order. I bumped my elbow on something sharp but brushed myself off and felt around.

I used Iranoct again, and it pulled me to the side. Walking quickly, I tripped over something—a leg.

"Destrian!" I hissed, patting around. Two legs. A torso. His head.

"Destrian, wake up!" His hair was matted and wet.

One arm lay limp beside me. The other seemed to be buried by rubble. I carefully pulled stones off. He was nearly free when the whole wall rattled.

"No!" I yelled, grabbing his shoulders and dragging him back as a cascade of stone came tumbling down. I pulled him as far as I could, then collapsed next to him.

I knew I should go after the pack, but I was too exhausted. I didn't want to lose Destrian again, either. What if an animal came to investigate all the noise? What if Destrian worsened? I couldn't take that chance. So, I sat, Destrian's head in my lap, and I waited. As I waited, I thought.

The shadows.

The shadows had helped us. Perhaps they weren't evil like we'd initially thought. I considered all my learnings about the Nightlands, but nothing had mentioned talking shadows, or spirits, or whatever they were. But why did they help us?

"Who are you?" I whispered to the darkness.

A long silence drew a veil over me. I wondered if maybe the shadows had abandoned me once I'd discovered Destrian. Perhaps they counted that as their good deed for the day. But then, a hiss came from beside me.

"*Lost.*"

Lost? They'd gotten lost in the Nightlands? So had most of the other adventurers who perished. Was that who they were? The other adventurers?

But then I remembered.

The voice in the library had said the same thing. Gooseflesh prickled over my skin.

I couldn't be sure, but I seemed to register the presence of more than one. "How many of you are there?"

"*We are half*," the voices said.

That didn't make any sense. Half a person? How could half a person be lost?

Destrian moved, diverting my attention.

"Are you all right?" I whispered. Poor Destrian. It seemed Imor was intent on injuring him time and again. Was it my fault? Was Imor testing my loyalty? I supposed if it meant letting Destrian die, or worse, killing him, then I would happily fail. Consequences be damned.

"No," Destrian moaned. His hand searched, grabbing my leg, then arm, before finding my cheek. "My wrist is hurt, and I think I'm blind."

"You're not blind," I said. "There's just no light in the cavern. Has any of your strength returned?"

"I don't think so," Destrian said, settling back. "I need to rest awhile. At this point, I don't even care if I die."

"Don't talk like that," I admonished. "I care. I didn't go to all the trouble of finding you, just to have you die on me."

Destrian's hand groped my leg then found my hand. "Do you really care?"

I let out an exasperated sigh. "Of course I do. Anyway, I need my rest too." I turned back to the darkness. "Shadows, can you let us know if something terrible is near?"

"*We watch*," they hissed.

Relieved, I settled down next to Destrian. He curled his arm around me, hugging me close to his side. I didn't think I'd be able to sleep, but knowing the shadows were watching, coupled with the darkness, put me to sleep almost instantly.

Chapter 25

I AWOKE WITH A START. Flailing wildly, I hit something. It turned out to be Destrian trying to calm me. "Nightmare?" he asked after I'd quieted and sat up.

"Yes," I replied. I'd dreamed of the man being killed again. I tried to warn him, over and over, but he never moved. I wondered if he could hear me but just ignored it. Why would he want to die? "How are we going to get out of here?"

Destrian's gem glowed, illuminating his face. A small fire appeared on a rock, which Destrian picked up and handed to me. "I've gotten some of my energy back, but I'll need to take it easy for a while."

I nodded. "Same here."

Destrian was quiet for a moment, sitting with his arms casually wrapped around his knees, staring at the fire. "I didn't know you could use your sword with lightning."

"Trust me, I didn't know I could do that either."

"May I see your blade?" Destrian asked.

I nodded, unsheathed my sword, and handed it to him. Destrian ran his hand along the edge. "Looks to be in order. I wonder if the bitter steel helped transfer the energy." He handed Iranoct back to me.

"We need to get going," I said, winding my time tracker in the dim light. "We've been down here for more than a day."

Destrian nodded. "What about our packs?"

I rose and sheathed my sword. "There's one over the wall. I've no clue where the other one is."

The rock wall seemed much smaller in the light. I climbed it and fetched my pack. With only a little trouble, I managed to heave it over to the other side and slide down.

Destrian was slicing through a portion of the snake's body that had been lying near him. He trimmed the skin from the meat with a dagger and laid it by the fire to cook.

"They're back," Destrian said, using the dagger blade to point at the shadow in the firelight.

I sat on the pack. "The shadows helped me find you. I don't think they mean to hurt us."

Destrian stopped butchering and gave me his full attention. "You spoke with them?"

"If you could call it that. I asked who they were, and they kept saying lost." Remembering the woman from the library, I decided not to tell him that she had said the same thing. Destrian always acted strange when I mentioned her. I wondered if she was warning me about the shadows in the north. Did she know about my journey?

"Lost," Destrian mumbled, staring at the ground. He

shook his head. "No, it can't be."

"What is it?"

Destrian was still shaking his head as more shadows gathered at the edge of the firelight. "How well do you know the legend of the lost tribe?"

"Mainly what we learned at Solridge. I didn't think much at all was known," I answered.

"I'd read about the lost tribe while waiting for you to come from Espiria. The Morganites were stuck when the Lyricans advanced north. Apparently, one of the tribe members had visions. He told the clan that the way to power lay through the Nightlands. So, the king, Joab, took the man and half the tribe north to find a way around the Ballerian Sea. He left his son, Philemon, in charge of the half who stayed. Joab and the rest of the tribe never returned."

I nodded. "Philemon managed to take the surviving tribe west over the sea and founded Helena."

The shadows crept closer.

"Who was the man with the visions?" I asked.

But it was the shadows who answered, multiple voices rising together in a loud murmur.

"*Morius.*"

That didn't make any sense. I'd read the book, *Morius*, and it made no mention of him in the Nightlands. Then again, how did he get his gem?

"The opals were calling to him," I said, looking to Destrian. "They called him to the Nightlands, but he thought the vision was for the tribe to escape!"

Destrian was watching me. "What did you read in that book at Helena?"

I looked up, trying to remember. "He bore a black opal, two actually, one on the back of each hand. He didn't spend much time at Helena. He had a wife, but they never mentioned her name. It was mostly about how he helped negotiate the treaty with the Woltari."

I turned back to the shadows. "You're the lost tribe? How did Morius survive, but you all did not?"

There was no answer.

"Well, I suppose we should find our things and figure out a way to get out of here," Destrian said when the silence crept on for too long. He laid the last of the snake meat near the fire.

"*We help,*" the shadows whispered.

I raised my brows. "You will? Do you know where our things are?"

The shadows seemed to hiss to each other. "*We show you.*"

I picked up the firestone. "How will they lead us?"

"They left footprints before. It's dusty enough that we could follow their steps," Destrian said, pointing to the ground.

The shadows were indeed leaving footprints in their wake. Little clouds of dust rose from the ground as a shadow began running toward the corner of the cavern. I followed until it stopped at a pile of rocks. I dug and found the other pack.

"Is there anything else?" I asked, tossing the pack over my shoulder.

"*Come*," the shadow replied. It led me to our pot that had gotten loose in the scuffle. I also found several skins, my whetstone, and one of Destrian's waterskins. My search brought me to what used to be the entrance of the tunnel that had been transformed into a giant pile of rocks.

Frustrated, I returned to Destrian, who was wrapping most of the meat and shoving it into his pack. At least he'd managed to butcher and cook a great deal of it. We wouldn't have to worry about food stores for a while.

"I've been chatting with our new friends here," Destrian said, glancing up when I returned. "They said they can lead us out of the mountain for payment."

"What payment?" I asked.

"*Water*," the shadows whispered back.

I furrowed my brow. "Why on earth would you need water?"

Destrian started putting his pack together. "It may be ancient magic. I've heard of a power that allowed someone to tie a soul to the land, and the person would live on in a queer sort of half-life. The scrolls that detailed the ceremony have been lost for hundreds of years, and a necromancer about fifty years ago exiled most of the shadow souls into a different realm. From what we've seen, the Nightlands are plagued by drought just like the rest of the empire. If the land is struggling, it could be that these souls are fading."

I looked back to the shadows. "I can bring rain, but I'll need my gem, an opal from the Land of Iriset. Can you help?"

The shadows hissed among each other before rising as one voice. "*We help.*"

Destrian and I pulled our packs back on and began following the shadow souls into a tunnel that hid behind a stalagmite. Destrian's light hovered around his knees so we could see the prints as we followed the shadows deep into the mountain. Destrian had to duck as the tunnel became smaller and smaller.

The ceiling got so low, we finally got down on our hands and knees and crawled. Our going was clumsy. Sometimes our packs would catch on a rock, forcing us to stop until we got unhooked.

We crawled for ages, our knees bruising as we crept over the rocks and pebbles littering the tunnel floor. At least the air was warmer, so we shucked some of our leathers in favor of our linen tunics and breeches.

Finally, the tunnel widened dramatically as we emerged into a cavern. Destrian's fire blazed, the light so bright that I had to shield my eyes.

"Destrian, what are you doing?" I cried.

"Sorry, I don't know what happened," Destrian said, the fire dimming. A moment later, he gasped, "By all the gods."

I peeked from between my lashes and my eyes widened. Enormous, milk-white pillars the size of trees protruded from the ground in every direction. Some had grown diagonally from the ceiling, while others formed a jeweled forest, rising from the cavern floor.

"What are they?" Destrian asked, stepping onto one to get a closer look.

"Crystals," I said, reaching out to touch one. "There were some in our caverns at home, but I've not seen any nearly this size."

Destrian made a noise that was a cross between "What" and a scream. He stumbled back, startled by something he found.

"What is it?" I asked, drawing my sword and leaping next to him.

It was only a small salamander, its pale white body camouflaged by the milky crystal it sat upon. The salamander regarded me with squinted eyes then scuttled away. I looked down at Destrian and laughed.

"Sorry," he said, his face flushing. "It just startled me was all."

"Oh, I believe you, my lord," I said with a chuckle.

Destrian opened his mouth to say something, but I cut him off. "Don't worry, I won't tell anyone at home about that fearsome little guy." I held out my hand.

Destrian shook his head with a smile and let me pull him to his feet. "You were ready to save me, weren't you," he murmured with a grin. He brushed away a lock of hair that had been pulled from my braids.

"Of course, we're partners, remember?" I said, patting his cheek a touch too hard.

Destrian grabbed my hand, brought it to his lips, and kissed my palm. "Partners," he agreed, meeting my eyes.

My breath caught in my throat. I didn't know what to say, so I just stood there. Destrian stepped down from the crystal to follow the shadow souls while I pulled myself together. It didn't escape my notice that he'd found an easy way for me to overlook his embarrassment. I shook my head and followed him into the tunnels.

Chapter 26

W E'D STOPPED IN A LARGE PORTION of tunnel where we could stand. Crawling was beginning to wear on our knees, and I relished the opportunity to stretch my back.

"Rebuild the Temple of Imor," I said, stirring my soup.

"What?" Destrian asked, looking up from the fire.

"You asked what you could do to help unite the Morganites and Lyricans. When Gillius and I traveled through Helena last year, the Temple of Imor was dismantled. You could rebuild it to the same level of splendor as the Temple of Sol as a symbolic gesture. Man the temple with Morganite guards and Imorati. If you really want to gain support, start training Morganites as city guards alongside the Lyricans."

Destrian's gaze went back to the small ball of red flames that sat between us. He probably thought the idea was stupid. Could he trust Morganite guards? Would his father even let him go through with it? Not to mention, it might work for the Morganites already living in the city, but that didn't mean the rebel tribes would see it as true change. It's possible that the Morganites in Helena wouldn't even visit the temple anymore.

"That's an excellent idea," Destrian said suddenly, ripping me from my thoughts. "I wonder if I could get it done by the Winter Solstice."

My stomach somersaulted. "If you asked the Morganites in the city to help, I'm sure you could accomplish it," I offered.

Destrian was nodding. "We could make a celebration of it. Light up the Temple of Sol and Temple of Imor, have each blessed by their priests. Prepare a feast for everyone." Destrian smiled at me. "I'll speak to my father about training Morganite guardsmen. He'd be against it for the castle, but I bet I could convince him for the city guard."

"You might also consider a Morganite judge," I suggested. "We have priests and men of law who would be fair."

Destrian dipped his spoon in his mug, swirling it around. "It's customary at the solstice for Sol's Temple to light a bonfire. We could set it up between the temples."

I raised my brows. "It's our tradition to fill morwood pine trees with lit candles so our ancestors can find their way to the celebration, and it mimics the stars."

Destrian nodded. "There are a few morwood trees in the city, so we could continue the tradition. Let's have both celebrations instead of one. Invite all the nearby clans. Could you speak to your uncle about Espiria joining the festival? I bet Solridge would let you come home for a bit."

I swallowed. "Maybe," I said halfheartedly. What if Baylin went through with his threat and gave up my guardianship to the empire? Would the emperor let me stay at Solridge or return to Espiria? I hoped that Conal would convince Baylin against it. What would the other clansmen say, or Urdua, if they found out what he planned on doing? What would Ferris say?

"What's wrong?" Destrian asked, leaning forward.

"Nothing." I refused to meet his eye.

Destrian cocked his head. "Don't do that," he murmured, setting his mug down. "I don't like how you evade me. It makes me question you."

I sighed. Was there harm in telling Destrian what Uncle had told me on my last day at home? I was tired of keeping things from him. I took a sip of the soup but still couldn't meet his eye. Instead, I watched the bits of rice and beans swirl around my cup. "My uncle plans to give up my guardianship."

I peeked up through my lashes. Destrian's mouth had fallen open. "To whom?"

I shrugged, casting my eyes back to the ground. "To the empire. I'm hoping that my return will change his mind, or that other members of my clan will stand up to him. But it may already be too late."

"No," Destrian said. "We can stop this. You'll be in your majority soon."

I finally found the strength to meet his eyes. "I'm a girl, Destrian. It doesn't matter what age I am. I belong to someone. When I'd left before, I'd run away, and that suited Uncle. But this time . . ." I shook my head, thinking back to my uncle's words. "This time is different. He's gaining something from this, and he's convinced himself it's what's best for the clan."

"I'll appeal to the emperor then," Destrian said. "You're Morganian, after all. If he took over your guardianship, it would make sense for him to pass it to my family."

I scoffed. "What, so you could own me? What good would that do me, Destrian? How is that freedom?"

Destrian's face fell. "Do you really have such little regard for my honor? I would give you freedom. Whatever you wanted would be yours."

I raised my brows. "Provided what?" There it was again. The secret. Destrian was keeping something from me. Whatever it was, it gave him power over me in some way, I just knew it. There was also the niggling suspicion in the back of my mind, of words that Gillius had spoken so long ago. *The Consulship of Helena owes this girl all the wealth you've gained in profit for your land.* Was Destrian offering his assistance to help me, or to gain my power for Morgania? "What would I have to do to earn my freedom? I'm not naïve, Destrian. There is a cost to this. You're just afraid to say it."

"Provided nothing!" Destrian exclaimed. "What must you think of me?"

I gritted my teeth. "It doesn't matter anyway. It's your father who would have to vouch for me, and you and I both know that would never happen."

Destrian frowned, studying my face over the firelight, his brows creased in lines of worry. "Don't give up," he whispered. "We can find a way out of this."

A tear coursed out of the corner of my eye. I brushed it away angrily, leaning my forehead on my knees to hide my tears. "I've been dreaming of freedom since I ran away. Yet, it's taken me this long to realize that the most freedom I'll have in life has passed. I don't think I'll ever get it back again."

"Don't say that," Destrian said, reaching out to me. But something caught my eye. Over Destrian's shoulder, on the stone wall behind him.

"What is that?" I pointed a shaky finger.

Long feelers were dancing in the air. A portion of the wall that I first thought was rock moved. Now studying it, the patterns and shadows seemed too precise.

It wasn't rock at all. Widening my gaze, I realized the

entire wall was coming alive with hundreds of bugs. Given the reddish body and wide legs, they looked to be giant cockroaches, the size of my arm.

Destrian turned slowly. One of the creatures scuttled forward. The feelers reached out, brushing Destrian's shoulder. Destrian jumped to his feet with Phyranox in hand.

I was frozen. I didn't realize I had a petrifying fear of giant bugs before. I supposed it was something that came up when it presented itself. The insects we saw in the Plains of Moranoct had been far away, and not numbered in the hundreds, and not climbing into my hair!

My hands flew to my head. I grabbed the bug, threw it to the ground, and stamped on it as hard as I could. The feelers spasmed around my foot, but the nightmare wasn't over. Something fell onto my back from the ceiling. I shrieked as I scrabbled at my back, trying to get a grip on the insect. More spilled into the chamber from a hole in the tunnel, lured by Destrian's light and our food.

Forgetting Destrian, my pack, everything, I bolted down the tunnel into complete and utter darkness. A few feet more, and the path, now wet with a slick layer of moisture, inclined steeply. I fell gracelessly to my bottom. Giving in to instinct, I widened my feet while covering my head. My sides barked on jagged pieces of rock and stone. Gaining speed, I careened through the tunnel as tumbling rocks echoed around me.

I smashed my head against a stone before I shot out of the tunnel and plummeted for several terrifying seconds before plunging into water.

Chapter 27

I OPENED MY MOUTH TO SCREAM, but water filled my throat and lungs, choking me. I pumped my arms trying to find the surface, with no idea of where it actually was. My fingers reached air first. I thrust myself up and took a big gulp of air before going back under, only to rise once more. Looking around, I could see nothing, no bank nor light.

There was no point in panicking, so I slowly swam in the direction my gut was telling me to go. I wasn't a strong swimmer, but I'd learned in a spring near home when I was younger. Luc, Ferris, and I would go there to play as children, and Mother made sure to teach me, as her mother had taught her. Grandmother had said she swam all the time as a little girl. She hadn't told me much of her childhood, but she'd mentioned that.

Behind me, I heard a call. I turned to see a dim light in a cavern entrance above the lake. My gut had been wrong. I turned and started paddling the other direction, finally finding purchase for my feet about a hundred yards from the bank. I stood, walking toward Destrian's outstretched hand when I felt something slide over my ankle.

The color drained from my face.

"Come on, Rowyn!" Destrian shouted, splashing in after me.

As he reached me, I was pulled under. I kicked whatever was ahold of my foot several times, but it wouldn't let me go. Instead, it towed me through the water toward the deeper part of the lake. I kicked and flailed, panicking for air. The water was pitch black as I grappled with the dagger at my waist.

Finally, the dagger was in my hand. I curled toward my feet and stabbed down hard at whatever had my ankle. Pain lanced through my foot, but the creature let me go. I burst to the surface and gulped in air. Another arm, or tentacle, or whatever it was, wrapped around my hand, pulling me back underwater. I was quickly losing air, and with one last thrust, I stabbed the creature again.

A blinding light appeared above me, and the creature retreated into the water's darkness. A hand grasped mine, and I was pulled up. When I broke through the surface, I took a great, gasping breath. Destrian pulled my arms over his shoulders and swam toward shore.

Destrian began carrying me when his feet found purchase. I could do nothing but be thankful as I coughed up water and relaxed in his grip. It seemed he had removed his shirt and boots before jumping into the underground lake. His chest was bare, and his breeches dripped with water. Kneeling, Destrian laid me softly against the wall and cupped my cheeks in his hands.

"Are you all right?" he asked, concern etched over his features.

I nodded shakily. The ball of fire had followed us to the bank and was burning above me. Destrian lifted my bleeding hand and shook his head. "I left our packs in the tunnel. I'll need to get them to treat your wounds."

Destrian pulled his boots back on and walked to his ball of fire. He grabbed a flame and looked over his shoulder. "I'll be right back," he said before turning and climbing up to the tunnel entrance.

I took a deep, slow breath despite the energy that still pulsed through me. My heart continued to race, and my hands trembled uncontrollably. The water in the underground lake had gone still. Not even a ripple disturbed the surface. The creature must've been afraid of the light for it to give up so easily. I wondered what other monsters lurked in the black water. Unsheathing my sword, I set the blade over my shoulder so it would be easy to grab.

By all the gods, how could I have been so stupid? To go off without light was reckless and indefensible. I'd never acted like such a coward in all my life. Still, I shuddered at the memory of the horde of bugs skittering over the wall.

There was a scraping noise, and Destrian appeared at the tunnel entrance. He climbed out, pulling our packs after him, and tossed them onto the bank. He leaped down and brought our bags over.

While I dug through my pack for the right herb sachet, Destrian crouched in front of the fire, still distractingly shirtless, filling the pot with water and placing it on the flames. His shoulders and arms were corded in muscle, and a dusting of red hair covered his chest.

I giggled nervously then clapped my hand over my mouth.

"What?" Destrian asked, his brow furrowed. He stopped working and stared at me over the fire.

"I can't place it," I said, shaking with nervous laughter. "You look like some kind of hero out of fairy stories."

Destrian shook his head. "You've gone mad." His lips curled into a smile nonetheless.

I let out peals of laughter. That was the moment I knew I was going crazy. The lack of sunlight had turned me into a crazed and helpless girl who was afraid of bugs. They were *giant* bugs, though.

I sat on the ground, sputtering in my laughter as I pulled off my boots and examined my bleeding foot. Seeing it, Destrian kneeled to investigate. Ignoring my giggles, he grabbed the tunic he'd been shredding the whole trip and ripped off another piece to wrap around my cut.

"Just stop getting hurt," Destrian said, chuckling softly.

More laughter from me. "I know. I don't know what's gotten into me."

Destrian was ignoring my outburst. That was probably the best course of action, to be honest. "This needs to heat up for a moment," he said, pointing to the pot. "We should probably get into some clean clothes."

He was right. I dug into my pack, pulled out dry clothes, then changed behind a large rock. While Destrian did the same, I laid my wet clothes by the fire to dry and checked the pot. The water was boiling, so I removed it from the fire and stirred in the herbs before setting it down to cool.

Uncoiling my hair, I let the black waves fall loosely over my shoulders so they would dry faster. I stared at the flames, using my fingers to absentmindedly comb through the dripping locks.

Destrian emerged from behind the rock, thankfully fully clothed. "Are you cold?" he asked, eying my wet hair. I didn't need to respond, for the blaze suddenly grew warmer.

I thought Destrian would sit across the fire, but instead, he settled next to me. Grabbing the pot, he lifted my foot into his lap and began smearing the herbal paste onto my cut before wrapping it in linen. When he was finished, he moved on to my hand. I couldn't look him in the eye, but I could feel him watching me.

"Are you all right?" he asked, guiding my hand so I held it up.

I nodded, my hand trembling at his touch. "Sorry about getting so scared."

Destrian smiled. "You weren't the only one. I blasted those damn things as soon as you disappeared."

The silence stretched between us as Destrian worked. He gently cleaned the blood that had trickled down my arm before applying the medicine.

"There, all better," he said when he finished wrapping my wrist in the linen scrap.

"Thank you," I murmured, expecting him to move away, but he didn't. Destrian kept hold of my hand. Reaching up, he lifted my hair and draped it off my shoulder.

My heart raced. I was sure he could hear it. The *thump-da-thump* pounded in my ears. Little sparks of feeling danced over my skin as though it reveled in his touch.

Destrian leaned in to close the short distance between us.

Luc. I still felt his soft lips. His hand clasping mine. Suddenly, it was impossible to breathe. It felt as though I were falling. I scrabbled to keep hold of my emotions and cling to my defenses. I didn't dare venture into another unknown.

"Please, Destrian . . . don't," I whispered, looking into

his eyes.

"Why?" he asked, tracing the imoret on the outside of my eye.

"We could never be," I murmured. "Your father could never accept me. My family would sooner kill you than see us together."

"I don't care," he said, lowering his hand.

I sighed. "Yes, you do. You care what your father thinks, not to mention the other soldiers at Helena and your friends at school. Why pursue something that could never work? It will only hurt both of us."

Destrian released my hand and studied the fire. "You and I both know that's not the real reason." He stared at the flames for a moment then rested his forehead on his fists. "By all the gods, I can't believe I'm losing you to Pedr Tore."

I felt a swell of fury. I cloaked myself in it and tried to forget the cloud of emotions in my mind. Rising, I crossed my arms. "What does Pedr have to do with anything?"

Destrian stood to face me, his eyes narrowed. "You've always chosen him over me. Before we left, we were supposed to be training together, practicing with our packs, and learning to trust each other." Destrian shook his head. "But you didn't care about that. You would walk every evening with Pedr instead. You never even asked if I wanted to join."

"That's absurd," I retorted. "How many times do I have to tell you that we're merely friends? I promise you that Pedr Tore and I don't have a thread of romantic feelings between us."

"How do you expect me to believe you when everyone else says otherwise?" Destrian growled, the tips of his hair smoking. "You must think me a fool."

I threw up my hands. "You're so blind, Destrian! What of Ingrid? What of Fin? You hold their affections and yet so easily make fools of them for the sake of your whims. There are plenty of ladies who would claw my eyes out to be with you. Why persist in having my heart as well?"

"Ingrid? She's a simpleton," Destrian scoffed. "She cares more for the title than the man. Most of the women at Solridge do. I haven't any interest in that kind of partnership."

"What of Fin then?" I asked. "You see the way she looks at you. You're always so kind to her, yet you have no feelings." The memory of Fin's eyes softening when Destrian spoke plagued my thoughts. It was clear she harbored deep feelings for the heir-consul of Morgania, despite what she said. He couldn't be blind to it all.

Destrian scowled. "No, Fin and I could never be. I don't love her. Even if I did, my father would never allow it. There's no way."

"Will you listen to yourself?" I exclaimed, my voice

rising a full octave. "You think your father would allow me? My death would be his dearest wish! Fin may be a dishonored child, but my father committed treason." I thrust my finger to my chest. "I have traitor's blood coursing through my veins, and yet here you are, telling me it doesn't matter."

Destrian glared at me. "Traitor's blood, yes, but there is more, Rowyn. You know there is. If we return with your gem, you'll be one of the most wanted women in the realm. You don't have titles, nor lands, but in this age, rain and water are worth more than gold and silver. In that, your wealth cannot be measured."

"Is that all you want from me, my power for Morgania?" I asked, furrowing my brow. "You don't have to give me your affection for that. I've told you I plan to return to Espiria. Morgania would benefit from that plan."

The ball of flame grew white-hot as Destrian slammed his hand into the cavern wall. I jumped.

"How can you say such things to me?" he shouted. "You know that isn't all I want! You know I care for you more than the hordes of other men who'll come courting at your feet!"

I shook my head. He seemed so sure. "I think you're wrong," I told him. "There are many men who wouldn't be happy with me. They would want an Ellora, or an Ingrid, or a Lisbet."

Destrian grabbed my shoulders. "Why won't you even give me a chance?"

I brushed his hands away. "Because your father would happily toss me out a window and dance on my grave."

Because the wounds of old love were still as fresh as the day I'd found out Luc was never coming back.

Because I couldn't bear feeling shattered again.

As sure as my name, I knew that Destrian and I stood no chance south of the Last Dusk. We'd have to run away and forsake all who knew us to get a fresh start.

Destrian would never do that.

I would never ask him to.

"I was honest about my feelings months ago," Destrian said, his eyes filled with pain. "For weeks I'd lain awake, wondering what I'd said that could've possibly been so abhorrent to you, but now I understand. You're keeping something from me."

What was he talking about? Our conversation in the marketplace was nothing but a small moment in a traumatic day. There were certainly none of the stirring declarations that he spoke of. I was missing something, just as I was missing why I tried to leave Solridge. It had to be tied into the memories that had disappeared from that week.

Destrian turned to face the lake and ran his hands through his hair. "Maybe you're being truthful, and it's not

Pedr. But I know there's someone else. Our families aren't the only chasm between us."

My heart skipped a beat and I stopped thinking about my missing memories. "I don't know what you're talking about," I said. I couldn't stop my voice from wavering. Had Fin told him about Luc?

"Don't lie to me," Destrian said, scuffing the ground. "Arda told me."

Damn that woman. I picked at the wrapping on my wrist, trying to order my thoughts.

When I didn't respond, Destrian took my silence as affirmation. "Who is it?"

I gritted my teeth. "It doesn't matter anymore. He's gone."

Given Destrian's expression, that wasn't the answer he anticipated. "What happened?"

I sighed. I'd been holding back from Destrian this entire journey. I could give him the truth. I owed him that much. "He was from home. Two years ago, he was taken to the war by doghunters."

Destrian shook his head. "I suppose that, too, is my fault," he muttered softly.

"I didn't say that." Of course, I'd thought it plenty of times. "Anyway, it doesn't matter. I'll never see him again."

I could practically hear the puzzle pieces snap together

in his head. Why I pushed him away, even when it didn't make sense. Why I spurned his feelings. Why I kept no eyes for the other nobles and knights at school.

Destrian studied me. "Why didn't you tell me before?"

"You act as though you aren't keeping secrets yourself. Why should I be honest with you?" I snapped. "You've been withholding from me since we first met."

"Rowyn, I've kept something from you because I didn't want to put you in danger."

"How could knowing something put me in danger?"

"Don't underestimate the other sorcerers in the realm," Destrian reproached. "Vianne isn't the only mind reader, though she's probably the kindest."

By all the gods, Vianne, kind? "Is it really so bad?"

Destrian shrugged. "I've met Vianne's old mentor, Agramon the Divine. He's constantly using people to get what he wants, and I'm pretty sure not all his desires are honorable, nor legal. The man is utterly terrifying. But I promise, when we get to Helena, I'll give you the book. You can keep it for all I care. Just . . . be careful. If something happened to you because of it . . . I don't know what I would do."

"You'd survive, as you've always done," I said, meeting his eyes. "You'd marry Ingrid, and rule Morgania, and forget all about me."

Destrian brushed his fingers over my cheek. "Have

you listened to nothing I've said? I'd sooner forget my-self."

I thought Destrian would persist further, but he didn't. His hand fell away, and he turned his eyes back to the lake.

I didn't know what to say, and that was the problem. I was confused about my feelings for Destrian because I never let myself think about them. I always replaced the thoughts with how Fin would feel, or my family, or the other students at Solridge. I considered it an impossibility. But if it wasn't, did that change how I felt?

Chapter 28

I COULDN'T ESCAPE MY THOUGHTS as Destrian led the way through the underground tunnels. I stared at the back of his head, trying to sort through my feelings. Destrian was right. I only considered the thoughts of others. Was I attempting to cast blame elsewhere so I could escape my emotions?

All my life Luc and I had been told that Imor had aligned the stars in our favor, that we were fated for each other. In hindsight, it only made us complacent. We didn't think anything could touch our love, but we'd been wrong. My belief in fate had left me wounded beyond repair.

There was no doubt in my mind that I cared about Destrian, but I knew heartbreak. I knew what it felt like to have your dreams ripped apart, leaving behind only raw shards.

But in our time in the Nightlands, Destrian insisted on healing me. He was beginning to piece me back together into a person. A person who could be broken again.

I dreaded falling for the heir of Helena. Everything about our lives doomed us to failure. From society, to our family, to our friends. If we fell, we would have nothing to hold onto but each other. I didn't have faith it would be enough.

SEEING THE NIGHT SKY lifted my spirits when we emerged on the mountainside, but the distance that had grown between Destrian and me dulled the feeling of elation. It also didn't help that we were still in the mountain range that I'd hoped we'd passed completely through.

I called the snow. The white flakes calmed me since we wouldn't have to worry about water for a while. I enjoyed watching the footsteps of the shadow souls skipping and dancing through the powder that collected in drifts over the mountain path. Kneeling, I shoveled snow into the waterskin that Lord Alexander had gifted me. When it was full, I rummaged through my pack and pulled out Galena's pouch of silphium. I pinched the herb between my fingers and sprinkled it in with the snow. I capped the waterskin, shook it vigorously, then let it fall to its place at my side. Looking up, I noticed Destrian watching me as he leaned against his pack on the other side of our fire.

"What was that?" he asked.

"Nothing," I said, my cheeks growing hot.

That only made it worse.

Destrian raised his brows as he dragged his fingers

through the snow. "I thought we were going to be honest with each other."

My heart skipped a beat when I saw the hurt in his eyes. He thought I didn't trust him. "Honestly, Destrian, it's something for girls. You really don't want to know." I didn't know how much truth there was to that statement, but it would be unbelievably embarrassing for me to explain.

He shot me a strange look. "If you say so."

I sat back and ate, at a loss for what to say next. I peeked up and found Destrian eying me.

"What?" I muttered.

"We need to move past this," Destrian said, waving his spoon between us. "We're all each other has right now, and if we continue this way, we'll go crazy."

I met Destrian's eyes. Dare I tell him what I feared? That if I let myself feel what every bone in my body was urging me to feel, we would be hurtling toward utter catastrophe? No, I didn't dare.

"I want to focus on my gem," I said, ignoring the hum in my bones. "Can we not just be friends?"

"We are friends, Rowyn. I'm sorry I can't help how I feel, but I've said my piece. I am yours until you send me away." Destrian stretched his hand toward me. "In whatever form you need. I won't bring it up again."

I took his hand. "Thank you," I said, relief flooding

through me. There was safety in the shelter of friendship.

Destrian leaned back and scraped his mug clean of the soup. "Now, what is our next step? We aren't as far as we hoped we'd be."

I pulled out the map and studied it. Standing, I looked toward the mountains to the south then turned north. "Do you see that?" I asked, pointing to an orange glowing light on the horizon.

Destrian rose and stood next to me. "What is it?"

"According to the map, the Land of Iriset is guarded by a mountain of fire."

"Fire, you say?" Destrian repeated. He was trying to mask the excitement in his voice, but I wasn't fooled.

WE TRUDGED OVER THE MOUNTAINS FOR TWO DAYS. The orange glow grew brighter, which let Destrian take a break from using his magic.

The mountain of fire belched ash and smoke that filled the air with noxious fumes for leagues. Molten rivers streamed down from the great peak and cast the land in ghastly shadows. I stripped off my cloak and furs when the heat ballooned to such an intensity that my clothes were soaked in sweat.

Destrian kneeled and captured flames on his finger-tips, studying the lava creeping over the ground.

Ash stung my eyes, and I waved a black cloud away from my face. "Let's hurry up and cross," I said, my eyes on the sky. "I have a bad feeling about this place." The clouds of ash meant our visibility was limited. It hadn't escaped my notice that animals in the Nightlands dwelled near heat sources.

We skirted around the flaming rocks. The poisonous smoke was near unbearable, but Destrian pulled me next to him and thrust a linen rag over my mouth to shield me from the worst of it. I shot him a grateful look then focused on not burning a hole in my boot.

We were halfway across the lava field, where the smoke was at its thickest, when I tripped over something and nearly fell into one of the flaming rivers. I screamed and rolled away from the lava as my pack caught fire. In an instant, the flames were gone, and I sat up coughing. My head ached as the scent of burned hair filled my nose.

"What happened?" Destrian demanded, pulling me back to my feet.

I coughed and pointed to an oval-shaped rock. "I tripped over this." I looked closer. Rocks weren't completely smooth.

Destrian reached out to touch the stone as a shrill ring of alarm filled my mind. The smoke was closing in, masking the land around us.

A whisper of a growl reached my ears.

"It's an egg," Destrian said, not noticing that I was frozen, facing the ash-filled cloud, as the growling grew nearer.

"Destrian," I whispered, my trembling hand grabbing his shirt and shaking him.

Destrian looked up, saw the look on my face, and pulled Phyranox from its scabbard as he rose. "Rowyn, we need to get out of here."

I nodded, my heart racing, and slowly pulled my bow down.

A snarl ripped through the air.

"Go!" Destrian shouted, shoving me forward. I bolted through the smoke, trying to find my way without running feet first into a stream of lava while dodging several other groups of eggs scattered over the land. I wheezed as ash filled my lungs and clouded my vision.

A feral shriek reverberated off the mountain and sent chills down my spine. I stopped running, my eyes wide, and grabbed Destrian.

"That didn't come from behind us!" I shouted, trying to listen. I wished my heart would stop pounding in my ears.

"Where did it come from?" Destrian crouched beside me, Phyranox clutched in his shaky hands.

My eyes were on the black clouds above. I grabbed an arrow. "The sky."

The rhythmic beating of wings passed to our right, but we still had no visual of the creature. Another unearthly shriek resounded through the air.

"There, look there!" I shouted, pointing to a silhouette barely visible through the black smog. It skimmed through the cloud before disappearing into the smoke. My heart stopped at the size of the creature. It was massive.

"Run!" Destrian shouted.

My heart pounded with the rhythm of my feet as if to make up time for its inaction before. We raced across the lava field, our eyes on the black sky, trying to outdistance the beast.

Something slammed to the ground in front of us, spraying molten rock into the air. We skidded to a stop, and I threw up my hands to shield my face. My skin sizzled as droplets of flames landed on my arms. I screamed from the burning pain, matching the guttural screech of the animal.

Large, leathery wings were poised over the beast's back as it crouched on all fours, its feet ending in claws the size of swords. Bright, amber eyes glared at us as the beast took a step forward and thrashed its spiked tail.

"A dragon," I breathed. The picture I'd seen painted in a book hadn't nearly done the creature justice. My nerves danced beneath my skin as the wind from the wing-beats took my breath away. It was the most beautiful, yet frightening thing I'd ever seen. The beast's mouth opened, revealing a glimmer of flames.

"Get behind me!" Destrian yelled, his arms outspread.

We were engulfed in fire. I covered my head and sank to my knees. The flames scorched past, but I didn't feel the heat. A red glow had materialized—Destrian's fire ward.

The flames ended but the ward remained. I tried to calm my racing heart as I stood shakily and turned.

"You have to stay with me. I won't have the power to ward us both if we're not together," Destrian said, holding his sword in both hands.

I nodded. My brain moved at the speed of a snail as I tried to comprehend the sheer size of the dragon. The impossibility of the battle began to cripple me. Destrian could only hold out for so long before his wards would be useless.

My power, drummed up by fear, shot upward in a burst of lightning. Ice-cold rain streamed from the clouds, taking the dragon by surprise. The rain sizzled and hissed as it met the molten rivers.

The dragon locked eyes with Destrian. It spat another wave of flames from its jaws while I huddled behind Destrian's fire ward. By all the gods, I was being such a coward. I couldn't let Destrian take on such a creature on his own. If I were to die, it wouldn't be crouching in fear.

I sped through my memories of what I'd learned about dragons. Their hides were impenetrable, just like the snake's had been. We needed to hit its weakest spots. Thinking back to our fight with the snake, I realized what I should've done differently.

This time I wouldn't waver.

The blast of fire ended, and I rose with determination, picking up my bow and arrow. I stepped out from behind Destrian to face the magnificent beast.

The dragon's nostrils flared as though it was confused as to why we hadn't been burned to cinders yet.

It leaned forward to get a closer look. I took aim.

The dragon sniffed the air, then blinked.

I took a deep breath.

The dragon took another step, growling and baring its teeth.

I shot.

The dragon reared onto its hind legs, wings flapping, and sent a column of flame to the sky. Lightning streaked above, followed by a blast of thunder. My arrow had landed true, embedded in the dragon's eye.

I gave a shout of exuberance, but it was too early to celebrate.

The dragon slammed back to the ground and spun, its

massive tail whipping behind it. Destrian and I dove to the ground, rolling away as wind and rain from the tail's path swept over us.

I jumped back to my feet, and my blood ran cold.

In our scramble to get away, Destrian and I had separated. The dragon started to turn. I had to make a split-second choice. Destrian could survive the dragon's flames. I could not.

I ran behind the beast, throwing my bow and arrow to the side, dropping my pack, and unsheathing Iranoct. Leaping over sizzling rivers of fire, I ignored the steamy rain and raced to get to the creature's back.

I passed the dragon's front legs and darted toward its hindquarters. Its beaded hide was the black of onyx, glistening from the rainwater rolling off it. The spikes on the tail ran up the dragon's spine and crested at the top of its head in a series of frills.

Suddenly, the dragon's wings smashed into me, knocking me off my feet and into a puddle of water. A moment later the wings drew back up, and I scrambled to grab Iranoct. Something slammed next to me. I turned, thinking it was the wing, but it was one of the dragon's hind legs.

I was under the creature. I stood, Iranoct in hand, and glimpsed Destrian facing the dragon. He held a pillar of fire.

Phyranox.

Destrian swung as a claw swiped at him. Sparks burst from the sword, meeting the dragon's hide.

Destrian and I locked eyes. He held so much trust in his gaze. If I stopped moving, fear would take over. We would be finished. I couldn't fail Destrian. I couldn't take the time to think. I had to act.

The dragon roared, then snapped its teeth, and Destrian's eyes were back on his adversary.

I bolted. Sliding out from under the creature, I turned and scanned the back of the dragon.

It was lucky I'd grown up in the mountains. I sheathed my sword, backed up several paces, then shot forward and scrambled up the hide where the dragon's hind legs met with its body. Leaping from side to side, I scaled the beast, slipping once or twice from the rain-slicked scales.

I made it to the base of the wing before the dragon realized I was on it. It reared on its hind legs, roaring and twisting its head. I grabbed the bony joint and held on. The dragon drew itself up, higher and higher, until I was dangling in the air.

I held in my scream as I looked down at the perilous drop below. One slip, and I would land on the lethal ridges lining the dragon's tail. My muscles strained, and I held on as tightly as I could. I closed my eyes and prayed to Imor to keep me safe. But Imor's face was hidden behind the clouds of ash. He couldn't see me.

The dragon's hind legs couldn't bear its weight for long. It slammed back down on all fours and nearly knocked me off. A blast of fire smashed into the dragon's face, exploding in a shower of flames that quickly extinguished in the rain still streaming above.

Bless Destrian, he was doing his best to distract the thing. I sent a quick prayer for his safety then scrambled to my feet and darted to the ridge growing from the dragon's spine. It was much easier to keep my footing on the ridges than the wet beaded scales.

I reached the head, pulled myself up onto its frills, and unsheathed Iranoct. My arrow was sticking out of one of the dragon's eyes, a thick stream of blood still gushing from the wound. I braced myself against the frill as it flung its head about.

The dragon stopped shaking its head and shrieked. It lifted its foreleg then stumbled. Destrian must've wounded the beast. I took that moment to hold Iranoct aloft. Rain beat down, and a burst of lightning surged from Iranoct's point. Energy pumped through me and I flipped the blade down, the arcing light dancing with it. I plunged Iranoct into the dragon's other eye.

But something was wrong. Though the dragon was blinded, the lightning didn't seem to have any effect on the creature. I pulled Iranoct out and was promptly flung off the beast. Luckily, I landed in a soft puddle of mud, not two feet from a sizzling patch of molten rock.

The dragon was now on a blind rampage. It twisted about, flinging its tail from side to side as giant feet stamped into lava rivers, sending molten rock flying. I had to jump up and stagger away as a claw nearly skewered me.

Suddenly, Destrian was at my side.

"I'm failing!" he said. His skin was gray, and his face was caked in blood from a nosebleed. "We need to run!"

Neither Destrian nor I would be able to outdistance the creature, exhausted as we were. The dragon was frantically sniffing the air, trying to find us. Though the beast was wounded, it still had all of its weapons at its disposal.

Destrian was completely spent. But I wasn't.

Cold. Dragons hated the cold.

The dragon caught our scent and turned on us, its ruined eyes seeping. It snapped its teeth.

I faced it and raised my hands.

"What are you doing?" Destrian cried, grabbing my arm to pull me back.

"Trust me," I shouted, shaking his hand off.

I concentrated on the heavens, wielding the enormous mass of power that boiled above.

Heart pounding and muscles strumming with magic, I focused completely on the task of bending the forces to my will. A blast of icy air hurled me back, flattening me to the ground. Wind swept over the mountain, yanking my hair from its ties and whipping it in every direction. I looked for Destrian, shielding my eyes from flying sparks and debris.

The dragon roared then took flight, spooked from the sudden burst of wind. Circling, the dragon spewed another torrent of flames. The heat singed my tunic as Destrian's fire ward sputtered.

I focused in. I had to take control. I pushed more and more power above until I had nothing left. The gale raced in a circle, transforming into a massive spiraling funnel. Lightning danced within the spinning cloud, and the air itself seemed to roar with life. It grew as the dragon desperately tried to flap its wings to get away.

But it was no use. The dragon was pulled into the cyclone. It bellowed as it twisted and spiraled helplessly. The wind thundered in its intensity, matching the dragon's bellow. I tried to keep hold of the force, but the power slipped from my control.

Suddenly, the dragon was hurled into the side of the mountain. An explosion of fire and rock enveloped the creature and careened down the mountainside. The cyclone disappeared into a cloud of smoke and ash.

The dragon gave one last anguished bellow, its wings beating uselessly in the molten lava before it sank into the molten rock. The rain continued to fall in sheets, freezing drops that steamed and began to harden the liquid stone around us, sealing the dragon in its tomb.

I collapsed to my knees, gasping for each ragged breath. My mind was mud. The only thought that managed to flit past my weariness was that Destrian was safe. It was a welcome surprise that we were both alive and mostly unharmed from battling such a formidable adversary.

Destrian knelt beside me, Phyranox dangling from his hand. "By all the gods," he muttered, his eyes on the mountain. "We survived."

Destrian swept me into a hug. I tried to catch my breath and calm my pounding heart as Destrian clutched me to him and whispered, "Rowyn the Morganite, slayer of dragons."

Chapter 29

MY BOW DIDN'T SURVIVE the attack. The smoking wood lay splintered on the ground, arrows scattered everywhere. I kicked the broken pieces into one of the lava flows, unable to shake the cloak of melancholy that had settled over my shoulders. I should be happy to be alive. I should feel blessed that I succeeded in a task that others had not. But I couldn't dredge up even a drop of happiness to lift my mood. The rain was being an utter nuisance, drenching me to the core and sending a chill through my bones. My dripping hair would take an eternity to untangle, and since the wind had died away, the whole place reeked of rotten eggs.

And Destrian. Destrian insisted on being ever the perfect nobleman. Always there when I needed a hand. Always mending my raw wounds. It was exhausting reminding myself why my feelings were wrong and that I should ignore the warmth flooding my veins at his every touch.

"I found our pot," Destrian muttered next to me. He watched me out of the corner of his eye, perfectly reading my mood and keeping his distance. I wished he wouldn't do that. He should do something wrong for once so I could go back to nitpicking the reasons why I didn't like him.

Destrian set the pot down to collect rainwater. I glowered and turned away, trying to suppress the urge to scream. I didn't relish killing the dragon. I'd just wanted it to leave us be. What would Fin have said if she'd seen? I envisioned her, tears streaming down her face at the destruction of such a beautiful creature. If I'd focused more with Master Gillius, if I'd taken my training more seriously, I wouldn't have made such a mistake.

I sank and rested my head on my knees, clutching Araceli's key in my hand. I knew I should be thankful I was alive, especially considering everything we'd been through, but I couldn't shake the suffocating misery.

"Rowyn," Destrian said, kneeling next to me. "What's wrong?"

"Nothing," I whispered, trying to hide the tears running down my cheeks. I prayed to Imor that the rain would hide it.

Destrian draped his cloak over me. Sweeping my hair to the side, he wrapped his arm over my shoulders and drew me to him. I wept into his chest.

"What is it?" he whispered, tilting his head to glimpse my face. "You can tell me."

"I don't know," I sobbed. "I just feel so hopeless."

"It's the sun," Destrian murmured. "Here, drink this." He shoved a mug into my hands. It was filled with water and had bits of herbs and mushrooms floating in it. "All this time I thought you were putting the sun remedy in your waterskin. I didn't realize you were using something different until we left the mountains. You should've been drinking this the whole time."

"Oh," I said with a sniff, surprised. "I'd forgotten." By all the gods, how stupid could I be? I'd remembered to use Galena's gift, as useless as it was, and had completely neglected to take the one thing that would stop me from going crazy in the darkness.

I took a large gulp and began laughing and sobbing at the same time.

Destrian's chest vibrated as he chuckled. "It's all right, you've had a lot on your mind." His hand smoothed down my hair and drew me closer.

Destrian's heat poured into me, filling me with strength. I'd never felt stronger, more invincible, than when I was with Destrian. Not even Luc had made me feel that way. I took deep shuddering breaths, my tears dying away with the rain. I should tell him how I felt. That I couldn't ignore my feelings. I steeled my resolve and faced him.

"Destrian, about what you said in the caves . . . about us."

But Destrian shook his head and cradled my cheek in his hand. "You were right. I've thought about it, and we should just focus on your journey. We'll have plenty of time to talk about us at your quest's end."

"Wait . . ." I began, but Destrian was already getting up. The heat seeped away in his absence as a chill crawled across my skin.

Destrian shook his head. "Rowyn, I made the mistake of thinking this quest could be about us. But the battle with the dragon made me realize that I was wrong. This quest isn't about us at all. It's about you. It's my job to guard your back, not distract you from your purpose."

I sighed, looking back into the mug as Destrian gathered the rest of our things. He was right. I needed to focus. We'd have plenty of time to talk about us later.

THE LAND OF IRISET LOOKED just as it did during my Trial by Stone. The clouds of ash and haze had wafted away, leaving a blanket of stars and the face of Imor. It had probably been a shallow sea in ancient times. The plain was carpeted with sand and sediment while giant boulders loomed across our path. My muscles trembled with excitement, and a high ringing sounded in my ears. I could only attribute it to one thing—opals.

"Something should call to you," Destrian whispered

next to me. "Listen for it."

I let myself go, dredging up how it felt during the Trial by Stone. Something tugged at my feet, so I walked, stepping carefully. We headed deeper into the boulder land till I nearly despaired. Was I deluding myself? Perhaps I was going mad with sun sickness.

Then, the glow appeared. It shone in the distance, a multicolored light that beckoned me. I walked faster, Destrian in step beside me, his eyes dancing over our surroundings for any hidden threats.

The light emanated from a giant boulder threaded with veins of color. I walked around it, running my hand over the rough surface. I couldn't see color in the dim light of night, but I could tell something was there, hidden beneath the rough sandstone.

"What do I do?" I asked, seeing no small pebbles on the ground to choose from.

Wordlessly, Destrian handed me a small pickax that was strapped to his pack. I took it and furrowed my brows. "Where should I cut?"

Destrian eyed the boulder, his eyes traveling over the veins in the stone. "Maybe just close your eyes and swing?"

More directions would have been nice, but I trusted Destrian. I tossed my pack to the ground, hefted the pickax over my shoulder, and closed my eyes.

"Wait! Let me get out of the way first," Destrian said, backing away.

I glanced behind me to make sure he wasn't in the line of my swing, then closed my eyes once more. My heart skipped with excitement as I took a deep breath and swung. The ax made a chink, but the rock stayed true. Wrestling the ax back out, I swung again, and again, and again, until a piece of rock fell away and split at my feet into three pieces.

The light from the boulder faded away while the pieces at my feet retained their glow. I kneeled to the ground and studied the stones. Which one was mine? I was supposed to have one stone for the embedding ceremony, but the three shards glowed even brighter when I held them. Cradling them in my hands, I looked up to Destrian.

"Which one?" he wondered, just as stumped as I was.

"I don't know," I sighed, turning each jagged stone over to inspect them. I would have to refine one before I attempted the conversion, but which one?

"Well, we might as well camp here then," Destrian said, dropping his pack and calling a fire. In short order I had the three rocks soaking in water and had pulled out the cleaning kit that Solridge sent with me. Perhaps my stone would reveal itself when it was clean.

Destrian leaned against his pack, watching me lay out all the materials. "Are you planning on doing all three?"

I nodded. "I don't know how else I'm supposed to figure out which one to use."

Destrian cooked some weak gruel while I worked, scraping the stones until pieces of rock fell away from the gems. I was fascinated by the veins of orange, green, and blue threaded within the dark surface. The three gems were easily the most beautiful things I'd ever held. I quickly ate my bowl of gruel before going back to work on my gems.

I could choose what shape the stone was, so I decided on ovals. Most of the women's stones were ovals or circular, while the men opted for the more masculine rectangular- or square-cut. Taking my polishing brick, I rounded the edges, using the light from the fire to aid in my task.

Destrian left me to my reverie. He lay down to catch some sleep so I could work undisturbed. I toiled for hours, not pleased until the stones were perfectly smooth, their inner colors shining brilliantly at me. Turning to Destrian, I went to show him, but he was fast asleep, snoring away on a pad of furs.

Disappointed, I closed my eyes and called to the stones. I was hoping they would do something like jump out of my hands, or maybe two would explode, leaving me one to use. Opening one eye, I looked down and found all three gems emanating their wonderful colored light. Sighing, I set the stones down to investigate them one by one.

"They all seem so perfect," I said to myself. "How can I choose just one?"

"*Do not choose*," whispered a voice in the breeze.

I jumped. I didn't think I would ever get used to the disembodied whispers of the shadow souls, despite the fact that they'd become allies on my quest.

"I thought you left us in the mountains." Shadowed hands reached out to touch the stones . . . wait . . . not the stones, my *hands*. I stared at the shadow and remembered my dream of Morius. He had opals on the back of his hands, not his head.

"Can you all send me dreams?" I asked the shadow.

"*We see, dreams speak.*"

"It's you, isn't it? You're showing me things in my dreams. Are you saying I am supposed to use all three?"

"*Three stones*," a shadow echoed. I understood they could only speak in short fragments, but I wished the words they chose made more sense, or at least clarified something.

Then, I remembered the dreams hadn't started in the Nightlands. The dreams began in Helena. "Are there more of you south of the river?" I asked, recalling the woman who haunted the library. The voice who had whispered to me in my sleep the year before. A long pause followed as I waited patiently for the shadow to respond. Others had crept toward me, listening and watching.

"*One*." They whispered together. "*One more*."

"Who is she?"

"*The faithless one*."

That explained absolutely nothing. I realized they wouldn't give me much information, so instead I looked back down at my gems, resolved to tackle one obstacle at a time. Three. I had to use all three.

Destrian stirred on his pad, awoken by my conversation. When he sat up, bleary-eyed, I asked, "Why would a sorcerer put gems on their hands?"

"I don't know," he said, yawning loudly. "Most of the sorcerers in the west used the backs of their hands before the conquering, but Lyrica took out most of the rebel sorcerers. We use the gem in your forehead because you have more control there."

"What is the advantage to them being on your hands?"

The shadow souls leaned closer. I turned my head to listen carefully as the whisper came like a breath on the wind.

"*Power*."

My eyes widened and I turned back to my stones. Three stones. Two for my hands and one for my head. I had never heard of such a thing. But all the sorcerers had made it seem as if I didn't choose—the stone chose me. So why were all three glowing?

Destrian beckoned me, so I sat beside him on his pad.

He took one of the stones and admired it in the light, complimenting my refining work. "Have you decided which one yet?"

"Have you ever heard of someone having three stones?" I asked.

"No," he replied, studying my face in the dim light.

I looked back down at my gems. "It feels as though all three have chosen me."

Destrian shook his head. "That's impossible."

"You have to admit they aren't giving me much choice," I insisted. "What if it's what I was meant to do— one for control, two for power. How will I be able to take on the drought without them?"

"That's madness!" Destrian said, practically spitting with agitation.

I looked down, studying each splurge of color within the dark stones.

When I didn't speak, Destrian grabbed my arm. "Rowyn, you can't have three stones."

"I read of Morius using his hands. In the book from your library."

"All right, so it's true with the hands, but why all three? You'll get killed if you take on too much power!"

"No, I won't. The gem on my head will help me control it," I replied. "Don't you see, this is how it was meant to be. All three have chosen me." Why couldn't Destrian simply calm down and listen? He could see for himself that the stones weren't giving me a choice.

"This is the stupidest idea I've ever heard. Maybe we should wait till we get back to Solridge and get the council's advice."

My eyes widened at how quickly the discussion was deteriorating. "No, we can't. I have to make my payment to the shadow souls. The Nightlands need water, and I won't be able to do it without all three gems."

Destrian grabbed my arm but I pulled away. "This is your *life*, Rowyn. You could lose your *life* over this. Why are you being so foolhardy? Maybe the Lyrican way is best! Why else would it be the only method used?"

"Don't be an idiot," I fumed. "The single stone is the only method because you Lyricans wiped out anybody who thought differently. You've been doing it for centuries! If it's a choice between Lyrica and Morgania, I will always go with Morgania, always. It's in my blood."

"Now what are you talking about?" Destrian yelled, throwing his arms out. "You know, Idris had a point. Lyrica brought schools and structure when they took over. Morgania and Adair warred with each other constantly before the empire brought them peace!"

"At what cost?" I debated hotly. "Our freedoms, that's what. Your father was appointed to rule us, like his father before him. Our traditions are all but lost as you strip our lands and take away our food to send to the fat nobles at the capital. Peace gained through war and destruction is not peace at all! It's fear —fear that if we try to rule ourselves, the Lyricans will storm in and tear us all to pieces!"

Little sparks of light shot from Destrian's fingertips. He dropped one of my beautiful stones and rose quickly to his feet. "*Fine*! I don't even know why I bother arguing with you!" Destrian stormed away, his hands on his hips as he watched the horizon, running his hand through his smoking hair.

I seethed as I picked up the stone and placed it on my lap with the others. After a moment, Destrian came stamping back.

"Why three?" he asked.

"I don't know."

"Rowyn, you don't need all three. Listen to me," Destrian pleaded.

I gritted my teeth. "It wasn't my decision. The gems chose me. You can't stand in opposition to fate."

"You told me yourself you didn't believe in fate," Destrian argued.

He had me there. "I don't . . . not really. But even I can't deny what's in front of me." There was no way my uncle would be able to sign me away with three stones.

Destrian rubbed his face with his hands. "Is there nothing I can do to dissuade you?" He eyed the stones angrily.

"No."

"Then stand."

I handed him the stones and Destrian pulled a dagger from his belt, his gem aglow. "Hold out your hands," he demanded.

I did, and he sliced his dagger over my skin, opening two deep cuts into the backs of my hands. I sucked in my breath. Tears stung at the corner of my eyes, and blood dripped on the ground.

"Which stones?" he asked, his eyes on me. I pointed a bloody finger to the two closest to us. Destrian lifted them and uttered words in a language I didn't recognize as he crushed the stones into my wounds.

A high hum filled my ears, and the gems burst forth with light. White-hot pain lanced through my hands and up my arms. I fell to my knees, dragging Destrian with me. My hands were on fire, burning with crippling pain that surged through my body.

Destrian grabbed my chin and lifted my face. He slit my forehead with his blade and thrust the last opal into my brow, muttering in the foreign tongue. I grabbed Destrian's arms, clawing at him to let me go as the pain seared through my vision. He forced the stone deeper until I blacked out.

Chapter 30

"YOUR EXPENSES ARE BEING taken care of by another, somebody from Somme. My guess is it comes out of the emperor's purse in some way." Fin watched me closely. "I thought you would've figured it out yourself."

"He deceived me," I whispered, despair pulsing through me. It was worse than I thought.

"I thought you knew," Fin repeated anxiously.

I dreamed, but I'd never felt more awake. The images flitting through my mind weren't dreams at all. They were memories.

"The seer says she will gain her gem . . . so help you if she manages to escape."

"Who is my real sponsor, Lady Vianne? Who is keeping me clothed and paying my way here? I know it's not Gillius. Is it the emperor I'm indebted to?" My eyes locked on hers.

Lady Vianne smiled, patting my cheek with her warm hand, and my fears ebbed away. "We promised we would take care of you, and we will. We don't want anything to happen to our Rowyn."

"My heart is drawn to you like a moth is drawn to a

flame." Destrian quieted, lightly touching my finger, then, after a moment's hesitation, held my hand. "You lure me in, and were I to touch you, I would be consumed." He met my eyes. "But I would burn happily, a thousand times over, to know that you are mine."

I AWOKE WITH A START. It felt like the whole world was crumbling beneath my feet. Vianne had stolen my memories. She'd turned me into a puppet, willing to do whatever the empire asked. How dare she! How dare they all work to turn me into a slave to their whims!

Never again would I trust anyone at Solridge. My eyes had been blinded to the actions of the council. Within my memories I felt the return of something I hadn't known was missing. Anger. It festered within as my power did, swelling and offering me strength. Had I not been so ig-norant, I would never have stepped foot into the Night-lands. I would have made my escape and ran as far away from Lyrica as I was able.

But what could I do now that I had my gems? Even if I survived the journey back, which was no small thing, what did I have waiting for me? Was it really too late to escape the empire? I studied my hands. The gems lay just below the surface of my skin, centered below the joints. I touched one, then the other. There was no blood, nor scabs. Not even red, swollen skin marked the injuries from the embedding ceremony. I felt my forehead, brushing my finger over the gem. It was fused to the bone of my skull, never to be separated, even in death.

"You're awake," a voice said.

I sat up.

Destrian was twisting a dagger in his hands, staring at me from across the fire. I expected him to say something more, but he didn't.

My heart is drawn to you like a moth is drawn to a flame.

It was as if I'd been punched in the gut. The words I'd screamed to him at Solridge were burned in my mind. *What am I to say?* I'd ripped his heart from his chest and ground it beneath my feet, crushing him in its wake. What had I done?

I studied Destrian in the firelight, unsure of what to say next. Should I tell him what Vianne had done? Apologize? Insist I hadn't known? In the end, I said nothing, not even knowing where to begin.

Destrian held out a bowl of soup. "How do you feel?"

"Good. Better than I've felt in a long time," I said, refusing to meet his eye. Vianne. Her name was as acrid as metal on my tongue. It was easy to hate her.

I finished my soup in silence, then stood and walked

away from our makeshift camp, rubbing my hands to-gether. I didn't want to think about Destrian anymore. He'd been right about putting the discussion off. We would have plenty of time to talk about what happened later. Recollections aside, I had work to do.

I shoved the power at my core. By all the gods.

An explosion of energy shot out of my fingertips with an ear-shattering blast that shrieked over the plain. Arcs of light crackled and danced over my hands, the strands of my hair, even my eyelashes. Suddenly, the lightning wasn't just dancing over me. Great ribbons threaded over the sky. They multiplied, splitting from each other and returning to earth, alighting the ground with crackling energy.

Wind drove into me, knocking me to my knees with a roar and sending snow and ice swirling through the air. The wind grew stronger, and I knew I was near a breaking point.

I was out of control. But I had my third stone.

I grabbed my head in my hands and sent power through the gem on my brow.

I was connected to *everything*. I saw the path from the arcs of energy, and the route the wind blew as it thundered past, sending stinging ice into my eyes. It made it hard to concentrate. I envisioned the route and tried to grasp it with my mind.

"Rowyn!" Destrian yelled into my ear. "It's too

much!"

He was right. I couldn't rise to my knees. I could barely breathe. I wasn't yet ready to take on the stones. I'd not rested enough.

Off—I needed to turn it off. I ripped myself away from the forces, smothering the power flowing from my gems to the sky. With a great wrench, I cut everything off and opened my eyes.

Everything was still. Small flakes of snow hovered in the air. The night was still and silent.

Destrian knelt in front of me. "Are you all right?" he asked, his breath turning to fog.

I was shivering. I hadn't realized how cold it was till the snow soaked my breeches.

"Here," Destrian said, wrapping his cloak around my shoulders. "You won't be able to master the stones if you catch a chill."

I let him pull me up and walk me back to the campfire. Destrian motioned me down to the pad of furs he'd made. I sat, clutching his cloak around me and watching the fire.

The power came much too quickly for my taste. I'd have to master drawing just a bit and fashioning it to my needs. I'd never been able to grasp the paths of the different elements before, so that was a welcome development. I looked back down at my hands. The stones, with their dark coloring, contrasted with my pale skin. The threads of color—red, blue, and green—gave the dark gems welcome color.

"Did it work how you thought it would?"

I shrugged. "It was a lot to keep track of. I wonder if I'll be able to call a single element, like wind, if need be. It makes me think that it's a possibility."

Destrian nodded then went back to staring at the fire, the dagger spinning over his fingertips.

I shivered, drawing the cloak tighter around myself.

"Come here," Destrian ordered, holding his arm out.

I hesitated. I couldn't shake the memory of his confession from my thoughts. I'd meant to distract myself, but that proved unsuccessful. I should tell him the truth.

I scooted into Destrian's arms. I was trying to work up the courage to tell him about Vianne when he rested his head on mine and breathed deeply.

"Are you . . . smelling me?" I asked, momentarily distracted.

Destrian's head lifted. "Sorry," he mumbled. "You probably get that a lot."

"What do you mean?" I sat up and faced him.

Destrian's brows furrowed. "Has no one told you?"

"Told me what?"

"You smell like rain." Destrian flushed. "I noticed it the first time we met in Helena ages ago. I can't believe no one has said anything to you."

"No, no one told me," I said, more shocked than anything.

Destrian's eyes fell. "Sorry, I didn't mean to make it awkward."

"It doesn't have to. I just didn't know," I murmured, but I rested against the pack instead of leaning back down in Destrian's arms. I wrapped my arms around my knees and rested my chin on them, staring at the fire. "Vianne made me forget why I left Solridge after the attack in the marketplace."

"Oh?" Destrian said. He slouched against his pack, his knees up. "You remember now?"

I nodded. "I snuck into Gillius's room and found a letter from someone at the capital. They were warning him of the consequences if I escaped. Someone there knows about me and has been paying my way. Gillius must have written to them as soon as he found me."

Destrian stared at the fire. The dagger was back in his hands, and he fiddled with the hilt as he thought. Dancing flames reflected in his dark eyes and his red gem glowed. "There's something not right," he admitted. "You think Gillius wrote to them after he found you?"

I shrugged. "How else would they have found out about me?"

Destrian met my eyes. "I don't know, but when Lord Alexander and I traveled to Yliria to gain my gem, we stopped at the capital on the way back and Gillius was there. Thinking of it now, it seems odd."

I tilted my head to the side. "I thought most of the sorcerers and students routinely traveled to the capital. Why would that have been odd?"

"Lord Alexander and he kept leaving to meet with the Council of Five on some urgent matter. Then, one morning, Gillius up and said he was going to join me in Helena in a few weeks."

My stomach dropped to my knees. "Are you saying Gillius knew about me before he even reached Morgania?"

Destrian met my eyes. "I don't know, but thinking about it now, it seems that way. What other matter would've been so important for him to come to Helena? The council at Solridge doesn't normally visit students' homes and escort them to school. We have guardsmen for that."

"How would he have known?"

"I've no idea. My father and I didn't know about you, and I can track magic a bit. I'm not as good as Marc or Gillius, but I can tell when magic is around. I passed by Espiria on the road to Helena when I got back and didn't feel any trace of you."

I rested my head on my knees. "I feel so . . . trapped," I said. "If Baylin signs me away, I'm done for. Everything I hoped for my life will be gone."

That's where Baylin got the guardianship papers from. My mysterious sponsor was now seeking claim to my body and person. It felt as though I'd stepped off a cliff and the ground was fast approaching.

Destrian rested his hand on my shoulder. "Rowyn, we'll find a way out of this. I don't want you to worry."

I wanted to believe him, but what could I possibly do to escape my looming fate?

Chapter 31

WE DIDN'T STAY LONG in the Land of Iriset. After resting, we packed and began the return journey with hopes that it would prove faster than the six weeks we'd been away. I practiced with my gems as we traveled over the flaming rivers, calling snow and ice to fall around us. If there were any more dragons, they stayed well away from the onslaught of cold weather that I brought to the land.

Following the path of the wind, I learned to temper it until just a gentle breeze swept my hair back and sent it dancing behind me. With a flick of my mind, rain went from a monsoon to a dense fog. Playing with my range, I sent the clouds boiling from the mountain of fire and across the Land of Iriset as far as we could see. I could reach for leagues—every gust, every snowflake, entirely at my whim.

The shadow souls splashed and danced in the puddles, relishing their promised payment as we followed the stars back.

We attacked The Dires, climbing with a fervor. The mountains were just as treacherous traveling over them as they'd been tunneling through. We didn't rest. Instead, we thought only of returning to the south before the autumn wind blew in.

Finally, we stopped to rest in a cave. In an unspoken agreement, we set up camp by the entrance. We certainly didn't want to get lost in the caves again.

"How's your power coming?" Destrian asked, dipping his spoon into the soup. "Do you feel the three stones were worth it?"

"I do," I said with a nod. "The stone on my head helps me turn it off whenever I want. I've never had that type of control before, and my range!" I smiled. "My range is incredible. I'm trying to figure out a way to control each element simultaneously. I think that's what will take the most work."

Destrian nodded. "It's certainly something to behold. I can't wait to see what you do south of the river. The drought is as good as over."

I took a sip from my mug. We hadn't spoken of the capital again. Instead, we traveled in comfortable silence. I didn't bring up the memory of his declaration either. We seemed in tune with each other in a way that had eluded us before, and I didn't want to be the one to break that spell.

We bedded down soon after we finished eating. Destrian was lying on his side, his head resting in my lap, while I kept watch. I wasn't thinking of anything in particular, just letting my mind wander over my gems, seeing Fin and Pedr again, the sea voyage back to Solridge. The fire popped and crackled; otherwise, the cave was soundless . . . until I heard faint scratching.

I froze, my hand on my sword, and peered into the cave's menacing darkness. It was silent again, but I was already alert, breathing shallowly, my ears craning to pick up the tiniest noise.

Rustling was followed by more scratching, even closer than before.

"Destrian," I hissed, nudging him awake. "Destrian, wake up!"

Destrian sat up groggily. I put my finger to my lips to quiet him and pointed to the interior of the cave. Destrian's eyes widened. Fully awake, he stood and drew his sword then leaned down and helped me to my feet. Our eyes were glued to the emptiness. The fire on the ground slowly lifted and traveled back into the cave.

Something hissed then scurried away from the illumination. Destrian and I looked at each other and raised our swords.

"Should we get our packs?" I whispered. "I think we should get out of here."

"We could," Destrian said, "but I don't want their weight to make it hard to move if we need to. We've made that mistake before."

A shadow passed beneath the light as something bounded toward us. The creature had a pointed face, with large teeth and whiskers set before black piercing eyes. Behind it whipped a long tail. By all the gods, it was a rat the size of a large dog.

Stepping in front of Destrian, I swept Iranoct up, cleaving the rat's head in two as it charged.

Destrian held out his hand, eying the darkness as the deafening hissing reverberated off the cave walls. A colony of the damnable beasts hurtled toward us. We turned, standing back to back as we met the horde.

I ducked as one leaped. My sword dug into its ribs, and I used its momentum to send it flying behind me. Raising my sword again, I beheaded another that'd charged toward Destrian. Blood sprayed everywhere while Destrian mercilessly chopped off the limbs of animals that dared come near.

I sliced and stabbed, meeting each creature with the end of my blade. One rat captured Destrian's arm in its teeth. I thrust Iranoct into the beast's throat. The animal's death throes pulled the sword from my hands.

Another rat charged.

I grabbed the dagger hanging at Destrian's waist, pulling it out as the rat collided with me. We both went rolling onto the ground. It snarled, its teeth snapping inches from my face. I drove the dagger into the animal's jaw. Blood streamed over me, coating my face and hands. I shoved the dying rat off and pulled Iranoct from the corpse before meeting the next assault. But it didn't come.

I wiped the blood off my face with the sleeve of my tunic then glanced at Destrian nervously. The fireball brightened, illuminating the live rats huddled around the bodies and limbs strewn around us.

"What are they doing?" I whispered.

"They're eating the dead," Destrian said, wrinkling his nose. One of the rats lifted its head and stared at us with beady eyes, flesh dangling from its bloody maw. The rat ducked its head back down and fed as I watched in horror.

Destrian grabbed my arm. We gathered our packs and ran from the scene. Destrian stood guard, still watching the feasting rats while I scrambled out of the small entrance. Once Destrian got out, we hoisted our packs onto our backs. We rushed down the mountain, trying to put as much distance between the rats and us as possible. I didn't want to be around when their supply of dead flesh ran out, and there was no telling how many there were.

Destrian grunted behind me, and a stream of rocks and pebbles cascaded over my path. When I put my foot down in a panic, I wobbled on the loose stones and fell forward. Landing on the steep slope, I scrabbled for purchase, but the pack was my undoing. It gained momentum as I hurtled down the mountain at a sickening speed, crashing into boulders and rocks. I felt two of my ribs break and prayed my spine and skull would go unharmed.

Finally, with a loud crunch, I met with the side of a large rock tower. I gasped for breath, but thankfully I was alive.

I couldn't even attempt to sit up. The pack pinned my back down, and my body shot pain from every direction. Fine, I wouldn't move. That suited me splendidly at the moment anyway.

Some all-powerful sorcerer I turned out to be. I'd just gained three of the most powerful gems one could have, and I was nearly defeated by a damned mountain. As I lay there, I noticed Imor looking down on me from the heavens.

He was laughing at me.

Chapter 32

AFTER WHAT SEEMED AN ETERNITY, I heard the pitter-patter of stones falling. A light shone like a beacon, steadily growing brighter as it neared me.

Out of the light came Destrian's face, crouching over me in a panic. "Rowyn! Where are you hurt?" he asked, looking over the wounds he could see. I was sure I looked a sight. Not only was I crumpled in a heap, I was covered in rat blood. Well, some of it could've been mine.

"My shoulder, ribs, knees, and elbows," I croaked as I tried to sit up. Nope, too painful. I lay back as tears found their way to the corners of my eyes. My whole body was one big ball of hurt.

Destrian shook his head above me, frowning. "It's my fault. I'm so sorry, Rowyn. If I hadn't slipped . . ."

"Just get me out of this pack," I snapped. All I wanted was relief from the pain, and I wanted it *now*.

Destrian delicately eased my arms through the loops until I was free. He lifted my shoulders and rested me against the pack, facing the fire that burned on a piece of rock.

"I'll need to look at your wounds," Destrian said softly, eying my clothes. The leathers had at least protected me from the worst cuts, but there would be considerable bruising, not to mention the bones I'd definitely broken. Destrian was already pouring water into a pan to heat and digging in his pack for the herbs.

I tried to lift my arms. My breath stopped as muscles screamed their contempt at me. I dropped my arms with a gasp, ignoring the tears crawling down my cheeks.

"Let me," Destrian said. He gently divested me of my furs. Heat radiated from the fire, making the cold bearable. Destrian pulled off my boots and socks. Holding one of my bare feet, he turned it gently, testing the bones and muscle.

I trembled, and it wasn't just from the pain.

Destrian eyed my breeches.

I tried to untie the strings holding the pants to my waist, but as soon as I tensed, pain assaulted my senses. I let out a gasping sob.

"Shh, I got it," Destrian said, leaning forward. He untied the string and peeled the breeches down, revealing the pale skin underneath. At least I still wore my undershorts. There weren't any injuries under them except a bruised rear. I choked back tears at the sight of dark bruises already forming over my skin.

Destrian turned back to the fire, dumped a large amount of herbs into the water, and stirred them to form a paste. He turned back to me and hesitated, unsure of himself, before meeting my eyes. "Can you do it?" he asked, holding the pan out to me.

I shook my head, swallowing a fresh set of tears. "I can't," I gasped.

Destrian's mouth hardened into a grim line. He dipped his fingers in the medicine and dabbed it onto my skin. I tilted my head back, unable to watch as my breathing grew shallow. Pain eased out of me from the medicine and Destrian's hands.

I relaxed and let him go about his task in silence, but I couldn't look. It would've been too personal. Too embarrassing. Destrian's fingers swept tentatively over my thighs. I sucked in my breath and held it.

Scooping out more medicine, he went to my lower legs. I couldn't breathe, my heart racing as he stroked my calf.

"Done," Destrian said before long, sitting back on his haunches. He was eying my tunic with a frown.

I tried to lift my arms to pull up my tunic, but it was no use. My arms screamed the moment my muscles grew taught.

"Do you need me to help you?" Destrian asked. Though the night air was chilly, tiny beads of perspiration speckled his brow, and his cheeks were flaming scarlet underneath the glow of his gem.

I nodded, unable to speak from mortification.

Destrian straddled my knees and tried to lift the tunic off. When he raised my arms, I screamed as pain lanced through my shoulder. Destrian quickly lowered the tunic back down.

Sitting back on his haunches, he pulled his dagger out. "I'll have to cut it off."

"Fine," I sobbed. The fabric was torn and dirty anyway. I had others in my pack that I could use, so it shouldn't matter.

But it did.

Luc hadn't even seen me with so little on, and I'd been closer to him than anyone. But the pain was excruciating. I prayed to Imor that I didn't have any lasting internal damage. If I ever wanted to make it out of the Nightlands, I needed the medicine, and the pain was *everywhere*.

Destrian met my eyes. "I'm sorry," he said, lifting my tunic and running the blade of his dagger from the collar to the bottom seam. He leaned me against his shoulder and gently pulled my arms out. The ruined fabric fell to the ground, leaving only my short corset.

My breath caught in my throat. His fingers lightly brushed the shadow falcon tattooed between my shoulder blades. My nerves fluttered as if another touch would set me ablaze, but pain tempered those thoughts.

"Let me get your back first," Destrian whispered as I rested my weight against him. I nodded, blinking back a fresh slew of tears. Destrian went back to work, smearing more of the herb over me. I could only breathe into his shoulder, finding comfort in his smell as his fingers swept over my skin, raising gooseflesh as they went. Pain and humiliation blazed through me. Did he notice how I reacted to his touch?

Destrian gently lowered me back down. The flames from the fire turned blue as heat rolled off in waves.

Destrian labored over my arms, only meeting my eyes when he hit a tender spot. I turned my head to the side and squeezed my eyes shut. The only reason I could bear it at all was because Destrian seemed as uncomfortable as I was.

"You said your ribs?" Destrian asked, frowning at my corset.

"Yes," I whispered.

Destrian couldn't get his fingers under the boning that lined the bottom of the fabric. Wiping the back of his hand over his brow, he sighed. "I'll have to untie it."

"I know," I said. Corsets were made to be tight. There was no getting around it.

He untied the strings, loosening them just a bit before he reached under the fabric. I sucked in my breath, my hands trembling, which he was sure to notice. He eased over the bones, pressing lightly to find the broken ones. His fingers brushed my lower bust and I gasped.

Destrian emitted a strangled noise and his hand shot back. "I'm sorry," he said.

I looked away, unable to meet his eye.

Finally finished, he leaned me forward, picked up my cloak, and wrapped it tightly around my shoulders. Grabbing my discarded furs, he layered those on as well until I was warm again.

"Thank you," I muttered. I'd never been so mortified in my life. I shrank into the cloak as though it could restore every shred of dignity I'd lost.

"It's nothing," Destrian said as awkwardly as he stood. "I'm going to walk around for a bit."

He stepped away, leaving me to watch the fire. I breathed deeply, trying to collect my wits. At least the pain had dulled. As angry as I was at Master Gillius, as much as I hated him for lying to me, I was grateful for the medicine he and Lady Madeline sent with us. I leaned my head back and stared up at the stars, listening to Destrian's footfalls as he wandered farther up the slope.

It felt as though the thin veil between Destrian and me had been ripped away. I'd told myself that nothing would happen on the journey. That there would be no substance to the gossip and rumors that preceded the quest. But I couldn't say that anymore. At least not convincingly.

It took a while for Destrian to return, but when he did, he sank at my side. "How are you feeling?" he asked the fire.

"Better," I mumbled. I began to hate myself. Destrian and I had finally gotten to a place where we could be comfortable in each other's presence, and I went and ruined it by falling down a mountain. I had to ease the tension, for both our sakes. After all, he could've taken advantage of the situation, and he didn't. "How was your walk?"

Destrian finally met my eyes. "Unfulfilling," he said. "I'm sorry about having to . . . you know." He waved his hands helplessly in the air.

I couldn't help but laugh, then cry as pain shot through my ribs. "If Vianne had seen, she would've been apoplectic."

A shadow of a smile crossed Destrian's face. "I was trying to think if any of Vianne's classes or my tutor's decorum book covered such a situation."

I glanced up at him. "Was that the first time you've seen a girl?"

"Rowyn!" Destrian choked, his face flaming red once more. That was too bad. It had just returned to its normal color.

I sighed. "Sorry, I suppose that's a personal question." Then again, he'd just gotten pretty personal with me. But that wasn't his fault.

Destrian was still shaking his head. "Yes, as a matter of fact, it was."

For some reason, relief flooded through me.

Chapter 33

I AWOKE TO THE FACE OF IMOR gazing down on me from above, flanked by an ocean of stars that illuminated the stone rising above us. We'd curled up on a soft blanket of snow and cloaks with furs piled on top of us. I recognized the melody of Destrian's sleep. The soft, even breaths whispering over his lips. His arm drawing me in, enveloping me in his heat.

I breathed a sigh of relief. A dull pain burdened my ribs, and my left knee ached, but at least I could use my limbs again. I celebrated my freedom of movement by turning and wrapping my arm around Destrian to bask in his warmth.

I'd fooled myself into thinking I could shield my heart in a fortress, but my weapons proved useless. My defenses crumbled at his every touch. The moment I'd let down my guard, my heart strained to escape, crying out for Destrian to steal it as his own.

Destrian's breath caught and he stirred. Opening bleary eyes, he focused on me and smiled. "How do you feel?"

"Much better," I said, returning the smile. I could have lain there forever.

Destrian sat up. An inward scream turned into a squeal as a rush of cold swept away his warmth. *I should be in a hurry to escape the Nightlands. I should be rushing toward the sun, ready to put the horrors of the Nightlands behind me. But I'd found more than terror in the land of darkness.*

"Will you be able to walk?" Destrian asked, calling a fire to start breakfast.

I nodded, wishing Destrian could read my thoughts. He was doing his best to act as though things hadn't changed between us. That couldn't be further from the truth. *I* had changed. I could finally see what had been in front of me the whole time.

But I couldn't muster the courage to speak. My fate would be sealed at their utterance, and catastrophe loomed on the horizon. What would happen if Baylin sent me away? What would happen if my mysterious sponsor arrived wanting something from me? I would be left broken, and Destrian with me. So I chose silence. Silence was safest for both of us.

We spent eight days traveling over The Dires, trekking over mountain after mountain. We always camped where I could practice control of my gems. I worked feverishly, unleashing heavy snow over the whole range, exhausting myself so completely that by the time I was finished, I would collapse next to Destrian and crawl into his warm arms.

I refused to think about Vianne and my mysterious sponsor. I refused to try to explain away my relationship with Destrian. I refused to think of anything but mastering my gems. If I were to have any hope for the future, if I wanted to be able to decide my own fate, I had to have complete control. I needed to be a force to be reckoned with.

The landscape had changed drastically from our short time in the Nightlands. The Dires, merely gray shadows before, were now capped with a glittering layer of snow. Though I didn't understand how most of the animals thrived here, the water would bring new life to the dark wilderness. I could see why the shadow souls helped us in exchange for water. They wanted a return to their home. The Nightlands had a terrifying beauty about it, if one was brave enough to look.

Finally, we reached the last peak and began our descent into the valley. The going was slick as we navigated the treacherous terrain hampered by the recent snow.

"What will you do first when we reach civilization again?" Destrian asked as we crossed over the boulder-ridden mountainside. He always had a question to encourage conversation during a lull. I still hadn't mentioned the memory of his declaration. I hadn't found the right time. Honestly, I didn't know what to say afterward. Did it change our future? Or lack thereof?

"I'll sink into a feather bed piled with pillows," I replied, looking over my shoulder with a smile. "What about you?"

"I'm going to eat a load of vegetables. A feast of anything green."

I laughed. We'd been subsisting on beans for weeks. I'd be delighted never to see another bean in my life.

Destrian chuckled with me. "When we get to Helena, I'll tell Daisy to bring you some extra pillows."

I grinned. "If you give me extra pillows and a hot bath, I'll never leave."

"Don't tempt me. I'll hold you to that."

My heart skipped a beat. If I left, it wouldn't be of my choosing. Was it my chance to speak? I opened my mouth to confess my feelings then stopped. We had a long way to go before our next rest time. Maybe I'd tell him then. When we could speak face to face. "I still have to gain mastery. You wouldn't keep me from that."

"Watch me."

Something caught my ears. I held up my hand as the low rumble grew louder. The ground around us was vibrating, and blood turned to ice in my veins. I recognized the sound. I spun, my eyes on the mountain. The face of Imor loomed over the precipice, and a wall of snow barreled toward us.

"The snow's breaking!" I screamed, grabbing Destrian's hand and dragging him to the side as fast as my legs could carry me.

Was this how I would die? It would be poetic. Killed in a snowslide, the same way I'd killed my father. Energy pumped through me, even as fear clouded my mind. I only had one thought. Run.

"Can we outrun it?" Destrian yelled.

I shook my head. "We have to get to the side!" I shouted over my shoulder.

We scrambled over the rocks but, seconds later, were overcome by a river of snow. I scrambled frantically when Destrian's hand slipped through my fingers and he was carried away by the force of the snowfall.

I screamed Destrian's name, but he disappeared from view, replaced by a swirling white cloud.

No. It wasn't supposed to be Destrian. It was supposed to be me taken by the avalanche. I couldn't let it happen again. I couldn't kill someone else with my powers.

I couldn't lose him too.

But if I wanted to save Destrian, I had to save myself. It took everything I had to remind myself of what I knew from home.

I swam upward, trying to slow my descent and stay aloft as the icy powder clouded my vision. I gasped for air as the snow tried to smother me. My body screamed, my pounding heart bursting through my chest. I managed to stay above the snowfall. The frozen river swept into the valley and slowed before finally stopping. What felt like forever, was only mere minutes.

Luckily, I'd been swept to the side. If I'd been caught in the middle, I wouldn't have stood a chance. I dragged myself away from the snow and discarded my pack before unsheathing Iranoct. There wasn't a moment to lose.

My hands trembled uncontrollably from the cold and nerves. It was happening again. A memory flashed through my mind. Me, frantically digging through the snow and pulling out frozen bodies. When we'd found my father and the other clan members, it had been too late. Tears rolled down my cheeks and froze into tiny droplets. I couldn't lose Destrian. It couldn't end this way.

I took a deep breath and thought of Phyranox. Iranoct seemed to recognize my urgency. The sword practically towed me into the lake of snow that had collected at the base of the mountain. I ran awkwardly back up the mountain pass, ignoring the cold in my fingers and toes, clutching the sword with both hands. I had to find Destrian.

I was losing too much time. Destrian had only minutes if he was buried. I couldn't lose hope. I had to find him.

The direction of Iranoct changed and pointed downward.

I dug as fast as I could, slowed by the cold that dragged the energy out of me. My hand connected with something.

Destrian's hand.

I furiously swept the snow away, my fingers brushing over his frozen hair. He didn't move.

I began to sob while unearthing the rest of his body. At least he'd been upright. I pulled him up by his shoulders, but he was far too heavy to lift. Using Iranoct, I dug a slight ramp in the snow. It took time, but it helped me slide Destrian out of the hole. My arms under his shoulders, muscles screaming in protest, I dragged him across the snow and back in the direction I'd come. We reached the edge where my pack waited, and I laid him down.

Destrian coughed. My heart beat again. He was breathing, at least, though the breaths were shallow. But he was far too cold.

Looking up to Imor, I sent a prayer of thanks and swept the snow off the both of us. I piled a nest of furs on the ground then pulled Destrian on top, crying as I went. Frantically, I dug through my pack and pulled out every piece of clothing I could find. Sitting next to Destrian, I ripped the outer coverings from both our bodies, leaving only our tunics and breeches. I draped the cloaks over us, then my clothes, and lastly, all the furs we had left. Finally, I rested, drawing the pile of clothes and furs over our heads to capture the heat from our breaths.

I couldn't see in the darkness of my nest, so I felt around and placed my hand over Destrian's mouth. He was still breathing. I sent another silent prayer above then wrapped my arms and legs around him as best I could, hoping against hope that my heat would be enough.

"Rowyn?"

I raised my head in an instant as Destrian started to moan.

"What happened? Why can't I see?"

A tear of joy escaped my eye. "You got swept into the snowfall."

"I'm freezing," he said, only now seeming to realize it. "I can't bring fire."

I clutched him closer. "I know. I'll keep us warm, I promise."

I hated that Conal's words chose that moment to enter my mind.

The heir's death could bring our people new life. You must decide where your loyalties lie.

Chapter 34

"ARE YOU AWAKE?" I whispered to the dark. I'd just woken from a brief respite, already feeling better having rested.

My hand lay across Destrian's chest. He was hot. I groped around and found his face.

He was far too hot.

Ripping the furs away, I examined Destrian in the light of Imor. Perspiration beaded over his face and cheeks, dripping into his hair. His face was red, but not from his gem.

"Destrian?" I asked timidly, shaking him a bit. But it was no use. A fever had taken hold, drying his lips and sending his body temperature soaring. He was far hotter than anyone I'd felt before. How long could he last in that state?

Destrian mumbled something indistinct but never opened his eyes. I crawled to my pack where my waterskin was and poured a little into my cup. Crawling back to him, I lifted his head gently and tried to get him to drink the cold water. He took several sips before his head fell weakly back into my lap.

Our medicine. I needed to give him medicine. I ran

back to my pack and ripped it open. My hands shaking, I dumped out the contents and laid them in the snow.

The herbs weren't there. Destrian had put the medicine into his pack after my last healing.

I'd never found Destrian's pack.

Time stood still. I couldn't wrap my head around the fact that Destrian's pack, with all of our medicine, our money, and most of our food, was gone. The medicine stores had saved our lives countless times. What in all the gods would we do without them? All I had left was the silphium Galena had given me. What good was that for him?

Then, hope flickered in my mind. I'd been so absorbed with Destrian that I hadn't thought to look for it. I stood and surveyed the field of snow, trying to see if there was a dark speck that looked promising. I ran to a shadow near the base of the snowbank, but it was merely a boulder brought down by the force of the avalanche. The next shadow I tried was an overturned skeleton from the dried riverbank the snow had crashed into. The last dark spot brought me to the middle of the snowfall. I hiked to it, my breath curling out of my mouth in a fog as the cold closed in.

The crust of snow broke below me and I fell, disappearing into the deep snowdrift. Biting cold pierced through my clothes. I slammed my fists against the snow and screamed frustration to the sky. Gasping sobs tore through my lungs as desperation and fear clouded my mind.

I had to get out. If something happened to me, Destrian was as good as lost. I spread my legs as wide as I could and swam at an angle. The snow crumbled at my touch and made it difficult to find purchase, but I couldn't give up. Destrian needed me. I had to get back to him. To keep him safe. To give him a chance.

Finally, my hands met with something I could grab. A rib cage of a large animal. I used the bone to leverage myself out of the fallen snow. I kneeled, trying to catch my breath. The flicker of hope died in the wind. Destrian's pack was gone, our medicine with it.

I couldn't take any more chances. I had to get back to him. I was all he had.

I staggered to Destrian's side and collapsed, defeated. Tears coursed down my cheeks and froze as the cold overtook my senses. I shivered. What could I do? I was no healer. But I wouldn't let Destrian die.

The face of Imor stared down on me, and for the first time on our journey, I refused to pray.

"You can't have him!" I shouted to the sky, brushing the frozen tears from my eyes.

Imor didn't answer. He only watched.

Cold snaked over my skin. I wiped away more tears

then crawled next to Destrian and covered us back up with furs.

Destrian would get better. Destrian *had* to get better. There were too many things left unsaid. There were too many chances that I could have taken but didn't. And now, it felt as though I'd run out of time.

I COULDN'T SAVE DESTRIAN at the base of the mountain. The sooner we got going, the better. The cold weather was due soon, and I could take much better care of Destrian back in Morgania . . . if he made it that far. There wasn't a moment to lose, so finally, with something to do, I made myself busy.

We were in the river valley that served as an open graveyard for the animals. I returned to the enormous rib cage sticking out of the snow nearby. The animal it belonged to had to have been colossal, whatever it was. I took Iranoct with me and hacked at the bones until I had the pieces I needed.

Dragging them back to Destrian, I laid the two longest pieces parallel to each other then placed several smaller pieces inside. Going back to my pack, I went through my supplies to see what I could use. I only had one length of rope. I needed more. Quite a bit more, in fact. I looked at my clothes. They would have to do.

Destrian wasn't any better and he wasn't any worse. I would take it as a welcome blessing. I pulled the dagger from his belt and went to work, shredding my clothes and tying them around the bones to create a makeshift sled. The only articles of clothing I kept, other than the clothes on my back, were my cloak and the dress my mother had fashioned me. I put down a layer of furs then looped my own rope through the creation. Surprisingly, it didn't take very long to create.

The hardest part was heaving Destrian onto the sled. Though we'd both lost a ridiculous amount of weight in the Nightlands, he was still heavy and much taller than me. A couple of times, I accidentally bumped him a little harder than I intended, but I finally got him situated. After I piled the rest of our furs on top of him, I shouldered my pack, pulled the rope around my waist, and took a step. The sled glided across the snow. I hadn't a moment to lose.

The going was much slower than I would've liked, but it could've been worse. The sled moved easily enough over the snow, so I let the soft flakes fall, carpeting the path.

One day passed as I made my way over the plain, wishing with all my heart that Destrian would get well. That day turned into two, then three, then four.

Destrian gradually fared a bit better. He'd said one or two things through his delirium, like water and food. After I gave him what he wanted, he simply drifted back to sleep.

As I walked, dragging my silent companion behind me, I took comfort in the knowledge that he would do the same for me, for the first time thankful for the memories that plagued my mind.

"I am yours until you send me away," Destrian had said, stretching his hand toward me. "In whatever form you need."

Destrian wouldn't have abandoned me.

The silence was oppressive. His shallow breathing was the only sound, the shadow souls having disappeared long ago. Sometimes I saw an odd footprint here or there, as if one or two were still keeping track of us, but the rest had gone on as soon as they'd gotten what they wanted of me. It was only Destrian and me, as it was in the beginning. The only company I had were my thoughts.

I missed his jokes and laughter. I missed the feeling of safety when he walked by my side. I missed the way he smiled at me, the warm light from his eyes and the feeling of being in his arms. How warm and soft and *right* it felt. Why had I deluded myself for so long?

I'd tried so desperately to hold on to the life I'd had. Growing up, I'd molded myself into the image of the chief's daughter, betrothed to his would-be heir, trained to rule Espiria with Luc at my side. Luc, against all of my pleas, left to visit Helena and never returned. I knew it wasn't his fault, but I couldn't keep holding out hope for something that would never be. When Luc disappeared, I was certainly shaken but still regarded myself as the natural successor, just as Father had taught me.

For a year, I'd been living the false ideal that I was important to my clan, that I was needed. I'd ingrained the notion that all I had to do was learn control, and the Morganites would welcome me back with open arms. My life would go back to normal. I would be with my family.

I'd given myself false hope, completely ignoring the fact that my clan had whispered their wishes for my absence for years before that fateful winter when my family had perished along with so many others. By all the gods, my only living family was itching to cast me off to the empire. Why would the presence of my gem change that? I thought I was holding on to the life I'd had, not even realizing it was already gone. I was an outcast of outcasts, without a home, without a family, without love.

I couldn't even wish to return to Solridge. What was there for me but more lies, more manipulations? Though I would see Fin again, and Pedr, and Araceli, and . . . Destrian wouldn't return. Apart from Fin's and Pedr's friendship, Destrian was all I had left. I'd been consumed with worry, holding on desperately to what I had left in my life. But, since my memories returned, I realized that the only person keeping me from plummeting, the only person I had left to hold on to, was Destrian.

What would happen if Uncle Baylin signed me away?

What would happen if my sponsor called for me?

We'd been putting off talking about *us*, but what if the Nightlands were all we had? How many weeks had I wasted, holding back my feelings? If Destrian survived, there was one thing for certain. The moment we left the Nightlands, the world would do its best to tear us apart. My time was running out.

THE GLOWING VINES from the vents had faded when I reached them on the sixth day after the avalanche. The chill of the snow had worked its magic, and I was pleased that I wouldn't have to worry about them, nor the insects that they fed off of. Everything was quiet and still in the frigid night.

We passed the vents without incident, and I was congratulating myself on a relatively peaceful journey when a nefarious chittering carried with the breeze.

I stopped my reflections, my eyes on the sky. A

shadow was circling above me. My hand grasped at a bow that wasn't there. Cursing, I untied myself from Destrian's pad as the bat fluttered overhead, its giant wings beating the air while it tracked us. Soon, it was joined by another, and another, and another, until a veritable colony darted and circled as I watched helplessly from the ground.

My breath caught in my throat. I should've known the quiet was too good to be true. It was only a matter of time before something dire would get in the way of me keeping Destrian safe. But I couldn't give up. I had to give him a chance at life.

Dropping to my knees, my heart racing, I dug into the snow as quickly as I could and wrestled Destrian off the sled and into the hole before covering him with the cloak and furs.

Using my newfound power, I threw up my arms and a blast of lightning streaked overhead. The gems burned in my hands as I directed it to my winged adversaries. A bat swooped down then was hit by a bolt of lightning that blasted across the sky. The current swept through the bat, arcs of light sizzling and dancing over its fur, revealing the bones within its wings. Another bolt flew from my hands and scrawled a line of white light across the sky.

Suddenly, I was lifted from behind. A bat rose with my pack in its clutches. Fear seized my throat, and I screamed as the ground retreated at a horrifying speed. I clutched my pack and clenched my eyes shut.

By all the gods. I was going to die. I couldn't possibly blast the thing with lightning. I would get caught in it, and that would be the end of me. If the creature managed to get me back to its roost with the rest of its brethren, I was as good as finished. I had to do something.

Opening my eyes, I glanced down. Bad idea. The icy plain was a long way away.

I caught hold of the bat's fur. The beast screeched in my face, razor-sharp teeth snapping within inches of my nose, but I landed a wild punch to the mouth. We fell several feet before it regained its flight, me holding desperately on to its fur and trying not to vomit. I hauled myself up, hand over hand, until I was perched atop the bat's back.

The height was dizzying. I clenched my eyes shut, trying not to panic. The bat, sensing it had lost control, was swooping this way and that, trying to unseat me. I plastered myself to the animal's back, holding on tight to the fur and praying that I wouldn't get thrown.

Shakily, I let one hand go. The bat sensed my release and shot to the side. I grabbed fur as the animal rolled and swooped through the air.

After a moment, it flew straight again. Taking a deep breath, I raised my foot and grabbed a knife from my boot. I placed the blade in my mouth and grabbed hold of the bat as it veered to the side.

It straightened its course and I took my chance.

Heaving myself up, I stabbed the back of its neck.

The bat shrieked then gurgled before rolling toward earth with me on top of it. I held on.

By all the gods.

My gems.

Wind.

Frantically, I thought of the wind's path. My gems seared into my hands as something roared beneath the bat and me, spinning us through the air until we landed with a sickening crunch. I bounced off the beast and rolled painfully away.

Broken wings and bodies littered the ground. Staggering to my feet, I turned back to the sky as clouds boiled without my direction. At the sound of thunder and force of the wind, the bats that remained began flapping back to the safety of their mountains. Luckily my pack was close enough to see, so I shouldered it and went looking for Destrian. I came across several bodies of bats as I scoured the dark in earnest.

I was about to pull out Iranoct when I saw a flicker of light in the distance.

It couldn't be.

"Destrian!" I shouted his name, running as fast as I could to the beacon until I saw his outline in the glow.

I'd barely been able to hope that Destrian would get well. My heart, lured at the sight of him, pulsed with renewed vigor. Relief flooded every fiber of my being as tears ran unchecked down my cheeks.

Destrian was alive. He was walking and using his power. I wasn't too late.

Destrian's face was a ragged mess. Behind him, a dark figure swooped in the sky then descended.

"No!" I screamed, reaching toward Destrian as the bat was about to sink its claws into him.

Lightning blasted from my fingertips, hitting the animal with a deafening explosion. The bat was thrown back, slamming into the earth, its body sliding through the snow before it came to a stop.

I hurled my pack to the ground and collided with Destrian, wrapping my arms around him and reveling in the fact that I wasn't dreaming. Though I'd tried to save those closest to me, I'd failed each time. I'd failed Luc, my grandmother, my father, and my mother. But Destrian would live. I hadn't failed him, and that had to mean something.

Power vibrated from my gems as heavy snow drifted around us. Destrian stiffened in my arms, a confused expression on his face. After a moment, his arms encircled my shoulders and squeezed me tightly. The burdens I'd carried with me for days fell away. I couldn't waste another moment.

"I was so afraid," I gasped, looking up at him. "I was afraid that you would be lost to the shadows before I could tell you . . ." I couldn't go on. I couldn't breathe. My courage was failing, but his dark eyes urged me to continue. "I'm tired of pretending I don't love you," I whispered, unable to silence my beating heart. "Can you forgive me?"

Destrian cradled my face in his hands, his weary eyes looking deep into mine. "Since we've come to the Nightlands, every thought, every step, every breath has all been for you."

His lips were on me. Sparks danced over my skin at every point we touched, and I gasped against him. I'd fought this moment for a year, and now that it was upon me, I surrendered completely. He leaned closer, lifting me off my feet, and I threaded my fingers through his hair.

Destrian pulled away, still gripping me in his arms, and leaned his forehead into mine.

"Tell me I'm not dead," Destrian said huskily. "Tell me this isn't all a dream."

I wrapped my arms around his neck. "You're not dead. I dragged you back from the afterlife myself." I made him meet my eyes. "If you take nothing else back from the Nightlands, Destrian Everett, know that you will have taken my heart."

Destrian sighed. "Say it again."

"I love you."

Destrian lowered me to my feet and smoothed my hair back, his fingers hot on my skin. He chuckled. "It's a funny thing . . . I've dreamed of this moment every night for the past year. There was so much I longed to say. But now I can't think of a single thing to tell you, except that I love you, and I would gladly cross every measure of nightmares if it meant that I could walk by your side."

Destrian's lips fell on mine, and I melted into his arms. Heat roared through me as the world stilled. Snowflakes hung in the air, sparkling as if they were stars, illuminating the night just for us.

Chapter 35

DESTRIAN AND I STARED at the night sky as we lay in the nest I'd made of furs and cloaks. My head rested on his chest, his arm around my waist. I'd taken the sled and brought back one of the dead bats. After butchering it, Destrian managed a small fire that we used to cook the meat and eat before retiring for a much-needed rest. Destrian would still need time to heal to full strength, and I was drained in every possible way.

I didn't know how Destrian had healed. I'd simply made sure to give him as much water as he would take, kept him warm, and fed him as best as I was able, given the circumstances. His life was a miracle to me. I couldn't help but wonder if perhaps Imor was looking out for us after all. If, perhaps, he was listening and cared what I had to say.

"How many days have I been sick?" Destrian asked, his fingers playing with my hair.

I squeezed him tightly, relishing his scent and warmth. "At least six. By all the gods, I'd no idea whether you would make it."

Destrian didn't speak for a long time. I wondered if he'd fallen asleep, but then he said, "You've been dragging me behind you for six days?" His voice cracked with disbelief.

I propped myself up on my arm and met his eyes. "What else could I do?" I whispered, my voice trembling as I relived the fears of the past week in a rush of emotion.

Destrian frowned. "Why didn't you leave me?"

"You know why," I insisted, running my fingers over his chest.

Destrian laid his hand against my cheek and traced the imoret marking the outside of my eye. "I knew it was only a matter of time till I broke you down."

I choked out laughter at the unexpected joke. Destrian grinned then raised himself on his elbow and kissed me softly. All my senses drew comfort from his nearness. His smell, how warm he felt when his fingers brushed my skin, the sound of his voice, and the way his eyes looked into mine.

But I broke away, unwilling to harbor any more secrets. Holding everything in was exhausting. "There was a reason it took me this long," I whispered.

Destrian leaned back. "What is it?"

"After my fight with the golgeman, when you visited me in the healing house . . . when Vianne made me forget about why I tried to run away, she took the memory of you and me in the healing house too."

Destrian froze, studying my face. "You didn't

remember that?"

I shook my head. "If I had, I wouldn't have behaved so dreadfully toward you."

Destrian lay back, his eyes back on the sky. "You didn't remember," he repeated, his brows furrowed. Then, he looked at me and smiled. Relief softened his features.

"I'm so sorry about all of that," I said, gripping his hand. "I can't believe how cruel I was."

Destrian shook his head. "Why should I care about the past when the only future I have is with you?"

I never thought I would hope for anything more.

We couldn't rest long. The Bitters loomed on the horizon, and over The Bitters . . . home.

"Unhand me this instant!" Destrian bellowed as I wrestled him back onto the sled. If he'd been at full strength, he would've easily overpowered me, but he was still so weak that it took almost no effort at all. I layered the furs on top of him and tied him down so he couldn't escape.

Destrian complained loudly for the first hour of our journey. Every once in a while, he would jerk at the leathers, trying to get free. But I needed fire more than I needed him walking.

I dragged him for a full day before agreeing to make camp at the base of the first mountain. The night air seemed less chilly as I collapsed next to Destrian and undid his fastenings.

"Finally," he said grumpily, shaking his arms loose from the straps. "You know, I could've traveled at least part of the day."

"No, you need to keep your strength. I don't need you incapacitated because you pushed harder than you should've."

I pulled out a frozen hunk of bat meat and warmed it over a small fire. As we ate, I looked over the vast plain. Though I'd initially worried it would be awkward after the kiss, Destrian acted the same as ever. Resting had done him good, despite his protestations. He was nearing full strength, which we'd need for the remainder of our journey.

"I wonder," I mused, chewing slowly, "how small a storm I could make. Gillius was always trying to maximize my range at Solridge. Here it seems to go on for leagues, but I've never actually tried to temper it to a smaller size."

"It'd be worth it to figure out," Destrian replied. "In case you want just to water a garden."

I chuckled then brushed my fingers off and stood. My gems glowed, and I threw multicolored light into the darkness. It had become so easy. Just a dab of power and the clouds began bubbling and frothing above us. I followed the path of wind that had eagerly begun to blow at my touch. I calmed it into a gentle breeze to carry the snow that blanketed the plain on the path we'd already traveled. Lightning danced at my fingertips, but I pushed it back.

I focused on the gems in my hands first. I suppressed the flow until it was only a whisper of blue light eking from either side. The clouds above were thinly spread across the sky. Focusing through the gem on my brow, I nudged the clouds a bit, pushing them together, tighter, until snow fell once more, only this time, the area it fell on was roughly the size of Solridge and its grounds.

Turning back to Destrian, I smiled, pleased with my progress.

"Can you move it?" he called.

I turned back to my work and concentrated on the wind. I allowed a bit more power through my hands and used it to give the clouds a push.

They shot across the plain with a roar and disappeared over the horizon.

Oops. I hadn't meant to use that much power. Looking back to Destrian, I found him laughing at me. Shaking my head, I tried it again.

And again.

And again.

Until I was exhausted.

"You don't give up, do you?" Destrian asked when I took my seat next to him after working for an hour.

I raised my brows. "How else do you become good at something?"

But Destrian's mind was on other things. He beckoned me to him. I crawled over and rested my head on his arm, watching the small fire.

"Your father was chief. Does that mean you were meant to rule Espiria after his death?" Destrian asked, curling a lock of my hair in his fingers.

"In a way," I said, fiddling nervously with Araceli's good luck key and Pedr's chess piece.

Destrian pulled away to look down on me. "What does that mean?"

I thought to brush Destrian off. I loathed talking about my past after just getting him back. But I'd promised myself that if Destrian got better, if he lived, I wouldn't lie to him anymore.

"Luc, the boy I had back home, would've taken Father's place when he was gone."

Destrian stiffened. But I wasn't going to leave anything unsaid.

"Our fathers were close friends, and they'd always promised each other we would marry. Everything seemed to fit into place, before it all got ripped apart."

"You were betrothed?" he asked, clutching me tighter as if hearing the story would rip me from his arms. He had nothing to fear. I'd held out hope for so long, but in the end, I knew the truth. There'd been hundreds of wardogs plucked from Morgania, and none had ever returned. They either died in the wars or perished farming the Fields of Forgotten Men.

"We'd been promised to each other for as long as I can remember. It wasn't forced on us, you know. It was just understood. Luc was my closest friend and confidant growing up."

"Then he was taken," Destrian finished. "How did the doghunters get him in Espiria?"

I sighed. "He wasn't in Espiria when he was taken. He'd gone to Helena to see the Equinox Festival and never returned. Ferris, my cousin, might've been lost, too, if his father had let him go, but Baylin is overly protective of his children."

"Do you still love him?" Destrian asked, his voice soft.

I met his eyes, knowing I could break him with one word. But I would never see Luc again. Was it wrong to try to find happiness? Who could blame me for trying to pick up the pieces of my life and find some semblance of bliss amid the grief?

"No wardog has returned to his homeland," I said, looking away.

"Is there room in your heart for me?" he whispered, a finger caressing my cheek. "Or will you long for him always?"

"Destrian, you have to understand, I spent my entire life thinking he was who I was meant to be with." All of a sudden, I found it hard to breathe. "What will they say?"

"Who?" he asked, brushing a strand of hair from my face.

"Everyone."

Destrian smiled. "Does it even matter? If there's one thing the Nightlands has shown me, it's that none of that matters. Not to me anyway. Not anymore."

"I don't want this journey to end," I murmured. "How can I let myself hope for us?"

Destrian pulled me toward him. "I'm not like you. I've never felt this way about anyone." Destrian pressed his forehead to mine, our gems meeting in the middle. "I've never felt so sure of anything in my life. You and I are meant to be. I won't let them tear us apart."

He seemed so sure. I wanted his certainty.

My lips met his. I could barely move in his embrace, my bones turning soft as butter. The warmth awakened a gnawing want at the base of my stomach. Destrian held me as though the Nightlands themselves were trying to tear us away. The fire blazed, tossing sparks into the air. Though the Nightlands had been as terrifying as I'd dreamed, I dreaded leaving. Everything was simple in the land of night. It was Destrian and me against the world.

I still couldn't help the feeling that we were hurtling toward a crossroads. One that would leave us irreparably scarred.

Chapter 36

LEAVING THE MAKESHIFT SLED on the plains, we began climbing the mountains in earnest, knowing our journey was near an end. Near the top of the first peak was where I first saw that all may not be well. I was eating next to Destrian when a flurry of snow whipped about near my feet, rising as though something was drawn through it. I elbowed Destrian and pointed before rising to inspect it. My jaw dropped. Gooseflesh prickled over the back of my neck and chills shot down my spine.

Stay had been written in the snow.

My eyes wide, I glanced at Destrian who shook his head.

"You know we can't stay," Destrian said loudly, looking around.

I hadn't even realized the shadow souls were still following us. I assumed they'd stayed in The Dires to celebrate the snow I'd been calling each time we rested. It had been days since we'd seen footprints, but the whispers were unmistakable.

"*Stay!*" This time it was hissed. I jumped, looking around wildly.

A chorus rose around us, each whisper voicing what was written in the snow.

"*Stay.*"

Each word a curse to my ears.

"Let's go," Destrian said, grabbing my pack and leading me over the snow, the voices haunting us.

"Please! You know I can't stay. I must return home," I shouted, pleading with them to silence their haunting whispers. As soon as it began, it hushed until I could hear nothing.

"Thank you," I whispered, slowing my walk beside Destrian.

He stopped me with his hand and made the fireball brighter, illuminating the ground. *Stay* was etched over and over in the snow, as far as our eyes could see. I hadn't thought of how many shadow souls there could be, but from the looks of it, there were hundreds.

We ran, the cold air biting our lungs as we tried to get away from the shadows that now haunted us. *Stay* continued to be drawn in the snow, carpeting our way over the mountains.

Even when I slept, I dreamed of the shadows. They whispered and pleaded for me to stay in the Nightlands until I thought I was going crazy. They sent me dreams, visions of me pleading with them, of the snow whipping around my feet and me frantically hurrying away.

"Go!" I finally screamed, dropping to my knees, my hands on my ears as the whispering continued to invade my thoughts. "Leave me be!"

"Rowyn," Destrian said, kneeling next to me and pulling my face to his. "You have nothing to fear from them. You've given them payment as far as I'm concerned. They shouldn't be treating you this way."

"Maybe if I send more rain, more than they could know what to do with, they would leave me be."

"You could try," he replied, warily eying the darkness around us. "If it doesn't work, at least we know they can't follow us south of the river."

I nodded. "You said before that they are tied to the land. That means they can't leave, right?"

Destrian shrugged. "If it's the same spell I'm thinking of, then yes."

I took a deep breath and raised my hands to call a great storm. Lightning danced over the sky as the rain poured down on the lands to the north. I filled the clouds with all of the energy I could muster, letting it flow through me and be absorbed by the black mass above until I finally drained of power for the first time since I'd gotten my gems. I cut myself loose and collapsed next to Destrian who was rubbing his eyes.

"*Stay.*"

I jumped when I heard the whisper and grew angry.

"If you pester me one more time about staying in this godsforsaken place, I will end the rain right this instant and you can rot in your dry land!" I shouted.

Destrian chuckled to himself.

I didn't hear anything and grew sorry for losing my temper. "I thank you all for helping me get my gems. Destrian and I couldn't have done it without you, but I have to return. We cannot survive here. We are family. Let us part as such."

"*Family*," the shadows said.

"Yes, we are family, and as a daughter, I thank you. Maybe I'll return one day, but till then, I must go. So, thank you, and may the gods bless you."

I waited a moment, surveying the darkness around me, but I heard nothing else.

I breathed a sigh of relief when I realized it was just Destrian and me. The shadow souls had truly gone. My payment to my ancient family was over.

It wouldn't be long till we reached the Last Dusk. Just a few mountains more, and our journey would be over. I was determined to cherish the last few days before life took its hold on me.

We stopped to camp at a rocky outcrop that overlooked the Nightlands to the north. We were a day away from the Last Dusk, maybe two. Destrian and I were stopping to rest more the closer we got to our destination. It seemed neither of us wanted the journey to end. I preferred not to think about what waited for me south of the mountains. In the Nightlands, I'd finally found the freedom I craved.

Destrian was heating up some meat over the fire. I sat across from him, my knees drawn into my chest, silently contemplating what I planned to say to my uncle when I returned to Espiria. Destrian offered to let me stay in Helena for the remainder of summer until I was ready to sail back to Solridge, but I knew time was short before Uncle signed my guardianship away. If it wasn't already too late.

Perhaps I should stay in Helena with Destrian. My heart warmed at the thought. What if I didn't return to Solridge after all and just stayed in the north where I belonged? It would be a welcome change to be away from all the lies and deceit, not to mention the ever-present threat of the empire hounding my thoughts.

"What are you thinking about?" Destrian asked.

Drawn out of my reverie, I raised my head. "Nothing," I muttered.

Destrian furrowed his brows. "I meant what I said. I will protect you when we return."

I nodded. I didn't doubt Destrian's sentiment; I just wondered how helpful he'd actually be. Destrian was used to being from the richest family in the west, which meant he often got his way. I sensed his sway with the empire wouldn't be enough to keep me on the western shore.

"Do you hear that?" Destrian asked, looking over his shoulder.

"Hear what?"

Destrian stood. "That dripping noise."

He was right. There was a soft dripping sound, carried to us through the breeze.

Destrian climbed over one of the rocks that formed a wall to our campsite. The face of Imor looming behind him silhouetted his tall figure. He looked down at me and smiled.

"Come see," he said, kneeling and extending his hand.

I let him pull me up the wall. Standing next to him, I found what caught his attention.

Steam rose from a vent in the mountain. The snow I called had melted, forming a deep pool at a low point in the rocky landscape. Destrian called a ball of fire. The water was crystal clear, revealing nothing but stone at the bottom of the basin.

Destrian stepped toward the water and kneeled, dipping his fingers into it. He looked back up at me and his smile grew. "It's hot."

My skin tingled. I sank next to the pool and tentatively immersed my fingers in the water. The warmth was jarring given the chill in the air.

"I feel filthy," Destrian said, eying the water with

longing. "Do you think we should take our chances and bathe?"

"Bathe?" I repeated nervously, reaching for my hair and feeling how greasy and dusty it was.

Destrian stood and began shucking some of his furs. "You don't have to, but I figure now is as good a chance as any."

I turned away, feeling a blush creep up my cheeks. Not even Luc had seen me completely bare. My fingers shook as I uncoiled my hair and combed through it with my fingers. Something soft hit my shoulder and fell into my lap—his tunic.

"I'll get the soap," I said shakily, dropping the tunic and hurrying down the wall. I pressed myself against the stone and felt the warmth rising in my cheeks. Destrian whooped above me as he splashed in.

I stared at the sky, wondering if I should go back up. I wanted to— there was no doubt about that—but was it wise? It would only give credence to the gossip.

My mind went to the women at Solridge, sold away in marriage at their family's will. What would happen if Baylin *did* sign away my guardianship? Women in the empire had to have a guardian, no matter their age. If marriage was considered, I couldn't possibly hold out hope that I would be given a choice, a rarity in the empire. My life had always revolved around duty. That wouldn't end with a new guardian; the duty would merely shift. But I loved Destrian. I wanted the choice, at least for the moment.

I dug out a comb and soap from my pack and brushed my locks until they were smooth and untangled. Knowing Destrian was naked above me absorbed my thoughts.

"Don't look," I said when I clambered over the rocky bank. Destrian stood in the pool, the water reaching up to his bare chest. His beard made him look more like a Morganite than the Lyrican I'd first met. A gnawing sensation formed at the pit of my stomach.

"On my honor as a noble," Destrian said, turning away.

I pulled off my furs, then tunic, and finally wriggled out of my breeches and underthings.

Rising, I said, "No peeking or I'll stab you."

Destrian laughed. "Is that any way for a lady to speak to a nobleman?"

"Just don't turn around. I mean it." I couldn't help the smile creeping across my face.

"I won't," Destrian murmured, lowering himself in the water.

Standing, I grabbed the block of soap and dipped a toe in the water. Gods bless it. I couldn't possibly resist.

"Still not looking," Destrian said to the boulder in front of him. I sat and scooted myself into the pool, sinking in until the water covered my chest.

"All right," I said, wetting my hair.

Destrian slowly turned, his eyes falling instantly on my markings. Chills crept over my skin and I shivered, but I refused to look away.

A ring of fire blazed around the pool, shielding us from the Nightlands and warming the brisk air.

"You just wanted to see better," I accused, splashing water at him.

Destrian shook his head. "I just wanted to be warm for once."

I sank back into the water, letting it envelop me. The oily soap did quick work of the grime that had collected on my skin and hair. In mere minutes, I began to feel like my old self. Being clean had always given me courage.

Destrian dunked his head back. Though he'd cut his hair quite short before we left, it had grown in. When he rose again, rivulets streamed down his red hair, over his broad chest, then traveled down his stomach and back into the water.

The gnawing sensation grew. In that moment, I wished with all my heart that I were just a simple girl, and Destrian a simple boy, living in a world where we could be together. I wanted him so badly, the fear of being broken if I lost him seemed to melt away. I was exhausted from putting off any form of happiness for fear that I would lose it. It was no way to live, and now that I'd given it some form of priority, it overwhelmed my thoughts with all its desires.

"Soap?" I asked, holding the bar toward him.

Destrian nodded. He curled his hands together as though to catch it, but I refused to throw. Instead, I slowly waded to the middle of the pool, a river of hair trailing behind me.

I saw the longing in his eyes. I refused to look away.

Destrian stepped to meet me, his hand outstretched. I wore my courage like a cloak and held the soap away from him. Destrian lowered his hand again, his brow furrowed. I took one last step and stopped directly in front of him. Raising the bar, I ran the soap over his chest. Destrian turned to stone under my hands as though he were under a spell. I couldn't even feel him draw breath.

His eyes never left mine, even as I worked the soap into a lather.

"Do you ever wish you didn't have power?" I asked. "Do you ever wonder what your life would've been like if you were just . . . normal?"

It took him a moment to answer as my hands moved up to his shoulders. "For a long while, yes. But I haven't felt cursed for quite some time now," he said, studying my face.

"What changed?" I whispered. I always wished I were normal. I hated my power and all the evil it seemed to bring into my life. If I could've given it to somebody, anybody else, I would've done so in a heartbeat.

Destrian finally moved. He sank to my height, letting the soap disappear into the water. Reaching out, he brushed my wet hair over my shoulder. My skin was near singing at his closeness.

"If I didn't have my power, I would never have met you," he whispered, looking into my eyes. "I wouldn't have come here."

I shook my head. He held so much trust in me. I couldn't help but feel it was misplaced. I was cursed from the day I was born. Nearly every person I loved seemed to meet a terrible fate, and it was all because of me. "This journey nearly killed you."

Destrian cupped my cheek in his hand. "How can I regret the very thing that brought me closer to you?" He leaned in, but it was at that moment my courage failed.

"Destrian," I said, pulling back. He stopped, watching me in the firelight as I fumbled with what to say. "I know what people say about me, but . . . I haven't . . . I mean, I've never . . ."

Understanding swept across his face. "Nor I," he said, sinking back into the water. "We don't have to, you know . . . do anything. I just want to be close to you."

But I could see the embers burning behind Destrian's eyes, ready to burst into flame at the slightest provocation.

Ready to roar to life, consuming me in their heat.

I leaned in and tentatively kissed him. Destrian returned it with a hunger and clutched me to him, lifting me from the water as his hands ran down my back. Energy traveled through me as I wrapped my arms around his shoulders.

I would never be unafraid of the fire, but I realized I wanted to burn.

Chapter 37

I WOKE UP TO DESTRIAN'S FINGERS tracing the shadow falcon tattooed on my back. Relishing his warmth, I smiled, tangled in his arms as he curled around me. It had been so long since I'd felt so . . . happy. Returning to the south held no allure for me anymore. I'd have to face my clan and convince them that I was an asset. I'd have to face the council at Solridge, not only about my three gems but about the fact that they had lied about my sponsor to keep me complacent.

Ayastaren would seek retribution for Elias's death, probably as soon as I stepped off the ship at Seaport. The council may have deferred their vengeance, but it was only a matter of time till Duke Roland Lyon came seeking blood.

"What are you thinking of?" Destrian mumbled into my hair.

I sighed. "What will happen when we return." I inspected the back of my hands, running my fingers over the gems. I was already used to them, as if they'd always been a part of me. "What do you think they'll say about my gems at Solridge?"

Destrian captured my hand in his and rubbed his

thumb over the opal's smooth surface. "What can they say? Gillius has been complaining all along that you needed control."

"They may have to send me to my sponsor at the capital after this. The three stones might have sealed my fate."

Destrian propped himself on his arm and looked down on me. "But you don't wish to go to the capital?"

"No, I don't," I whispered, lying on my back to look up at him.

Destrian brushed the hair from my face. I flushed, remembering the heat of his skin enveloping mine. His hands gripping me so tightly I could barely breathe. The thrill of moaning his name into the darkness.

"I won't let them take you," he said, leaning down to kiss me. I wrapped my arms around his shoulders and immersed myself in the moment. I desperately wanted to believe that Destrian could save me from my fate and we could have a future together. If they took me from him, what would I have left?

"Are you ready?" Destrian asked, shouldering my pack and holding his hand out to me. I nodded, taking it and following him up the mountain.

My gems emanated their steady glow, the light rising toward the clouds as they rolled across the sky. I grew weary, stumbling and slipping on the rock purchases as I followed Destrian toward the summit.

Giving my last directive, I sent the thunderheads farther north, just enough away from us not to hinder our journey, before I cut off my power. Dragging myself over the summit, we took one last look at the Nightlands.

Destrian's arm was draped over my shoulder. We surveyed the land, and I couldn't help but think back to everything we'd endured. Every hurt we suffered. Everything we saw. Turning to Destrian, I found him watching me.

He smiled. "Are you sure you want to return?"

"Would you stay with me?" I asked, not entirely joking. The only thing waiting for me in the south was betrayal.

Destrian tilted his head. "Honestly, the Nightlands weren't as bad as I thought they would be."

I pursed my lips.

Destrian laughed. "No, what I mean is, there is so much beauty here. It was a privilege for me to experience."

"You almost died," I reminded him again, "more than once."

"But you brought me back to life," he whispered, kissing the top of my head.

I heard voices as we crested the final peak. Torches lit up the night air, and a cheer rose from a crowd when they spotted us. Their shouts and applause reached my ears as I neared the rope bridge.

"What's going on?" I asked over my shoulder as Destrian stumbled behind me.

"I've no idea," Destrian said, his eyes on the crowd.

I crossed the bridge shakily, letting Destrian go before me. As soon as my foot stepped to the other side, I felt an indescribable burden fall from my shoulders and into the river behind me. I was free. The Nightlands was over.

The crowd looked on in awe and reverence, whispering about my gems. Many backed away as I neared, though the children grabbed my hands and pressed their fingers on the smooth stones. People peppered us with questions and herded us toward the inn. I shot Destrian a worried look and saw he was smiling with ease as we entered the establishment to an uproar.

The light in the inn nearly blinded me. It was moderately lit, with candles flickering on the walls, but Destrian and I had been so used to the dark that the light was overwhelming. Not to mention the noise and the bodies and the indescribable smell of actual food. My mouth watered.

We shoved through the crowd and were finally able to wrangle a room. Ducking through the door, we slammed it shut and I locked the bolt. Turning to Destrian, I was sure my eyes spoke volumes.

"What are they doing here, Destrian? What do they

want with us?"

"They saw the storm begin several days ago. People gathered to watch," Destrian said, discarding the pack. He pulled the bottom of his tunic up and over his head, baring his chest.

I heard a knock and opened the door.

"We are preparing baths for you," a girl said, peering around me to ogle at Destrian.

I ignored her ogling and followed the girl down the hall to a tub filled with steaming water. The kitchen maid helped me disrobe, and I sank into the bath with a sigh of relish. I was warm, I was safe, and by the gods, I was being pampered. The maid washed my hair and poured water over me from a basin while I used their perfumed soap.

When I was finished, the girl toweled me off and held out my mother's blue dress. I smiled, holding my arms up before the aging fabric fell over my shoulders. The dress was loose around my figure, and I felt a pang of regret for how bony I'd become.

After combing my hair, the girl led me out into the hall where our company waited. Destrian stood near the corner around a throng of other young men. His hair was damp, and it looked like someone had given him a change of clothes. The simple white tunic and breeches suited him. His eyes found mine, and he gave me a smile of adoration.

Destrian elbowed his way to me and took my hand. "You look beautiful," he said, rubbing his thumb over my gem. "You should always wear your hair down." I couldn't help it—I glowed.

Someone thrust a goblet of wine in my hand and sat me down at a table to eat. Destrian was pushed down next to me and a hush fell over the crowd.

"Your story, please, let us hear it," the innkeeper said as all of the people sat at attention. Their hands were filled with spirits of all kinds, but their voices were quiet.

I nudged Destrian with my elbow. I was no storyteller. Destrian nodded and began with the sable panther. Several of the women gasped, and a young girl shot me a look of pure admiration, something I never thought I'd see in earnest. When Destrian spoke of the shadow people, I was relieved he didn't mention my connection to them, or to Morius for that matter.

The people were very interested in the shadow souls, and when I mentioned the storms I created were in payment to them, those listening murmured in disbelief.

When the tale ended, I rose and walked through the crowd, sipping my goblet as the warm fire filled me with energy that had been lost since crossing the river. The people parted before me, nervous about the gems and my successful journey. They were much more comfortable with Destrian who spoke easily, laughing over our misadventures.

Someone poured more wine into my goblet just as the innkeeper's son pulled out a fiddle. The night was clear, so the innkeeper lit several bonfires in front of the inn while the crowd of well-wishers flowed outside in their merriment. The fiddle played happy songs, jigs that set my feet to tapping. Although I was normally impartial to dancing, the people seemed to jump and leap beside the fires, letting their spirit guide their steps rather than rules that I could never remember. One of the young men asked me for a dance and I accepted, spinning out with the rest of them and laughing as we switched from hand to hand in a reel.

Switching partners, I found myself face to face with Destrian who grasped my waist with one hand and my palm with the other.

"It's over," he murmured, spinning me in the firelight.

"We still haven't made it back to Helena," I warned, smiling up at him. "Who knows what we could meet on the road back."

Destrian laughed. "If it's another giant creature, I'm going to pack up and move somewhere else. I've had enough of animals trying to eat me."

I giggled as Destrian lifted me off of the ground and spun, making it feel as if I were flying. We spun, stepped, and laughed together in the moonlight until all that remained of the bonfires were a few glowing coals.

WE STUMBLED INTO OUR ROOM and shut the door. Exhaustion had settled in my bones, but the wine had lifted my spirits. I heard Destrian lock the door as I tried to undo my laces. My arms were stiff, and I couldn't seem to get my fingers around the knots.

Feeling Destrian behind me, I froze, holding my breath. His big hands took the laces and worked to undo them. I felt them loosen, then his hands pushed the shoulders of my dress off, and his warm fingers rested lightly on my back. He leaned down, his beard tickling me, and lightly kissed my neck. My skin tingled as an alarming thrill surged through me, starting from my neck and shooting to the tips of my toes.

"Destrian," I breathed, capturing him with that one word.

"What is it?" He wrapped his fingers in my hair, pulling it aside before kissing my shoulder.

We weren't in the Nightlands anymore, but I realized I

didn't care. Turning, I met his eye. "Nothing." I leaned forward to meet his lips. I felt the curves of his flesh through his breeches and my thin shift.

Destrian lifted me, wrapping my legs around his waist, and pressed me hard against the bolted door. My breath quickened as his hands shifted underneath me, his breathing slow and steady.

Could he feel the hammering of my heart through my chest? I was sure he could sense it. It seemed to be pounding so loudly, I could hear it in the room.

The trials of the south loomed before me, but I pushed those thoughts aside, melting once more into Destrian's arms.

The south could wait. It was Destrian and me against the world.

Chapter 38

I T WAS STILL DARK when we awoke the next morning, but the promise of dawn called us. Dawn. I'd waited so long to see it that I sped through packing and stood at the door a moment later.

We hurried down the stairs to the large eating room where the innkeeper's wife was keeping watch.

Destrian spoke to the robust woman as she delivered food to the tables set up in the great room, bartering with him over prices. Exasperated, he nodded and came over to me.

"We lost all of our money with my pack. She wants one of the horses we left. She's already been using it for plowing."

I shrugged. I couldn't argue that the woman deserved some form of payment. Destrian left with our pack to ready the horse, and I wandered until I spied Arda sitting in the corner with a younger woman. I walked over and sat across from the seer with a smile and a greeting.

Arda waved the woman away, who seemed glad to leave the old crone to my care while she went to a handsome young man. Turning back to Arda, I noticed her eyes were even odder in the bright light.

"So, you made it back, I see," Arda said, smacking her lips after she took a sip of water. "I also see the fog has been lifted."

"Indeed, I feel as though I am a new woman. Do you see my paths now?"

"I do. There are many—too numerous to count. Your life is very complicated, my dear," Arda said. Her eyes moved from my forehead to my palms. She seemed to nod to herself in satisfaction. "Tell me about your gems."

"You know, I was always told I wouldn't have to choose my gem; it would choose me. But when we reached the cavern of the opals, I broke the stone into three pieces by accident. From then I couldn't choose, and the shadow souls made me think I had to have three."

Arda was nodding while I talked. "Of course, you needed three. They are as tied to your fate as they are to each other."

"What do you mean the stones are tied to my fate? What is the semblance of the three?" I hoped for an answer less cryptic than her previous ones.

"You are a keystone, Rowyn. Whoever rules you will carry the fate of the world. You must learn to distinguish true friends from enemies if you seek to stay true to yourself. Until then, you will always be a pawn, subject to others' scheming."

"How can I tell friends from enemies?" I asked, almost

stamping my foot in frustration.

"That's simple enough. Enemies are those seeking to bend you to their will."

My mind raced, thinking of Vianne and Baylin, my dreams, and finally, to Destrian. "That means damn near everybody," I muttered, making Arda chuckle.

"You must ask yourself, what do *you* want in life, Rowyn?"

"I don't know, really," I admitted. "I haven't thought much about what I wanted, because I've had to focus on what others wanted from me. I suppose, in the end, I want what everybody wants—to be happy."

"Well, that isn't necessarily what everybody wants. Some seek power, others fame, most seek to better their placement in the world. If they can use you for it, they will."

I nodded, seeing the wisdom in her words.

"I notice you don't speak of helping others," Arda hissed. "Do you not wish to do some good in the world as well? Would this bring you no happiness?"

My eyes widened in surprise. "Well, I suppose I should want that." I caught myself, realizing how callous I sounded. "I mean, I do want that . . . to help others, that is."

Arda scowled at me. "Do you forget the people of Seaport? You ended the drought, saved lives, and helped them begin to prosper once more. You used your powers to help them, and they repaid you with unflinching loyalty. If all you seek is freedom and happiness, then you must fulfill the task Imor put you on this earth to do. You have a duty and a choice. Using your gift to help others is the only road to freedom now."

I was struck dumb at the sound of my mother's dying words being thrown back into my face. Thinking back, I realized Arda's words were true. I hadn't even known I was revered by the people of Seaport until I'd needed assistance the most. Then, they had stepped forward and protected me against the ills of the Lyon brothers. They'd killed noblemen, putting their own lives at risk, to help me.

"I see you have a big decision ahead of you," Arda added, eying me closely with her four pupils.

"Will I at least be able to avoid the empire?"

Arda's face grew serious, studying my gems as she thought. "I've already answered that question," she said slowly. "Imor has tasked you with helping all people, not merely Morganites, my dear."

Arda glanced behind me and waved to her attendant who left the man begrudgingly. I realized that was as clear a dismissal as any. I leaned down and kissed Arda's cheek, but she grabbed the front of my dress.

"The red one loves you," she croaked in my ear, "but the lost one hasn't forgotten."

It took me a moment to register her words. All else left my mind, and a hundred more questions poured forth.

"Luc is alive?" I gasped, kneeling beside her. "Where is he?"

But Arda shook her head.

Suddenly, Destrian was behind me. "Are you all right?" he asked, eying Arda as I rose.

I couldn't look Destrian in the eye. "My apologies, ancient one," I muttered to Arda before following Destrian to the barn.

DESTRIAN AND I RODE AS FAST as we were able, crazed for sunlight. It was several hours before the first edges of light gleamed over the horizon. Arda's words resonated through my mind, along with my mother's words. I was blessed with gems from the north, tasked with helping the people of the realm.

And Luc.

Luc was alive.

Destrian pulled the reins back and slipped down from the saddle, his arms outstretched toward me. With barely contained excitement, he walked me to a cliff that overlooked the road and the eastern horizon.

The first rays of sunlight were pure bliss. I took a deep breath, feeling Destrian beside me as we faced our first sunrise in two months.

Destrian wrapped his arms around my shoulders. I wanted to remember everything about the moment. The beauty of the sunrise and the smell of sweetgrass on the dew-laden air that filled my lungs and seemed to give me new life.

"I'd forgotten what you look like in the sunlight," Destrian whispered in my ear.

I turned to him. "I barely recognize you." Cupping my face in his hand, he bent and delicately kissed my cheeks, leaving me breathless. Then his mouth was on me again. Resting his forehead on mine, he breathed deeply as the soft rays warmed my flesh.

But Arda's words prickled at the back of my mind. Luc was alive and hadn't forgotten me. By all the gods, what could she see in her visions that she hadn't shared? Destrian and I had already crossed a bridge that we couldn't return from. I gazed up at Destrian's face, brushing back his hair before resting my head against his chest. I wished the seer had just kept her damned mouth shut and let me remain happy and ignorant, reveling in the bliss I'd chosen for myself. I refused to second-guess it. I'd made my choice.

We held hands, watching the sun for several minutes

before mounting the horse to continue our ride to Helena. We traveled slower, enjoying the golden light over the mountain peaks. We spent our last evening cozily recounting our experiences with the shadow souls. Without a tent we lay propped up against a stone wall facing the fire. I wrapped my arms around my legs, my long hair blanketing me while I watched the stars winking down on us.

"I can't believe it's over."

"I know," Destrian answered, playing with his dagger. "It feels like our last night, doesn't it, before reality."

"Yes." I leaned back, my mind wandering to what lay before me. "I'm excited to see Fin, to find out how her journey went."

Destrian grinned. "Me too. I hope hers wasn't half as eventful as ours, poor girl."

Reality slammed into me when he spoke those words. He looked at me, embarrassed. Yes, poor girl. I knew she had feelings for Destrian, and yet the journey made it seem as though it was inevitable for us to form an attachment. I hated knowing everyone had been right.

I heard the moment when Destrian fell asleep, his breathing soft and even as he snored quietly next to me.

I needed to speak to my uncle. I hoped to all the gods it wasn't too late to stop him from signing me over to the empire. I knew Destrian thought he could sway his father to speak for me, but I didn't dare hope for that.

No. I had to speak to my clan and prove they shouldn't toss me to wolves.

In the morning I stayed quiet as I flung my pack onto the horse and stepped up into the saddle. Destrian settled behind me, his arms wrapped around my waist. At least he knew when I wanted to remain silent. We rode hard over the rocky landscape toward Helena.

Chapter 39

A S WE APPROACHED THE GATE, I saw them. Another crowd of people craning their heads toward the entrance to the city. When they spied us, a cheer went through the crowd, chanting our names.

Women reached toward us and shouted, "Lady Rowyn! Lady Rowyn!" I held out my hand and a woman grabbed it, kissing the gem. Others followed, pulling my hands toward them. Our furs were being tugged from the pack to be taken as souvenirs. Arda's words blazed through my mind. The key to freedom was helping others.

"See, we're heroes," Destrian murmured in my ear, waving to the people of the city.

I waved back, but receiving excessive adulation didn't come as naturally to me as it did Destrian. I forced a smile, though, and waved both my hands, trying not to meet anyone's eye.

All of a sudden, a troop of city guards rode over to escort us to the citadel. I recognized the young men, Asher and Karl, from before. Their eyes widened when they saw my gems, and though I waved a hello, they averted their gaze. It almost felt like they were scared of me. I didn't know what to do as people continued to scream my name.

Finally, we reached the gate to the castle and were ushered inside by the troop. Riding into the ward, we dismounted.

People spilled from the castle doors, the consul included. They slapped Destrian on the back and shook his hand, welcoming him home with honors. I was mostly ignored, which was a relief. At my elbow I saw the maid, Daisy, bidding me to my room. I followed her and she took me inside, set my pack near the bed, then left me in blessed peace. The only thing I could think to do was collapse on the bed and sleep.

I DREAMED IN A BODY that was not my own.

"He is here?" I gasped, clutching my throat. "He lives!" I ran to the door and pulled it open. A man in rags stood there. He regarded me with weary eyes.

"It's you," I breathed, frozen to my spot.

The man reached toward me and I caught his hand. On the back of his palm, embedded into his flesh, was a black opal. I kissed his fingers, crying with joy, trying to convince myself that he wasn't a ghost. But his eyes held no joy. Only sorrow.

"The others are lost to the shadows," he said gruffly.

"The journey was far too perilous. We shouldn't ever have attempted it."

I shook my head. "But you're alive. All thanks to Imor, you are alive."

"My lady?" A woman stepped from a doorway and curtsied. The bundle in her arms waved a tiny fist and wailed softly. "Little Mony is hungry. Can you feed him?"

I turned back to the dark-haired man who only regarded me with grief.

"I'll stay long enough to regain my strength," he grumbled, "then I'll be on my way."

"Wait, Morius, please!" I pleaded, grabbing his arm.

He shook his head. "I'd already heard from the people in the street. They worship you, as I did. How can I take their queen from them?"

"I waited for you," I said, my voice rising in anger and regret. "Weeks turned into years. I thought you were lost. I didn't think there was any way you could survive."

Morius cupped my face in his hands and looked into my eyes. "I'm not entirely sure I did survive, Helen. The better part of me died in the north. But I know I can't stay here. I can't bear to see what might have been."

"Please don't leave me again," I whispered, tears coursing down my cheeks. "Please stay."

But Morius shook his head. "I've met with the Woltari. In exchange for me calling rain to the land, we'll have peace. Our people will thrive here. But I'm sorry, I can't stay. To stay and watch you with him would be like a dagger to my heart. It will end me, and there is still some good I can do in this world."

He let go of my face and turned to stride down the hall and out of sight.

I sank to my knees, clutching my heart and weeping. I knew then that my life would be forever tainted with mourning what might've been.

I OPENED MY BLEARY EYES. She was in the room with me. I felt her.

"You've been sending me memories, haven't you?" I whispered to the room.

There was no answer.

Walking to the window, I looked out to the city below. People crowded at the gate, trying to get a glimpse of the heroes who'd just returned. I shuddered, training my eyes instead to the sky, the sun glowing brightly over the treetops, not a cloud in sight.

My eyes went to my reflection in the window. Somebody stood behind me.

I peered over my shoulder thinking it was a servant,

but there was no one there.

Looking back to the reflection, I saw the hooded figure, and my mind went back to my dreams. It was her.

She gazed at me with her empty black eyes, the hood hiding her face in shadows. I didn't know what to do, but I knew I had to know why she haunted me.

"Helen?" I asked, staring at the reflection of the first queen of Morgania.

The woman lifted her hands to her hood and peeled it off, revealing her face. I recognized the lines in her cheeks, the long and regal neck. I'd seen the face so many times before at Espiria, the lines etched in stone. It was the girl, the woman from my dreams.

I looked over my shoulder and saw nothing, just as before. Turning back to the window, I jumped when I noticed she'd moved closer, standing right behind me, almost to my ear.

"Why do the shadow souls call you the faithless one? How did you come to be?" I asked.

The specter leaned in, her lips touching my ear, and she whispered, "Morius."

"Morius turned you into a shadow soul?" I asked, watching her reflection. The specter nodded slowly. "You waited for him but still he came too late. Are you warning me of Luc?"

The queen shook her head again. She leaned in. "You

were what might have been."

She was gone like a wisp of smoke. I strained my eyes over the glass, searching for her face, but to no avail. "Why do you haunt me? What must I do?" I almost yelled. By all the gods, what did that mean? How was I what might've been?

"Rowyn, what are you going on about? I've been looking all over for you," Destrian said, standing at my open door and glancing around my room warily. "Who were you talking to?"

"No one," I said, then forced myself to laugh. "Do you often barge into ladies' rooms without knocking?"

At least Destrian had a sense to look contrite, if not for all of a moment.

I changed the subject. "How is your father? Happy you're back, I warrant," I said, going to sit on my bed.

Destrian smiled. "He is well, and yes, happy I returned unharmed. I told him of how you saved my life. How you brought me back from the dead and, you know . . ." Destrian shrugged. "Carried my almost corpse for six days. He should leave you be now that we're both indebted to you."

I gave Destrian a queer look. "How are you indebted to me? You saved my life as well, if you remember."

Destrian merely shook his head. "I came to tell you Father is holding a feast tonight to celebrate our return. He's already invited most of the great people in the city to attend. You, of course, being our guest of honor."

"A feast? I suppose I could pull out my dress once more." I forced a smile. I was already tired of crowds and being gawked at. Did helping people mean I had to be put on display at every moment? "I admit the food has more draw to me than the company."

He laughed. "No matter. They want to hear our story. I shall come to escort you to dinner as soon as the sun sets. Daisy will help you get ready if you don't mind."

"Thank you," I said. "I shall see you at dusk then."

"At dusk," Destrian repeated, bending to kiss my cheek before leaving me to my thoughts.

I sat on the comfortable mattress to think. Queen Helen was trying to tell me something. That was what the dreams were about. I just didn't know what. I wondered if she was like Arda, warning me about Luc.

But I made my choice. I wasn't the same girl who fell in love with Luc in Espiria. I'd changed, and I'd made my choice in the Nightlands. I was in love with Destrian. Nothing would change that. I was tired of going back and forth. I was tired of putting off planning my life for something that would never be. Luc was my past. Destrian was my future.

Chewing on the inside of my cheek, I wondered what exactly Destrian had told his father. Would the consul speak for me if Uncle signed me over to the empire? Did

I want to be indebted to the consul in that way? Looking around the room, I realized I had to make a home for myself somewhere. Why should it not be in Helena, the home built by my ancestors? Then again, I believed Destrian overestimated his ability to sway the consul in my favor.

Or, I could ride to Espiria and convince Uncle not to sign me away. Convince Urdua and Conal and the rest of the clan to speak for me. Perhaps, I could even convince them to find peace with Helena and Consul Colman. I'd lost hope in the Nightlands, but since our return, seeing the people's reactions to me fed the burning need to finally find acceptance at home.

Chapter 40

I FELT THE SILKEN CLOTH of the dress and balked at wearing something so fine.

"Lord Destrian requested it," Daisy said in a voice that hinted I didn't have a choice. "It's one of his sister's. 'A lady of such renown shouldn't have to grace my hall in rags,' he said." The girl stood, waiting expectantly for me to disrobe.

I looked down at the blue dress my mother had embroidered so long ago. It was true it was worn down in the elbows and didn't fit right anymore, but still, I couldn't bear to think of it as a rag. I remembered watching Mother as she laid the pieces of cloth with care. I even helped her position some of the black design.

"So be it." I sighed as she helped hoist my old dress off, then pulled the silky black cloth over my head. As she tied the laces, I admired the sparkling silver stars that decorated the skirt. At least Destrian knew what would look good on me. Daisy made small adjustments, pinning the length of the skirt delicately so I wouldn't trip and embarrass myself at dinner.

While she worked, I gazed at my reflection in the mirror. My black hair lay in curls down my back and over my shoulder. I was paler than ever before, thanks to my nighttime adventure. It was taking me a while to get used to seeing the opal on my face. It stood out starkly against my skin and made my blue eyes seem small in comparison. Luckily, with my black hair, the gem somewhat complemented my features. The dark veins of color seemed almost to glow within, accenting the reds, yellows, blues, and greens laced throughout the circular stone. Turning my head, I realized some might say that it made me look frightening. I figured that wasn't so bad. There were people I wished would fear me.

Daisy finished setting my hair over my shoulder and left me in peace to wait for Destrian. He'd made it clear he would escort me to dinner. While I waited, I fretted, trying to come up with arguments to use against my clan. I was a "lady of renown." I'd conquered the Nightlands. They should be proud to call me their daughter and should welcome me to their hall once more.

I sighed gustily as I gazed out the window at the darkening sky and continued to ponder my impending future.

Belatedly, I remembered I didn't have any weapons on me. I searched the room but didn't see anything offhand to take. I figured I would probably be all right, seeing as how if anyone really irked me, I could simply blast them out of the window with lightning. The thought lifted my spirits somewhat.

There was a knock. I opened the door to Destrian. My heart skipped a beat. He'd dressed up in a rich black overcoat with a fine white shirt underneath, made of a thin, soft material. He'd finished his look with plain black breeches and fine black leather boots with silver cuffs ringing the top. It set off the color of his hair, I supposed, like a flame in the night. He'd trimmed his beard so the red framed his face. He looked quite handsome.

A small crease gave way between his eyes. "I figured that would look good on you," he said gruffly.

I was able to draw up a small smile, though I had no idea why I was suddenly shy. "Thank you. I had nothing else to wear. It was very thoughtful and kind," I said, all the while feeling guilty for taking offense earlier.

Destrian swept the curls off my shoulder. His fingers traced the Morganian rose blossoms tattooed over my neck. "I just want you to look the part. Our story is being told even now across the Lyrican Empire. The two sorcerers who braved the Nightlands and came out unscathed. We have to start acting the part." Destrian held out his arm for me to take. "Are you ready?"

I eyed him with apprehension. We were back in the real world. It wasn't just us anymore; it was others, always watching, always judging.

Destrian was proving to be very insistent, though. He continued to wait, this time wiggling his arm a bit to get my attention. I sighed with a grin and placed my arm dutifully under his.

As we entered the great hall, the guests around the richly decorated tables stood and applauded. Destrian bowed deeply to the assembly. I took my cue from him and curtsied, hopefully with grace. At least I didn't wobble. Thank you, Araceli.

Consul Colman still eyed me with obvious distaste, but he chose to ignore me as a page pulled out my chair and I sat on Destrian's other side.

After we were settled, the servers brought in food and the tables became heavy under succulent roasts of pheasant and goat. Destrian talked animatedly to those around him. Everyone wanted to hear of our adventure, but I couldn't bring myself to join in. Many people eyed my gems with wonderment. I didn't know if there had ever been a sorcerer with three gems before. The people's fear ensured their reverent silence toward me, for which I was thankful.

I silently picked at my food, half listening to Destrian. He was trying to include me in the storytelling, but I proved obstinate. I wasn't in the mood for it.

"What's wrong?" Destrian whispered after a bit. Under the table, he took my hand in his. I cast my eyes to the hall and noticed that most of the assembly watched him. Heat rose to my cheeks and I gently pulled my hand away.

What was going through their minds? Several of the ladies' eyes had narrowed, and they whispered to each other behind their hands. I began to tremble, my hands clasped in my lap.

"Nothing, I'm just tired is all."

Destrian frowned but moved on with his story, drawing the ears of those who'd wandered. I continued to nibble on a fruit tart Destrian insisted I try while wishing myself back in my comfortable room, sprawled out on the delectable feather bed, and away from all of the people's stares.

Destrian turned to me again after the table was cleared of the platters and whispered, "There is a surprise for you."

I wrinkled my brow. Destrian should know by now I hated surprises. "What is it?" I asked as I eyed the room. Pages were moving some of the smaller tables to the walls to clear a large space in the center of the hall. I turned back to Destrian, my temper rising hot. "I'm not dueling again, Destrian. How could you expect it?"

Destrian looked puzzled. "Duel? Of course not, Rowyn. Dancing. There is an accomplished musical group in town. We'll have dancing tonight." Destrian's face changed again to one of delight. "I demand your hand for the first one."

Belatedly I felt my face fall. I didn't know which I

counted worse, dancing or dueling. I wished I'd remembered to slide a knife in my sleeve. At the very least I could have used it to threaten Destrian to let me alone to my thoughts. But, I could tell by Destrian's body language that he would insist. I fixed my expression with a gracious smile as I nodded.

"Of course, what was I thinking? Dancing would be wonderful."

Destrian's eyes lit up. My heart fell.

I should be overjoyed to be back here with Destrian. He was paying me every respect, spoiling me even, but it only made me absurdly uncomfortable. I couldn't stand all the stares. It reminded me of . . . home.

It was as though I'd been punched in the gut. Wherever I went, whatever I did, others would always be staring at me, judging my behavior, whispering behind their hands.

I watched the small group of musicians take their place at the back wall. Destrian helped me out of my seat and led me to the cleared floor. I could barely control my trembling hands, my eyes darting around the room as the hiss of whispers filled the hall. The consul was staring at his goblet.

The musicians played a song of medium tempo, thankfully not so fast I would lose my step and not too slow to give the people in the audience the wrong idea.

Albeit I wasn't good, I was certainly tolerable. At least, you couldn't say I was embarrassing myself. Destrian of course moved with the grace of someone who had spent years dancing in courts of all sizes. Hopefully some of his skill would rub off on me and make me look good. Maybe then the others would stop staring so.

"I know you're not just tired," Destrian said as we moved together. By now other couples had joined the dance, so I didn't feel so on display. I circled around Destrian in time to the music before he took my hand again and we lunged forward, waltzing in step around the hall. "What is it you are not enjoying?"

I looked away as we separated. This time he circled me as I clapped in time to the music. When we connected once more, I tried to answer in a way that wouldn't hurt his feelings. "I just hate all of the attention."

Destrian nodded but didn't seem convinced. "I thought all ladies loved attention."

I frowned. "Not all ladies have received the attention I have in my life."

When the dance ended, he asked if I wanted to do another, but I shook my head. "I think I'm ready to retire, Destrian. Please, continue without me," I murmured, trying to pull away from his grasp. His hand didn't budge.

"No, before you go to bed, I want to show you something," he whispered back, leading me through the doors.

As soon as the doors closed, I let out a sigh of relief. It was just Destrian and me once more.

"What is it?" I asked as Destrian pulled me down the hall.

"A special place here in Helena. You'll like it, I promise," Destrian replied. I heard excitement in his voice as he let go of my arm, trusting me simply to follow him. We had reached a small winding staircase. Destrian held out his hand, and I took it while we climbed the staircase together, winding our way up a large tower. Out of the arrow slits in the wall, I saw small lights from the city below.

Destrian stopped at a door at the top of the stairs. Pulling a key from his overcoat, he fitted it into the lock and turned it deftly, pushing the door open with a creak before he smiled down at me and led me through the threshold.

It had to be the highest tower in the citadel. It rose above all others, the wind blowing in warm gusts, picking up my skirts and curls and tossing them in the breeze. The dim outline of the mountains surrounded the city. The stars twinkled at me, a mirror of Helena below, which made the view all the more breathtaking. I walked to the edge and looked down. People walked through the streets, but I couldn't hear their shouts, their voices carried away by the wind.

The wind. It carried with it the sweet scent of

morwood pine. Behind me, a tree grew out from the top of the tower, its needles rustling as the sweet perfume seemed to wrap me in its embrace and make me think of only one thing.

Home.

"How does it survive here?" I asked, marveling at the beauty of it.

Destrian found my hand and drew me down on a bench beneath the tree's fragrant branches. "It's always been here, since when the castle was first built. They brought it to honor the forest where they'd come from."

"By all the gods, I had no idea," I whispered, overwhelmed by the height of the tree, the beauty of the view, the fact that he'd thought to bring me to such a perfect place of solitude and wonder.

"What's this?" he asked, his voice wavering as he touched the single tear that had rolled down my cheek.

"It's just so beautiful." I sniffed.

Destrian hesitated then laid a soft kiss on my lips. My heart hammered, and the heat from him swept through me. Energy seemed to ricochet within, bouncing around until I was a mess of jangled nerves. I didn't think I'd ever get tired of kissing that man.

Destrian broke away. "There is something else," he whispered, his voice so close to my ear that his hot breath flowed over me. I shivered as gooseflesh rose over my skin. "I made you a promise, and I mean to be a man of my word."

Below the bench, he drew out the book that I'd wondered about for the past year. The history of the last reigning family of Morgania. Destrian slid his finger under a shred of silk that marked a spot near the back of the book and opened the page.

"Here is why I kept it from you," he said, meeting my eyes. "I didn't mean any harm by it. I'm sorry I didn't tell you sooner, but you have a right to know."

I looked down and gasped. The marking on my neck, the Morganian rose blossoms that symbolized my mother's family, they'd been carefully drawn in the book.

"What does this mean?" I murmured, tracing the lines of the blessing.

Destrian looked down at his hands. "I've looked into all the records from The Fall. You know that Lyricans are vicious conquerors. We were successful in our conquests because of how diligent we were at wiping out the royal families. They wanted no heirs popping up to cause trouble later and had no qualms with murdering youths." His face flamed red, as though he was ashamed. He well should've been too. His family had been part of the conquest, though it was over fifty years ago.

"They stormed Helena and left no prisoners. Theramon, his wife, oldest daughter, and three sons were killed. But his youngest daughter wasn't there. Though she was assumed to have been killed, her body was never found."

"What was her name?" I asked, clutching at my heart.

Destrian met my eyes. "Her name was Rhoswyn."

I choked. Rhoswyn was my grandmother's name. She hid behind the shroud after the invasion with a host of other Morganites. Was she the lost daughter of Helena? Would she have been heir to the throne?

I'd been named for my grandmother. Realization hit me like a galloping horse. That meant my father was descended from Morius, and my mother was descended from Helen and Philemon I. Queen Helen's words swam back into my mind. *You were what might have been.*

I couldn't breathe. I couldn't think. I couldn't stop my racing heart. What did it all mean?

Destrian grabbed my trembling hands and kneeled before me, his eyes on mine. It took me a moment to realize that his hands were shaking too.

"Stay with me," he murmured. "Helena is where you belong. We'll find a way for you to gain mastery. You can come into your own, have freedom, whatever you want. Just let this be your home. Help me unite Morgania—Lyrican and Morganite, together as one."

I gasped, tears streaming down my face. Was that what he'd planned all along? Was that how he would convince his father? A voice in the back of my mind wondered if the argument would work. A much louder voice hoped it would.

"Don't answer now. Just think on it," Destrian said, brushing the tears away. Here he was, giving me his heart, and all I could do was sit and cry.

"I'm sorry," I whispered, clutching the book to my chest. "I just feel so overwhelmed right now. I'm so sorry."

Destrian sat next to me. "Think of it, Rowyn," he urged. "Just think of what it could be like, here with me. Your family could be honored guests in our halls. All this could be yours," Destrian said, sweeping his hands to the city lights flickering below.

"Your father," I managed to gasp, but Destrian knew what I meant. His father would have nothing to do with me.

"Don't think of it. I'll make him love you, as I do."

Destrian's smile made me hope against all else. My resolve failed me and melted into a dream of what could be. Perhaps whoever sought to control me from Lyrica would lose interest or be swayed by Destrian's offer to let me be. My family would be free to return to the city in peace and live out their days in the comfort the citadel of Helena could afford them.

A pleasant fantasy to say the least, but I knew it would

never come true. Whoever had their grip on me in Somme wouldn't release me so soon, not without getting their payment in return. Destrian's father, although so easily dismissed by Destrian, was none too small an enemy. He wouldn't want me as a daughter, no matter how much his son stood by me. I was sure Consul Colman would find a way to end Destrian's relationship with me if we became betrothed.

Despite all of our trials, I yearned for hope. I'd lost my entire world when I met Destrian. I'd been so used to the darkness, I didn't see him holding out his hand, urging me back into the light.

Destrian turned my face to his, tracing an imoret with his finger. "Say you love me," he whispered, leaning down and kissing me tenderly. The scent of morwood pine curled through the air as his warmth enveloped me. The city below mirrored the stars' sparkling lights, and I didn't feel adrift anymore. It felt as though I were home.

Chapter 41

"I MUST TAKE YOU to your room," Destrian whispered. It was getting late. I couldn't focus on one thing. I could be a lost heir of the Morganite throne, passed to me through my mother and grandmother. I could stay in Morgania with Destrian and take my place among my people once more. Perhaps I'd been worried for nothing and there was hope for me after all.

My heart sang within my chest, lifting me with its song until I was floating on a cloud, drifting through the castle of my ancestors. The castle where I belonged.

We stopped outside my door, the book clutched in my hands. I leaned against the wood, looking up at Destrian in the torchlight. He glanced around the hall, making sure no one was around, then leaned a hand against the wall next to me and kissed me lightly.

"Just think on it," he whispered once more, running his fingers over the gem on my hand.

I couldn't help but beam at him. I was about to invite him into my room but thought better of it. Destrian didn't expect it either. He kissed me softly on the cheek then walked slowly down the hall, turning once to smile at me before going around the corner.

I sighed. Bliss seemed to fill every fiber of my being. I ignored the cruel thoughts that tried to voice their reasons why it would never work. I wanted to believe that, in a world that had always been cruel, I had a chance at happiness.

I stepped through my door and shut it softly behind me, locking the bolt with a smile, still remembering the way Destrian's lips felt.

"There's the girl," a voice said from the corner.

It took everything I had not to scream. I dropped the book and clutched at my heart, my back against the door as I surveyed my room.

"What in all the gods?" I asked, my eyes adjusting easily to the darkness. I recognized the voice but couldn't place it.

An old, stooped figure sat on a chair in the corner. His yellow gem glowed, emitting little bursts of light that danced over his dark wrinkles.

"Lord Obi," I exclaimed, rushing to him. "By all the gods, what are you doing here?"

Lord Obi's hand reached out shakily and grabbed mine, crushing my fingers in his grip. "You poor girl, you don't see."

"See what, Lord Obi?" I quickly lit a candle on the table next to him, my fingers fumbling with the tinder. "How did you get in here?" I couldn't find the courage to question *why*.

Lord Obi grumbled, though it seemed he spoke to the wall. "They think I don't have my powers; they think I'm weak, but I'm strong enough for this. I used to be a league leaper, you know. I've been all over the world."

I frowned. "League leaper? I thought you could move objects and such." I'd seen him often enough in the library. He could move books or candles with his mind. I hadn't seen much more from him, though, and I'd never heard of a league leaper.

Lord Obi grabbed my hand again. "He is coming for you. I came to . . ." Lord Obi noticed the gems on my hands. "Yes, good girl. It might be enough. It might work, if you're careful."

I leaned down, my hand on Lord Obi's knee, and tried to look him in the eye. "Lord Obi, what are you talking about? How did you get here? Where is Pedr?"

Lord Obi glanced to the door. "She told me to give this to you." He pulled a delicate silver chain from the folds of his robe and held it out to me.

I took it from his hands and studied the silver filigree. Little clear stones sat in casings every inch or so that sparkled in the candlelight. "What is this?" I asked, looking back at Lord Obi.

"I don't . . . I can't . . ." Lord Obi trailed off then placed his head in his hands.

There was a small scroll attached to the chain by a ribbon. I carefully undid the knot and rolled out the parchment, squinting in the candlelight.

This is the Girdle of Ephema. Keep it with you always, hidden under your clothes at your waist. Never let another soul see it. Never say anything to anyone about it being in your possession. I wish I could do more, but at least this will keep you from being turned into a complete puppet.

"Lord Obi," I said gently, placing my hand back on his knee. "Who sent this?"

Lord Obi shook his head. "I can't tell you."

I frowned at the old man. Why, in all the gods, had the person who sent the Girdle of Ephema, sent Lord Obi of all people? Who traveled all the way from Solridge with him? It seemed cruel to put the man through such an adventure.

A knock sounded on my door.

Lord Obi's eyes widened. He clasped my hands in his. "Remember girl, tell no one, and wear it always."

Suddenly, the pressure from his hands disappeared, and he with it. "Lord Obi?" I looked to the corners of the room, but he wasn't there.

By all the gods, where did he go? I even looked out the window to see if he leaped from the sill, but the window had been closed and there was nothing below. He simply disappeared.

The knock sounded again.

"One moment!" I shouted, pulling the Girdle of Ephema over me. Though Lord Obi was not of sound mind, he'd said that someone was coming, and it played right into my greatest fears. If Lord Obi was right, then the girdle would protect me. If he was wrong, then nothing would happen. Hopefully it wasn't poisonous, and Lord Obi wouldn't get lost finding his way home.

As soon as the chain settled over my hips, it disappeared into my clothes. I could feel the weight of it but saw nothing. Frowning, I touched it. I barely felt it. Somehow the hard edges of the chain and stones softened against the fabric.

I ran to the door when the pounding became more agitated and opened it. I was surprised to find Old Bernard shoving his way into my room. The elderly knight who had befriended me a year ago was absent at dinner, and though I wondered why, I'd been so absorbed with everything else that I hadn't thought much of it.

Bernard slammed the door shut. Startled, I stepped back, wary of him.

"We missed you at the feast," I said, pulling my sword belt down from the wall. I couldn't help but send a silent thanks to Imor that I didn't invite Destrian to my room.

He would probably take issue with the number of men traveling in and out of it. "Are you well?"

If Bernard caught my fear, it didn't show. "My lady, I need ye to come with me. It's urgent that someone speaks with ye."

"Who?" I asked, hackles rising on the back of my neck. "Who needs to speak with me in the middle of the night?"

"My lady, please. Just trust me. I promise no harm will befall ye." Bernard reached his hand out to me.

I hesitated but belted Iranoct's sheath to my waist and followed. He led me through several corridors and into a room bare of everything but a roaring fire, a table, and two chairs. At the sight of who filled one of the chairs, I froze and refused to move farther, palming Iranoct's hilt.

"I won't hurt you," the consul said, waving his hand to the seat across from him. Bernard nudged me forward. I glared at the two of them.

"What is this about?" I asked, my voice tinged with anger as I took the chair across from the consul. Destrian had said he would speak to his father. Perhaps the consul was prepared to buy me off in exchange for rejecting his son. After all, he was the wealthiest man in the Western Empire. I sat back, prepared to rebuff his offer. What surprised me was Bernard's involvement. I thought him better than that.

The consul held his head in his hands. His eyes were

red, and the puffy bags under them looked as though he hadn't slept in weeks. Nodding to Bernard, who moved to stand by the door, the consul took a deep breath.

"My son says you saved his life." He looked across the table at me. I found my revulsion for the consul rising in my throat. I hated how his eyes were like Destrian's. It was unkind to his son. "I first want to thank you for that. I thought for sure . . ." The consul took a deep breath. After letting the breath out, he dropped his hands and picked up his goblet. "I was convinced he wouldn't return."

I raised my eyebrows. "Is that all?"

The consul glared at me then shook his head. "No, I would like to apologize. I'm sorry for how I've treated you in the past. I'm sorry for the things I've done."

A part of me said to accept his apology. Destrian was going to try to convince his father to allow us to be together. I should be doing my best to stay within the consul's good graces, however I'd gotten there. But I also couldn't ignore the torment my clan faced from the consul over the years. I couldn't ignore the last rattling breath of my grandmother. My mother's dying words before the fever and boils took her. The way he squeezed my throat, ready to push me out of the window before we'd left. I had pride after all, and the consul wouldn't have bid me from my room in the middle of the night simply to apologize. There was more than he was letting on.

"Apology not accepted," I said, rising. "You murdered my family and half the clan. I didn't save Destrian's life for you. It was because Destrian's life was *worth* saving. I would have left you to die in the Nightlands and not looked back."

The consul stood as I turned to the door. "Wait, that wasn't all I brought you here for."

Finally, we were getting to the point. I faced him. "What do you want?" I demanded.

"You saved my son's life. I know you owe me nothing, but all the same, I must ask you to save it again."

My heart faltered as ice shot through my veins. Destrian's life was in danger? Whatever I was expecting, it wasn't that. "What are you talking about?"

"Please, have a seat. I must explain."

I glanced to Bernard, who nodded. Stepping back to the seat, I sank into it. "You'd best get to the point."

The consul nodded and leaned forward. "The Ayastaren army has marched on Espiria."

A buzz filled my ears, soft at first, but it rose until it roared through my mind. Ayastaren was marching on Espiria. Duke Roland Lyon wasn't going to wait till I returned to Solridge to enact his vengeance. He was going to reach me where it would hurt the most. My family. My home.

"How are they able to get in?" I asked, trying to calm

my racing heart. Only one thought was able to sneak through the clamor in my mind. I had to return home.

Consul Colman shook his head. "They aren't trying to break through the shroud. They plan to turn the mountain to rubble."

Anger swelled and I began to shake. My gems emanated a multicolored light that I had to temper. Lord Obi had just warned me that someone was coming for me. I wondered how the Girdle of Ephema would protect me against the Lyons. "I must warn them," I said, getting ready to rise, but Bernard put his hand on my shoulder, keeping me seated.

Consul Colman leaned forward. "They've been warned, I swear to you."

"How?" I asked, unable to control the tremor in my voice. I had only one thought. It was my duty to help my clan. I couldn't let them fall to the wolves.

"That girl of yours," Bernard said above me. I looked up. "Ena. I snuck her to the Espirians before the army closed in. She's there now."

My eyes widened. "You sent Ena! She could be killed!"

Bernard held up his hands. "They wouldn't have trusted me. I had to send one of their own for the warning to be taken seriously."

I looked to the consul, my eyes narrowed. "Is that all?" I asked, itching to steal a horse and be on my way. There wasn't a moment to lose.

"No," the consul said, his eyes on the table. "My son says that your uncle is planning to sign your guardianship to the empire. He asked me to intervene and accept the guardianship for Morgania."

Nervous energy ricocheted within me. My leg bounced. I was running out of time. "I knew you wouldn't accept guardianship, and I'll be honest, I don't want to be tied to you in that way," I said, still palming Iranoct's hilt, ready to be gone. I had yet to see what his words had to do with Destrian.

The consul nodded. "I might have considered, except for the present circumstances. I won't hold you here, though it's my duty since Espiria is a rebel faction. I've already risked sending Ena as it is. But you understand that if you go, if you intervene with Ayastaren's attempt to bring your clan to justice, I won't be able to speak for you. Even attempting it would brand me as a traitor. It would put my land and titles at risk. You will be on your own."

"I've never asked for your help, Consul Colman, though I appreciate you warning the clan." I glanced at Bernard and nodded. "I won't lower myself to ask for it now."

The consul sighed. "But you know my son will follow you. He will want to help."

"And why shouldn't he?" I asked. "The Espirians are

your people, too, whether you like it or not."

"I know this," the consul growled. "But he must not follow you. It's a trap."

Of course, the Ayastaren army would attempt to trap me in my homeland, to drive the dagger where the damage would be deepest. But, the expression on the consul's face gave me pause. "What do you mean?"

"Duke Roland has been eying the wealth of Morgania for years," the consul explained. "He tried to gain it through a union, but I refused to marry Onora to his son. I wouldn't have ever seen her again. Now, he's trying to take it by force."

"How do you know this?"

Bernard cleared his throat. "We have spies in the Ayastaren court. When Seith returned home, he spoke at length about Lord Destrian's partiality to you. That was all the duke needed to make his move."

I couldn't wrap my head around what they were saying. "How can he take Morgania by force if he marches on Espiria? Wouldn't it make more sense to come here, to Helena?"

Consul Colman shook his head. "Duke Roland is using Espiria as a guise to stamp out a rebel force. He sent his son, Teilo, to explain the terms, and he's already sent news of his plans to the emperor. They demanded to bring the traitors to heel, and since Duke Roland is my overlord, I wasn't to stand in their way. If Destrian fights against the duke, if he's involved in any way, it would be an act of treason."

Heat burned my cheeks. "He would lose the consul-ship," I breathed. "Everything he's worked for."

Consul Colman shook his head. "He would lose his life. If Destrian moves against him, Duke Roland will execute him, imprison me, then assign his son, Teilo, as Consul of Helena."

I gripped the black skirts with white-knuckled hands as all feeling left my body. I'd thought the Nightlands held the greatest dangers I would ever face. I had underesti-mated the nobles of Lyrica, even when Marc tried to warn me. Destrian executed?

The bliss I'd felt earlier was replaced by a sick sense of dread. I'd known it was too good to be true. I'd known that our happiness would be brief when we were returned to the cruelty of the real world. I just wished I'd had more time.

But I had a duty to my clan. It didn't matter that they were going to cast me off to the empire. I couldn't let them feel the sword of Ayastaren. I had a duty and a choice.

If I didn't help them, if I stayed in Helena with Destrian and let them be slaughtered, I would never find the hap-piness I so desperately sought. Our love would be tainted by the souls of the dead. I was the daughter of Morius and

Queen Helen. My place was fighting beside the other Morganites, not hiding behind the walls of Helena with Lyricans. I had a duty and a choice.

"Have you told him?" I asked.

The consul shook his head. "I know my son. He'll follow you regardless, no matter what I say."

"I can't stay here. I can't abandon my people." Tears welled up in my eyes, but I refused to cry in front of the consul.

"I know, but please, Destrian must not know," the consul urged.

"How will you keep him from finding out?" I asked.

"We were planning on riding through Helena in the morning. We can be gone for most of the day, which will buy us time. If Destrian finds out, I'll chain him." The consul rubbed his knees with his hands. "Bernard has a horse saddled for you in the ward. You can leave tonight."

"He will hate you for this," I said. The consul had warned me, so I thought it only fair to warn him. "If you chain him, Destrian will never forgive you."

The consul nodded. "I know, but I'd rather him hate me than be dead."

I met the consul's eyes. "Thank you."

"An eye for an eye," the consul said before taking a drink from his goblet and hanging his head. Destrian had always said that to me. All hope of happiness seeped out of me at the consul's words. Destrian and I could never be. If I rose against Ayastaren with my family, it would forever taint my name. But I had a duty and a choice. I loved Destrian, but I had a duty to my family. My choice, yet again, was made for me.

I strode through the door and followed Bernard back to my room. In short order I changed into a tunic and breeches, my weapons strapped to me, and the pack slung over my shoulder. I sat at the table, grabbed a piece of parchment and a quill, then wrote, letting the tears I'd been holding back flow down my cheeks. I didn't know what I would say when I began. I let the words move through me. I couldn't leave Destrian without saying goodbye. Not after everything we'd been through.

When I was finished, I held it up to the candlelight.

Destrian,

A duty to my family and clan has called me away from Helena before I could tell you goodbye. Despite my best efforts, I know that there are things that have been left unsaid. I know that you are probably angry with me for leaving without an explanation, but I have to honor my duty, no matter the cost.

Our time in the Nightlands now seems like a dream. Despite the terrors, despite the fear, I will always treasure the memories that I had there with you. I didn't think that I would be able to love again, but I was happy to be wrong.

To the question you asked me to think on; were it a different world, one like the Nightlands, where it was just you and me, the answer would be yes. I would have been honored to stay in Helena with you. But I've known that this world is not a one where that's possible. You must fulfill your duty to your family, and me to mine.

Do not follow me. If something were to happen to you because of me, I would never forgive myself. Do not doubt my love. I wish, with all my heart, there were another way.

Yours truly,

Rowyn

I wiped my eyes on my sleeve and folded the parchment. Walking to the bed, I placed the note on top of the black dress that I'd delicately lain out. I approached Bernard who fidgeted by the door, his eyes on the hall.

"When he finds out, please make sure he receives that," I said. Bernard nodded then led me out of my room and down the hall. It was the middle of the night, and the corridors were dark with dancing shadows in the sparse torchlight.

"Nobody else knows of this, but it won't be long before Ayastaren's presence is known," Bernard whispered as he led me out to the ward.

"Thank you for all you've done for us," I said, grabbing the old soldier's hand. "Keep watch over Destrian, and don't let him do anything foolish."

Bernard squeezed my hand and kissed my cheek. "Yer a fearsome lass. Make 'em regret it."

I tossed my pack onto the horse's back and jumped up. I looked over the castle. There was so much left to say, but I'd finally run out of time.

Bernard slapped the horse's hindquarters, and we galloped out of the gate and into the night. The feeling that I was being hurtled down a dark abyss came over me again, and I seemed to be dragging Destrian and everyone I loved with me.

Chapter 42

I RODE HARD, THE NEED to reach Espiria spurring me forward. I couldn't fool myself. It was my last chance to stop my uncle. My last chance to prove I could be an asset to them, rather than a curse. It was a chance to earn my place among my brethren.

I loved Destrian. I dreamed about finding my place in Helena, but that didn't mean I wanted to lose my true home either. The place where I'd grown up. The place of happy memories and a childhood of love with my family, before they were gone. I had yet made things right with my clan, and now they were trying to cast me off. I had to show them I was one of their own.

I considered Lord Obi and the mysterious gift around my waist. The Girdle of Ephema lay under my clothes. Though it was loose to get on, it seemed to shrink around my hips. I wondered again at its use. Was it a shield against weapons? How would it protect me against the Lyons?

I used my gems to call a thick fog to settle on the road behind me, just in case anyone decided to follow.

When my horse tired, I snuck into a merchant's camp and stole one of theirs as they rested, leaving my travel-worn animal in its stead. I ate only the small rations that

Bernard had thoughtfully packed in the saddlebag. I refused to sleep. I only had one thing on my mind: I had to make it home.

When I grew close to Espiria, I turned off the road and wove through the trees, alert to every sight and sound. Haplin found me sneaking through the brush near the western edge of the shroud. He stepped from the trees, his staff in hand, and stopped my progress with one look.

"What are you doing here?" he asked, his eyes flitting to the gem on my brow.

"I've come to help," I said, dismounting. "How is everyone?"

"Ready for battle," was his only reply. He walked with me through the mist until we emerged on the other side to a city in chaos.

Men and women darted about, shouting as they made preparations for battle. Our blacksmith was overseeing several of his apprentices sharpening swords at their wheels. A stack of quivers leaned against the side of the mountain entrance, full of arrows tipped with the gray feathers of shadow falcons.

"Why have you not tried to escape?" I asked, turning to Haplin.

Haplin refused to look at me. "Escape to where? This is our last stand."

"No," I said, grabbing Haplin's arm.

But Ferris was at my side, his eyes wide. "Rowyn," he said, grabbing my hands. His fingers brushed the gems and he looked down. "By all the gods," he breathed, eying the gem on my face. "What happened?"

I tried to smile, but I didn't have the energy for it. "Quite a bit, but we'll have time later to talk. I must speak with Uncle. What does he have planned for the Ayastaren forces?"

Ferris dismissed Haplin and led me through the throng of Morganites who stepped out of our way. The whispers began. The whispers that seemed to follow me, no matter where I went. Narrowed eyes darted in my direction then averted their gaze as soon as I met their stares.

"Rowyn!"

Ena ran out of the throng, her arms filled with long-bows. "I told them you would come!"

I threw my arms around her, blinking back tears of relief. "Oh, Ena, you shouldn't have risked so much in coming here. It's far too dangerous."

Ena shook her head. "Bernard got me through right before Ayastaren got here. The army has been camped on the western road for the past day, but now that you're here, Ayastaren won't stand a chance."

"But your family," I whispered. "They wouldn't want you to risk it."

Ena looked down at the bows. "I've always wanted to

feel as though I'm a part of something. Besides, you're my family now too. They understand that."

"Thank you for warning the others," I said, leaning in to hug her again. "I'm so lucky to have you."

Ena blushed. Taking the bows, she left me with Ferris who had watched Ena hurry into the fortress, his eyes on her every step. When he turned back to me, my brows were raised.

"What?" Ferris asked, seeing my look.

I shook my head. "Don't break her heart."

"I didn't say anything," Ferris sputtered, then added, "So she's not betrothed or anything?"

"No," I said sullenly, sending a prayer to Imor for Ena's safety. Though the thought of Gillius still made my blood boil, I couldn't fault him in his choice of Ena as my companion.

Uncle Baylin stood with Urdua and Conal, his arms crossed over his chest as we approached. I stood before them silently, my back straight and sword ready at my waist.

"What are you doing here?" Uncle asked finally when the silence had dragged on for too long.

"I've come to help," I replied, palming Iranoct's hilt.

"Haven't you done enough?" Uncle Baylin grumbled, sweeping his arm to the groups of Morganite fighters. "We are in this mess because of you! Yet again, Morganite blood will be spilled because of *you!*"

Boiling rage bubbled within my gut, but I pushed it back. "It's not because of me. It's because Duke Roland is trying to take Helena for himself."

Uncle Baylin raised his brows then glanced at Conal, whose narrow eyes regarded me with skepticism. "How do you know this?" Conal asked. "How do you know if that's what he truly seeks?"

Of course, he would ask me to explain myself. By all the gods, how had I gotten myself into such a mess. "Consul Colman told me," I said finally. At least I had the grace to meet his eyes when I said it.

Conal's face turned scarlet. "Yes, you and the Everetts have been getting along quite well, I hear. News of the heir of Helena returning in good health and *blissful* spirits reached us yesterday."

By all the gods, news traveled fast in this damnable empire. I met his gaze and decided to lie. "The opportunity never presented itself to . . . to end his life," I said, still trying to stand tall.

Conal shook his head. "You expect us to believe that? This was our chance, Rowyn. This was our one chance to retake Morgania for ourselves. You let those silver-tongued nobles lure you into believing that you're their friend. You've let the wolves in, and we'll all be consumed!"

"No, I haven't. I'm here, ready to battle. I can help, so let me. What do you have planned?"

Throughout the conversation, Urdua had remained silent. She was wearing her own battle gear, the great sword of her first husband strapped to her back. Urdua met my eyes and nodded as if deciding something. "The Ayastaren forces have taken the road from Darkport. Teilo Lyon leads them."

"Have they offered terms?" I asked, already knowing the answer.

Urdua shook her head. "They sent one of our lookouts back with a missing hand and a message. We are traitors to the empire and hereby sentenced to death."

I bit the inside of my cheek. "I need someone to show me their camp."

"I will," Ferris offered, stepping forward.

Uncle Baylin eyed his son. "No," he said firmly.

"Father, you can't keep me safe forever," Ferris protested. "At some point I'll have to live."

Urdua turned to Baylin. "If you have any desire for Ferris to rise as chief after you, he must be seen as a leader, not cowering in the shadow of his father."

Baylin glared at her, gritting his teeth and mulling her words. "Fine," he said. "Ferris can show you the camp, but make no moves against them."

We nodded and turned away, me breathing a sigh of

relief. I didn't know what I expected in my return to help them. I didn't realize they blamed me for the entire mess. But wasn't it my fault? The only reason Ayastaren was making a bid for Helena through Espiria was because of me and the role I played in the death of one of the seven sons. At least that was the excuse they were using. I'd hated Elias in my time at Solridge. He was an evil bully. When he and the youngest brother, Seith, came across me in the market, they beat me within an inch of my life. It wasn't my fault that the city folk from Seaport came to my rescue and killed Elias in the brawl.

Of course, Duke Roland would blame me for everything. I'd seen it during my awful trip to Ayastaren a year ago. The way his eyes crawled over my body. The fact that he'd sent soldiers to my room to kidnap me and hold me hostage in Ayastaren. Then, the final act of evil, the family he'd hung on the wall as a warning of who was in charge of the Western Empire. I never forgot that message.

But he'd gone too far. He'd come to my home, in a land he had no right to be in, cloaked in the guise of bringing a clan of traitors to heel. Treason or not, I wouldn't let Ayastaren harm my clan. He would have to go through me and all of the new power I brought with me.

"Has Ayastaren made any further moves?" I asked as Ferris and I walked through the crowd of Morganites toward the shroud.

"They've tested the shroud several times—lost a dozen men."

I nodded, slipping silently into the mist and staying quiet until we emerged on the other side and found the coast clear. Leaves cast dappled sunlight over the forest floor. The shriek of a shadow falcon hunting at dusk reached my ears. I watched the bird circle the trees before it soared away over the mountain.

I hadn't realized how much I'd missed home until I was actually there. Still, I wished Destrian could see it with me.

"Rowyn," Ferris whispered, pointing through the trees. A band of soldiers in Ayastaren livery rode straight toward us. Ferris and I ducked behind the trunk of an enormous oak.

I patted Ferris's shoulder and pointed up. He nodded.

Wrapping my fingers together, I leaned down. Ferris placed his foot in my hands, and I launched him up to grab the lowest branch of the tree. Its boughs were full of leaves, offering perfect cover. In my experience, soldiers from the empire rarely had the sense to look up. I doubted Ayastaren men would be any different, especially given the lack of trees in that barren land.

Ferris's hand came down and hauled me up next to him. We climbed higher until the leaves and shadows of the coming dusk concealed us from the ground.

"Message said the sorceress is back in Helena," one of the men said.

"Lyon said she wasn't due back till the frost," another mumbled, his horse snorting.

"What is wrong with you two? Afraid of a mere girl?" a gruff voice asked. "Teilo Lyon will show her a thing or two about what it means to fear."

The men trotted off. It looked as though they were making rounds around the shroud in case any Morganites tried to escape.

I met Ferris's eye. "It may not surprise you to know that many people fear me."

Ferris snorted. Of course he knew that.

But I went on. "We can use that fear. If I spook them, we could scare some away."

Ferris clutched the longbow, running his fingers over the smooth wood grain. "You need to get close enough to see?"

I nodded.

"Father said not to do anything, but if it's not an all-out battle, if it's just magic, I don't see anything wrong with it."

I rolled my eyes. "Did you want to go ask Uncle Baylin's permission?"

Ferris scowled. "Of course not. Let's go. This oak is part of the tree passage."

The Espirian tree passage was one of our secrets. The empire was used to doing battle with armed men on horseback, but we Espirians used the forest itself as our means of passage, our cover, even our weapons. Since horses were a rarity in our clan, we moved through the woods, using a tree passage made up of a series of large hardwoods that we affixed with knotted ropes and long, wooden hooks.

Ferris and I climbed higher. We reached the hook and rope of the tree we were on. I lifted the hook above me from its holster and squinted, trying to find the rope in the tree next to us. There, it hung beneath a thick branch. I used the hook to draw the rope to us, then hung the hook back in its place. Swinging through the air, I landed on the sturdy branch of the other tree then tossed the rope back to Ferris, who did the same. We moved quickly through the forest, swinging silently through the canopy while evading the Ayastaren guardsmen who prowled below. Before long, we reached the edge of the road where a large encampment of Ayastaren soldiers sat to dinner.

I scanned the troops. There appeared to be over a thousand soldiers. Not much for a full-scale attack, but the Espirians numbered only in the hundreds. I couldn't see the dreaded trebuchets, but they would be fiercely guarded and prone to early attack. The Lyons were evil, not stupid.

The sun had already fallen behind the mountains,

casting long shadows over the road and giving Ferris and me plenty of cover as we spied on the soldiers.

"What are you going to do?" Ferris whispered, his eyes on the campfires flickering through the trees.

"Like I said, I'm going to spook them." I balanced carefully on the branch and rubbed my hands together. I pushed the nagging weariness and hunger to the back of my mind and concentrated on the soldiers below.

The sorcerers at Solridge might've been able to explain away my traitorous actions before I'd become a student, but if I rose against Ayastaren, I'd be sealing my fate. Not even the Articles of Clemency, the law stating that accidental bouts of magic from novice sorcerers couldn't be tried as crimes, would be able to save me. But I'd already decided to help my clan, treason or no. I would think about the empire's consequences later.

But what about the consequences I would have to face with Destrian? Would he be able to forgive my choice? Would I ever see him again?

My gems glowed. Clouds swelled above us, blocking out the stars and the face of Imor. The wind picked up, gently at first, making the campfires in its path flicker. I wanted the soldiers to know that the storm was unnatural. I wanted them to feel my presence. Following the clouds, I made sure to push them away from Espiria's mountain so as not to hinder my clan's preparations, then turned my attention back to the sky above. I painstakingly fed my power to the clouds as they grew to enormous size, layering on top of each other.

The soldiers had yet to notice my work. Good. Let them enjoy their nice meal. Let them think we were just a vagabond band of heathens. They would rue the day they judged me as just another infidel, powerless in the hands of the empire. I wanted to show them just how wrong they were, empire's laws be damned.

"Ferris, you better hold on to something," I murmured, feeding every last drop of power I had to the sky. The black masses of clouds were so close they touched the treetops.

Ferris braced himself against the tree. I was going to try to keep the worst of the storm across the road, but my control wasn't what it could be . . . yet.

I unleashed the tempest. Bolts of lightning slammed into the earth, threading through the soldiers' camp with great explosions of energy as sparks and arcs of light danced around the men. The wind roared, ripping my hair from its braid and flinging it behind me. Deafening thunder shook the ground, and the screams of men filled the air.

The soldiers scrambled to put out their fires. Horses pulled at their tethers, their eyes bulging as they tried to flee. Several got loose and galloped away. Tents rolled in the gale and went spinning into the trees. I sent another bout of lightning to dance over their campsite with its blinding light.

Then, the rain began. It was a veritable downpour. Within moments, everyone was soaked. I gave one more nudge to the wind, forcing the air to cool. I wanted them absolutely miserable.

"Rowyn!" Ferris shouted in my ear. "We should go!"

Ferris's face was shrouded in fear. His eyes were wide, watching the men pointing to the sky and waving wildly toward the trees.

Yes, they knew it was me.

I cut myself off from the storm and sank to my knees on the branch, trying to catch my breath. I'd forgotten I hadn't really eaten, nor slept. Exhaustion screamed through my muscles, raging against me.

"Let's get out of here!" I shouted to Ferris, who was all too ready to follow my orders. He swung away, then tossed the rope back to me. I caught it and leaped from the branch. As soon as my muscles strained at the weight, I knew I'd overdone it. The rope slipped from my hands as I fell to the ground.

Chapter 43

THE CRACKLE OF A FIRE woke me and I squinted groggily. Though I was wet, warmth spread over me like a blanket as I investigated my unfamiliar surroundings. I was in a canvas pavilion. The thunderous beating of rain pelted overhead, and my hands were bound behind a wooden pole erected in the center of the tent. It meant only one thing—I was a prisoner.

The rope scratched my wrists while I struggled with the fetters. In a moment of relief, I realized my knife was still hidden in my sleeve.

"So, the all-powerful sorceress," a voice said. Teilo and Seith Lyon sat in chairs on the other side of the fire. The brothers shared the same chestnut brown hair and watery gray eyes. Seith had lost weight since I'd last seen him. His eyes were shrunken and glassy, as though he'd had trouble sleeping for the past several months.

Teilo looked just as I remembered. His hair was pulled back from his hawk-like face, his eyes glittering with malice. Unlike Seith, he was able to grow a beard and trimmed it close to his face in the Lyrican style. I narrowed my eyes at his smile. Not only had Teilo killed a woman's family in Ayastaren, but he'd also murdered Pedr's sister, Thedra.

Teilo was evil in human form. I wanted to blast him where he stood, but when I tested the reserves of my magic, I found it all but empty.

"You should kill her now, brother," Seith whispered, his eyes on me.

Teilo scowled. "You heard Father. We need her alive." He turned back to me. "So Lord Destrian comes to her rescue."

"Destrian isn't coming," I snapped. "He may not even know I'm gone yet."

Teilo shook his head, clicking his tongue. "I highly doubt that. He'll be here, just as Seith predicted. He sees things, you know. Things that have not yet come to pass."

I glanced at Seith. "I never heard that before."

Seith glowered. "I saw that you were going to be a plague on my family from the minute you stepped into our lives."

That made more sense than it didn't. I always wondered why Elias and Seith gave me so much trouble at school. I'd assumed it was because I didn't act like the other girls. Then again, would Elias be dead if they hadn't tormented me for the better part of a year? It seemed they had both sealed their fate on that one.

But I hoped he was wrong about Destrian. I wanted Destrian as far away from Espiria as I was able to get him. If he died because of me . . . no. It was too painful even to think about. Destrian had to live.

"I don't like this. We don't know what she's capable of anymore," Seith whined. Teilo looked back at Seith, and I feverishly worked the knife in my sleeve loose.

"I'm fairly certain the storm was the best she had. You said it yourself that she just calls rain and snow. Besides, no sorcerer has an unlimited source of power," Teilo snapped. "Obviously she's tapped out, or she wouldn't have fallen out of a tree!"

Damn him, he was right. I could feel the power start to return, but it was coming so slowly, there was barely anything for me to work with. I wondered how long it would take me to regain my strength. Hopefully not long.

But the Lyons thought I was defenseless without my powers. That's why they didn't thoroughly pat me down. If they had, they would've found more than Iranoct on my person. The sword hung on a hook by the entrance of the pavilion, right over Teilo's shoulder. Because I was a woman, he assumed I was defenseless without my magic. It was a mistake I didn't intend to let him repeat. I finally had the knife in my hands and began to saw clumsily at my binds, my work blocked from the Lyons by my body and the fire.

"How many men did you lose to the storm?" I asked. I wanted to keep them talking. If I could do that, I would have a chance to escape.

Teilo sneered. "That was a neat little trick you pulled. Sadly, the men know they have more to fear from me if they desert than some sniveling whore from the wilderness."

"You Lyons are probably experts at whores," I scoffed, "given that nobody would sleep with you free and willing."

Teilo didn't like that at all. He unfolded himself from the chair, stepped forward, and punched me across the face. It took everything I had to keep the knife hidden behind me as pain shattered my senses and a ringing filled my ears.

Teilo squeezed my cheeks between his fingers. I tried to focus on him, but he was a fuzzy blur. He leaned into my ear. "I've heard it gets quite cold in the Nightlands. I bet Lord Destrian kept your bed warm in the north." He breathed deeply, inhaling the scent of my hair. "If I were a betting man, I'd wager he grew accustomed to seeing every little inch of you."

Teilo Lyon would die for his words. I was sawing eagerly now. Teilo gripped me tighter as if my movements were an effort to lean out of his grip. I was nearly there.

Seith glared at me over his brother's shoulder. He didn't look as comfortable as his brother that they held the upper hand. Seith might've been smarter than I ever gave him credit for.

"I will enjoy every moment of killing you," I whispered,

meeting Teilo's eye. I fully planned to avenge the family from Ayastaren, Thedra Tore, and the fact that he would try to use my clan as pawns in a feckless power grab.

"Brother," Seith hissed, his eyes on me. "I don't think this is worth the risk. She's bound for the empire."

Teilo glared at Seith. "You saw this in your dreams?"

Seith turned to me with a smirk. "You should see what the gods have in store for you at Somme," he sneered. "If you think we Lyons are the worst the empire has to offer, you're in for quite a surprise."

Teilo grinned. "Perhaps, after we finally take Morgania, Father will put you in my charge instead of sending you away. Would you like that?" Teilo let his hands drift down to my neck, running his thumb over my throat. "Now that you've grown accustomed to filling a nobleman's bed, I would hate to deprive you of the pleasure."

"If you so much as touch me, not even the gods will be able to help you," I retorted. I made a show at readjusting my bonds while cutting the ropes. "I don't need Destrian's help in defending myself."

Teilo laughed. "When Morgania is mine, I'll be sure to hang all the fallen Espirians on the walls of the castle. I think it will be quite the poetic end, don't you? Given our history?"

Anger seared through me, giving me strength. If anyone deserved death, that person was Teilo Lyon. I spit in his face, then wrenched the bonds loose, breaking the last few threads of rope. Hurtling myself into Teilo, I sent him flying into the fire where his tunic caught flames.

I turned on Seith, who threw up his hands and shrank back into the corner. "Please," he said, "I wanted none of this. I told them it was folly!"

I grabbed Iranoct and darted into the rain. A group of soldiers hunkered beneath a canvas cloth, trying to stay dry. When they saw me, their eyes widened and they reached for their swords. I had only a little bit of power, so I used it to make my gems glow.

"Come near me, and I will turn your bodies to dust," I said, letting the colored light envelop me. The men stood stock still, their hands in the air.

I ran to the trees, toward safety. Hoofbeats splashed behind me, but I didn't turn to look. I slipped over wet brush and went careening into the mud. Scrambling up, I sprinted through the trees, trying to find my way through the pounding rain. Breath tore through my lungs, and exhaustion dulled every muscle of my being, but I couldn't stop. I had to get away from Teilo Lyon's sneering face.

A horse grunted behind me. I dared a glance over my shoulder and saw two Ayastaren soldiers riding after me.

Despite all my protestations, my body was slowing. It had given me the last that it had, but it wasn't enough.

A cry of pain rang through the forest.

I turned and squinted through the rain. One of the men had fallen from his horse, an arrow in his chest. The other soldier looked at his companion then scrambled for the crossbow at his side. Two arrows whistled through the air. The man slumped forward on his saddle, unmoving.

Ferris swung down from the trees and kicked the soldier off his horse.

"Come on!" he shouted.

I ran to the other horse and mounted. We galloped through the forest, not slowing until we finally reached the shroud.

"THE ARCHERS MIGHT BE ABLE to hurt their ranks here," Uncle Baylin said, pointing to his little stone totems on the map. I picked up one of the tokens. It reminded me of Pedr. Instinctively, my hand reached to my necklace, to the queen-shaped chess piece that hung there.

Conal eyed the clan members around us. "They're here on a blood errand." His eyes paused on me before darting away. "They won't care about taking prisoners, so don't expect mercy if you're captured."

I could tell my chances of Conal speaking in my favor were slipping away. The next morning's battle was my only chance to prove to him that I was worth fighting for. What Morganite would send their kin to the empire? If my uncle did cast me aside, what awaited me across the Ballerian Sea?

Queen Helen's words drifted through my mind. *You were what might have been.* Dare I tell my family what I'd found out in Helena? The clan had known that my grandmother Rhoswyn had been a wealthy girl outside of the shroud. But I didn't think anyone suspected she'd been heir to the throne of Morgania. Arda's words held me back from telling them. People would try to use me. Why would my clan be any different from anyone else who sought to bend me to their will? Would it even make a difference to Uncle Baylin? He was more likely to use it as one more arrow in his quiver of reasons why it was risky to keep me in Espiria.

I tuned my ears back to Uncle Baylin, trying to concentrate on the plan, not even realizing his eyes were already on me.

"How can you help?"

I looked from Urdua, to Uncle, and finally, to Conal, whose disappointment had been etched on his face ever since I'd returned and he found out Destrian lived. "I can provide us cover. The danger is the trebuchets he's brought. He could do quite a bit of damage to the mountain if those go unchecked. I think the cavalry unit should try to break through their ranks here and attempt to get to the trebuchets. Once we break through, I might be able to help bring them down."

Uncle Baylin glanced at the rest of the council. "What do you think?"

Everyone nodded. It didn't escape my notice that I stood at one side of the map, completely alone save Ferris. The others cast distrustful glances in my direction, their eyes on my gems. My clan had feared me before. Now it seemed that fear was matched by complete distrust. I couldn't even blame them. I'd left for the Nightlands with one of our greatest enemies and orders that Destrian not live. I returned with Destrian in tow and three gems. I was surprised the shroud even allowed me on the path anymore. Yet, there I was on the eve of battle, ready to fight side by side with my fellow Morganites.

My heart sank at the thought of Destrian. Had Bernard given him my note yet? Had his father gone through with his claim of chaining him? I prayed to all the gods the chains would hold. With Destrian safe and out of the way, I could focus on what my clan needed. I hoped, one day, he would forgive me for leaving. Perhaps I would get another chance at his love, once everything settled down.

But a nagging thought came to my mind. Would the empire even let me live after such a display of treason?

Ferris turned to me as the rest of the clan members filed

out. "Get some rest," he said, his hand on my shoulder. "Tomorrow we fight for our home."

Chapter 44

WE LEFT BEFORE DAWN. Ferris brought me a bow, and I grabbed a quiver of arrows from our weapon's cavern, which was nearly empty. What few horses we had were saddled. Morganite men and women had assembled with quivers and bows slung over their shoulders, or newly sharpened blades at their sides. Urdua, flanked by Pria and Ena, ushered the children inside the safety of the mountain fortress. But the fortress wouldn't be safe for long.

Espirians silently swooped through the trees, me with them, making our way through the forest canopy. Nearly every warrior of the city was coming, including Uncle Baylin and Conal.

My throat tightened. The plan, so detailed before, became a blur in my mind. We'd never attempted such a large assault. They outnumbered us more than two to one.

But we had the forest. I pushed back my fear. I let the anger at the Ayastaren invasion feed my energy.

They had no right to come to our land. They had no right to use us to get to Morgania. They had no right to use me to get to Destrian.

I fought for Destrian's life as much as I fought for the

lives of my clan members. I was a daughter of Queen Helen and Morius the Black. I would not let myself fail the people I loved.

Finally, we reached the road. I stood next to Ferris, looking over the lines of Ayastaren soldiers standing ready for battle. They wore plate armor, which was enough of a deterrent against our longbows to give me pause. We would have to shoot strong, aim for the neck and face, to break through their lines. The wind picked up, stirring the purple flags. They snapped to attention, the golden griffon of the Lyon family looming over the soldiers below.

Silence descended on the forest. The only sound was the wind whistling through the leaves as everyone settled into position. I looked to my left and right, marking where other clan members stood, their eyes dark, ready for battle. Several glanced at me then averted their gaze.

I clutched the bow. Morganites would die in battle. A battle we faced because of me. Though I fought for Baylin not to forsake me, I couldn't help but feel that it was the final straw for my clan members. There were too many lives laid at my feet. I began to second-guess myself. Perhaps Baylin was right. I seemed only to bring death to those I loved.

A sinking feeling began in my gut as I watched the soldiers. I couldn't dwell on it anymore. If I were to be of any use to my clan, I had to have courage.

Ferris and Conal were perched on another branch of the tree I'd hidden in. Someone hooted a message. The guards below heard the noise and murmured among each other, their wide eyes staring into the forest. Shields were propped in front of them, overlapping to provide cover to the man on their side. It didn't escape my notice that Ayastaren's soldiers were well trained, but these men were used to battle on an open field. They were woefully underequipped for a battle in the forest.

Ferris held up his hand. I took the bow off my shoulder and nocked an arrow, waiting patiently for another signal. My eyes crawled over the Ayastaren camp, searching for Teilo Lyon. He was nowhere to be found. It wouldn't surprise me if he watched the battle from the rear, letting the other soldiers do the fighting for him. But the only thing keeping the Ayastaren soldiers in Helena was fear of Teilo Lyon.

The sound of groaning wood filled the air. There was an ominous thud, followed by a loud whistle. I looked up at the sky. A large black ball soared high over the trees, trailing black smoke. The ball slammed into our mountain with an explosion of fire.

The trebuchets were up. Several more balls were flung into the air, each blasting into the side of the mountain, catapulting rock into the shroud.

Ferris's first arrow whistled through the air. The rest

of us followed. I shot until my arms grew weary. We picked off soldier after soldier until they were too densely packed to shoot through the shields. Their archers stayed low since our height advantage and the trees offered us excellent cover. Even with those blessings, one of the Morganites on the tree next to me fell with a scream, an arrow pierced through her shoulder. A long pike shot out of the row of shields, and the woman's scream was abruptly cut off.

I sent a couple of shots toward their cavalry unit, but the mounted soldiers were too far away. The element of surprise was over. It was time for me to move.

Another whistling ball soared overhead, followed by a sickening crash. The sound drove me back into the forest.

I swung through the trees. Passing a large branch, I grabbed the ax thrust into my belt and swung it into a piece of rope, severing it. An enormous ball of spikes careened through the branches, carried by a rope attached to a tree farther on. The ball hurtled toward the line of soldiers, along with several others that had been unleashed along the tree line.

I didn't have time to watch the effect of the traps. There was no time to waste.

I swung and leaped through the trees until I reached Uncle Baylin. Scrambling down the branches, I dropped myself onto my horse and grabbed the reins. Ferris and

Conal manned the trees with the archers, but I had Baylin and Haplin with me. Urdua remained in Espiria, taking charge of the clan who couldn't fight.

Uncle Baylin eyed the other Morganites. Judging by his darting eyes, he was nervous. Baylin never was one for battle. Haplin glanced between Uncle and me, waiting for orders.

I wished that Destrian were with me. He'd fought alongside me against so many terrors in the Nightlands. It felt as though my right hand were missing. But I dismissed the selfish thought and instead sent a silent prayer to Imor. *Don't let Destrian follow me. Keep him safe in Helena, where he belongs.*

I swallowed then took a deep breath. "I can cover us as we go in, just make sure you all stay behind me."

Uncle Baylin nodded, looking at the rest of the warriors on horseback. The other Morganites shifted in their saddles, clutching their reins with white knuckles. "If this is our last battle, let it be a good one."

The mounted Morganites traced their imorets then raised hands high in blessing. Fear prickled down my spine as I looked to the sky. Another ball of black flames hurtled toward the mountain. It landed with a deafening crash. If we were to protect the rest of the clan, we had to ride.

I grabbed the reins, nudged my horse into a gallop, and dodged the trees toward the road. Baylin was to my right and Haplin to my left, riding a horse's length behind me, followed by the rest of the mounted warriors. The rustle of leaves and creak of branches above signaled other Espirians darting through the tree passage, following our assault.

Two more black balls of fire soared through the air. My stomach wrenched at the sight, but I wasn't afraid anymore.

Teilo Lyon was not a creature of nightmare from the Nightlands. Teilo Lyon was merely a man. A man I intended to skewer at the end of my blade. He'd come to rip everything I held dear from me. My home, my clan, even Destrian were targets of his murderous barbs. I had only one intent in my gallop through the forest. I would find Teilo Lyon, and I would finish him.

My gems glowed. Fog billowed around me as I rode, blanketing the trees and concealing the Espirians above and behind me. The rumble of hoofbeats compelled me forward, matching the beating of my heart as time slowed.

I breathed deeply, feeling the rush of wind over my hair. The scent of morwood pine filled my nose, calming my trembling hands. The horse grunted beneath me, its hooves swallowed by the fog that ballooned before us.

I saw the road through the trees. The faces of men watching me behind their shields. Archers rose behind them.

An arrow whistled over my shoulder and disappeared into the fog. I heard a cry but couldn't turn. I could only focus on the road ahead.

Unsheathing Iranoct, I held it aloft. Lightning crackled out of the blade and shot into the sky. A blast of thunder reverberated through the trees. The fog swelled around me.

The pounding of hoofbeats and the rumble of thunder announced our attack. The soldiers braced themselves.

My horse and I leaped from the tree line. I pointed Iranoct at the first row of men and let myself loose with a war cry. Lightning blasted from the point of my sword and struck the line of shields. Blinding arcs of light crackled over the metal in bursts of sparks. The wave of energy blossomed out, flitting from the middle shield toward each end of the line. Soldiers convulsed with the surge, the light twisting and crackling as the men dropped their weapons and fell to the ground.

A line of Espirians swung out from the trees and dropped themselves behind the row of soldiers. Pulling swords from their sheaths, they began battling with a vengeance.

I leaped my horse over the line of fallen men and into the row behind them, leaving the cloak of fog behind to cover my brethren in the trees.

I took another deep breath. The panic of battle held

me in its clutches. Cries of wounded men and the sharp smell of blood filled the air. Time seemed to race forward at a breathtaking speed.

An ax swung in my direction. I kicked down the soldier wielding it and let my horse trample him, then stabbed Iranoct into another.

A mounted soldier rode toward me, his sword aloft. A few paces away his body was peppered with arrows and he fell. I glanced gratefully over my shoulder to the trees, still shrouded with fog, then turned my sights back to battle. I galloped forward, weaving through my brethren as they fought, trying to make it to the trebuchets.

Someone bumped into my leg. I didn't think. I stabbed Iranoct down before I looked over my shoulder and saw Uncle Baylin pulled from his saddle. I reined my horse around. Rearing, I trampled one soldier then thrust Iranoct into the back of another before pulling the blade out and kicking another one down.

"Get back on your horse!" I yelled at my uncle.

I stood guard, cutting down another soldier who ran toward us, giving Uncle the chance to remount.

Something swung toward my head. I ducked as another mounted soldier passed, swinging a mace. I had no shield, so I pulled a knife from my boot and flung it into the man's arm as he reared back to swing again.

"Rowyn," Uncle Baylin shouted. "What do we do?"

His eyes bulged and his cheek was painted in blood.

Where was Teilo Lyon?

Casting my eyes over the battlefield, I saw a Morganite get stabbed through. Another fell out of the trees from a stray arrow shot into the fog. A whistling ball of flames soared through the air toward our mountain.

We were close to the trebuchets.

A trumpet sounded, and I reined around as a line of mounted soldiers hurtled toward me. I pointed Iranoct and sent a blast of lightning into their charge. Soldiers and horses were hurled to the ground. I leaped over their bodies, ignoring their screams, and sent another bolt through the cavalry. I used Iranoct to cut through what remained of the line before galloping into the trees toward the trebuchets.

Looking over my shoulder, I found Uncle Baylin riding after me, his ax in hand. At least I wasn't alone.

Chapter 45

THE SOUND OF CREAKING WOOD filled the air as I galloped through the trees. Men were shouting, loading a giant ball onto the trebuchet's sling. Pack horses were driven back, cranking the arm of the machine. Shouts of fire filled the air.

I pointed Iranoct and blasted the damned thing.

The arm still pitched forward, though the wood collapsed around it. The flaming ball was lobbed to the side and crashed into another trebuchet standing next to it.

The blast launched me from the saddle. I shielded my head as I landed and slid through the mud. Sitting up, I couldn't help but let out a cheer of victory. We had two trebuchets down.

"Get up!" Baylin said, grabbing my hand and hauling me to my feet. "We have to get the others!"

One of the soldiers manning the trebuchet ran toward me brandishing a sword. I gripped Iranoct in both hands and cut him down with a swing. Baylin dispatched another, and we headed toward another pair of machines farther in the trees.

Someone on horseback emerged. He wore plate armor under a purple tunic embroidered with a gold griffon. The visor on his steel helmet was gold and molded in the shape of a griffon's beak.

Teilo Lyon.

Uncle Baylin stepped in front of me. "Go!" he yelled over his shoulder. "Save the others."

"No!" I shouted, trying to pull him back. But Baylin pushed me away and ran.

Teilo spurred his horse forward and charged at Uncle Baylin.

"Stop!" I screamed, but Uncle ignored me. I couldn't let someone from my family fall at the hand of a Lyon, no matter how little I cared for them. But I didn't have much power left. I'd not fully recovered from the night before, and my early use of sorcery had me nearly tapped out.

I sheathed Iranoct and darted forward, running next to Uncle Baylin. Pulling my ax from my belt, I flung it into Teilo's mount. The horse fell, catapulting Teilo off with a crash as another trebuchet flung an enormous ball of fire through the air.

"Help the others!" I yelled at Uncle, gesturing to the trebuchets beyond us.

Uncle Baylin looked as though he wanted to argue, but when the clamor of battle grew closer, he nodded and ran through the trees.

Soldiers rode in our direction. I stepped closer to Teilo and used what energy I had left to call a wall of fog to encircle us.

"Get up," I ordered. I unsheathed Iranoct in trembling hands.

Teilo scrambled to his feet, grabbing his sword as he went, and swung wildly toward me.

"The emperor will have your head for this!" Teilo shouted. He advanced, but his movements were clumsy and stiff from the armor. I stepped to the side as he swung again, and I slammed Iranoct into his back. Sparks flew when my sword met the plating.

Teilo stumbled but regained his footing quickly. "My father is convinced I should let you live, but I'm starting to realize that Seith might be right," Teilo said from behind his visor. "Perhaps I should just kill you now and ask for forgiveness."

He darted forward and swung again. The muscles in my arms screamed at the weight of his blows. I deflected, but it wasn't just my magic that was failing. Teilo had obviously waited till I was already battle-worn to pick a fight.

I gasped for breath, straining to shove Teilo's sword back. I screamed and threw him off, but Teilo was swift. He slashed forward, opening a deep cut in my arm.

I refused to let the sharp pain overwhelm me. I didn't even bother looking at the wound. Instead, I raised my sword and narrowed my eyes at Teilo. "Lyons will never take Morgania as long as there is breath in my body."

Teilo lifted his helmet off his head and threw it into the wall of fog surrounding us. His hair was soaked in sweat, plastered to his red skin. He smiled. "Let's remedy that for you then."

He raised his sword, his eyes filled with enmity, then brought the sword crashing down on mine in a rapid series of blows. I gritted my teeth as the wall of fog evaporated around us, trying to block him as my wounded arm began to fail me.

Teilo kicked me down. I lost my grip on Iranoct and flew back into the dirt.

Another ball of fire whistled above.

I'd failed my family.

I'd failed my clan.

I'd failed Destrian.

I sat up and looked into Teilo's eyes as he stepped toward me.

But he was taking too long. He was relishing the moment, his eyes closed as he breathed in the scent of blood and smoke and death.

What a fool.

I took the opportunity to pull a dagger from my boot. Teilo's eyes widened. He brought his sword down, but I rolled out of the way and leaped to my feet behind him.

"This is for Thedra," I said, then drove the blade into his neck.

The sword fell from Teilo's hands. I stepped in front of him, so he could view the girl he'd underestimated. I wanted my face to be the last thing he saw before death. His eyes squinted at me before he dropped to his knees, clutching my tunic.

A large fireball hurtled through the air above Teilo, but this one wasn't launched by the trebuchets. It was heading straight for them. The massive blaze slammed into one of the machines in a shower of flames. Black smoke billowed from the debris, and I felt the earth give beneath me.

There was a glimmer of red as someone rode toward me. I yanked my tunic from Teilo's grip, letting him fall to the ground.

Destrian had come.

I grabbed Iranoct and staggered toward Destrian. Blood dripped sluggishly down my arm. I glanced at the wound and realized it was worse than I'd initially thought. I clenched my hand over the fabric, trying to staunch the flow.

Destrian dismounted a pace away and caught me in his arms as I stumbled. "I prayed I wasn't too late," he sputtered. "I thought I'd lost you for good."

"You shouldn't have come," I protested. "I can't have you punished for this."

"How could I forgive myself if something happened to you?" Destrian demanded. "What life is worth living if it isn't with you by my side?" His hands on my shoulders, he leaned away and caught sight of my arm. "By all the gods above, what have they done to you?"

"It's nothing," I said, "but Teilo Lyon is dead. I don't know where Seith is, but Teilo is gone."

Destrian's nostrils flared and he paled. "Did you slay him yourself?" he asked, his tone measured.

I nodded.

Destrian pulled me back into his arms and rested his chin on my head. "We'll figure a way out of this, I promise."

Destrian tossed me onto Valor's saddle and leaped up behind me. We began riding back to the road, passing Ayastaren forces running for the trees to the south of the western road. I ignored the retreating men as exhaustion settled into my bones, and the loss of blood in my arm made me lightheaded.

"Father came with me," Destrian was saying in my ear. Despite my alarm at Destrian's presence, I was still comforted by his familiar warmth. "I left him on the road."

"He was supposed to chain you," I said grudgingly.

Destrian cleared his throat. "Oh, he did. Father drugged me first, then chained me, but I melted them off as soon as I realized what his plan was. After that, I convinced him that we'd be able to sway the empire in our favor given Father's impeccable service record."

I sighed. I could only hope it would be so easy. Destrian always had a propensity to be overconfident.

Fallen men and horses filled the road, both Espirian and Ayastaren alike. The fog in the trees had dissipated, and the clan members who remained were catching their breath or searching over the battle scene and pulling out fallen comrades. Black smoke billowed from large areas that looked as though they'd been burned.

Uncle Baylin walked ahead of us. He looked over his shoulder at the sound of our approach, and when he noticed Destrian behind me, his eyes went from warm to cold in a matter of seconds.

Silence descended over the road as other clan members rose to watch Destrian and I ride toward them. I refused to look away from their stares. Destrian had come to help us. Surely they understood that.

But the look in my clan members' eyes still had meaning. In attaching myself to Destrian, I had severed their bonds with me.

I was lost to them forever.

Guards from Helena had clustered around Consul Colman who dismounted, watching Destrian and me with a frown. He clenched his teeth as we stopped before him.

"I did my best, but he wouldn't stay away," Consul Colman growled, eying me as I slid from Valor's saddle to face him.

I glared at the consul. "The Espirians want peace," I announced, glancing at Uncle Baylin, who was clapping Ferris on the back. "Will you give it to them?"

Consul Colman looked over the field of fallen men. Flies were already buzzing around the corpses beginning to bloat in the sun. A wagon lumbered through the trees to help carry our dead back to the shroud. I had no idea what we would do with all of the dead Ayastaren soldiers.

"We've been warring with our own people for too long," Destrian said, jumping down from the saddle. "This is our chance to unite Morgania under one banner. We would be fools to waste it."

Consul Colman was nodding, his eyes on the Espirian warriors who watched the Everetts with uncertainty.

My eyes fell to Conal, who glared at us. He gripped a longbow as his eyes darted from Destrian to me. He lifted the weapon then reached over his shoulder to retrieve an arrow.

It took me a moment to realize what he planned, and by then it was too late.

His eyes held mine, his fury at my betrayal written in his scowl. He nocked the arrow and pulled the string taut.

Conal would never forgive me.

"No!" I screamed, throwing myself at Destrian and knocking him nearly off his feet.

Destrian gripped my arms tightly, steadying me.

"What is it?" he said as I felt along his body to make sure he was unhurt.

The soldiers beside us shouted. They drew their weapons, their eyes on Destrian, waiting for orders. I panicked, looking around for the next threat when something grabbed my arm and pulled me down.

Consul Colman fell to his knees, my sleeve in his grip. His other hand reached up to touch the arrow buried in his chest. His gaze swept to Destrian and he fell back.

Destrian's eyes widened in panic. He loosened his arms around me and dropped next to the consul.

I couldn't think. I couldn't breathe. Even my heart seemed to stop as I stared at Consul Colman, my mouth open.

"Father," Destrian whispered, gripping the consul's hand.

The position of the wound was fatal. Ice shot through my veins as I met Conal's eyes. He scowled at me, daring me to challenge his decision. Even Baylin stared at his Imorati with disbelief. But I could see it in Conal's eyes. He saw every action I'd taken with Destrian as the ultimate betrayal of Luc.

I turned my attention back to Destrian. His face was white with shock.

"Tell the girls," Consul Colman grunted, then a gurgling sound filled his throat. Flecks of blood sprayed from his mouth as he leaned his head back into the dirt. "I'm sorry I didn't get to see them . . . one last time."

The consul's chest heaved once, then stilled.

We all watched in silence as Destrian bowed his head, his father's hand still clutched in his grip.

The Consul of Helena was dead.

Chapter 46

ESTRIAN'S HAIR BEGAN SMOKING as he rose from the ground. Sparks crackled at his fingertips, and his eyes glowed red as he looked over the Morganites in the road.

"Destrian, wait!" I shouted, grabbing his hands. But my fingers burned at his touch.

"Get out of my way!" Destrian yelled as a ball of fire grew in his hands.

But I couldn't let him lose control. I'd gone through so much to save my clan. I couldn't leave them to Destrian's anger. No matter how much I loved him.

I had a duty.

"Run!" I shouted over my shoulder to the Morganites behind me. The Espirians scrambled toward the trees. I prayed to Imor that I could stall Destrian long enough to allow the others to escape.

Uncle Baylin and Conal remained. My eyes widened. "Go!" I shouted, running to them.

"No," Uncle Baylin said, his eyes on me. "I do not fear him."

Conal clenched his teeth. "I made my choice. Let him have me if he wants. What have I to live for anymore?"

I couldn't let it come to that. There had already been enough bloodshed. I stood in front of my brethren and faced Destrian. "I won't let you hurt them," I said, my voice breaking.

Destrian glared at me. "Move!"

The fireball launched itself toward us. I unsheathed Iranoct and tried to knock it away. Sparks rained down on us, and I hissed with the pain.

"Please," Destrian said, his eyes dimming. "I don't want to hurt you. Please, just move."

I met his eyes and shook my head. "I can't do that, Destrian. I'm sorry about your father, but I can't let you hurt them."

Destrian hurled flames into the forest. Trees were transformed to dust and ash as the wall of flames burned.

Suddenly, the sound of trumpets filled the air. Destrian turned to the sound, and the flames disappeared into the wind, leaving a charred trail of devastation. The guards from Helena were gaping over my shoulder. I turned with Uncle Baylin and Conal as a line of soldiers circled around us.

I gripped Iranoct, assuming the men were from Ayastaren. Perhaps it was another Lyon brother coming to fight in Teilo's stead. But I focused on one of the soldiers' tunics and stopped breathing entirely. It felt as though every organ in my body screamed to a halt while my eyes made their way to a richly dressed man riding a white horse toward us.

The soldiers' tunics were white with a golden sun embroidered in the center. The sigil of Somme, the capital of Lyrica.

"It seems we missed the battle," the richly dressed man said, dismounting from his horse as the empire's mounted soldiers pointed their spears toward us. His features seemed wholly unremarkable at first glance. His hair was neither blond nor brown. He was neither tall nor short. He was neither old nor young. Even his eyes looked muddy and forgettable.

But the gem on his brow, a mix between pink and purple, glowed as he studied our group. His eyes darted to the consul on the ground, and to Destrian who, in his shock, was frozen and staring at him.

"Duke Agramon," Destrian grunted, bowing before the man. I furrowed my brows. By all the gods. It couldn't be.

The duke ignored Destrian and turned to me. He studied my clothes, my sword, then noticed the gems on my hands. Raising his brows, he met my eyes. I expected him to say something, but he didn't. Instead, his gem emitted a blinding light. I shielded my eyes with my arm and didn't put it down until the light died away.

"Rowyn the Morganite," the duke said as I blinked,

trying to see through the stars in my eyes.

"Your Grace," I said with a curtsy. I couldn't show fear. I couldn't show anger. I stood in stony silence, assessing the duke as he assessed me. The nobleman was draped in fine white fabric stitched in gold. His fingers were heavy with rings, and he held a staff with an amethyst globe at the end that was an exact match to the one on his brow.

The duke tilted his head to the side, perplexed, then turned to Destrian. His gem shone brighter as Destrian stared defiantly into his eyes.

I shook my head. Duke Agramon was the most feared sorcerer in the empire, not because he could read minds, but because he could bend others to his will. Fin had told me a story of a servant who had accidentally spilled wine on the duke. The man strode through the city and walked himself off a pier, even though he couldn't swim. They dragged his body out of the sea three days later.

The hackles on the back of my neck rose as the duke finished assessing Destrian and turned back to me. The only thing keeping me to my spot was the fact that Uncle Baylin and Conal were behind me.

"I meant to arrive sooner," the duke said, pulling a piece of parchment from a pocket of his golden robes. "We received the Lyons' plans. I see that Ayastaren was unsuccessful in their assault."

Nobody said anything. Instead we let the bodies littering the road speak for themselves. I watched the duke warily, realizing what he'd traveled across the sea for.

Duke Agramon turned to Uncle and Conal and smiled. After a moment, he said, "Baylin, I presume?"

Uncle Baylin nodded.

"Have you the document I sent you?"

"Y-Y-Yes," Uncle Baylin stuttered, pulling a roll of parchment from his tunic. I recognized the scribble of writing on the guardianship papers.

"No," I said to Uncle Baylin, shaking my head. "Please, Uncle, please don't do this!"

Uncle Baylin's face reddened as he looked away from me. "It's for the clan."

It hit me all at once. Uncle Baylin had always hated battle. Right now, I could see what drove Uncle Baylin away from such a thing.

"Conal, don't let him do this," I pleaded, but Conal's eyes were cold.

"You have feelings for this . . . this boy who sits atop the throne of your ancestors, soaked in their blood?" he shouted, flinging his arm to Destrian who bristled at his words.

"Conal, no, it wasn't like that!"

"They took Luc from us!" Conal yelled, pointing a quivering finger at Destrian. "They stole my son from me, your family from you, and now you lower yourself to bed such vermin! You are no Morganite! Imor curse you for this betrayal!"

"No, Conal, please! Destrian would never—he didn't know!" I sobbed as Conal turned his back to me. "No, please don't forsake me!" I reached out to grab Conal's cloak, but he strode between the soldiers and into the trees toward Espiria.

Baylin stepped forward. There was remorse in my uncle's eyes, but it was brief. He had a duty to the clan, and the Blythes' mantra was clan first; before pride, before family, before life itself, clan first.

Uncle Baylin handed Duke Agramon the parchment.

The duke held out several scrolls. "Deeds for the valley and Caymir's Rook. I will ensure that the new Consul of Helena honors our agreement."

Uncle Baylin nodded then met my eye. "Imor cursed us when he brought you into our lives." His eyes glimmered in relief. "You're the empire's burden now."

I sank to my knees as my uncle followed Conal into the trees. My family had abandoned me.

"My dear," the duke said, taking my hand and forcing me to rise. "It is done. You are henceforth my charge since your relations have signed it as such. Don't make this harder than it has to be."

"Please!" I screamed, tears streaming down my face as

my family retreated into the forest. "Don't leave me to him!"

But they were gone.

"How could you turn my own family against me?" I whispered. I was weary of always being in the dark, weary of being a pawn.

"You can't take her," Destrian said, unsheathing Phyranox. The mounted soldiers stepped forward, their blades aimed at Destrian. Agramon gave them a small shake of his head then angled narrow eyes at Destrian.

"It's a shame that you were involved in the fight against your overlord. The moment you gain the consulship of Morgania will be the very moment you lose it. What do you think the emperor will say about such open defiance?"

"I don't care," Destrian said, gritting his teeth. "I won't let you take her."

The duke looked at me, raising his brows as if he expected something. I didn't understand. When I didn't do whatever it was that Duke Agramon was hinting at, he glowered and turned back to Destrian. "So be it. If you want to make this harder than it needs to be, I will inform the emperor of your betrayal and you can have a trial at Somme. The *least* they will do is strip your title."

All of a sudden, I remembered Lord Obi's gift.

The Girdle of Ephema.

The words in the note.

I wish I could do more, but at least this will keep you from being turned into a complete puppet.

Duke Agramon had no control over my mind.

I sucked in my breath. Destrian was still shaking his head at the duke. He met my eyes. "Come home with me, Rowyn."

Finally, I realized what the duke was trying to communicate. He was giving me a chance to save Destrian.

"No," I said simply, wiping the tears from my eyes. Destrian was all I had left. If I wanted to save his life, I had to let him go.

Destrian shook his head. "I know you don't want this. Please, come with me."

I stood tall. "I'm sending you away." I couldn't waver. No matter that my heart was shattering in my chest at each word I uttered. If I wanted Destrian to live, there was no other way. I couldn't let him follow me.

I met his eyes. "We never could've been. You see that now, don't you?"

Destrian's eyes brightened as his sword burst into flames. "I would give my life for you!"

I realized I still had one question that lingered in my thoughts. It took me a moment to regain my courage, but when I did, I was proud my voice at least was clear and unwavering. "What you said so long ago, about fate being real? Did you honestly believe any of that?"

Destrian shook his head. His eyes fell to his father's body lying next to him in the road. "I don't know what to believe anymore."

I wished to all the gods I hadn't said what I did. I wished I'd thrown my arms around him and begged him to take me away—to run with me and live together in another place, a world where we could both be free. We could go back to those feelings in the Nightlands, where it was just us and no one else. Where I could love him, for him, and not for the consul he would become. Not for the lands that he would rule, but just for him as he was, the man who I'd grown to love.

But I didn't do that. Instead, I let my broken heart harden to stone. Love had only brought me sorrow and pain. I hated the emotion and all the betrayals that went with it. I wasn't living for love anymore. I simply had to survive. Destrian's life would be my last gift to him.

I took a deep breath. "You told me that you were mine until I sent you away. I will hold you to that promise. It's my fate to go to the capital. I've known it for some time now, just as I've known we were never meant to be. Go home, go rule Morgania, and promise not to think of me anymore."

I turned my back on Destrian and began walking away. Duke Agramon came up beside me and matched my steps, watching me as dusk settled over the forest.

I looked up at Duke Agramon, the sponsor Solridge had concealed from me for the past year. His eyes glinted, but his expression didn't change. "It is time to pay your dues."

I surprised myself at the strength in my voice. "With respect, Your Grace, dues were not outlined to me when I was brought here. I had no knowledge that I was indebted to someone as . . . illustrious as yourself."

Duke Agramon studied me a moment longer. "That may be so, but the dues will be paid all the same."

"And what do you command in return? What is it you feel that I 'owe' you?"

"I'm afraid I can't even begin to explain the full extent of your debt."

I refused to shout. I addressed him in the most even voice I could manage. "Yes, you can, Duke Agramon. Someone in this godsforsaken empire needs to start telling me the truth." I surprised myself at how calm I sounded. Still, all I could feel was the ebbing pulse of hate brewing within me.

The duke smiled. "You will be moving to Somme with me. You will be my student there, and we will practice your delightful skills all over this realm. You will study at the Great Library of Somme, rub shoulders with all the great families of the empire. As your guardian, I will clothe you, feed you, and protect you. So, all decisions regarding your welfare will now go through me."

"What all did my uncle gain from this?" I asked, though I'd already known the answer.

Duke Agramon laughed. "It was a simple request. The Morganites will be pardoned by the empire for past crimes, and they will be given some land back. Espiria will be declared a sanctuary, and no consul is allowed to attack it unless provoked. I would've given him much more in exchange for making my sponsorship so simple, but such are the predilections of simple men."

"Peace in exchange for my freedom." I laughed. A cold, biting sound with no warmth to it. "That must've been an easy offer to accept." I sucked in my breath. I'd never known such hate in my heart as I did in that moment. I found it easy to hate everyone. My mind teemed with all of the lies I'd been fed. How willingly I'd dismissed my fears. How content I was just to soldier through without asking the right questions.

But at least I had my mind. I wondered how long it would take for him to figure out that the Girdle of Ephema was what eluded him.

A soldier led a horse to me. I stepped into the saddle as Agramon mounted next to me.

"Thank you for your kindness in sparing Destrian's life," I whispered, meeting his eyes.

The duke raised one eyebrow. "Why, my dear, I think that's the first time anyone has ever called me kind." His eyes hardened in the orange rays of the sunset, and my skin grew cold as I found the glimmer of evil within. "I assure you, it will be the last. But, since we're in the spirit of the moment, would you like me to erase you from the lord's memory? It might make it less painful."

I looked back at Destrian who watched us in the fading light. His cheeks were wet as Phyranox dangled at his side. He didn't speak, he didn't waver, he only watched as I left him on that bloody road.

"You might as well. You've taken everything else from me," I said. Perhaps it would be better that way. If Destrian could forget me, he would live a safe life away from the capital. It would give him a chance.

Agramon looked over his shoulder then turned back to me. "On second thought, nothing gives a man greater pleasure than the look on another's face when you've taken that which he loves. I live for these moments."

I refused to cry in front of him. I didn't want to give him the pleasure of seeing my pain as well.

Even if cruelty won my life, I'd never let it have my soul.

WE WOULD LEAVE BY SHIP IN THE MORNING. I was curled up on the floor of my room clutching Araceli's key. A candle flickered at my side as dusk peeked through the window. I couldn't lift myself from the pain inside. Every step I took was taking me further from the life I'd dreamed. Everything I held dear had forsaken me.

But I resolved to fashion a new dream. If my journey to the Nightlands taught me anything, it was that I needn't be frightened of capital bullies, no matter the stories that preceded them. If I could survive the Nightlands, I could survive anything.

Arda's words. Vianne's lessons. Pedr's chess games. All had revealed one vital truth.

If I was the most powerful sorcerer in the realm, then it was time I stopped letting myself be a pawn.

The flicker of the candle caught my eye. The melted wax had pooled, unnoticed on the ground as I succumbed to my thoughts. It had pooled in the shape of a single word.

Family.

By all the gods.

Gooseflesh rose over my skin, and my eyes darted around the room. "How did you follow me?" I whispered. "I thought you all were tied to the land?"

I held my breath. Finally, I spotted a shadow creeping next to me and leaning toward my ear.

"*The stones.*"

I looked at my hands. The shadow souls were tied to the land. But the stones *had* been part of the Nightlands for thousands of years. By all the gods, did that mean? Were the shadow souls now tied to me?

"Are all of you here?" I whispered to the dark, watching the shadow in the flickering candlelight.

"*One.*"

One shadow soul had followed me from the Nightlands. What would Duke Agramon say when he found out? But if he couldn't read my thoughts, how would he?

Why did it follow me in the first place?

Then, I remembered. They were able to show me what they saw. I rose with the candle in my hand. The shadow lengthened beside me.

"Can you show me what Destrian is doing? Can you send word that I'm sorry, that I was only trying to save him?"

"*No,*" the shadow whispered. "*Too far.*"

I blew out the candle and collapsed into the bed, letting despair take complete control of me. The look on Destrian's face upon hearing my words completely broke my courage. What was the point of surviving when there was nothing to live for?

"I'm lost," I told the shadow. "I have no one."

"*Sleep.*"

THE DREAM TOOK ME BACK TO THE NIGHTLANDS. Destrian held me tightly in his arms as I slept, his head resting on mine. His fingers absentmindedly played with my hair as he watched the fire with a warm smile.

Suddenly, we were in the caves. Destrian had just made me laugh. I turned away, chuckling. Destrian reached out as if to touch my shoulder but let his hand fall away.

We were at the underground lake. Destrian carried me out of the water before falling to his knees.

Then, I was swept to the Land of Iriset. Destrian stood in front of me, embedding the final gem into my brow. I fell, only to be caught in his arms. He brought me down slowly and cradled me before ripping a piece of linen from his shirt and wiping the blood from around my gems. He swept the hair from my face before dipping the rag in water and going back to his task.

The dream revealed every gentle look, every touch, every tender moment that Destrian and I shared in the Nightlands until I reached a room lined with stone in

Helena.

The Everett family sigil hung on the wall above the burning hearth. Destrian stood in the ornate overcoat he'd worn the night of the great feast. The consul sat next to him, a dog's head resting on his leg.

Destrian palmed Phyranox's hilt, regarding the consul with urgency. "Father, Rowyn saved me in the Nightlands. She had every opportunity to let me fall, yet she pulled me back from the darkness."

The consul stared at the fire. "I know you care for her, son, but you must temper these feelings of lust. You're meant for greater things."

Destrian shook his head. "You once told me that love made you a better man. I saw what a crushing loss it was to you when Mother died. I understand how the absence of her love changed you. Don't ask me to suffer that same fate."

"She's not nobility, son. Consuls rule through the grace of the emperor. You can't marry a traitor to the crown."

Destrian sat in front of his father, leaning toward him. "You once told me that peace would never be had in Morgania. If Rowyn and I ruled together, we could unite all under our banners. The Morganites would honor it. They would follow us. Can't you see this is the only way?"

"You really love her?" the consul asked, frowning.

"You love her enough to ask this of me?"

Destrian's eyes fell to the floor. "When I'm around her, all I see are the possibilities of who we could become. How we could bring justice to this world. Rowyn has made me into the man I've always wanted to be. If she's taken from me, you will be taking the only future worth fighting for. I'll be left with nothing. I don't want to live in a world where she isn't by my side."

The consul's hand swept over his face. I saw the thoughts of anger, resentment, and fear. I knew what they meant.

I WOKE UP TO THE COMING DAWN, my pillow soaked in tears. Ship sails stretched high in my window, ready to carry me to the place I dreaded most.

All I had left were dreams of what might have been.

The End

THE LAST DUSK

The story continues in Tempest Rising Book 3

A Gilded Cage

Preorder today on Amazon.com.

Please be sure to leave an honest review of
The Last Dusk
at Amazon.com or Goodreads.com.

Follow us online!

https://www.elliottvandruff.com

https://www.facebook.com/elliottvandruff/

https://twitter.com/EVandruff

Make sure to sign up for our newsletter to receive communications on new releases and special content!

Acknowledgments

I would like to take the time to acknowledge several individuals who made *The Last Dusk* possible. The first is my father's friend Lou. He received early rough drafts of the novel and took the time to painstakingly leave comments and edits in the margins, then mailed me the hard copies of those notes all the way from South Korea. I know my father has always appreciated his friendship, and I was blessed with his early support in writing the beginning drafts of Tempest Rising.

I would also like to thank my three beta readers, Patricia Jeanne, Aureece Einfeld, and Patrick Wolfgang, who took the time to provide support all the way up to the submission deadline. Patricia's sensitivity and character feedback were instrumental in cleaning up the relationship development. Aureece's detailed edits and honest criticism helped me make numerous improvements to the plotting and pacing. Patrick's chapter analysis kept me laughing and provided engaging ideas for me to make the story truly shine. Those three were my rock stars, and I have unconditional gratitude for their support and insight.

Additionally, I would like to acknowledge the fantastic work by my editor, Cayce Berryman, from Kingsman Editing. It was a pleasure working with her to refine the story.

There were many evenings that my mother, Rachel, and sister, Olivia, spent with me out on the porch to brainstorm and bounce ideas. Many situations within the novel were developed and plotted during these sessions.

Finally, I would like to thank my husband, Bryan, for his support of my dream. He took on more than his fair share so that I had time to write and has been my unfailing cheerleader from the beginning. Without him, *The Last Dusk* would not have been possible.

www.ingramcontent.com/pod-product-compliance
Lightning Source LLC
Chambersburg PA
CBHW032301020726
47495CB00001B/195